WILD
APPLES

WILD
APPLES

Lucinda Franks

Random House New York

This is a work of fiction. Names, characters, places, and
incidents are the product of the author's imagination or are
used fictitiously. Any resemblance to actual events, locales,
or persons, living or dead, is entirely coincidental.

Library of Congress Cataloging-in-Publication Data

Franks, Lucinda.
Wild apples / by Lucinda Franks.
        p.   cm.
ISBN 0-394-57578-4
I. Title.
PS3556.R3518W55   1991   813'.54—dc20   90-9080

Manufactured in the United States of America

First Edition

for Bob
for Joshua

ACKNOWLEDGMENTS

I wish to thank the people who provided me with support, encouragement, and, in many cases, room to write this book. Thank you to Ken McCormick, Ray Morris, Eleanor Bergstein, Arthur Gelb, Nick Gage, Tom Franks, Lee Crespi, Nick Pace, Suzanne Kopp, and Pauline Wais for their help and advice through the years. Thank you to Renia Hylton for being always by my side, to Penny Franks for her love and sharing, and to Jill Comins and Molly Haskell for their time and tender encouragement. Thank you to Alison Dye, who made so many things possible.

Many thanks to those who provided me with a place to work: to the Writers Room in all its liberating incarnations, to Jerry and Reece Mason for the use of their "milk house," to Eileen Mayhew for her Quitsa Pond cabin, and to Judy Rossner for her cozy back room presided over by the little fertility goddess.

Thanks to my agent, Elaine Markson, for her passionate belief and her brilliant commentary, and to Kate Medina, an editor with an unsparing taste for excellence and complete devotion to the shaping of her books; she spurred, goaded, and inspired me forward.

My deepest thanks goes to Bob, for those weekends he became a single parent, for his hours of loving involvement and forbearance. And to my small son, Joshua, who was patient and understanding to the last and who drafted the plans for a splendid "writing robot" that could, in the future, do all that writing for me.

WILD
APPLES

CHAPTER  1

The auctioneer was waiting when the farm truck full of Woolsey-Beans and their valuables came bobbing into view like flotsam from a shipwreck. Fifty years ago, the auctioneer's father had waited for the Woolseys in a gleaming new automobile, chauffeured them to starlight balls, polished their boots, and lowered his gaze before their haughty stride. His grandfather had labored in the Woolsey brick factory until his child's hands were raw. But now it was a DeCarlo who stood tall while the good folk who had humbled his father and his grandfather came to him like beggars. Need can make the richest blood run thin; the grand old Hudson Valley estates that the DeCarlo Auction Barn had sold off bit by bit to the relic-hungry masses had already built Dominick DeCarlo a custom-designed house and sent his boy to college. As long as families like the Woolsey-Beans kept disintegrating, there would be no more chauffeurs or shoeshine boys in the DeCarlo clan.

In all truth, it had been a sad day when Lydia Woolsey-Bean, the last Woolsey matriarch, had died three months ago. The news had passed quickly through the valley, and on the day of the funeral, people mobbed the Episcopal church, some of them recipients of Woolsey philanthropy, some whose lives were saved when old Cornelius Woolsey, the family founder, gave them food and jobs during the Depression, some who had more recently been snatched from disaster by the large-spirited Lydia. But even those who knew Lydia only by sight lowered their knees to the rail, for in this year 1977, Woolsey Orchards was the closest thing to an old-fashioned Romantic Idea that the town of Stonekill Landing had. Although developers had marred its pristine beauty, Stonekill Landing was still a jewel of a little valley within the larger Hudson Valley, a riverbank paradise of rolling pastures tucked into the Wappappee Highlands, low, pillowed mountains that made one think of a family of giants who had fled New York City to slumber a hundred miles upriver beneath the quilted turf.

Set on the town's highest hilltop, the Woolseys' Victorian mansion with its towers and cascading apple orchards could be seen for miles around, announcing its status as the first and finest home ever built in the region. Lydia herself had inspired respect, even awe. The great-granddaughter of Cornelius Woolsey had been grand and generous—and mesmerizing. She was literally larger than life. Tall and heavy, she carried her weight like a regent carrying her robes; her bulk was never unpleasing to the eye. If she had a sharp tongue and a superior air, she was nevertheless not too proud to get down on her hands and knees and mop up other people's detritus; she had volunteered in the labor room at Wappappee County Hospital for so many years that in the end she had helped deliver most of the babies born to the county policemen, who allowed her to speed around in her white vintage Imperial, never giving her a ticket.

But Lydia had been a woman of contradiction, an enigma. Warm and enveloping, she inspired people to pour out their hearts, but would never unburden her own. Behind her warm light, a cold draft blew. Although the Woolsey homestead had once been the site of lavish teas and dances, by the time Lydia had become its mistress, the family fortunes had dwindled. Lydia turned inward and though she never stopped venturing forth to minister to the town's poor, she came to shun its increasingly middle-class populace for a few close friends, most of whom she cultivated upriver, in fancy horse country. She kept her multigenerational family private, closing the doors of her turreted home behind them.

Of course, no amount of Woolsey grandeur or noblesse oblige could stop the persistent whisperings of family scandal. Though DeCarlo had always had a soft spot for Lydia, he could tell a secret or two about her, but never had.

Rumors abounded of extreme eccentricity in the family, of grandparents' senile ravings, of excessive drinking and philandering and even violence on the part of the men, four and five generations living under the same roof and no one, but no one, leaving the land that old Cornelius had sown.

Until Augusta. Lydia had two daughters, Augusta and Nellie, the fifth generation of Woolseys, and of all the generations of Woolseys, only Augusta had ever managed to leave home. She had gone to California and made a success of herself, but she had never forgotten her family. Until this past year, that is, when she had been oddly absent, not even returning for her mother's funeral. No one seemed to know why.

Augusta was back now, however, driving the truck into the auctioneer's yard, her younger sister Nellie beside her. Their father, Henry Bean, who ordinarily looked the part of a dignified gentleman, was bouncing about in the back on an old settee and could hardly keep his pipe in his mouth. Bean was considered courtly but remote, absent, as though he had never recovered from the realization that a name like Woolsey always carried more weight than a person, no matter how fine that person might be.

Augusta was out of the truck and taking charge of unloading the belongings. Just like her mother, DeCarlo thought: magnetic, with that blond silky hair, creamy skin, and those eyes, startling blue, that could fix you with such a stare it could cause you to swallow your plug of chewing tobacco. DeCarlo straightened his shoulders and went to help the family lay out their belongings for sale. You had to be careful with people like these Woolsey women. The loving way they were talking about their chewed-up heirlooms, the way they were endowing them with a value elusive to anyone but themselves—he would have to be careful. They could make you believe in anything. First thing he knew, they'd have convinced him to overprice things. Here he was already, expressing gratitude to them when he should have expressed irritation. Who else but the Woolseys would dare deliver chipped spongeware and quilts full of holes and expect people to pay good money for them?

Nellie brushed a clump of red curls from her eyes and held up an egg-shaped instrument polished smooth by the oil of many hands. "Augusta, surely you didn't intend for us to sell Great-grandma's sock darner, did you? Nobody could bid enough for the memories this thing contains. Don't you remember how Great-grandma used to clutch it? She carried it around like a baby. Oh, think back, the governor's visit, how she floated up to him, smiling that sweet smile of hers and saying she saw a spot of light shining through his sock. And he just took it off and let her darn it. Don't you remember things like that?"

Augusta sighed. "Nellie, why do you want to remember Great-grandma at her worst?"

"The Tunbridge tray!" Henry suddenly exclaimed, moving his hands lovingly over a large, intricately inlaid rectangle. Was this the same tray upon which Lydia had placed steaming cups of coffee to deliver him from his morning alcoholic hazes? He never remembered it so beautiful and he held tight to it. "We can't sell this," he said curtly.

DeCarlo made a decision then and there: this might be the valley's first family, but unless DeCarlo took control now, the

Woolseys would end up exploiting him as they had exploited his ancestors. "Now wait just a minute," the auctioneer said. "You can't start taking away the only stuff of value, or we ain't having no auction."

Augusta looked at DeCarlo through half-lidded eyes, and he felt himself shrink within his clothes. But she took her father aside and gently removed the tray from his hands. "Daddy. We have to let go of some of our memories, or we won't have any future." Even as she spoke, Augusta was struck with the weary familiarity of her family role: the mediator, the pacifier, the one who saves the day. Here she was, trying to soothe DeCarlo into believing they had things worth selling, and her family into believing they were worth letting go. Unify the world into a working whole, Augusta, even if your own soul fragments in the chaos. As a child she had worked feverishly to bring her warring parents together, swallowing her own anger and fear, even going so far as to deflect their rage at each other onto herself.

Nellie was standing there staring resentfully at Augusta. Their mother had always made Augusta feel guilty, made her feel that nothing she did was good enough, and now Nellie had taken up their mother's baton. Augusta found she could not even return her sister's stare; she was stuck like a pig in a mudslide of guilt.

After Lydia died, their father had somehow been struck helpless, and Nellie, although she had tried to manage the failing orchards, had run them even further into the ground. Finally, true to the family pattern, Augusta had come to the rescue; she had quit her job as a senior talent agent at the Hollywood agency Celebrities International, and she had come home. She had arrived two weeks ago to discover there wasn't enough money in the orchard account at the bank even to spray the trees, which was necessary for a decent harvest. For years, Augusta had been sending her savings home to try to help keep the operation afloat, but now, with not a little trepidation, she had brought herself to insist that her family learn to manage on its own. She would not stay: she would not help them forever. She would stay only long enough to get them on their feet, and then she would take up her own life again.

Augusta had organized the auction, the first stage in a scheme to make the farm self-sufficient, a scheme that Augusta had assured them would work, although she actually was not sure at all. Her sister had been lukewarm about the plan; naturally, Augusta thought—people hate a savior, especially people who cannot seem to save themselves. And her sister's reasons for hating Augusta seemed endless. Augusta wished it were not so; when Nellie twisted her hair between her fingers that way, nervous, vulnerable, Augusta was filled with tenderness. She was tempted at such times to bury their differences, to take in her arms this little sister who had never left home, to tell her everything would be all right, as she had so many times when they were young. But they were not young anymore, and Augusta couldn't make things right; she fought against a surge of that old grandiose passion, that belief that if she just tried a little harder, she could.

Nellie was sifting through the cartons with a shocked expression on her face, though she had participated in the selection of the items to be sold and knew full well what they were. "Can't you take pity on us?" Nellie said, as Augusta and her father came over, "I feel absolutely sick about this, Augusta. Can't you just lend us a few thousand more so we can buy some time—buy the spray before the blossoms come?" Someday, Nellie thought, grappling to restore her fallen pride, she would be in a position never to ask her older sister for anything again. Not her dresses, not her makeup, not one penny of her money. But of course she always said that, and she always ended up just as she was now. "I know you've given us a lot, but these heirlooms are what we're all about—they're our family. They're Mother, they're the way we were brought up—to cherish our traditions, to take care of our own. And now to have an *auction* of our family's things! We're going against everything the Woolseys have stood for, we're giving away our heritage!"

"No we aren't," Augusta said. "We're getting rid of junk to ensure the survival of our heritage."

"I have a very spooky feeling about this. I have a feeling that we're going to be sorry," Nellie said, echoing Lydia's frequent warning. Nellie knew well Augusta's vulnerable spots. Nellie knew that, as a child, Augusta had believed even more strongly than Nellie did that their mother was a god whose magical eyes could see everywhere, who could exact punishment for every covert transgression. Right now, Nellie was trying hard not to let Augusta see the tears that she feared would splash down onto the little Victorian doll's surrey with the real leather seats and two iron horses to pull it. But telltale watermarks stained the carriage's satin canopy. "I can feel it," Nellie said. "Mother would die—if she weren't already dead."

"Nellie, this is ridiculous." Augusta took her sister by the arm. "We are *suffocating* with Woolsey junk—antiques, bric-a-brac, memorabilia. Lord, I'm surprised we didn't find framed fuzz from the first dust that gathered in that house. The money we raise tonight will take us through this spring's bloom. The next auction will carry us through the growing season. If mother were alive, this is what she would want us to do."

"I don't think you're in any position to say what Mother would have wanted us to do," Nellie said in an ominous voice. "Listen, I've changed my mind, that's all there is to it. There are things here I want to keep." Augusta would make Nellie beg for the things that belonged to her, Nellie knew it. She would not be happy unless Nellie got down on her knees and begged like a dog. "Look," she said. "I have my own rescue plan, Augusta. We could sell off some land—better that than treasures collected over a century. It's more dignified, too. Just give me a few weeks, and I can raise much more than we'll get in this cheesy auction barn."

"You and Daddy have had months to raise money, and you

didn't do a thing," Augusta said. "I'm used to running a business. If you want the farm saved, stay out of the way and leave things to me."

"Don't talk to me like that!" Nellie said, her green eyes flashing. In a family of blond, blue-eyed Anglo-Saxons, Nellie with her curly red hair was an anomaly. It crossed Augusta's mind, as it had after Nellie was born, dethroning her and disrupting all their lives, that maybe Nellie was a changeling, not part of the family at all, but just left on their doorstep to cause trouble for Augusta. Augusta's hands went clammy as she remembered something else: that scene with her mother, that tearful night when it was Augusta's legitimacy, Augusta's birth that was called into question. She quickly put it out of her mind, as she always did.

Nellie glared at her sister, knowing that Augusta did not believe that she could have a plan to save Woolsey Orchards: but it just so happened that she did. Nellie might be a part-time clerk in the local inn, but she would surprise them all. For Nellie's whole life, Augusta, born five years before her, had been the cherished daughter. Her mother had filled albums and journals with commemorations of Augusta's first years, yet there were no albums at all for Nellie; her one baby picture had been eaten by mice. Perhaps her mother had always overvalued Augusta, her first-born, but where had Augusta been when her mother needed her most? At the end, it had been Nellie who was there for her mother, Nellie who had come out of the shadows and been Lydia Woolsey-Bean's salvation, Nellie who had rubbed her back, cooled her forehead, tried to extinguish her pain with a daughter's perfect love. "Leave things to you!" Nellie fumed. "If Mother had left things to you, she would have died abandoned and alone."

Augusta took the surrey from her sister's hands. "Abandoned and alone! Mother always did say you were melodramatic." Since her homecoming, Augusta's feelings toward Nellie had shifted back and forth between pity and rage, and now rage won out.

Nellie had been the one to beg Augusta to come home, and Augusta had. But, like Lydia, Nellie was never satisfied with anything Augusta did. Augusta stayed away from home, left the family to Nellie, and Nellie despised her for it. Augusta came home, offered her help, and Nellie despised her for that too.

"Girls, girls." Henry Bean came over, embarrassed that people arriving at the auction were beginning to stare at his squabbling children. "Come on, now." Henry was at his best on the few occasions when he was called upon to be masterful; and his daughters, capable grown-up women, were transformed into children whenever they were thrown together, providing him with that rare opportunity.

They were so different! Lydia had said that Augusta, thirty-four, had classic loveliness while Nellie, twenty-nine, was a character; a funny little nose, a pleasingly crooked smile, a head of hair the color of a rusty scouring pad, and an iron determination to boot. As a matter of fact, both his girls had the Woolsey stubbornness, but Nellie was inclined to cloak hers in self-pity, and that in turn was overlaid by her practice of hamming things up, even as she stumbled over chairs and misplaced her belongings. Henry wondered whether she was aware that her clumsiness made her appear at times clownish, bizarre. She must, for why else would she cling so fearfully to the familiar? Henry happened to know that, behind her scatterbrain exterior, Nellie was at heart very careful, very reserved, a distant observer—just like himself.

Henry moved his gaze to his first daughter. Augusta had her share of whimsy too, though she tended more toward the ethereal—but mostly, she was the type to jump right in where no one else dared. Augusta was the more obvious success story in the family; a polished career woman whose glamorous work had kept her away this last year, a crucial one for the orchards—and for his wife. But people always undersold Nellie and no one more than Nellie herself.

Nellie had joked that she was the daughter who had flown

back *into* the nest, but in the face of his own lethargy during the final months of his wife's life, Nellie had taken over. While Lydia was alive, the only thing he'd been good for was nursing her, and after her death, he hadn't the stomach to even take a drink. If the orchards were now in a mess, at least Nellie had kept them going, not to speak of managing the household and the Hopestill Arms, where three days a week she virtually ran the inn. Still, he was relieved that Augusta was finally home. They desperately needed her strength, as they had always needed it.

Henry had never been as expressive as Lydia, and he wondered whether his children really knew how much they meant to him. As they stood here under the shelter of his arms, as he watched the sun coming through the barn window and lighting their hair, he thought that he would never again love two people as much as he loved his daughters at this moment.

"Your mother wouldn't have wanted you to be upset," Henry said to them. "Especially in front of her friends." He motioned toward the door where two women in similar tweed jackets and jodhpurs were standing. Peggy Steptoe and Betsey Blanquette lived in an exclusive town north of Stonekill Landing; they were part of that horsey My-Ancestors-Came-Over-on-the-Mayflower set that Lydia had pursued with such gusto. Henry had thought himself disdainful of them, but now that Lydia was gone, he found himself grateful for their attentions. It was a way of keeping his wife alive, he supposed, or perhaps he was, in truth, as intrigued by them as she had been. His wife had done everything for him—provided his home and his line of work, made his friends, handled his daughters; maybe she had felt his feelings for him also.

Peggy and Betsey came over now, calling, "Augusta, how lovely, welcome home!" Betsey embraced her. "Your mother was so proud of you and all your accomplishments." And then, noticing Nellie, she gave her a peck. "And you too, of course."

"What a shame you have to do this," Peggy said, looking

around at their belongings. Her voice had always reminded Nellie of a foghorn. "And after you watched your mother suffer so, with that cancer. Particularly at the very end, it was just terrible. And then to lose your grandmother so soon afterwards!" Just three weeks after Lydia's death, her mother, Amenia, the last surviving Woolsey grandparent, had dropped dead of heart failure. So much drama had surrounded Lydia's illness that Amenia's sudden passing, at age eighty-five, was frequently mentioned as a macabre afterthought. Peggy sighed and looked around with distaste at the cold, cavernous auction barn. "Well, maybe it was all for the best. It's certainly a blessing she didn't have to see this auction."

Nellie's cheeks reddened. "Oh, this is just junk we've been trying to get rid of for ages."

Betsey nodded. "It's about time somebody cleaned out that old white elephant. Lydia hated to throw things out, and she never did."

"That's because she loved her antiques, Betsey," Peggy said. "See that old beat-up Edison phonograph over there, with the horn and crank? It was her father's. They used to listen to records together when she was a child."

"They did? Really?" Nellie asked, suddenly alert.

"Girls," Peggy said. "Your mother was a most extraordinary woman. She would have handled this auction with grace and dignity. Only Lydia Woolsey-Bean could have been near bankruptcy and managed to pull off a debutante party that made everyone assume she was sitting pretty. She desperately wanted you to 'come out,' Augusta, and she used every scrap of ingenuity to do it. She certainly needed ingenuity since she didn't have any money! Picked wildflowers at five in the morning and festooned the house with them, and dressed your farm manager up as a butler!"

"The party was for me," Nellie said. "I was the debutante."

"Of course," Peggy said. "That's right. That's what I meant to say."

"Well," Betsey said quickly, "we'll go and have a look. We each want a memento of your mother and no, Augusta, don't try to give me anything. I'll pay just like everyone else. It's the least we can do."

As they were moving off, Betsey edged Augusta aside. "You must get that grass mowed, dear, where it shows by the road. Your mother wouldn't have wanted people to see the Woolsey place looking that way."

Nellie turned to Augusta and rolled her eyes as soon as the two women had left. "Actually," Nellie conceded, "I like Peggy and Betsey. They were good to Mother at the end, and at least they try to remember that I'm a separate person from you. Usually Mom's friends come up to me and say, 'Oh, tell us about life as a Hollywood agent, do you represent Cher? Have you met Audrey Hepburn?' "

"Don't pay any attention to them," Augusta said, and she sighed, stepping away so no one could see her face. It would come over her, this profound wave of depression, when she least expected it. Sometimes just looking at her father, who moved so slowly it seemed as if he might stop moving altogether, would do it to her. Sometimes it was the smallest thing, sometimes something bigger. Peggy Steptoe had said Lydia had suffered, and Augusta hadn't even been able to nod and say, "Yes, I saw her, she suffered at the end and it *was* terrible."

Although Augusta had left home after college, her mother's pull on her to return had been almost irresistible. Birthdays, Christmases, the illness of a grandparent, financial crises— Augusta felt that if she did not come home, the whole Woolsey family structure would crumble. When she was not at Woolsey Orchards, she constantly worried about the property and about her family. She had been desperate to leave home, to escape her suffocating enmeshment with her mother, the confusion of love and hate between them—but as soon as she did leave, she came up against feelings of rootlessness and guilt. She was afraid that without her to mediate, her parents' fights would end in tragedy; that Nellie would become overwhelmed by their unpredictable mother, by their weak father, by this family that on the outside seemed so invincible, but on the inside was swamped in misery and self-doubt.

When her mother fell ill five years before, Augusta's obsession had only increased. It would visit her swiftly and inconveniently, like lightning, often in the middle of lovemaking; she would go cold with fear for her mother and have to find a phone to call home. Her last thought when she fell asleep at night and her first upon awakening was always the same: My mother is going to die; what I feared all my life is finally happening.

Augusta secured a standing plane reservation home every week. She had been the one to tell her mother that what had been diagnosed as nerves was in fact ovarian cancer. She had brought her mother to specialists who operated and gave her two extra years of life when no other doctor would give her more than four months. But, finally, something snapped in Augusta. She was exhausted. She felt suffocated by the responsibility. She could not go on. And so she made a stand and made it at the wrong time. Augusta had stayed away, and her mother had died. She supposed that Lydia had never really forgiven her. It was certain that Augusta would never forgive herself.

"Are you all right?" Henry Bean came over and put his arm around his elder daughter.

"Fine," Augusta said, wishing she could tell him the truth: no, she was not all right, never had been.

"What do we do now?" he said. "I think there's still some stuff in the truck."

"Let's get it then," she said, slipping her arm around her father's waist. She was glad he was here beside her even though she could not really talk to him, had never been able to really talk to him.

Henry followed Augusta out to the truck. Did her fast, determined stride mean she was annoyed with him? He had been doing everything he could to avoid lifting the rest of the cartons out of the truck; now, he pretended to remove a pebble from his shoe so Augusta would unload the first of the remaining cartons. When she turned her back to go into the barn, Henry quickly tumbled another carton out of the truck and unobtrusively kicked it along the drive. He had sent Nellie to the train platform to meet Augusta two weeks ago so that his daughters would not see how much trouble he had lifting her luggage. One horribly hung-over morning a little while before his wife had died, his legs had slid out from under him, sending him flat on his fanny, and the pain in his left hip still hung on. Bone cancer, maybe. He had a friend whose bum hip turned out to be a signal that the throat tumor the doctors had "removed" had gone down the rest of his body. Henry went back to the truck, took out the last carton, which was filled with ancient linens, and heaved it up on his right shoulder, listing as though it were full of hardware. He saw Nellie looking at him admiringly. I'm an old fraud, he thought. This was the hardest part of his bad hip: he was known for his gentlemanly ways; even though he came from a middle-class background, his manners had outshone even those of the highborn Woolseys. But now it was often physically impossible for him to exercise the chivalry that had redeemed him.

But Henry really could not afford to dwell on his hip, for he had a much more pressing burden. He had lost his wife's rings. The diamond engagement ring that had belonged to her great-grandmother, and the huge, priceless star ruby ring. Lydia had given them to him before she died, instructing him to safeguard them for the girls. No matter how long and how carefully he searched, Henry couldn't remember where he had put them. He thought he had tucked them in the old mahogany secretary in the hall, but they weren't there. Augusta and Nellie had not asked about them yet; for now, their disappearance was his secret shame. But it was only a matter of time before he would be discovered as having failed them once again.

If he was not looking for the rings, he was looking to save face. For forty years, Lydia and he had run the orchards at a profit. Times had been hard for the little farmer, that was true; but was it only coincidence that as soon as Lydia got sick and passed full responsibility over to him, the orchards began to fail? He hoped that wherever she was, Lydia could not see what they had come to now. She would be so angry. He could taste her anger. Just then a chill breeze ruffled what was left of his thinning hair; there wasn't any wind anyplace else, he thought uncomfortably.

He went into the barn, where his daughters were examining a small iron gadget. "The old apple peeler!" he said, his eyes lighting up. He took an apple out of his pocket. "It's perfectly good. See how it works."

"Daddy, that thing has been hanging around in the cold-storage pantry forever, and you've never peeled an apple with it until this very moment," Augusta said. She felt herself weakening, and so made her voice sound more emphatic. "Look you two, it's dreams you're trying to save, not anything real—like apple orchards, for instance. If we still can't make ends meet by the end of this season, we'll be auctioning off something we really care about—the ground under our feet."

"Listen folks, you have to let us tag the rest of this stuff." DeCarlo walked up to them, his swarthy face seeming even darker. "I really don't know why you're all still here. At times like these, I advise the family to stay at home."

DeCarlo lifted up a portrait of a woman that Lydia had painted when she was dabbling in art, and carried it off. When Henry saw it he did a double take—the portrait was the spitting image of his secretary, the one he had had his first affair with. Only Lydia had painted her up like a hussy. He had never seen the painting before; the girls must have unearthed it from the attic.

Lydia had often accused him of revolving in a private orbit

of bees and trees and booze, and he remembered how devastated she was when she first learned that this world also included other women. Yet Henry could have sworn that Lydia, who had a terror of sex in general and of sex with him in particular, had directed him right into that secretary's arms. But she claimed that the affair had broken her heart.

He had been having another affair when Lydia's illness began five years ago, and had promptly broken it off and devoted himself to Lydia from then on. But he would always wonder whether she had known about this last other woman, and whether it had caused her to get sick.

The barn was filling up now. Barn swallows winged through the rafters, but their screeching was lost in the twitter of human voices. The first two rows of folding chairs were taped with the names of auction regulars. Augusta had forgotten these faces, the look they had, and how much she had wanted to escape their sameness; pale doughy skin, thin mouths, pointy chins. The people of the county looked so inbred, though it might have simply been that the similarity of their existence had bred a similarity of look. DeCarlo stepped onto the auction block and turned on the clothesline pulley contraption by which the auctioneer could run notes of who bought what for how much back to the cashier. Then he tested the microphone.

"I'm sitting in the back," Augusta said, heading toward the cashier's window. "The less obtrusive we are, the better."

"I think we ought to sit up front so no one dares say anything nasty about our things," Nellie said, but she followed her sister and father to the back row.

DeCarlo straddled himself on a tall stool, and the room became hushed. It was a fine evening for early April, and a hint of spring was rustling the air. People knew they could count on DeCarlo for a performance; he would take them places only an evangelist could go. For some, this would be the only entertainment of the month.

DeCarlo had been pleasantly surprised to find some gems

among the Woolsey castoffs. There was a gooseneck tin teakettle which looked Shaker, a couple of Early American hooked rugs with pictures of dogs sitting like people, and a coffee table made by Lydia's father, a would-be inventor, out of an old maplewood sled.

Still, there was so much junk and damaged antiques that he would have to employ a technique reserved for such mixed auctions; he would be blasé about everything. He would use humor to keep his bidders off guard, so they would never know when he was being serious. If they thought something of value had gone undetected by DeCarlo, was it his fault? Long ago, he had learned that people like to believe they can think for themselves, and if they imagine they have thought themselves into a discovery nobody else has made, they go wild.

Of course, he would also, as he always did, include in the main estate sale paraphernalia from other sources: leftovers from previous auctions, odd unpeddled pieces such as a new bench, which had been chain-whipped into antiquity, or the contents of small houses. It saved the families embarrassment—who would know that those were Aunt Gertrude's watercolors which didn't sell? And it helped him—if those watercolors were thought to have hung above the mantle in a famous mansion, then they might sell after all.

Henry leaned over Nellie to speak to Augusta. "Did you tell DeCarlo we want certain things back if he doesn't get a minimum price?"

"Don't worry, Daddy, I explained about your bee box." Bean had volunteered to contribute one of the first hives he had ever devised, on the chance that there might be someone in the audience who shared his apiary interests.

"Okay, folks," DeCarlo began. "You know why we're here tonight. We're here to pay homage to one of the great families in the valley. The things you'll see tonight may be ugly or they may be beautiful, they may be priceless or they may not, but they are one of a kind. Their value is that they will never be made again. Some of these items are the personal furniture and memorabilia of Cornelius Woolsey, who over a hundred years ago came to this corner of the Hudson Valley and cleared the property upon which some of your houses now stand."

In spite of herself, Nellie felt pride rising to overtake her shame. She had to admit she liked the way DeCarlo had lingered over her great-great-grandfather's name. Nellie had been christened Cornelia after old Cornelius, who had lived until Nellie was six. He had planted rows of trees down by the river and called them the Christmas Orchard in celebration of Nellie's birth on December 19, 1947. Nellie's own secret plan for rescuing Woolsey Orchards required her to sacrifice this symbol of her value, however, for she had found a French organic farming expert who regularly stayed at the Hopestill Arms, and she had interested him in buying that orchard.

The first items were auctioned off quickly. There was a mahogany-and-brass lap desk with mother-of-pearl inkwells and a false bottom disguising a secret compartment; it had been used by the early Woolseys for train travel. There was a funny old foot warmer with a pierced iron door, which DeCarlo was able to talk up to twice its worth by remarking that you would never find one that still had its tin cup for the hot coals. There were old Cornelius's calling cards in a leather case, some fringed piano scarves, boxes of embroidered linen, a lovely copper washtub, sets of Staffordshire china, a Sheraton highchair, footstools with covers needlepointed by Nellie, brass rubbings, and coin silver.

When the energy level in the auction barn was at a pitch, DeCarlo began sneaking in the junk, timing its interspersal with the fine stuff so subtly that eager bidders had no idea their normal prudence was being drowned in a flood of passionate excitement. He held up a brass samovar that had a bent spout from when Nellie had run over it with roller skates. "A beauty, ladies and gents. I understand that the estate this comes from—no, I can't reveal which one—got it from a Russian princess."

"Russian princess, my ass," Augusta said. "Mother bought that at one of Dominick's auctions ten years ago!"

There were no opening bids. DeCarlo put the samovar down. It was time now to change tactics and do a little bully-ing. "Okay folks," he said, striding up and down the platform, lifting his hands expansively. "Think of this lovely old piece like you'd think of your grandmother. A little worn, a little unsteady, but would you ever let her go just like that? Sell her down the river? If the answer to that is yes, I'm going to go home right now. The royalty of Russia will never come back. The glory that once belonged to families like the Woolseys is gone too: some of their homes are now museums. Think of this barn as a museum which suddenly threw open its doors and invited people to steal its treasures for pennies."

DeCarlo heard fifty, the bidding rose fast and grandmother went for $145.00, at least a hundred more than it was worth.

Then DeCarlo's men brought out a long bench with rockers, and Nellie sucked in her breath. The "mammy rocker" had been given to their great-grandmother by their great-grandfa-ther with the idea that they could rock on the porch together with their baby, who was kept from rolling off the bench by a little guardrail. It was his last gift to his wife, for shortly afterwards he walked out of her orchards and never came back. Great-grandmother Millie had banished it to the the base-ment, where the rockers had contracted dryrot and fallen off. "Now look at this gorgeous thing," DeCarlo said, stroking the back of the bench. "Yes, I know, it's missing the rockers, but you can still sit in it. Personally, I think it's better this way, for the baby won't go flyin' out if the mom and dad get rocking too rough."

DeCarlo knew whenever his humor had caught the sails of the audience; the bidding would race along like a sloop. He held up a painting of a bearded scholar bent over the Talmud. "It's signed Goldman. Here is Mr. Goldman doing his first income tax." This had been hanging around for several auc-tions, and he hadn't until now found the right line to make it go. It went now for five dollars and after all five dollars was five dollars.

He held up a modern spotlight lamp which resembled a serpent. "Here we have the latest in designer lamps," he said, holding it far away from himself.

"Oh, I have one like that," someone called from the audience. "It's absolutely wonderful!"

"Must be the owner," Nellie whispered.

"Oh really?" DeCarlo replied to the caller. "I wouldn't be caught dead with one." It sold for fifteen dollars.

The auctioneer held up another painting, this one belonging to the Woolsey-Beans. It was a brightly colored oil on thin canvas, of a pale woman with rouged cheeks and very yellow hair clutching a red handkerchief. Henry slumped in his seat. Surely, he thought, some old-timer would recognize her as the woman who was his secretary thirty years ago.

"I think she has hepatitis but I'm not sure," DeCarlo said, wincing at the portrait. "But who's going to open their arms to this poor girl?"

Amidst general laughter, Augusta leaned over to her father and said, "I don't know what possessed Mom to paint that! It's completely out of character for her." Henry suddenly looked pale. "It looks like it belongs in a Spanish bordello," she concluded.

The portrait was bought by a restaurant owner. Henry saw the man carrying the painting away, with its brassy, angry brush strokes, and felt immense relief. He wondered if Lydia had also felt relief just by painting it.

Now that the painting had been sold without anyone discovering who the portrait represented or why Lydia had painted it, Henry began to relax. To tell the truth, he was starting to have some fun out of all this. Not that he would have admitted it to his daughters—he wanted them to remain safe in the illusion that he shared their reverence for the Woolsey legacy. But in fact he felt almost buoyantly relieved, as if he were a boat being unloaded of too much cargo. All of this stuff had been cherished by his late wife, of course, and he had to respect that fact. But he'd be damned if he wasn't getting a bit of a thrill watching all the debris of their lives float off into the unknown.

Augusta looked over at Nellie's wry face and at the amused expression on her father's, and she realized that they had actually begun to enjoy this auction. And, in fact, Augusta herself felt lighter with every item DeCarlo sold. She realized then, although the thought filled her with shame, that she had felt lighter, too, after her mother's death; it had opened up a kind of opportunity. While Lydia had been alive, it had been impossible for Augusta to truly separate herself from her mother, but now she would have to separate or perish as well. Piece by piece, she would sort through the house; she would get Woolsey Orchards in order; and she would order her own soul as well. If she was able to accomplish all that, did she dare to hope that she could then create a life that really belonged to her and not to her family?

Augusta leaned over to Nellie and said, "This isn't really so bad, is it? It's kind of fun to see the old stuff get this kind of a send-off instead of going unceremoniously into the garbage pile." As soon as Augusta had spoken, she wished she hadn't.

Nellie turned a cold eye on her sister. "It's *my* garbage, Augusta. Things that I value and you don't. Did it ever occur to you that maybe DeCarlo is right? That we are a local legend, but we become just like anyone else when we lower our standards of behavior this way? DeCarlo himself is effectively declaring the Woolseys dead—good-bye to the valley's first family. The British have a monarchy because they need someone to look up to. When was the last time the Queen sold her broken lorgnettes to the highest bidder?"

"What standards are we lowering? Whose?" Augusta shot back. She was thinking of the house as it was when she was a child, with its catwalks, its hideaways that had nourished her, secreted her away. Her sister didn't even know how much she loved that old homestead—Nellie would be thinking, "It's the old Augusta, no feelings, made of iron." No one knew how afraid Augusta was of the power that house had to pull her in and drown her. "Nellie," she said. "The standards are already gone. We live in a decrepit house with an orchard whose crop hasn't been any good for years. Our home is an eyesore, Nellie, and our apples are lousy."

Henry, sitting between his daughters, raised his hand to silence Nellie before she could respond, so instead she sat back, her cheeks coloring. In a single moment, Augusta had spoiled the fragile peace she had made with the fact of this circus. How could her sister be so cavalier with Nellie's distress? How could she be so insensitive? This auction was like the nightmares she had had as a teenager, of showing up at the prom wearing only her bra and girdle. She hated the fact that Augusta's pronouncements had so much power over her; DeCarlo was holding up the Haviland pitcher they used to pour mulled cider from at Christmas, and all Nellie could see now was its shabbiness. Things that throughout her life had remained as new and wonderful as the first time she'd seen them were now revealed to be stained, chipped, secondhand. She realized she probably looked that way too.

"No, no!" DeCarlo was shouting. "I don't want to see a penny more than ten dollars bid on this. We have to protect the customer from himself here." He held up the bench that had been chain-whipped and stained. From a distance it looked as if it might have come from an attic in Pennsylvania Dutch country. In spite of his protests, the bidding continued to escalate. "A ten-dollar bench and you're bidding fifty? You shouldn't even be thinking of bidding! You can get it for nothing with green stamps."

"Oh no," said Nellie, who had seen the bench up close. "People are going to think that thing's ours!"

"Now here's a real honey," DeCarlo said, presenting a child's desk that had been painted pink and highlighted by decals of Donald Duck. "Early American in persuasion, I'd say. This is your vintage Norman Inkwell."

"That *is* ours, isn't it?" Nellie said below the laughter. "You didn't tell me you were including that!"

"It's not ours, Nellie," Augusta answered.

"Isn't that my childhood desk? I had a pink desk once."

"No," Augusta said impatiently. "Ten times, no."

"Take a look at this," DeCarlo barked. "For all you collectors, you'll never see anything like this anywhere. Handmade by a famous apiarist—that's a doctor who fits glasses on apes— handmade by a famous apiarist, or beekeeper to us plain folks, this special grade-A wooden beehive can hold hundreds of nice, friendly, cuddly honeybees."

There were a few respectful twitters—it was known that Henry Bean bred bees. He kept at least two dozen or so beehives in a clover field across from the orchards—but this sample of his apiarian homebuilding talents, a hive about the size of a small filing cabinet, brought no bids.

"Come on, you nature lovers," DeCarlo said, opening the hive and lifting out the frames of creamy white beeswax upon which the bees would draw comb. Henry had carefully embedded the sheet of wax into wire supports so the bees would have a sturdy foundation upon which to lay out their brood and make honey. "This is a perfect present for little Johnny or little Mary. What's a sloppy old dog or a silly cat when there are these nice little pets that don't take up much space? Why have a guard dog, or a burglar alarm, when you can have an army of household bees? And think of all that free honey." There was silence. DeCarlo shrugged. "It could double as an end table. Or an extra seat in the garden. A special seat, a regular hotseat, for the tax collector, or your maiden aunt, or anyone else you don't want staying around."

The audience seemed to be moved to near hilarity. "Keep the noise down, please," DeCarlo said, "or we're going to take names."

Henry, who never betrayed much emotion, found his cheeks

reddening. He had worked hard on that hive. He had invented a new kind of trough feeder that fit inside and from which the bees could sip sugar syrup until they made enough nourishing honey from the first pollen of spring. Henry had invented little floats that the bees could perch on so they wouldn't fall into the syrup and drown. DeCarlo hadn't bothered to mention that innovative part of the hive.

Henry's bees were very special to him. For several years he had tended them religiously, and those high up in apiculture could testify that Bean bees were extremely healthy and highly productive: not only did they produce gallons of honey, a nice little source of household money, but they could be brought over to pollinate the orchards at blossom time, saving money on rental bees. Henry could also do a lot of tricks with his bees, and people loved these tricks. He could make the bees walk up his arm, he could even make them dance, and they never stung him. He could take the queen from any of his hives, put her on his chin, and the drones would come swarming around, creating a bee beard. This trick always sent his daughters into gales of fright and pleasure. He loved his bees, even when they were cross. They couldn't be wiped out by the weather, or by pests, for they constantly reproduced. And as long as nature bloomed, no matter what it bloomed—they liked any pollen, even skunk cabbage pollen—they made food for man. They never hit you with any nasty surprises, the way fruit trees, or people, did. He loved watching their little cities through the holes in the hive bodies he built, with the long elegant queen laying eggs and the drones surrounding the bee larvae in their hexagonal honeycomb cells with pollen of lemon and crimson and orange and purple. He thought about his bees a lot; he dreamed about them at night. They were the only predictable, orderly, and exquisitely precise thing in his life.

"Won't somebody give me a dollar for this unique bee contraption?" DeCarlo said with exasperation. "Sold! To the gentleman over there."

DeCarlo went on quickly to a couple of samplers, a tall pewter ale pitcher, and an old Dutch Cleanser poster with a muscular arm posed to beat the "RUB OUT OF SCRUB."

"Daddy, you didn't!" Nellie said when the auctioneer's assistant delivered the beehive to its new owner, Henry Bean. Henry kept on looking straight ahead.

"Well, then, I'm just going to put in a bid of my own," Nellie said. DeCarlo was holding up some sleigh bells on a cracked leather strap; Henry, dressed in a red suit and white beard, had jangled them on the roof each Christmas when Nellie was a child and still believed in Santa Claus. She got them for two dollars.

A few more items were sold, then the auction was over. The audience slowly filed out, satisfied with having collected enough gossip about what had been inside the Woolsey home to last for months.

The Woolsey-Beans were the last to leave, primarily because they had bid on and bought more things than any other group at the auction. They left silently, Henry with the bee box, Nellie with the sleigh bells and dressing-table mirror. Even Augusta had, at the last moment, bought back a Flexible Flyer sled with her name carved on its top.

DeCarlo sorted out his receipts, cleared the platform, and put the stuff that had not sold in the back for another auction. He chuckled to himself as he put a thick roll of cash into his pocket—his share, thirty percent of the proceeds. He had seen a lot of strange things in this business, but this was the first time that the seller had paid the auctioneer a commission for the privilege of keeping his own goods.

That night, Augusta had the dream again. Each time the details were different, but always its burden was the same: her mother was alive. In life, Augusta had neglected to take her mother to Europe, as she had always intended, but in the dream they were in the south of France. Lydia was frail and weak and she swam out too far. Augusta, intent on her own surfing, lost sight of her. Suddenly she heard her mother's tiny voice, saw her hands waving frantically, but Augusta stood paralyzed. She knew she could not reach her in time. She looked and looked, hoping to see Lydia's face spring up once more from the water, but there was only an even sea. Eventually, Lydia's body was swept up on the beach. Don't die, don't die, Augusta cried, then suddenly the body rose. Only it did not look like her mother anymore, it looked exactly like Augusta.

A wet spot spread over the sand beneath Augusta, sucking up everything that stood upon it. Augusta began to scream, a child's desperate screams, but the sand continued to swallow her up slowly, relentlessly, as she reached out in vain for the woman who was her mother and who had now become herself.

CHAPTER 2

Two weeks before the auction, Augusta had been on a train bound for home, careening along past the landscape of her childhood. She had left behind the quick, rich pulse of her life in Los Angeles, and now she felt as if she were traveling back in time. Her eyes became instruments of magic once again, turning the Hudson River into a moat of seething oil, the valley into a mortuary. The train whistle echoed like a pipe organ, the trees sprinkled snow upon the mist-shrouded old river, and the cliffs, with their ledges ascending like pews, looked like the stony faces of the bereft and rueful.

She had always dreaded this trip home up the Hudson. Movies and songs told her that home was a sweet haven, a place you went to for comfort and restoration before returning to the world. But home to her was a place that she was drawn to like an addict. She realized she had always felt this same fear, coming back—a fear like fish must feel at the deep unknown of a whale's belly. One day, she resolved, one day when she was rid of her past, she would get things the right way round again: her home, wherever it might be, would be a welcome spot; the lines would not blur, roses would be roses, children would be children, parents would be parents, and things would be exactly what they seemed.

But coming home here would always be coming home to Mother, and it was never so true now that her mother was dead. As the sun flashed across her eyelids, Augusta found herself invoking that oldest picture of all: the First Mother, the good mother, loving, true; the mother suffused in martyred holiness. Yet even as the wheels in their incessant circling chanted "saint saint saint," the train screeched around a corner and into view came the Other Mother, the one who saw Augusta as a symbol of the family's sin.

Augusta's First Mother had enveloped her in a phantasmagorical presence whose memory was less of a picture than a fretwork of feeling that even now could be called up to comfort her. This mother was always laughing, always caressing, causing the child to believe, to explore, to experience life as a hundred fingers playing gently over her being.

The Other Mother, who coexisted with the first, was in thrall to fury. To this Other Mother, Augusta was a pariah; her second, more acceptable baby, Nellie, was preferred. The Other Mother hovered inside Augusta even now, filling her with shame for being alive when Lydia herself lay dead in the grave.

To each mother, Augusta was the most important thing on earth. To the first, she had been the source of all joy; to the second, the source of all disappointment, the cause of all suffering. These two personas existed now within Augusta herself—she had internalized them. Lydia's contradictory behavior had made her feel permanently confused about whether she herself was bad or good; it had left her with a sense of self that was weak, fractured, ambiguous.

Her mother's personality had seemed to bifurcate like a tree. Hate sprang from love, kindness from cruelty; stodginess and practicality shared a bed with childlike romanticism. After her death, the condolence letters spoke of Lydia's loving generosity, her enormous capacity for fun; but not one of them had hinted at her darker, more self-absorbed side. In fact, of the hundreds of people who had filled the church for the funeral Augusta had missed, not one of them, not even Nellie, seemed to really know this double woman who was Augusta's mother.

They would be in the middle of a screaming, tearful fight, Augusta and her mother, and the telephone would ring. Her mother would answer it, chirping "Hi Doll" to Peggy or Betsey, content as a bird in May. Augusta could see her mother now, rubbing her hands together vigorously, excitedly, as though she had energy she could not dispel any other way, hooting with pleasure, uttering a wisecrack that would break up the room. Augusta had loved her mother and had longed for her all her life. But she had hated her too, with a remembered and dangerous rage.

For the First Mother, life was a festival of stories; the fantastic spun from the banal, the ordinary transformed into a shimmering apocryphal tale. Lydia's own childhood had been given the sheen of a fairy tale. Born into the prestigious Woolsey family, great-grandchild of the legendary Cornelius Woolsey, inheritor of his historic farm, Lydia had grown up in the orchards of indulgence. True, her mother was always off on cruises, but two great-grandparents, one grandmother, and a beloved father doted on her instead. She had even gone on living there after her marriage, just like every other Woolsey woman.

For Augusta, pleasing the First Mother, causing her to break forth in laughter, feeling her hands run gratefully through your hair, became an end in itself. When her mother was pleased, Augusta was magically endowed; stardust fell over her, and she could come to no harm. When Augusta was five, she fell out of a rotten apple tree, sliding down the bark until a branch had pierced her stomach like an arrow. She lay on the hospital table while the doctor eased the stick out of her and staunched the blood. Her eyes were fixed in terror on the needle and thread as it went in and out of her midriff. Her mother, trying to block her view, spied a cobweb on the ceiling and thereupon began a hair-raising story about the spider scurrying back to her spider children, who were doing dangerous acrobatics on the topmost strand. When the story was finished—the mama spider had spun an emergency thread to catch her children as they plummeted—the doctor had finished too. Augusta's fall, like everything else in their lives, soon became inflated to myth; each time her mother spoke of it, the branch seemed to have penetrated farther up into her chest, until it barely missed her heart.

Augusta thought of her mother in those days as a giant bird upon whose back she rode; they might escape the fussy presence of the grandparents and fly to the Land of the Supermarket, where Augusta could go racing along in a wire cage, buried in a mountain of colored boxes. Or they might fly to the Land of the Apple Blossoms, where Augusta, wrapped in a slicker and bee veil, was allowed to peer into her daddy's dangerous bee boxes and watch the bees make honey. When they rested, the Mother spread her big warm wings over Augusta, who was so happy she could never imagine life otherwise.

Augusta often thought about capturing her mother's magical personality on film, but instead she had gone on to be a talent agent, fostering other people's film careers instead.

It was when she turned six that things began to fall apart, and the First Mother seemed to disappear in a puff of fairy dust. It was then that Lydia's second child, Nellie, was born. And it was then that her husband, Henry, began a life devoted to committing adultery.

Lydia was very much in love with Henry, although, like all Woolseys, she was unable to express that particular emotion in physical ways. Instead of sheltering Augusta, her mother's wings now seemed to smother her, to leave her gasping for air.

Lydia's watch over her first child shifted from gentle to fierce; she would not let Augusta out of her sight. Augusta could not go to other people's homes; she could not leave the orchards. Lydia grew enraged when she expressed an opinion of her own, or attached herself to one of her grandparents. Yet, half the time, Augusta's mother did not seem to know she existed. The new baby, Nellie, now flew on her mother's back during those flights of love and fancy. Augusta's needs became mere annoyances; she even complained about picking Augusta up at school. Lydia's first child, her precious gift-child, had become as burdensome as a bad apple crop. It was as though the great embracing bird that was Augusta's First Mother, the Good Mother, had flown away, wishing to reverse time and events, to return Augusta to the egg, and the egg to her body.

Later, much later, Augusta still wondered whether she had imagined this withdrawal of her mother's love and presence; was it just a figment of her selfish infantile imagination? For not only did her mother deny treating her so, she also told Augusta that she was and had always been the center of her universe; that she had arrived as a gift-child after many miscarriages. Augusta never knew for sure whether the gift-child story was just another myth, but she loved taking it out and thinking about it, especially when all the other signs seemed to point to her uselessness.

Perhaps her memory had simply created this negative Other Mother. Now, as she looked out upon the sleepy river towns, the brick-front factories of her youth, she remembered how often she had been made to take part in her parents' miserable battles. Having risen to the sound of their voices, which the grandparents pretended not to hear, she would go and try to heal them.

For some reason, her parents' reconciliations often took place around the bathtub. Her mother would call Augusta to come into the big old bathing room upstairs. Floating majestically in the clawfoot tub, her stomach ballooning out, shiny as a helmet, her mother would say, "Go tell Daddy he is an icklebick." And off Augusta would run, carrying the image of her mother's hopeful face, pounding down the stairs to the only other bathroom in the house, where her father was ensconced. Sometimes Augusta would have to beg her father to participate in the game—"Tell her she's a mashed potato, Dad"—and then she would run back and forth between the bathrooms, eagerly, anxiously, transmitting messages, drawing them back together, sometimes nearly tripping over her great-great-grand-father Cornelius, who was confined to a wheelchair and liked to see activity.

With luck, by dinnertime tensions would have eased; as they sat down at the table, Augusta would watch, holding her breath. If her mother shifted her regal shoulders toward her father and asked, for instance, if the roast beef was rare enough for him, this was the signal that the war, for the moment, was over, that Augusta had done her job well, and that for this night, at least, the silence at the dinner table would not be so great that you could hear great-grandmother click her fork on her dentures.

One time her father actually disappeared. Went AWOL from Woolsey Orchards. The incident turned out to be her mother's finest hour. Lydia was always superb in the big crises. She was, in fact, always superb when she was the center of attention. This time the grandparents could not ignore what had happened, for it had actually happened in their lives before: Lydia's grandfather, who, like Henry Bean, had agreed to start his married life in the family home of his wife, Mildred Woolsey (Cornelius's daughter), had left suddenly "for a quart of milk" and had never come back.

Augusta's grandparents hovered over Lydia when Henry had left on this "indefinite business trip." And so had Augusta. "When is Daddy coming back?" Augusta had wept, with Nel-lie joining in. Their mother, who had been consoling herself with the compulsive consumption of cupcakes, had snapped out of her morosity, and taken her distressed children in hand. They made Welcome Home signs. They tied imaginary messages to their father on imaginary falcons. They made pictures of the kind of presents he might be carrying for them when he walked through the door. This healing instinct was the best part of Lydia Woolsey-Bean, this ability to inspire and to mend, to single-handedly lift them up and fit the pieces of their lives back into some exciting shape.

The trouble was, she was the one who often shattered them in the first place.

When their father finally did return, Lydia changed again and went on a rampage to punish him. She would cut him dead with a few words; she nagged, she belittled. Her fury seeped down to taint Augusta, who always felt that in some essential way she herself was to blame for her father's infidelities.

After this, Lydia became afraid periodically to answer the telephone. She would make Augusta answer it for fear the telephone lines would carry evidence of another secret betrayal. "Was it a woman?" her mother would ask, "wanting your father?" and Augusta learned to lie, to create a fantasy as instantly as her mother had created fantasies to console her desperate children. "No, Mother, it was the tobacconist in town. Daddy's cherry pipe-tobacco has come in, you know, the kind you like."

"Rubbish," her mother would say, tears forming in her eyes. "You know very well that I know it was a woman."

And so Augusta's relations with her mother alternated, throughout her childhood, between the sublime and the absurd. She seldom knew for sure when she got up in the morning whether or not she would find the First Mother, full of warmth and delights, advice and concern, or the morose, sullen woman who was the Other Mother, who would walk past her, frozen-eyed, or look her up and down with scorn.

In the quiet of her room at night, Augusta would write out prayers; she would make deals with God. She would do anything if he would grant her Most Precious Wish: that her father would love her mother, that her mother would love her father, and that her mother would love Augusta as completely as she once had.

By the time Augusta was eleven, she and her mother had stopped touching, though Lydia's intense involvement with Augusta did not abate. When Augusta graduated with honors from high school, her mother displayed copies of her certificate in three different rooms, and introduced herself as "the mother of the valedictorian." When Augusta's first serious boyfriend turned out to be William Hurley, the class president and the son of a prominent attorney, her mother was so delighted that she knitted him two sweaters and three pairs of socks. But often the involvement between mother and daughter was of a desperate kind, designed to make up for their frequent fights, which for a time replaced her parents' fights in their ability to cast a chill over the household. The deaf grandparents often missed Lydia's subtle degradation of Augusta, but even they could not help hearing Augusta's newly acquired four-letter words, delivered at the top of her lungs. The grandparents shook their heads, averted their eyes, and pursed their lips at the deplorable behavior of their Woolsey granddaughter. Then, one by one, they died: first the indomitable great-great-grandfather Cornelius, then his daughter, Great-grandmother Mildred, and finally Grandfather Augustus, all within three years. By the time Augusta went screaming into her fourteenth year, the Woolsey generations had shrunk to three, with Lydia's mother, Amenia, the only grandparent left.

After college, Augusta fled to the farthest point she could: California. Expecting that the distance would make her family recede and enable her to begin living her own life, she found instead that her stature at home took on near-gigantic proportions.

It was not only that she was the first Woolsey to venture outside the family circle—she turned out to be extraordinarily successful at it. At Celebrities International, a small but highly respected agency, she developed the knack of spotting good material and bringing it to the actors she represented, who loved her because she was subtle in a town where few people are. She didn't manipulate people or push them around, and she had an artist's imagination. She created the temptation of a story in which her clients could transform themselves, the way her mother had created glittering worlds for her when Augusta was a child.

Her family, with their eagerness for news of her, soon loomed as large in her life as her movie stars. Her mother fairly soaked up her stories of famous directors and producers refusing to deal with any other agent but Augusta Woolsey-Bean of Celebrities International. She overpraised Augusta, and exaggerated her importance (she had Augusta dating Robert Redford; she had her running the talent agency) and she barely acknowledged Nellie's existence.

Nellie had asked Augusta many times during this past year, as her mother gradually lost her battle with cancer, to take a leave of absence from her job. Her father begged her to just get on a plane and come home. Augusta had pleaded pressing work; she was putting together an important film package and could not break away. But that was not the truth. In fact, she had tried to go home, but somehow she kept missing the plane. She would actually get to the airport and then discover that she had forgotten her ticket, or locked her keys in her car.

She talked to her mother regularly on the telephone, but each time she lifted the receiver, the dread would nearly paralyze her. She felt that she was in a childhood dream; the wolf was coming at her but she could not move; her legs were frozen in place.

She did not want her mother to die. She especially did not want her mother to die before the Most Precious Wish was answered.

Somewhere, deep inside, she really had believed that if she was good, if she was able to transcend the bad selfish girl she imagined herself to be, God would make the wish come true.

But now that her mother was dying, Augusta the adult realized that Augusta the child never really had a chance. She had been tricked by this cancer, this illness that was taking her mother away.

Ironically, in the end, Lydia Woolsey-Bean had undergone a transformation of love. She had developed a passionate faith in God, and that faith had made her serene, grateful, and happy.

Augusta wished, oh how she wished, that she had been able to share in her mother's rebirth, had truly made peace with her. But she had not. At the time, it had seemed too late. The First Mother had died for her decades before. Augusta could not watch her die a second time.

She had gone home briefly for her birthday in September and then briefly at Christmas—her mother's last—but had found being home unbearably painful, even more so since her mother, now tolerant and loving, had, in spite of her physical agony, found the visits so fulfilling. Augusta prayed that her mother had not sensed her discomfort, that she had not once again spoiled things for her mother, spoiled her death as she had spoiled her life.

In mid-January, her mother had suddenly and unexpectedly taken a turn for the worse, then died abruptly. Augusta had been camping out, in the desert; the rugged nature-loving writer of the important film script she had been working on had gone there to rewrite his ending, and he had insisted he needed Augusta along for inspiration. The family had been unable to reach her until five days after Lydia was dead.

As soon as she learned of her mother's death, something profound happened to Augusta. She lost interest in her work and in her friends. Without her mother to encourage her, to devour her, her life seemed meaningless. Her world was suddenly peopled with greedy promoters, spoiled prima donnas, narcissistic authors, their products exploitative, derivative, homogenized. The entire movie industry, which before had seemed glamorous, exciting, laced with metaphor and Aristotelian principle, now just seemed cheap.

Augusta confronted what she had somehow known all along: she had become what she was for her mother. A child of the sixties, she had marched against the Vietnam war, had been outraged, had believed in a countercultural philosophy of moral integrity and the search for truth. But when her mother intervened through a friend and helped Augusta get a job as a talent agent, there was never any question that Augusta would take the job—although she had insisted on starting at the firm's Los Angeles office, not at the nearby New York one. Suppressing the inclinations of her heart, she had succumbed to her mother's version of her, to her mother's dreams of family glory within the Establishment.

Once her mother was dead, she saw that she had become in fact only a glorified salesman. She did love movies, but as she traveled to raise support for her latest package, she realized that she was a kind of Willy Loman, trading empty words over long liquid lunches, staying in hotel rooms with locked windows and ventilators that blew around the smells of spilled whiskey and stale sex. More and more, she despised herself for her persuasive charms, for her slick ability to flip things over so that the seller became the buyer and the beggar the begged for.

Augusta had a secret: she was, in fact, a sham; not even her beloved Grandma Amenia, who abruptly followed Lydia to the grave, still dazzled by her granddaughter, suspected the truth.

Augusta's enormous talent, her prodigious self-confidence, it was all just another family myth, like the branch that had threatened her heart. No one knew that in the beginning she had barely squeaked by at her job. She had hated and feared the high-powered desperate world she was plunged into. She hated selling herself. And she had grave trouble with basic arithmetic. She had always multiplied on her fingers, and could barely grasp the complicated finances involved in putting together an entertainment package. It was only by constant work, by working when every other young agent in the office had gone home, that Augusta kept up with and finally surpassed them.

Now, Augusta was terrified that she would come home, ostensibly to straighten things out, but actually to end up messing them up worse than Nellie had. Her mother had half-resentfully pointed out that Augusta was making more money early on in her job than the whole family had ever made from Woolsey Orchards and Augusta imagined she knew the real reason why. It was only by religiously seizing opportunities to impress her boss as a yes-person, a token woman who would cause no trouble and flatter on request, that she was promoted so rapidly. Her family labored under the illusion that her social life was fast and glittering, that she had men chasing after her, but in actuality every man she had ever loved during her fifteen years in Los Angeles had ended up sending her away. She would pick men who had some fatal flaw, alcoholics or gamblers, the raffish, the ambivalent, the ungiving, renegades who pretended not to need her but who needed her desperately. She came to the conclusion that she also had a fatal flaw: once emotionally hooked by a man, she would become so dependent on him that she would cancel herself out. She could never leave these relationships, and would linger inside them until her lover finally pulled out. For the last year, she had been so mistrustful of this propensity for losing herself to an unworthy man that she had stayed away from men altogether. But lately she had battled strange, restive feelings. When she got to the desert with the screenwriter, she had decided in her mind to let him make love to her upon the baking sands—but he had never even asked.

Two months after her mother died, Augusta sold her house in the Hollywood hills, quit her job to the protests of her boss and her clients, and responded to her family's cries to come home and help.

Now, as the train rolled into the Stonekill Landing station, her heart began to race. She could never go forward or change her life until she resolved what was behind her, until she rid herself of this woman who possessed her twice as strongly as she had when she was alive. Augusta saw her in every crowd: a familiar silk dress, a broad back, a silvery voice, a wave of honeyed hair. This woman who had created Augusta from a microscopic egg would never die. She had become, in a sense, the egg within the egg, an oval of swirling marble, orange blossoming yellow, soft sun rising to fire on the horizon. The egg was inside her for perpetuity. Sometimes it lay buried, its influence subtle; at other times she could feel its outline, hard and tender beneath the surface.

Catching sight of Nellie and her father on the station platform, Augusta felt the twin stabs of surprise and recognition. Her family always looked different from the way she imagined, and yet they were so familiar, like the look of one's own body; the mind knew them but did not remember them quite the way they were. Characteristically, Nellie and Henry were bumbling about. Her father seemed to be going back to the car, which she might have predicted; he always tried to avoid moments of emotion.

Augusta closed her eyes so that she too could delay the moment of reentry, the invasion into her world of this father, once tall and perfect, now as fragile as a late cornstalk, and this sister, his miniature self. The sight of them instilled more pity in her than fear, but the tightening of fear in her chest was what she felt when she thought of how easy it would be for her to get off this train and never get back on. Her mother had warned her, in a thousand different ways, that Augusta and she could never be separate from each other. And when Augusta had tried to separate herself, when she had not come home this last year, her mother had not blamed her outright. Instead, she had died.

Augusta clenched her jaw. She would not let Nellie and her father keep her here by playing on her guilt, by throwing up to her her final betrayal of her mother. This time she simply wouldn't let it happen.

She got out of the train, struggling with her bags. She was annoyed at herself; she had brought much too much stuff. She should have packed most of it in the trunks she had sent on to the farm for storage. She had made a promise to herself: no matter what, she would leave here by her birthday, September 25, six months hence. She would go to Europe, or Africa, any place far away, where she could figure out what she really wanted to do with her life.

Augusta's arm suddenly gave way, and she dropped her bags. She looked up and saw Nellie, face beaming, running toward her. And that old feeling of shame, of remorse, slid down inside her like an eel.

CHAPTER 3

Nellie followed her sister through the quiet rural station, marveling at how Augusta had simply assumed Nellie would carry her suitcases. But then Augusta had never really seen Nellie the person, the way you don't see your bellboy until he misplaces your bags.

For a few moments, when they had embraced, Nellie had almost believed that things might be the way they sometimes had been in the past: the Woolsey-Bean sisters, banding together whenever there was family stress, protecting, loving, enriching each other; best friends. While the friction between them was acute, it had always ceased in the face of threats from outside.

On the railroad platform, they had exchanged their stock greeting, each one saying she had never seen the other look so skinny. They were both afraid of becoming obese like their mother, and so these words were a comforting ritual, like warm milk brought to you in the nursery. But Augusta had not apologized for jettisoning her responsibilities to their dying mother onto Nellie; indeed, her confident progress through the station carried no hint of humility, gratitude, or regret.

"Daddy." Augusta came up beside her father, who was outside, opening the trunk of the battered old Imperial.

Bean drank in the sight of her, using all his small cheek muscles, which usually lay locked, to keep his face under control; he tried to drive from his mind the delicate feel of Augusta's backbone. His first daughter always moved him so, but God, he had forgotten how much she looked like Lydia ... his late wife emerging from the train station, folding herself into his arms, coming back, finally, to free him from self-recrimination.

"Daddy, let's take the scenic route home, let's give Augusta a homecoming tour," Nellie said as they drove out of the station. The sisters chattered excitedly, and Nellie grew more hopeful that perhaps this time they would succeed in a reconciliation. But then this was part of the pattern, wasn't it? At first they would have a strange and powerfully arousing effect on each other. Whether they were talking of clothes or the weather or childhood reminiscences, the cascade of words, the air around the words, always crackled like the air round incipient lovers. And when the air went dead, as it always did, it was as though an invisible grate had slammed down between them.

The valley farmland was having a disquieting effect on Augusta. The cornfields were alive, even in March, their stalks poking up through the powdering snow like old men sunk to their ankles in mud. Mount Freedom, where Augusta had picked laurel and watched the sun rise over the horizon, stood immense and matronly. Fog sidled up from the river, clinging to the trees and wrapping itself around the peak like an unrequited lover.

They were coming upon Woolsey Orchards now, the rows of trees dipping and curving like dancers, stark in their late-winter dignity. The dramatic rise and fall of the hills tugged at Augusta, filling her with homesickness and sorrow. You could still see the bleached red barn that Coert occupied.

Coert Van Voorhees, the beloved Woolsey farm manager, was Augusta's special friend. In just a few weeks, the barn would be submerged by the sudden bursting forth of apple blossoms, their bloom bringing a whirling cotillion of upturned petticoats to the hills. Out of the corner of her eye, Augusta saw Nellie staring intently at her, willing her, Augusta believed, to feel sorry that she had ever forsaken such bucolic glory.

Augusta hated the way this land, these trees were making her feel. She rolled up her window; the glass had been cracked years ago, and so to look out of it was to look upon the rushing of a shattered universe.

"You have to admit how beautiful this is!" Nellie exclaimed, unable to repress herself any longer. "You did miss the farm, didn't you, Augusta? Didn't you? Just a little bit?"

"According to the new issue of the *Wappappee Historical Society Magazine,* our place is the most scenic spot in the area," Henry said, his voice acquiring an authoritative timbre.

"In the *county,* Dad. In the whole *county,*" Nellie said. "Maybe even in the whole Hudson Valley. Not another estate, not another farm, not even the scenic landmarks in the state parks are as spectacular as ours. We're the only corner left unspoiled."

"How much?" Augusta asked. To her surprise, her question came out hard and fast, like a bullet. "How much is it going to cost to save all this beauty?" Her voice sounded, even to her own ears, uncharacteristically sarcastic.

Henry looked away from the road for a moment to stare at her with surprise. Then he cleared his throat and said, "We've got to buy the oil sprays; we have to smother the insect eggs while the trees are still dormant, and we have to do that in a couple of weeks. And then there's the fungicides. We have to have enough on hand to cover the orchard by the time the April showers come, or scab could wipe us out. We need ten thousand dollars, Augusta—at least."

Augusta looked out at the trees, which all at once looked

ugly, bent, thick with unpruned shoots. "I suppose I shouldn't even ask how much you have left from the sale of the fall harvest. Or where the last infusion of money I sent you has gone?" Augusta was amazed and a little frightened at her harshness. She should be acting like the penitent one, eager to make up for her long absence. But instead she was doing what she had never done before—calling her family to account. For years she had been helping to carry the farm, yet every time she sent a check, they all pretended she had not. Her mother or her father or Nellie would drop the gentlest of hints that they were in trouble, whereupon Augusta would offer to help, whereupon her family would say, "Oh no, we couldn't." Whereupon Augusta would end up begging them to take the money. This system not only saved her family's pride, it enabled them to take from her but to deny that they needed to.

Nellie was caught off guard by Augusta's bluntness, her departure from the established game, the carefully orchestrated denial. Nevertheless, she rose up from the backseat, set her shoulders in what Augusta noticed was an eerie imitation of their mother, and spoke quietly. "Do you mean to say that after a year's absence, and after only being here for fifteen minutes, before we've even reached the house, your first thoughts are about money? Not a word, a thought about anything or anyone else? Not a word about Mother, or Grandma, or missing the funerals? The only thing you can say is 'How much is it going to cost me?' "

"I didn't say that," Augusta said, suddenly feeling the roughness of the ash-burnt vinyl under her thighs, suddenly smelling the sickening, acrid odor of her father's pipes lined up on the Imperial's extra-wide ashtray.

"You, who are rolling in money, come home, with Mom dead only ten weeks, with Grandma Amenia freshly buried, and what are you thinking about: 'How much is preserving the family going to cost me?' " Nellie went on. "Let me ask you this, Augusta. How much did it cost you to abandon Mother on her deathbed?"

"You bitch! At least I gave her something to live for," Augusta snapped, and immediately she regretted it. Nellie was right—two minutes into her visit and Augusta was displaying the self-discipline of a wolf. Did she really have to lower herself to her sister's level? To fuel the old rivalry, the ugly primitive competition for everything, including, still, their mother's love?

"I suppose you mean that Mom fed off your phenomenal successes," Nellie retorted. "I notice that they didn't actually keep her alive."

"Stop, stop, stop," Henry Bean said, slowing the car and knocking his head in histrionic despair against the steering wheel. His deep baritone voice was the strongest, indeed the only weapon he had had for a long time, and it had served invariably to silence his wife. Now it silenced his daughters.

They turned into the drive that led up to the house, passing the row of Romes that Augusta's great-great-grandfather Cornelius had planted. The trees had then been exactly the same size as four-year-old Augusta; the idea was to see who grew faster. The trees had shot up, leaving Augusta behind, of course, but now they were an ominous umber color, half-dead or dying.

"We have a nice fresh-killed chicken from the game farm for dinner. I plucked it myself," Henry said to Augusta. "Just like your mother used to have for you when you came home."

"That's not all we have for you," Nellie said under her breath.

Augusta looked at Nellie's face. It seemed the face of a devil, red cheeks, pursed, V-shaped mouth. How many times throughout their childhood had this same stifling silence fallen over the Imperial, its passengers warring, its children forced to drown out the silence by concentrating on the rhythmic noise made by the tires as they hit the road grids?

Augusta had not expected it all to start so soon, but now that it had started, it felt oddly natural, familiar. A few hours ago she had been a leading Hollywood talent agent, making deci-

sions that affected the lives of millions of American moviego-
ers. She had been a wise, calm, soft-spoken adult. Suddenly, she
had undergone time-lapse photography, backwards; she was a
child again. If moments ago she had stood up to her family,
and refused to be cowed by guilt, it was not without a price.
Through Nellie's eyes now, she saw her worst self: a resentful,
acid-tongued adolescent whom it seemed Augusta had not
been able to kill off after all.

How could she expect to win against her past? Even though
the world had judged her a success, she might as well sit back
and sprout dark wool through her pores and settle her voice
into a permanent bleat. Her disguise was gone. The black sheep
of the family was home.

Augusta walked through the front door and was flooded with
the old smells: damp wood, leather worn soft, rich musty odors
like bread baking. The yellowed brocade wallpaper of drifting
ferns and hollyhock seemed to envelop her in its dreamy familiarity. And there was Jeeves, the big round newel post at the
bottom of the staircase, which had always looked to her like a
disapproving butler waiting to take her hat. Augusta's knees
felt weak; she sat down, and against the small of her back she
felt her mother's tapestry pocketbook, lying against the chair
exactly where it had always lain. She closed her eyes and,
resounding through the silence, she heard the bell-like voice,
hardly able to contain its excitement, pealing forth in exquisite
pleasure, "She's here! Augusta's arrived! Hurry, Henry, hurry
up . . ." And then the band, marching into the hall, the three
of them with Nellie bringing up the rear, banging the pot lids,
"For she's a jolly good fellow, for she's a jolly . . ."

Augusta opened her eyes, and there was only her mother's
absence; in the dust on the legs of the chair, in the empty
flower urns, in the tarnished picture frames that cried out for
Augusta to polish them; in this bulge behind her back, in her
mother's belongings—purse, sewing bag, scarf, even a couple

of the old-fashioned widened bobby pins she had used on her hair!—left carelessly around. It seemed a sacrilege. What could Nellie and her father have been doing all these months?

She opened a drawer of the bonnet-topped secretary and found the same mementos she remembered finding there for thirty years: flowers pressed into opera programs, envelopes with hair cuttings and children's baby teeth. The family founder, Cornelius, had begun the tradition of saving everything that might explain the awesome Woolseys to future generations, and the practice had been scrupulously followed ever since, down to the lace (preserved between two pieces of waxed paper) from the petticoat that Augusta's mother had worn under her wedding dress. This house of her childhood was reeking with seduction; she felt its tentacles closing around her neck.

She suddenly realized that the tarnished picture frames she had absently noticed when she first came into the hall were everywhere, on the walls, on the radiator cover, and they contained pictures of her mother: daguerrotypes of her in bloomers, carrying a parasol, in cap and gown; wedding pictures, baby pictures, old candids. Augusta remembered how her mother had never liked seeing photographs of herself; she would have hated this!

Nellie came down the stairs just then, having brought Augusta's bags up to her room. She made a silent vow: she would try again to make peace with her sister. "Are you admiring how clean the house is? I spent all morning on my hands and knees to get it ready for you. The dog is vomiting everywhere these days."

"What are all these pictures, Nellie?" Augusta asked. "And the candles around them?"

"Aren't they wonderful? I wanted to fill the house with Mom for you . . . and for us. For a while, anyway. Don't you love the one of me and Mom in the wading pool, isn't it funny?"

Augusta swallowed. "It's a little like a shrine, isn't it? Or an

Egyptian tomb, or one of those Italian crypts where everybody's drawer carries an old tinted likeness."

"Do you always have to make allusions to the exotic places you've been?" Nellie replied, looking so gloomy that Augusta felt ashamed of herself. She suddenly realized that Nellie had put up the pictures so that she could get in touch with a mother she had wished for but never known. Perhaps what Nellie was doing was no different from what Augusta was doing—trying to come to terms with the two mothers rooted in her being. If only they could reach out to each other, help each other. Lydia's black moods and rages had once literally driven the sisters into each other's arms; they had taken refuge under an old spreading Newtown Pippin tree that they called Auntie Mame, and they had pretended they were orphans huddling together for protection against a thunderstorm of apple blossoms. Now that Lydia was dead, maybe they could join together again to ease each other's pain, to resolve the tumultuous legacy she had left them.

"Nellie," Augusta began, carefully. "Do you remember, when we were little, sometimes we thought Mom was a saint because of what she had to suffer? Remember how she used to trudge heavily up those stairs, as though she carried some anguish we could never know? Do you ever think about the reverse side of her martyrdom? That she might not only be the victim, but also the victimizer?"

Nellie stared at Augusta and her cheeks grew pink. "Victimizer!? Martyr!?" Nellie held up the picture of herself and her mother in the wading pool, wielding it as though it were a knife. "This woman was in such agony that when I helped her across the room to the toilet, her elbows trembled. This woman had to have the telephone wrapped in a blanket, because its ring jolted the bones in her body. Still, she insisted on having it in her room in case you called. I daresay you, or even I, would have crawled under the bed and screamed for morphine in her condition. But did she? No. Instead, she made a needlepoint pillow! For you."

Nellie took the pillow out of the sewing bag and tossed it at her sister. "Even on days when she could barely hold the needle, she sewed and sewed because she wanted to finish it before she died. Each day she said, 'This will be the day Augusta comes home,' and each day she was disappointed."

Augusta fingered the pillow. Her mother's work had once been flawless, but Augusta's initials, stitched in the center in large spring colors, were rough and wavy. It was beautiful; Augusta held it to her chest and her head began to swim. She held onto the radiator for support.

"She loved my being in Hollywood, she loved hearing about the movie stars," Augusta said, her breath coming fast. "I couldn't have taken time off from my job to come home. I was afraid to. I was afraid that Mother would find me out, that she'd discover I was mostly a product of her fantasy."

"If you had come home, Mother would probably have held on longer."

"If I had come home, I might have blurted out the truth and the truth would have killed her," Augusta said. "Do you know I've never even *met* Robert Redford? I just deal with his personal manager. Do you know that most of what I do is two-bit bullshit? At first I lied about glamorous successes I didn't even have, then finally I didn't need to lie."

"Oh, we all know how well you've done," Nellie waved dismissively. "You're just flailing around trying to excuse yourself, but you don't need to. Mother didn't blame you. Up until the day she died, in her eyes you could do no wrong."

"And in your eyes I can't do anything right! You make me out to be this all-powerful indestructible force who could have kept Mother alive, but Jesus, Nellie, you're exaggerating my role the same as she did. Only you're doing it to make me feel lousy."

"Always thinking of yourself first, Augusta," Nellie said acidly, knowing this would get to her sister; it was the phrase Lydia had always used to taunt Augusta with. "If you feel lousy, I daresay it's because you crave something in this house that you can't get anymore. It's because the one person who hung on your every word is dead."

Augusta started toward Nellie, wanting to sock her, but all of a sudden Nellie began to cry.

"Don't you know what it was like for me?" she sobbed. "I needed you, we all did. I couldn't make her better. I wanted to make her better, but I couldn't make her feel good the way you could."

Augusta suddenly remembered a scene a few years ago: her mother introducing her daughters to the president of the Gristbrook Country Club. "This is my daughter, Nellie," she said, barely glancing at Nellie, "and this," she exclaimed, beaming upon Augusta as though she were buried treasure, "this is Augusta."

Augusta had felt mortified for Nellie then, and she felt mortified now; she would give anything if she could turn back time and tell her mother that she must, just once, make Nellie feel as valuable as her sister. Augusta took her sister's hand. "You've been wonderful, holding everything together all alone. But you won't be alone anymore. I'm home, Nell."

"Yes, you're home," Nellie said coldly. "Mother always believed you would come back on a white charger. It's too bad she didn't live to see it."

Nellie's hand in hers suddenly felt coarse, dead, and Augusta dropped it. Typical Woolsey, Augusta thought, soften up your victim so she reaches out to you and then punch her in the gut. "I don't know why you think you need me so much, you don't even like me. And I'm damn well not going to take responsibility for everybody's life here."

Nellie wiped her eyes, straightened her belt. "You don't need to, thank you. You may think nothing has changed around here, but I can guarantee you, plenty has." Nellie gave Augusta the family look, secretive, knowing, superior. "This house is different than it was when you left it, Augusta, in ways you cannot even imagine. I don't think you'll be too happy about it." Nellie picked up the pictures of her mother, one by one. "These frames need polishing. I think I'll polish them now," she said, then left the room.

Augusta stood for a moment, her hands going clammy with fear at Nellie's ominous words. That ridiculous old fear. How many times had Augusta stood in this house with those sentences rebounding from her head, words uttered by her mother to her, by her grandmother to her mother, by her mother to her father? "You'll pay for this"; "Do *you* have a surprise coming!"; "Mark my words, you'll be sorry someday!"—words that had the cruel power of the unknown, that could wrap you in an almost masochistic anticipation of the worst. But wait; Augusta shook her head. She wasn't six years old anymore. And her mother, her grandmothers, all the Woolseys with their knowledge of the torment of mystery, they were all dead. This was only Nellie, Nellie using the phrases she had learned, in order to impress her older sister.

Nellie was proud of herself and rightly so. She had grown and blossomed; her parents, accustomed to relying on Augusta, had turned to Nellie. Augusta had deserted, had relinquished her status as Most Favored Daughter. Nellie had the moral edge. And so what? Surely that was all Nellie's ominous words had meant, wasn't it?

Augusta looked at the door to the downstairs bedroom, her mother's sickroom, with a sense of foreboding. It had seen virtually every Woolsey die. The door was closed, but in her mind Augusta opened it, and saw her mother sitting by the window in a blue mohair shawl, her eyes bright, the sun tying ribbons of gold around her emaciated, unsteady body. But when Augusta opened the door, the room was dark and smelled of rotting flowers. There were used Kleenexes by the bedside table, along with a Bible and a laminated bookmark printed with the Lord's Prayer. By the window, the blue mohair shawl that Augusta had sent her mother from California was draped across the shoulders of the chair, as though Lydia would be back any minute. Augusta quickly closed the door.

She understood why Nellie had not touched her mother's belongings. Just thinking of removing that shawl seemed like another betrayal. You only empty a room when a person dies. At this moment, Lydia Woolsey-Bean seemed incapable of extinction.

She walked into the library, and there was her mother again, amid the gallery of Woolseys rendered in oil; Cornelius had insisted that his heirs grace the library walls. Looking at the portrait of her mother, painted when she was in her twenties, Augusta could see what people meant when they said that she and her mother looked like twins. They shared the same widely spaced eyes, a departure from the characteristic close-together Woolsey eyes that Nellie had inherited. They fell short of being beautiful, or even classically pretty, for their jaws and cheeklines were too long and their slender noses too strong; they had sturdy, even horsey, House of Windsor looks, but their coloring, rose and ivory skin with Dresden-blue eyes, made them striking.

The mother Augusta gazed at was slim, sculptured; it was only when Lydia reached her mid-thirties, Augusta's age, that she became overweight. Augusta's heart beat faster; would some similar disaster befall her, would she be plunged into the same kind of compulsive eating? Would she one day wake up and find that she had become the type of matron who spilled over chairs, who could only shop in oversize-clothing stores, who had to trap herself in girdles and long-line bras, who would never look in mirrors, who was caught on an eternal roller-coaster of losing pounds and gaining them back; who could embarrass her children by simply running to catch a train? Augusta suddenly felt diminished. Her mother had been a beautiful woman, everyone had said so. Augusta seemed to be the only one who had felt ashamed of her.

She looked around at the gallery of portraits. Four generations of Woolseys stood stolid: the family founder Cornelius, his daughter Mildred, her daughter Amenia, and her daughter Lydia, looking like four different exposures of the same negative, with their ponderous eyelids, their ironic mouths, their shoulders squared.

An especially ornate gold frame encircled Cornelius Woolsey, whose sideburns were brushed as luminous as a cat's back and whose eyes were rendered so skillfully that they followed you from one side of the room to the other. In his high-collared gray morning coat, he looked like an everlasting watchman, presiding over this house that he had built in 1873.

At a young age, Cornelius, dreaming of adventure and wealth, had left his job as an apprentice at the hattery of one John Bowler in the City of London, and made his way to the port of New York, then up the Hudson Valley. Dressed in his best Eton-style waistcoat and top hat, he had wandered into the Wappappee Hatworks Company, and, using paper and pins, put together a hat with an odd dome-shaped crown and curved brim; it was none other than the bowler, or derby, as it came to be called in the new country. Thanks to this whimsical lad from England, it was Wappappee County that had it first.

Cornelius went on to marry the daughter of the hatworks owner, and within several years, he had helped found the town of Stonckill Landing. He owned a brick-making factory, the Stonckill Landing Savings Institution, the weekly newspaper, and the village inn, which he named the Hopestill Arms. His wife had been so eccentrically devoted to her family (she was named Hopestill because her parents, after five daughters, were still hoping for a boy when she was born) that on her wedding day she wore a gown of silver-gray to symbolize her sadness at leaving her father's home. Augusta thought perhaps Hopestill had cast some kind of spell down through the generations, for no Woolsey woman ever again let marriage interfere with remaining in her family home.

But Cornelius built Hopestill something better than the house she grew up in. Amid 250 acres of farmland, upon which he planted several varieties of apple trees, Cornelius erected the centerpiece of his fortune, as a kind of shrine in which to ensconce his wife. Hopestill was a pale-skinned prima donna and the one thing in Cornelius's life that threatened to slip out of his hands. She had a sweet voice and such unique beauty that the very sight of her stopped the rocking of men's chairs in front of the post office. Luckily, Hopestill, who carried herself like a swan and had that bird's same voraciousness, was more than content to tinker and toy in loneliness with the earthly pleasures her husband could give her. There was, so it was said, no end to her demand for them.

Augusta's great-great-grandfather Cornelius had believed that life was a spiral of symbols, signs, and hidden meanings waiting to be revealed. The land he chose was in the shadow of Mount Freedom, on whose summit Revolutionary War patriots had lit beacon fires to give the signal for ambushing redcoats; in fact, a Revolutionary War cannon found on the property still lay in the barn. Cornelius got the stained glass for the windows of the tower from the First Presbyterian Church the day after it burned down; he got the wood for the outdoor cornices from lion cages after a circus went bankrupt; the foundation stones came from the ruins of the first Dutch farmhouse in the valley that was built under the Rombout Patent.

According to family legend, the Woolsey homestead was the envy of Wappappee County. It had the first telephone, the first hot-air furnace, and, as accident would have it, the first public library in town.

From a round table draped with fringed taffeta, Augusta picked up the ten-pound family Bible, with Cornelius's name inscribed on the frontispiece in a spidery script, along with names, added in blue ink, red ink, even in hurried pencil, of all his heirs as they were born down through the decades.

Cornelius had brought with him from England not only the Bible but a black walnut trunk of books; he went on to collect about two thousand volumes over the years, and the library became a rendezvous spot for townspeople, some of whom would borrow his Waverly novels and return them carefully wrapped in brown paper. They had not been touched in decades, and when Augusta lifted one out, it left her fingers black. We should get rid of some of this stuff, Augusta thought—auction it off. She had to come up with a strategy, to figure out how to make some money, clean out the house, and get out of there.

Augusta thought about Cornelius, how he had made all his dreams come true except for the one over which he had no power: Hopestill could not, and then would not, produce for him a son and heir. She delivered one daughter, Mildred, and declared that she would never endure the ordeal again.

The portrait of Mildred was, like her father's, uncannily lifelike: the same artist had captured her mulish chin, her rounded bosom thrusting out like a coat of mail, the heavily folded family eyelids, and even a wickedly rendered hint of her mustache. With the birth of Mildred, the Woolsey line changed forever from a patriarchy to a matriarchy, for from then on, only females (and strong-minded ones, at that) were born. Augusta's great-grandmother, Mildred, had been left virtually a widow by Samuel Beaumont, the one who had walked out for milk one day and never returned, leaving behind a small daughter, Amenia, Augusta's grandmother. Mildred legally changed herself back to a Woolsey, and her husband's name was never spoken in the house again.

Augusta remembered her great-grandmother Mildred as a redoubtable lady, stern, Victorian, and, like all the Woolsey women, prudish to a fanatical degree. Her abandonment must have softened her, Augusta reflected, for Mildred was an endless well of kindness. When her daughter Amenia repeatedly left her own small daughter, Lydia, for the lure of travel abroad,

Mildred stepped into the breach. She provided Lydia with kindness and care; then, later, when Lydia's marital troubles were visited upon her children, Mildred stepped in once again.

Augusta would fling herself sobbing on her bed after a fight with her mother, whereupon she would hear the familiar opening and closing of her bedroom door. Then, the wordless presence of her great-grandmother by her bed, the large arthritic knuckles massaging her back, the honey drops pressed into her hand. Later, when Augusta fought back more strongly against Lydia, Mildred left Augusta's corner and joined the other grandparents in silent condemnation of the monstrous curses that flew from this rebellious little Woolsey's tongue. As she looked now at the portrait of Mildred, Augusta realized that she loved her great-grandmother even for that—for her loyalty to her wounded granddaughter, Lydia, whom she had so abidingly mothered.

To the right of Mildred was the portrait of her daughter, Amenia, a rather homely but determined-looking woman with a small chin that had skipped a generation to land on the face of poor Nellie. Amenia had found her own path to independence from the family by marrying a penniless second cousin from Delaware. Although Amenia's husband, Augustus, was a Woolsey in both name and blood—as great-great-grandfather Cornelius was said to have remarked, "A splendid coup: a marriage of ourselves to ourselves"—it was soon apparent that Amenia had played a trick on the family. She had brought home a Woolsey who matched every Woolsey trait with its mirror opposite—or so Augusta's father, Henry Bean, had put it. Augustus was heartfelt and impulsive, shy and dreamy. And he was a spendthrift. In a household where old petticoats were cut up for handkerchiefs, where good horsehair mattresses were never replaced, even when box springs came in, where Cornelius rolled fireplace "logs" from old newspapers, Augustus's propensity for losing money infuriated everyone. He seemed to live in a wind tunnel, listening to his own echoes, his ideas and his wife's money flying all over the place. A would-be inventor, all of his inventions (the "papple," a cross between the pear and the apple, "gold bricks," which the new rich industrial barons were supposed to buy, but which only bankrupted the brick factory) came to nothing. Old Cornelius, who had been impressed enough with Augustus's ingenuity to turn over the family holdings to his care, lived to regret that decision. Within a few years, Augustus had lost the Hopestill Arms, the newspaper, and had nearly bankrupted the orchards.

At least one person, however, never lost faith in him. Lydia worshipped her kind, romantic father and named her first child, Augusta, after him.

Augustus's wife Amenia, however, had been disappointed by her husband's failures. When her daughter Lydia was still small, she had begun to spend a good part of the year sailing on great cruise ships. Amenia had abandoned her own daughter the way Amenia's father had abandoned her; but when Amenia's two little granddaughters were born, she showered them with attention. Augusta loved this grandmother for her stories of faraway places, for her tales of shimmering ice palaces and resounding amphitheaters, and monkeys that rode on your back, for the wonderful wooden shoes and jeweled vests and sachets full of spices she brought back. Amenia made Augusta dream; she gave her a taste for independence. Whenever her mother would hint that Augusta might do worse than stay on at Woolsey Orchards, Augusta would think of Grandmother Amenia, and she would vow not only to leave these lands for the lands of her imagination, but to leave them for good.

Augusta looked back at the portrait of Lydia, at the mesmerizing eyes of her mother. How could the color blue be so cold yet so hot? The artist had known, had captured her mother's secret, the Woolsey secret: keep showering your children with love, then keep snatching it away, and so you will have them forever. Augusta had known the secret too, and she had vowed never to let her mother's cruel love entrap her as other Woolsey women had been entrapped. By the time Nellie was born, Augusta had already begun rebelling against their mother; no wonder Nellie had such a negative view of Augusta's attitude toward Lydia. Nellie had never been able to understand what Augusta had suffered.

Augusta looked again, now, into the parlor. When she had first arrived, the porch, the staircase, even the floor-length arched windows seemed to have shrunk, but now that she had been here a little while, the furniture was swelling to normal size. Or could it be, she thought, that I am already shrinking? My vision diminishing, my world narrowing into the preserve of this valley, this family? As I go through this house, with the wide plank floors squeaking as they have always squeaked, I am aware of how easily time goes backwards. It is as though adulthood is but a ghost of our real lives, which remain somewhere in childhood.

She looked up at the massive chandelier and felt dizzy. Five generations of Woolsey women have felt dizzy like this, she thought, have replaced the crystal teardrops as they fell from the chandelier, dusted the white marble mantelpiece, received kisses on the brocade loveseat, baptized their children over the silver font, shook out the prayer rug that still lay over the piano. And who was she, Augusta Woolsey-Bean, to single-handedly break the circle? Who was she to rip up what had been lovingly sown and tended for over a century? Was Nellie right? Was money burning a hole in Augusta's heart? Could she really be so selfish as to let their heritage disintegrate, when it was only a matter of money, of paper that could not touch you? Each generation of Woolsey women, in spite of their weaknesses, had tried to leave this heritage stronger, to sustain something of themselves that existed outside of themselves; they knew that while they would surely turn to ash, something in this house that gave rise to each of them would endure. It was there before they were born and would be there after they were gone.

Augusta entered the dining room that opened off the parlor.

A breeze puffed up the glass curtains in the bay windows, and with it came a powerful memory. She was six or seven, and was being punished, made to stand in the corner by the windows for what seemed like hours. Her legs hurt so much that she thought she would scream, but she did not want to give her mother, who was sitting nearby with baby Nellie in her lap, the satisfaction. Suddenly, a miracle had come to release her. The sun flowed in through the glass and swam over the floor like a school of fish. The fish, palpable, moving, drew her in; come with us, they said, stop your weeping; come away and swim with us in the sun; and she did. And she had. She *had* swum away. She had escaped. She had created her own space in the world, and now she wanted to use it.

It wasn't just the money, it was the freedom money could buy her. It was the freedom to fly to ice palaces and amphitheaters and anywhere else she liked, and if she chose, never to look backwards again.

She would tell Nellie right now: they must start immediately weeding out this place. They must raise the money to get the orchard to produce, not by raiding the last of Augusta's savings, but by auctioning off some of this useless stuff. She might have to extend the length of her visit a little; there was so much to sort through, to sell, and she would have to see them through the beginning of the autumn harvest. But then, whether or not they had made a go of things, she would bid good-bye forever to the Woolsey estate.

She strode purposefully through the dining room, rounded the corner into the kitchen, and bumped smack into a tall man in a nubbly tweed jacket. She stumbled backward. There, before her, like an hallucination from the past-steeped recesses of her mind, stood the tempting figure of William Hurley.

CHAPTER 4

"I guess you didn't expect to find me in your kitchen," William said, steadying her. He looked at Augusta and smiled sheepishly.

"Not exactly," Augusta replied, and stared into the deep brown eyes of the first boy she had ever loved. She could feel the color draining from her face and she willed it to return. Was he dressed in the same checked wool jacket he had worn twenty years ago? She would swear that he was. And his smell—still sweet, tweedy, still powerful enough to make her heart dip.

"You haven't even changed," Augusta said. It had been ten, fifteen years at least.

"You have," William said, taking a deep breath. "You were always pretty, but now you're beautiful."

William had attended high school with Augusta, dating her in their senior year, and then he had gone on to Columbia College and Columbia Law School. He had been active in the burgeoning radical student movement, but after law school, he had come back to the comparatively quiet town he had grown up in and joined his father's small and staid law practice. His father had long been revered in the community and his boy soon gained the same reputation. To the needy, father and son never sent bills of more than twenty-five dollars, and they themselves lived like churchmice. Next door to their office was the Wappappee General Store, owned by blind Sam Perry. William would buy huge bagfuls of Sam's candy and hand them out to friends. If the Hurleys thought a family needed some clothes or a day or two of good hot meals, they would pick up the phone and call their most cherished fellow samaritan— Augusta's mother. But just two years after William joined his father, his parents were killed in a car crash. At age twenty-six, William had to sell everything to cover the debts left by his father, and afterward he had abruptly moved to Washington. Since then, Augusta understood he had researched hazardous wastes for Ralph Nader, been a watchdog for the EPA, drafted clean-air legislation for Congress, and had lately been lobbying to stop riverbank factories from dumping chemicals into the water. He had boundless energy, an enormous appetite, a good heart, and, as dozens of wistful women could testify, deadly charm. William might love women, but he was apparently too exuberantly busy for cumbersome attachments. There did not seem to be anything he did not want from life, but twenty years ago, after months of making puppy love to her, he had decided he did not want Augusta.

Just then, Nellie came in the kitchen door carrying herbs from the garden. She stopped when she saw William and her sister staring awkwardly at each other. "You remember William, don't you, Augusta?" she gushed, and then realized how inane her comment was. She went over to the dinner table and, moving awkwardly, self-consciously, she set places for four.

Augusta glared at Nellie, who refused to meet her eyes. Did she look infuriatingly smug, or was it just scared?

"Augusta," Nellie chirped suddenly, in a voice that nevertheless had the unmistakable ring of the mistress of the house.

"William's come back to the valley to live. He's going to help us save the farm."

"Well, I don't know that I'd put it that way," William said, looking shyly at Augusta. "But I'll add my hands to yours."

"You've actually come back here to live?" Augusta looked at him, disbelieving. "But why?"

"I couldn't stay away anymore, Augusta." Augusta noticed he had acquired a little Washington drawl. "I guess I'm a born-again Huck Finn, hankering after the simple life. But look, it's wonderful that *you* are back. We've missed you."

Nellie clattered a serving bowl down on the old mahogany dinner table and appeared at William's side, touched his arm, then turned to Augusta and faced her sister's cold eyes. "By 'we' he means 'me.' Since Mother died, William's been by my side. He's the one I called when she went into the last coma."

Augusta noticed that William let Nellie's hand rest on his arm, even as he was uttering soothing condolences to Augusta about the death of her mother. Then she remembered, with an unaccountable flash of anger, how physically affectionate William had been, always touching people, even in their adolescence in the fifties, when it was not common for a boy to squeeze a girl's arm or tousle her hair; he was demonstrative to all the girls, even if he was going steady with only one.

"I'm so glad I came back before your mother died," William said. "I'm so glad I saw her . . . and your Grandma Amenia. Your mother! Oh, was she stubborn. I loved that woman. I loved your mother. She was determined not to make it easy for her disease. Whenever I came, she would be propped up, ready to tease me and to reminisce about old times."

Augusta sat down heavily on a Sheraton dining chair. "You saw her before she died? Even you?" Her mother had adored William.

"Oh look," William said, embarrassed. He went to the door. "I shouldn't have barged in on you all so soon. I'll just go and see if I can find Coert."

When he had left, Augusta turned to Nellie. "Why did you invite him here on my first night home?"

Nellie smoothed out the napkin at the extra place setting. "William has connections and know-how. He'll be the one to get the farm on the right track. Besides, I want him here." Nellie was well aware that she had committed something akin to a crime in Woolsey theology. Woolsey homecomings and holidays were strictly for Woolseys. Not only was William not a Woolsey, years ago he had made Augusta Woolsey-Bean miserable.

"Couldn't I have gotten reacquainted with my home first? Couldn't I have had a little time to settle in? To absorb Mom's absence? To mourn?" As soon as she had walked into the house, Augusta had felt her mother's presence, and her passing, as acutely as if it had just happened. And now, in some black twist of fate, Nellie had delivered this shimmering specter of Augusta's past, hot as a fork of lightning, shot down to taunt her, to burn her out by the roots.

"You mean you would have liked to have been the center of attention a little longer," Nellie said coolly. "That's not going to happen anymore, Augusta. Every one of us in this house is important now."

Augusta struggled to keep her voice calm. "You didn't think it was important to mention to me that you had taken up with my old boyfriend?"

"That is coarse and absolutely ridiculous," Nellie said, suddenly feeling that she had gone too far. She felt the folly of letting her sister know how she felt about William before she had told William himself. "Augusta, William has saved entire wilderness areas. He's a famous environmentalist. And he's ours for the asking. Am I supposed to tell him, 'No dinner for you! Augusta has graced the door.'?"

"As I remember," Augusta said, helplessly, "he eats enough to feed a village in Biafra!" She followed Nellie into the kitchen, hoping she would manage to rise above her fury. "I know you're very angry at me for not helping with Mother at the end, but do you really want to make me feel so unwelcome, do you want to make me sorry I came back?"

"I have needed William," Nellie said, sounding equally calm as she deftly tossed breadcrumbs in a bowl. The set of her back reminded Augusta of their mother—the Other Mother— when she was in one of her steely arrogant moods. "I have had no one else," Nellie said. It struck her that actually she wanted William even more now that Augusta was home than she had when Augusta had not been around.

"You know what I think? I think you've brought William here to defend yourself against me, to punish me, even to avoid facing me," Augusta said, taking the thoughts right out of Nellie's head and causing her to snip the stems of the sage into the stuffing instead of the leaves. A sudden image crossed Nellie's mind: Augusta throwing out William before he'd had his dinner, just like Great-grandmother Mildred once threw a fishing friend of Henry's out of the house on Easter morning because he was wearing mudboots.

"How can you even entertain a flirtation with him?" Augusta said, realizing the black irony of the situation: during Augusta's previous visits home, she had found "poor Nellie" without so much as a date, and had spent hours coaching her, dressing her, urging her on. "It's incestuous! William was the biggest love of my life."

And of mine, Nellie thought, but she said, "I'm not saying I *want* him, I only want the right to want him. You've gone after professional success. I've stayed home. I want to get married. I want to marry someone wonderful. I may want to marry William."

"*You?* Marry William? You just want him because he was mine."

"I could damn well marry him if I wanted to! And he's *not* yours anymore. He is *my* friend now. He is staying at the Hopestill Arms, my place of work, where I got him a bridal

suite for the price of a single. He was here for me when you
were supposed to be, he's kept me going, given me hope. And
I have reacquainted him with the town." Nellie noticed she
was holding the raw chicken aloft, legs dangling, as though she
was about to hurl it at Augusta. Embarrassed, she put it down
and began to spoon the stuffing in. "I'm not the person you
think I am anymore. I'm not the helpless dope that used to be
your sister. I'm a whole different person, especially when I'm
not around you. Fill this room with people and you'd be
shocked at who I am."

Augusta watched Nellie's hands; beneath their confident,
graceful movements, they were shaking; she knew her sister,
she always had. And she knew that they were both afraid of the
same thing—of being repossessed; of having a sibling usurp
everything they had become as adults, of stripping them and
returning them to the raw painful clay of childhood.

"I know you're different," Augusta said. "So am I. And
maybe we don't really like that. Maybe we both hate the
thought of the other one becoming different, growing up,
improving herself. It's bad enough losing a mother without
losing a sister too."

Nellie dried her hands and turned to Augusta. "I don't know
what more you can improve about yourself. You're a winner.
You've always had men falling all over you."

But it hasn't meant anything, Augusta thought, they might
as well not have existed; it was men immune to her charms that
she would fixate on, and as soon as they were the least bit nice
to her, she was a goner. "If you only knew the real me instead
of the myth of me, Nellie, you'd have a good laugh. My romantic life has been one disaster after another, and you even know
about some of them. I'm butter in the hands of the bastards
of the world. I'm terminal. I can't be allowed out on the
market. I've taken a vow of celibacy. Don't look so skeptical,
I'm serious."

Nellie hoped her face was not registering the pleasure she

felt. Was it possible Augusta would leave William alone? Leave him to Nellie after all? "Oh Augusta, I know. I know you better than you think. I've watched you suddenly lose your own interests, your love of music and reading. Mother and I will call you and you'll suddenly be fanatically interested in sports or whatever else your man of the moment is into."

Augusta stared at Nellie, then turned away. She went over to the pantry window and saw William standing at the western edge of the lawn, looking down at the orchards. "I'm going out for some air," she said.

When Augusta walked across the lawn and came up behind him, William turned and smiled at her. "This is the heart of the valley for me," he said. They turned to gaze down at the alternating rows of McIntosh, Rome, Cortland, and Red Delicious; the grand sweep of trees moving in alternating waves of hills and ridges down to the Hudson River, the sun bleeding primrose and orchid over the spine of the Catskills to the north. "I feel like I'm back in my boyhood dreams. It's a kind of ache. Even after you and I stopped seeing each other, Augusta, I used to come here secretly. I'd go through the woods and cross the creek, then sit down in the Christmas Orchard with a book. I'd always be hoping you'd come by."

"I'm glad I never did," Augusta said. "It would just have gotten my hopes up. I'd have thought maybe you didn't mean to ask me for your cleat back." Augusta had worn his polished football cleat on a chain round her neck: it was a trophy, a love totem, it meant they belonged to each other.

"How could I have ever asked you something so stupid?" William said, brushing a fly off her ear. He stared at her. "Do you know that when I was with you I used to get this funny feeling in my shoulders, like I had just drunk something piping hot, something like hot chocolate? I thought it was teenage growing pains, but I'm fully grown and it's happening again."

"Nellie seems to think you came back for her, for Woolsey Orchards," Augusta said, stepping back. Yes, it was exactly like

hot chocolate. Coursing through her veins. He was still disturb-
ingly attractive. Age had deepened his appeal, flecked his char-
coal hair with gray, brought lines of kindness and warmth to
his eyes. He still had the cowlick and the curl that fell over his
forehead, and the dimples, oh those dimples, two of them. Her
mother (her mother!) had said they made her long to be young
again. Augusta saw him now through Nellie's eyes, his haunting smile and full sensuous lips; to a woman not yet thirty who
had trouble attracting all but the plainest of men, he must
appear like an alabaster god, like Michelangelo's David.

"For years so many of us suffered from sixties' hubris, from
revolution fever," William was saying. "We were so stuck in
the last decade that the seventies didn't even exist. I kept
thinking I was going to change the way the human mind is
programmed. I helped change things, I suppose, but they were
like the changes an ant makes in the landscape of a sandlot. It's
1977 and all over the country, Augusta, there are thousands of
chemical dumps ticking away like time bombs. One man in
Louisiana was asphyxiated by the fumes of wastes he dis-
charged from his truck. Companies use our waterways like
toilets. PCBs are in our cows, our milk, our fish, our soil. The
nation is being poisoned, but even an army of people like me
and Nader couldn't move Washington to really do something
about it."

"But you're not going to give up, are you? You're not going
to throw away your dreams and lie down and molder here in
Stonekill Landing?"

"Come here," William said. He walked back around the
corner of the house toward the south side, and pointed to the
distant cluster of housing developments. "Last year I returned
to visit for the first time in a decade, and it was like coming
back to a town on Mars. The sleepy country roads had become
highways and the fields were shopping malls. The big developers had crept up from New York City like giant centipedes.
Prefabs were everywhere, and those malls! With the same

Muzak you hear in the malls of Detroit or Sacramento, the same chemically treated clothes that don't need pressing, the ice cream that won't melt, the books that are going to crumble to dust, the electric fork-sharpeners and the automatic egg-peelers, and the Astroturf and the phony neon fires for the fireplaces." William's forehead was glistening. He drew his hand across it and smiled apologetically. "I get crazy about this. I can feel my blood rising whenever I talk about the fact that the town is not exactly as I left it when my parents died."

"Funny, I feel exactly the opposite. It makes me crazy that not one speck of dust has been moved in this old house since my mother died. Since anybody in the family died, as a matter of fact."

"After last year's visit, I went back to Washington but I couldn't get the county out of my mind," William said. "The memory of growing up here, watching birds with Dad, the fresh smell of the air when I went hunting in the woods down by your orchards. I kept thinking of how the land had been robbed of its gentle rural individuality, how the people were being forced off their farms. I thought about the old grist mill which they razed and replaced with a plastic barn that sells vinyl swimming pools that sit above the ground."

"I saw those pools when I came from the station," Augusta said. "They look like giant industrial drums! How could they swim in those things? It looks like people are going to climb up those ladders and plunge into a vat of oil or acid or something."

William laughed. "You always did have a way of getting to the truth. They really are poisoning their lives. People have gone suburban. The cookie-cutter middle class has flooded the valley. They're ripping out hand-hewn beams and letting them rot in the yard, they're putting up radar television discs as large as their cheaply constructed new houses. They're replacing old wooden shingling with aluminum siding, which has the advantage of never needing to be painted. The chemical compounds used instead of natural materials are leaching carcinogens into their homes. They're destroying the old and they don't know that the new will destroy them."

Down the hill, a mile away to the southeast, lay the factories of the Apex Electronic Corporation, which had been built on property adjoining the orchards. "That," William pointed to the complex, "is the nation's newest technological nightmare: the industries that poison more than they produce."

"A giant wound belching smoke," Augusta agreed. "Nellie begged my parents to buy the land Apex is on now. It used to be the Whiting dairy, you know, but the dairy went bankrupt. If we had bought that land back then, we could turn around now and sell it to Apex or whoever and keep the orchards. As it is, Apex keeps bothering Daddy with offers to buy *us* out."

"Apex is destroying the environment," William said.

"I know. Daddy said in the car that when the wind is right, the chemical smoke now comes right into the bedrooms."

"I'm talking about *more* than just air pollution," William said.

Suddenly Augusta did not want to hear any more bad news. "You were saying you went back to Washington and kept thinking about the rape of the valley. What did you do then?"

"I decided to stop trying to change the world, and instead to pay attention to what was happening in my own backyard," William said, thinking about his parents' old homestead, how they would never again make the kind of solid house that he had grown up in. It had been torn down for a car dealership. The towering maples and the peeling cherry tree he used to climb hovered like apparitions behind the rows of polished sedans with large cardboard prices on their windshields.

William told Augusta how he had come back to start an organization called the Hudson Valley Land Preservation Foundation, funded by both private and government conservation groups, devoted to buying open space and helping farms in the valley to keep operating.

"I've been staying at the Hopestill Arms. Your sister has spoiled me, getting me this palatial suite. And I have an office on Main Street for a ridiculously low rent. Half the stores are boarded up because everyone goes to the malls. Newbury's Five and Dime is about to close, and poor Sam has been forced to sell beer instead of candy. Even I can't buy enough fireballs to keep him afloat."

"Preservation," Augusta sighed. "It has a wonderful echo to it, that word. In Los Angeles there's nothing worth preserving. That city dreamt itself up. Nothing has been built or sunk into the ground, and when it has, the earth rumbles up and rejects it like a transplanted organ. You would hate it. Movies and cars and stories and mirages. Cars moving the mirages into stories, the stories into movies, the movies into money. The place is an hallucination."

"But now you're home," William said. "Real house, real people, real farm."

"Real problems," Augusta sighed.

As they watched the sun sink down below the hills, their shoulders touched and Augusta felt increasingly apprehensive. She was at risk; she would be obliterated again; already her legs felt unsteady. All she wanted to do was to free herself from the past, but the past kept looming up like countenances in a dream. First the House and now the Man.

Perhaps Nellie had subconsciously brought William here, not only to torture her, but to lure her back into the fold.

Augusta felt her sense of self beginning to leak away. Had it begun with William, this impulse to curl up inside a man, to hide in his pocket? No, she realized, it had begun with her mother. Lydia had been the first figure in her life to say "I love you" and then to turn away. William had been a powerful second. The two of them had put her on a train that had never stopped.

William had been in love with her and then he had not been: he had said she was wonderful and then he had found she was not; she was left once again with the old question: Can I trust someone to love me, am I worthy of it? Or will I always lose love in the end?

His leaving had set her searching for an answer, searching, in the arms of man after man, for an end to what Lydia and William had begun. Over and over, she had played out this pattern, this cycle of love and loss. He had complained that she was closed, but he had left her as open and raw as a tortoise whose shell had been ripped away. And now, just when she had forsaken all of that, had put aside this painful search for love to build an independent being, here he was, back again, the original lover, standing ready like an old question mark beside her.

"The Hudson Valley once fed the rest of the country," William was saying. "Your ancestors were the providers." He looked up at the rambling porch. The chain on the wooden swing was broken, the wicker furniture unraveling. "I used to think you were the luckiest kid in the world, growing up with all that family. I never even had a cousin, let alone a sibling or a grandparent. Nowadays, we shove our old people into nursing homes. I'll never forget your grandmother waiting on the porch for me with a plate piled with steaming pandowdy. She made such a wonderful fuss over me."

"That's because no one else in the family could abide her cooking. You not only ate everything she cooked, you asked for more! It made up for the fact you were not born a Woolsey." Augusta pointed to the house. "Did you know the great architect Calvert Vaux built that? He was a friend of my great-great-grandfather from his London days."

"I did. I read the *Historical Society Magazine* article," William said.

He did not want to be talking of architects while Augusta's skin was turning coral in the sunset. The memory of the one kiss she had given him so long ago suddenly registered deep in his belly. He had followed her into the cellar after they had had a fight over the issue of premarital petting—she had said it made her sixteen-year-old heart go cold with fear. But it was not fear that day that made her stiff body yield so quickly to him when he pressed her up against the cold cellar wall. He was shot through with a painful, violent lust. He remembered the exultant slipping of his tongue between her lips, the smell of the English cologne she wore, the feel of her tiny breasts, the rapturous reaching of their tongues, the desperation rising in his body; and then her flight, suddenly, from out of his arms. Up the stairs and out the cellar door she had gone, and as it happened, out of his life as well. She had never let him kiss her again.

It was inexplicable, really, it was damning. He was too unsure of himself even now to ask her why she had run away. In his worst imaginings, she said to him, "It was your braces. They were repulsive." But surely she had not acted repulsed, surely she had been as pleased as he by that magnificent meeting of their lips, their bodies. He remembered thinking, hadn't her face been moist with excitement, hadn't they actually fallen to the floor? He was never to know, for he had tried and tried to get past the virginal barrier which she subsequently put up, tried to soften her tight frightened lips. Then, finally, he had stopped trying. Perhaps all those Victorian grandmothers *had* been the problem. They had made her old before she had a chance to be young and free and daring.

"Are you sure you're Huck Finn and not Calvert Vaux reincarnated?" Augusta said cheerily. "Vaux was a rebel. He loved nature unspoiled, he loved open space, and he hated the stark new manor houses built by the industrial barons that defiled the banks of the Hudson with their phony Greek revival pillars."

"Yes, I'm Vaux," William said, deadpan, trying to recall what he had read about the Woolseys in the magazine. "God, did I hate those bald white cubes! And I hated those 1850s townhouses, with their low-ceilinged halls as ghoulishly dark as funeral parlors, and the rooms stuck on either side like spider legs. By George, I had to go down to the basement to accomplish my favorite activity, which requires a kitchen. I vowed to old Cornelius I was going to defy convention with this here house."

Augusta laughed. "I can remember riding the wheelchair from room to room, sitting on Great-great-grandfather's lap, looking up at these tall tall ceilings, and his voice booming, 'Calvert and I made them so's the Catskill giants wouldn't bump their heads.' "

"The magazine said your great-great-grandmother Hopestill put peepholes into the walls so she could spy on the maids." William gazed at the house and then turned to Augusta. "Did they spy on you, is that why you were so uptight with me?"

Augusta looked sharply at William, but he did not avert his eyes, so she turned and walked toward the orchards, talking quickly, heartily. "Hopestill died before I was born, so I only know her by reputation. She loved to be pampered. She would spend hours in this single luxurious bathroom she ordered Vaux to design, and half the time Great-great-grandfather had to resort to transacting his business under the gaze of the Almighty."

William put his hands on Augusta's arms and turned her around. Her hair was gold, shimmering strands of it. He remembered her skin, so soft next to his, her shoulders trembling. He did not think that he had ever been so aroused by a kiss as he had been by the one whose memory was arousing him now. "You are so beautiful," he said.

She took his hands and put them at his side. "It's your eyes," she said. "Your eyes are making things beautiful." She walked away and noticed that it was like walking away from a magnet. Keep walking, she told herself, and don't stop. She felt him coming up behind her and she spread out her arms defensively. "Just look at this. Vaux set this house so we could see a different aspect of the valley from each side: to the west, hills tumbling down to the Hudson, to the east, hills rising to Mount Freedom, woods and more mountains to the north and south."

"Blast Vaux," William said under his breath.

"William," Augusta said turning around. "You know I was in California when the car accident happened. When your parents were killed. Mother said you reacted with such dignity and courage, she felt like she was seeing your father alive again."

William dropped his arm; the sensual excitement drained out of him. It had happened ten years ago, but there was still that familiar punch in his gut when anyone mentioned the crash. He shrugged. "I was an only child. Only children are expected to be strong," he said. "No one to be weak for."

"You lost everything—the law practice, your beautiful old farmhouse," Augusta said. All at once she didn't know if she could keep herself from touching him. "You've never come to terms with what you lost, have you? That's why you've come back."

"Everyone worshipped Dad, he took care of everyone. Everyone but his own family," William said. "Do you know poor Mom never had a holiday outside of a few days in the Catskills? After he died, I found a drawer full of uncashed checks from clients. They dated back for years. That's why I left. I didn't want to end up like him."

"But here you are, back again, trying to help others," Augusta said quietly. "Maybe you were disappointed by your father, William, but you didn't forsake him. You have done as he did. You've always made a difference. I haven't your strength, or your conviction. I haven't been strong enough to save both myself and my heritage."

"You've helped your family keep these two hundred and fifty acres when everyone else was succumbing to the forces of progress," William said. "Your father even raises your own bees! Thank God for you, Augusta, thank God for your family."

"Coert!" Augusta suddenly cried, seeing a ruddy, muscular man in work clothes come out of the trees. The Woolsey farm manager, Coert Van Voorhees, had an overlong nose and a tangle of copper-colored hair rising from his forehead. A pair of sideburns sliced down his jaw like tomahawks. Over the years, he had set his mouth in a Calvinistic scowl, but any air of sternness was tempered by the slight, almost comic bulge of the cheek where he kept his chewing tobacco. His hands were calloused and stained from his painting, a hobby in which he obsessively indulged when he wasn't obsessively tending his trees. During the dark times of her childhood, Augusta would sit up in the loft of the barn where he lived, listening to allegories about his Dutch ancestors.

Augusta embraced him and then found she couldn't let him go. He was strong, he was safe, he was holding her as her father had once held her; as she had always wished to be held. And he was one person who would never ask anything of her. Tears ran down her cheeks now, until the wool of his lumber jacket was wet. "I messed up, Coert," she whispered. "I should have come home before."

"You were her pride," Coert said softly, patting her back. "You were the first one to go on the outside. That's where you belonged, outside. Not here."

"And now we're going to lose the farm," she said. Suddenly, Augusta had an ugly vision. She must have been watching too many outtakes in the screening rooms of Hollywood, for the vista of the orchards that spread out before her became a wide screen. The rows of apple trees dissolved into rows of pastel tract houses, crisscrossed with roaring exhaust-filled highways. The score was by Muzak, and she saw her name listed as producer.

"We can't lose the farm!" she said.

"With a little luck, we won't," Coert said, looking at William.

"I got the one-year whips, Coert," William said. "That agricultural station upriver says it'll donate them."

"Now that's a good bit of luck right there," Coert said, turning to Augusta. "Only way to save this place is to start all over again. Replant. Our crops aren't any good anymore, Missy. We used to have the best and biggest apples this side of the river, and now they're small, no good. Color's off, taste's not right. Trees are old, like your Dad and me. None of us is producing like we used to."

"Coert. The day you stop, we all stop," Augusta said. Like his father before him, Coert Van Voorhees was the backbone of Woolsey Orchards.

Coert looked out at the descending rows of Rome apple trees, with their drooping tip-bearing boughs, and he thought how much they looked like great geysers delivering themselves up from the soil. These trees were in his soul, his blood. He remembered how he had helped his father set them in the ground years ago, how his father had said, "Son, we are only planters. It's the hand of God from deep down in the earth that pushes his seed toward the sun." And now God was through with these trees.

"You have to talk to that sister of yours," Coert said. He began to chew his tobacco with more force, and shrugged his jacket down on his shoulders. "She thinks the poor deer should be allowed to roam free and nip the tops off the young trees. Every mouse in the orchard seems to be her friend. Your father just looks the other way. I can't keep up with the mowing when the grass starts shooting up, especially down by the river, and so I say I want to use this new herbicide. Approved by the federal government, perfectly safe. Not on your life, Nellie says, it kills the fish. I say *not* to spray kills the farm. She accuses me of exaggerating. Okay, so then I say we gotta cut down some of those old trees, the Newtown Pippins at the very least. No, says she, those old trees are sacred."

"You're not thinking of cutting down Auntie Mame, are you?" Augusta said, feeling suddenly defensive about Nellie. Auntie Mame had been the tree under which Nellie and she had taken refuge as children. "The Pippins are more than just trees. They were the first ones Great-great-grandfather planted."

"Well, Auntie's growed so big, she blocks off sunlight for the other trees. Them Spartans the next row down think it's night half the day," Coert said.

William cleared his throat. Nellie had always just been Augusta's funny-looking little sister, but now William had come to care for her. She had leaned on him, made him feel he was needed again, and welcome in his old hometown; she shared his vision of a clean environment and his intense love of the valley. "You have to understand Nellie," William said to Coert. "She feels attacked. She sees your insistence on razing the trees as a razing of the beauty and tradition of the orchards. I think sometimes she confuses you with the forces that are lying in wait to destroy the farm. Besides, she makes some good points; most farmers don't need to do as much saturation spraying as they do."

"Cornelius Woolsey might have planted those trees, but they are producing as much fruit as he would if he were still alive," Coert said, spitting a bullet of tobacco juice at the trunk of a Newtown Pippin a few feet away. "Speak of the devil, here she comes now. She's probably not talking to me because I told her yesterday I was going on strike until she let me run an orchard instead of a wildlife preserve."

Nellie came up and looked from Augusta to William to Coert. She had been the main woman in these two men's lives for the past few months and now they stood, their bodies kind of poised at attention, gazing with fascination at the homecoming queen. Nellie hoped her smile did not look as unnatural as it felt.

"Coert," she said sweetly. "I hope you'll join us for Augusta's homecoming dinner. I've fixed a cider-basted chicken."

"Ah, cider," William said. "One plan we've been talking about is getting a cider-press, Augusta. If you have as many russeted apples as you did last fall, they could be used for cider. Nellie says there's a new health-conscious market here that would buy additive-free cider over apple juice."

"Cider-presses don't grow on trees," Augusta said.

"You won't have to put up a dime," Nellie replied coolly. "William has located a used press and I know how we'll pay for it." Nellie moved nearer to William; just standing beside him helped to dissolve the lump in her throat. She and William had accrued three months of history, and it was current history, not two decades old. They had shared her mother's death, her grandmother's death; William had held her dying mother and he had held Nellie. She had given William one of her arms at the funeral, her father the other. Nellie was amazed at how easy and relaxed she had been with William, considering that she had kept a rather significant secret from him and Augusta all these years; she had been as relaxed as you can be with a man who had unwittingly given you your first French kiss, in a dark cellar when you were eleven, when he had thought (and probably still thought) he was kissing your sister.

"Pumpkins," Coert said suddenly. "I was thinking this morning . . . what about pumpkins? The seeds cost almost nothing, and people love them. We could grow corn, squash too, and eggplant for the Italian population."

"And what if they get wiped out like the peaches last year?" Nellie asked. "You know, half the time it's not the farmer's fault a crop fails. One late freeze or too much rain, anything unseasonal, could wipe us out."

"That's the truth," Coert said. "Look at the frost we had last week. The Red Delicious were hit the hardest. Fragile as babies. Half the pistils of the buds turned brown. They won't blossom, that's for sure. This time last year, the buds just dropped right off the stone fruit over in the North Orchards. No peaches, no cherries. Damnedest thing I ever saw. No earthly reason for it. Nothing like that ever happened here before." Then, more softly, he said, "Though my father might have said it was nature crying out in sympathy with your ailing mother."

"What *is* our biggest problem anyway?" Augusta asked impatiently. "Is it old trees, lack of help? Crazy weather patterns? Or some mysterious force that's jinxing the fruit? We have to get a plan of action."

"Augusta," Nellie said easily. "There is no simple answer. This is an orchard, not a movie."

"You can't get anybody to work on a farm, that's the problem," Coert said. "Nobody wants to work anymore. They get twice as much at Apex just sitting motionless at a desk."

"Speaking of Apex," William said, "I have reason to believe—"

"I could do it myself," Coert interrupted. "I could take care of the whole damn orchard alone, if my hands weren't tied behind my back . . . if I could use weed killers, and cut down them trees. I could—"

"Coert, I think your idea of pumpkins and vegetables is wonderful," Nellie said, too quickly and too loudly. She was afraid that Coert would start criticizing her in front of William, maybe even suggest that Nellie was to blame for the farm's troubles. "We could even do it without using pesticides. Research is being done on releasing natural predator insects to control crop-invading pests. We're killing all the natural predators with these heavy sprays, the ladybugs and the good insects, not to mention the bees who manage to make their way back to the orchard no matter how far away Daddy carts them during the spraying periods. I know we could experiment with other organic methods, like not waxing our apples with that fungicide-laced wax—you can never wash it off, you know."

Coert waved his hand. "It's the consumers who want their fruit to win a beauty contest. They won't buy fruit that ain't red and shiny and free of any blemish whatsoever. In the old days they would hang jars of molasses from the branches, hoping the bugs would drink and drown," he added, lifting his hairline with his forehead muscles. "My grandfather used an umbrella upside down on the end of a wheelbarrow and smashed the contraption against the trunk of the trees in hopes of shaking out the plum curculios, which would then fall in the umbrella. That was fine when you just had a few trees. Then they took to using arsenic and copper sulphate sprays, which is a damn sight worse than what we use now. How'd you like to bite into an apple glazed with arsenic?"

"Nellie, if we try to cut down on the spraying, the apples will be full of maggots and the tomatoes will rot off the vine," Augusta said. "Mother was never big on organic farming. She said it doesn't work well, you always lose on it."

"But Mother was always ready to at least *try* new things. If she hadn't, these trees would be ashes now," Nellie said. "When Grandpa Augustus nearly bankrupted the orchards, Mother and Daddy planted the stone fruits to increase revenue. This orchard had never had cherries or peaches before."

William nodded toward Apex. "I'm afraid your parents and grandparents didn't have that nightmarish Apex to contend with, either. Coert, isn't it odd that other orchards aren't having such bizarre problems with their trees? The weather, the vermin, the soil—these things aren't much different in Ulster or Columbia counties. Why are things so much worse over here?"

William pointed to the Christmas Orchard at the bottom of the hill. It was bordered by the state-owned woodland that ran from the ridge upon which the house stood down to the river, and that divided the Apex and Woolsey properties. "Augusta, I've been trying to tell you that I've just heard Apex is dumping tons of toxic chemicals somewhere in the woods down there."

"What? They are?" Nellie exclaimed.

"I don't know how near to your property the dump is, but

it's possible the toxins could be seeping into your soil. Even reaching the roots of the trees."

"You're not saying they could actually affect our apples?" Augusta asked. "We have enough legitimate reasons for the condition of the orchards without pointing to some fantastic plague."

"It may sound fantastic, but why don't we try to find out some facts?" William said. "If PCBs can make a rat embryo grow five ears instead of two, if tetrachlorides can make the fetuses of perfectly healthy women inexplicably abort, what do you think they could do to an apple?"

"William, you're making me dizzy," Nellie said, leaning toward his shoulder. Nellie suddenly saw her own secret plan to save the farm endangered—her negotiations with the organic farmer from France who wanted to buy the Christmas Orchard. "If the toxins are everywhere, what can we do about it? I've been trying to get Coert not to use so much spray, but this is much worse. If poison is in the soil, the grass, the plant food, it could be affecting the mice as well as the apples. It could be producing a mutant breed of supervole that can chew twice as fast! Maybe that's why there are so many trees girdled and dying in the Christmas Orchard."

"Oh Nellie, don't be ridiculous," Augusta said, suddenly wondering if her entire life, from her mother to motion pictures, had been spent in fantasy and illusion. She suddenly felt weary of it all. She wanted hard reality; she wanted to get on with it.

"Hmm. I wonder," Coert said. "Christmas Orchard *is* worse off than the trees up the hill and on the other side of the ridge. Those Macs came out mottled last fall. But poisoned apples, sounds like stretching things to me."

Coert liked William, but he wasn't going to give him too much rope; he might know his books, but Coert knew his apples. Besides, Coert could not forget how much William Hurley had once hurt his little Augusta; and by the jealous look on Nellie's face right now, by the tension in the air you could almost cut with a blade, the biggest poisoner of all in the Woolsey orchards might turn out to be William himself.

Augusta had taken a notebook and pencil from the pocket of Coert's jacket. "All right, we can worry about Apex later. Right now we have to formulate a plan to make some money, to get this farm on its feet. As soon as the ground softens and dries out, we plant vegetables, like Coert suggested. And Nellie, we could even have an experimental patch that you can grow organically."

"If you stagger the vegetables," William said, "you could get revenue as soon as June, with lettuce and zucchini. Then the corn in August, followed by your apples and cider."

"Right," Augusta said. "And as for the most pressing problem—buying the sprays—we'll raise the money by letting Dominick DeCarlo auction off some of the old stuff in the house." Augusta held up her hand before Nellie could protest. "Just the junk, the stuff we don't even see anymore, in the attic, the cellar, the stuff oozing out of the cracks."

"I think it sounds like a good idea," William said, looking at Nellie.

"We're all going to work together now," Augusta said. "We're going to use everything we can think of, including sheer will, just like Mom and Dad did when they got the orchards back on their feet before. The Woolseys have been growing apples for over a hundred years. If any little farm can beat the odds today, ours can."

Upstairs in the house, Henry Bean looked out the window of the master bedroom, the room that he and his wife had shared a long, long time ago. He had been searching again, under rugs, in drawers, behind pictures, anywhere that he might have secreted those rings away.

Now he gazed at his daughters talking with William and

Coert. He had always felt separate somehow, even from his family, as if he were a stray atom circling somewhere far away from the nucleus; but never more so than now. Often, he did not even feel in touch with his present, only with what it evoked; sometimes he recognized Lydia's presence in his daughters, and it made his heart jackknife.

Henry saw Lydia in the way Nellie automatically turned on every light in the room, leaving them blazing; in the scent of her wafting by; in Lydia's old scarves that Nellie would carelessly tie around her neck. In the way Augusta stood now, resting back on her heels, hips forward, the way his wife had so often stood. At these times, he would want his daughters to stay with him so badly that he could hardly restrain himself from asking, "You won't leave soon, will you?" But they could not stay, could not share his future.

His very name was like a vestigial tail on their names: half the time people forgot the Bean was even there. I will never be lost to them, he thought; but it won't be long before they are lost to me.

CHAPTER 5

"Go ahead, you go first," Nellie said, opening the door to the bedroom downstairs and giving Augusta a little push. Lydia had spent her last months in this room. She had died here, with Nellie and Henry in attendance.

The room smelled musty, but warm and strangely more lived-in than other rooms in the house. Augusta went over to the window and opened the brocade curtains. In flooded the brash April light, and a view of the silver-banked sky and of trees with their birdlet, lime-green leaves. Renewal was in the air, and Augusta suddenly felt a flash of anger at the floor-to-ceiling windows; that her mother, the life going out of her, had had to sit here and be reminded daily that nature only died to live again. The dusty furniture looked naked, surprised by the unfamiliar glare. Augusta, who had been asthmatic as a child, felt her bronchial tubes tighten for the first time in years.

"It's not really so bad in here after all!" Nellie said, standing in the middle of the room like a dancer embracing the stage. She ran her fingers over the heavy oak bureau. "It feels like we belong. I don't know why I put off coming in here for so long."

Augusta knew why. Interfering with Lydia's personal things seemed like an invasion they would have to answer for.

Since her arrival home eighteen days ago, when she had briefly peeked into this room, she too had been skulking past it like a malingerer by a police station, automatically averting her gaze from its weighty brass doorknob, deliberately ignoring her mother's purse that still lay untouched in the hall. Augusta had managed to tackle other things; she had sorted through attic and cellar, collecting things to sell; she had organized the DeCarlo auction three days ago, which had raised enough money to buy all the sprays for this year's growing season. But she had been operating on automatic pilot. She felt like a body moving underwater, through a sea of images, each possession a razor-cut of memory, her soul hiding out somewhere in the swampy deep. She felt she was in a dream, watching herself move numbly, dazedly, as the colorful rabble of her past— William, Nellie, her father, her mother, all these artifacts— rose up and beckoned her to swim to shore. If she obeyed, if she really gave herself up to them, she would never get away. She would end up like the unpicked apples you see in winter on the tree—brown, shriveled, forgotten. She would end up like Nellie.

"Mom loved fresh air," Nellie said, chattering eagerly and opening a window in the bathroom. "I'd always open this one because it sent a breeze wafting over her forehead. Oh God, look!"

Nellie pointed to her mother's nightgown hanging on a door-hook, with the wind puffing it up. "It looks like someone is in it! Oh Augusta!"

Nellie began to flitter manically around the room, from the bathroom to the dresser to the closet. She opened the door and took out a dress. "Look, look at this! Her clothes still hold her shape." She yanked open the top drawer of the bureau and grabbed a handful of lingerie. "Smell this, Augusta! It's got that special odor of Mom's, warm elastic and cologne. And here, her strands of hair are standing upright in this comb!"

She went into the bathroom and came out with a bath pillow. "She blew this up, Augusta. Her breath is inside. I can't stand this. I'm going to keep the air in this thing . . . Christ, you're going to have to take over." Nellie sat down on the bed and started to weep. "You know how she hated us to touch her things. She's here, Augusta, she's never left."

Augusta went over to her sister and stroked her hair. "Oh Nellie, I know," she said. "I know."

"Augusta, maybe we aren't supposed to be doing this. Do you know that three days after she died, Daddy and I came down one morning and found the family album lying on the floor with the photos scattered all around? It had been up on the library shelf, securely tucked away, and it couldn't have fallen off by itself! She knocked it down, I know she did, she wanted to tell us something, Augusta. But I can't figure out what it was."

"Your nerves are shot, Nellie. You took care of her, you watched her die. You've held Daddy and the farm together. And you've been all alone."

"I wish William would come," Nellie said miserably. "I don't know why he's been staying away. I can't even catch a glimpse of him at work, he's gone before I get to the inn and comes back after I've left. He's never worked so hard at that foundation of his before." Nellie caught herself; it was a constant struggle not to reveal to Augusta how strongly she felt about William. There had been a time when she had been naked before Augusta, when she had thought her sister the most dazzling, important, wonderful person on earth. Augusta had been the only one who had understood her first words; she had translated for her, had interceded for her, had protected her from the world and presented her to it. But that time was now gone. Nellie would never reveal—either to William or to her sister—that it had been she who William had embraced that day in the dark of the cellar, that it was she, not Augusta, who had held the promise of that kiss to her heart. If it turned out that William did not return Nellie's passion, Nellie would rather die than let Augusta see her humiliated.

"William will be back," Augusta said, trying to keep the tone of the martyr out of her voice. In spite of her desire for William, in spite of the powerful temptation to reclaim the man who had abandoned and hurt her most in life, Augusta had decided to snub William's advances; she had tried to make sure that when he did return, he would return for Nellie.

"Augusta, I have to say it, there's something here I really want." Nellie wiped her eyes. "I want it badly. I've been lying awake at night practicing ways of saying this to you. Mother's shawl over there, the blue mohair one you sent her from Sausalito. I think that if I could have it, I'd always remember her a certain way. We had trouble finding anything that was soft enough for her, her skin became so sensitive from the chemotherapy, and then you sent the shawl and she couldn't get over how soft it felt. We kept talking, that last day when she drifted in and out of the coma, talking about its being softer even than a baby's skin, and it was our way of fighting off death and her way of making things special, like in a story. It couldn't mean that much to you, could it? You never really saw her wear it, it couldn't mean what it meant to me."

"No," Augusta said, her heart sinking as she gazed at the shawl draped around the window chair. Such a simple gift, and it had apparently been able to reach down into the blankness and lift her mother's life up again as it drained out of her body. She could see Lydia fingering the shawl, imbuing it with love, like a talisman, so that it could comfort this daughter Augusta whom she would never see again. "You take it, Nellie," she said. "You've earned it."

Augusta turned and opened a mosaic jewel box on the bureau. "You know, one thing I'd really like to have," Augusta said, "is that little four-leaf clover pin. I wonder where it is. That's what *I* remember. It wasn't very expensive, but it was so green and it looked so real. I can see myself sitting on her lap, trying to pluck it off her breast."

"Oh Augusta, you make me feel awful," Nellie said. "I have

to make a confession. I took some things from upstairs in her old master bedroom. I took two crystal necklaces, and some love letters she had written to Daddy . . . and the four-leaf clover pin."

"You took that pin?" Augusta said. "That was one of my only memories of being on her lap! She wore it before you were even born. Why did you take it?"

"Well I *was* born, Augusta, and I sat on her lap too. All those memories of Mother aren't yours alone."

"Nellie, how can I possibly trust you, if you keep going behind my back?"

"Listen," Nellie said, rising from the bed. "I want you to know something. In spite of the fact that you deserted us, *this* room has been sealed since she died. That," she said, pointing to the huge mahogany armoire inlaid with satinwood fountains, "contains her most precious things. But I haven't even peeked. I knew that when this room was opened, it should be opened by both of us."

Augusta closed her eyes. She felt herself being sucked down farther into the past, like water through a drain. "You sound so much like Mother. The drums rolling in the background . . . the sacred sealed chambers of the glorious Woolseys are being opened. You don't have to bang the drums for Mother. Just be just plain Nellie, my little sister."

"And *you* don't have to be so condescending," Nellie said. "Just because you went off and became vice president of a big talent agency doesn't mean I've remained poor Nellie, a second-class citizen in our mother's house."

"No," Augusta said, "you've become vice president of it."

"President," Nellie said sharply. Then, moving slowly and deliberately, she extracted a key from beneath the corner of the rug, unlocked the mahogany armoire, and opened the doors onto her mother's most precious things.

A rush of smells swept over them: spicy sachets brought back in hatboxes by Grandmother Amenia, a musty velvet ball

gown, the dry, cracked hides of some small animals made into
stoles and hats, slippers and lap rugs. Old costumes and paraphernalia hung up and laid out, each pinned with a history like
treasures in a museum case: the white high-buttoned shoes that
Great-great-grandmother Hopestill had worn the night her
crafty and determined suitor, one Cornelius Woolsey, had
stolen her dancing card and substituted it for one that carried
only his name; Great-grandma Mildred's brocade wedding suit,
whose very severity foreshadowed the departure of her wild and
faithless husband; the gay cotton dirndl Lydia had worn on the
day she found herself pregnant with Nellie; the romantic and
hopeful silk pajamas she had given her husband on their first
anniversary. There were boxes and boxes—boxes full of bro-
chures of exotic places Lydia had longed for and only her
mother had gone to. There were riding crops and jodhpurs
from the last century, when the Woolsey estate had horses;
there were shooting jackets and chesterfields and gaiters and
ascots; there were ancient linens yellowed and spotted with
age: doilies, runners, handkerchiefs some Woolsey had
clutched at life's great epiphanies; lace tablecloths lovingly
pressed for the eyes of the Queen Mother; soft-skinned leatherbound books presented in hopes that the given to would never
forget the one who gave.

Rummaging in the back of the wardrobe, Nellie found two
long white boxes. One was labeled, in Lydia's distinctive script,
"Nellie," and the other "Augusta." They looked anxiously at
each other and then opened them.

Nellie pulled out Lydia's camel hair coat, the one with the
wide lapels, let out a little cry, and buried her nose in its silky
lining; it was her mother's beloved old "car coat," wide-cuffed,
voluminous, big enough for Nellie to hide in when she was
little.

But when Nellie saw what her sister had extracted from her
box, she dropped the coat. "Where did *that* come from?" she
asked. Augusta held up a pink satin robe trimmed with white

feathers. "It's so lovely! I never saw Mother wear a thing like that. Can I try it on?" Nellie removed her sweater and jeans so that she could fasten the little covered buttons that ran the length of the bodice. She wrapped it around herself and giggled behind the extravaganza of pungent goose down. "It's clear why Mother gave this to *you,*" Nellie said. "Do you remember how she always called you the Glamorpuss? Wherever would she have worn this? Certainly not for Daddy! Oh Augusta, do you think Mother had an affair? I've always wished it. Maybe she saved this for her clandestine rendezvous."

Augusta looked away uncomfortably, and when Nellie begged her to let her have the robe, she gave it up.

Augusta found several programs of Broadway shows: *Sail Away, My Fair Lady, Oklahoma!* She had to sit down because of the power of the memories they invoked: her mother, the Good Mother, sitting with her in the front row of the theater, enraptured with her by the phantasmagoria of color and sound and movement, afterwards finding record stores where they would buy record albums of the shows, singing in the taxi, singing down Fifth Avenue, imagining themselves into the snowy little Christmas scenes in the display windows at department stores, singing the songs again and again through the trees of Woolsey Orchards.

Augusta went through the rest of her box excitedly, expecting that her mother would put her in touch with more tender, forgotten times. But no; disappointment dawned slowly. In Augusta's box were the fine amber beads that had been too small for her mother's large frame; the beautiful carved jade earrings Lydia had shunned; Italian mosaic brooches Amenia had worn; wristlets of rare lapis lazuli, lustrous gold watches from Switzerland, clusters of garnets made into elaborate flowering pins and necklaces; cashmere sweaters from China threaded with pearls and embroidered red beetles. All of these things, Augusta realized, had been treasures given to Lydia by her mother, Amenia, and Augusta had never seen Lydia wear one of them. It was true that Augusta had always fussed over the foreign delights her grandmother Amenia had brought back, but now she saw them through the eyes of her mother and they seemed cold, meaningless; the oil of history had not been rubbed into them by loving hands.

But there—was that the Woolsey cameo? It was a huge brooch upon which was carved, by a leading artist of the nineteenth century, the delicate pink and white profile of Hopestill Woolsey, a halo of emeralds and diamonds round her head. It had been too extreme for even the substantial Lydia to wear.

And here, in an engraved silver cigar box, was the infamous hair jewelry—a nineteenth-century mourning convention popular in the upper classes—an array of filigreed brooches and earrings braided from the hair of Cornelius Woolsey's mother. Lydia had considered the pieces macabre.

Augusta was nearly at the bottom of her box; she looked over at Nellie, who was still working through hers, smiling at the discovery of heirloom after heirloom: a gold locket containing her mother's picture, her mother's favorite scarab bracelet, her mother's favorite white kid gloves, her painting smock, the muslin suit that she wore when she defied her family and went to work in a munitions factory during the war; even her bottles of Mitsouko perfume, which she began dousing herself with as a youngster in defiance of her grandparents, who still believed that one bath a week and a dusting of talcum was sufficient. Now Nellie was holding her fist aloft and sighing with pleasure at the perfectly coiffed head of hair arranged upon it; made in France, it had been Lydia's pride, Lydia's salvation when her own hair grew gray and thin with illness. And what, Augusta thought, a lump growing in her throat, was Nellie supposed to do with somebody else's wig?

"Oh look, Augusta!" Nellie said, pulling out the matching Raggedy Ann outfits that the sisters had worn one Halloween. "Mother left me both of them! I guess she thought I would be the one to get married and have kids. Don't you remember how we sat there with our arms and legs stretched out while she put rows of tape all down the sleeves and stockings, how it took her hours to dye the stripes into the longjohns and boil the mop-heads red? And how she and Dad hid behind the bushes at each house because they wanted to see what people would say about our costumes?" Nellie cradled the outfits. "No other kid had costumes like these. She wanted us to be perfect, to have perfect childhoods. Oh Augusta, she wanted to be a loving mother, she really did!"

"Why did she leave you Grandma's cane?" Augusta asked, pulling it out of Nellie's box. The silver head, shaped like a serpent, glittered in a shaft of sunlight.

"Surely you haven't forgotten my big moment? That day at your dancing school, Miss Ferguson's dancing school?"

"O-o-oh, oh yes," Augusta said, a vivid memory coming back to her. It had been the autumn after the summer of the Three Terrible Events: Augusta had shot up four inches, started menstruating, and developed bosoms that poked through her shirt like pencil erasers, all at the horrifically early age of eleven. She began wearing three undershirts and bending her knees slightly to shave off crucial inches. Her father admonished her to stand up straight, but he did not know that her permanent slouch saved her from what she perceived as complete deformity. Thursday night dancing classes, presided over by Miss Ferguson, a sternly amused matron with a mass of shiny gray curls rumored to be phony, was a nightmare.

On the dance floor Augusta felt about as graceful as a soup ladle. "One two three, one two three, wa-a-altz, wa-a-altz!" Fergie's voice could have been driving a stake into the ground; she patrolled the floor with a bamboo stick, tapping legs and arms that strayed from proper dance positions, while from the balcony above, families gazed upon this sea of pink chiffon and sweaty palms, wobbly heels and wrist corsages, watching their daughters, who mistrusted the Listerine they had gargled with earlier, exhale to the side, though they needn't have done this, for their sons held them a safe foot away.

Augusta's partner for the night was a slight, clumsy boy who she could have lifted up like a rag doll. She kept trying to whisk away her peau de soie pumps before his feet caught them, when suddenly Miss Ferguson, with a jerk of her ample bosom, ordered the music stopped; her heels made a penetrating click as she slowly cricled the room. "Someone," she trilled, "is *leading the boy.*" Augusta cringed for the hapless victim. Who could have been so stupid? The sound of the heels grew louder until they stopped behind Augusta. Fergie touched her shoulder and declared, "*This* girl was leading the boy."

The next dance was the last, and as the class waltzed out of the room, parading in front of the families waiting on the balcony stairs, Augusta, cheeks burning, saw through a watery blur the figures of her mother, grandmother, and Nellie. Suddenly, Nellie gave her sister a dazzling grin, snatched up her grandmother's cane, and, in what seemed like one motion, hooked Fergie's gray waves and weighed back as though she was bringing in a fish. Augusta waltzed past just in time to see Fergie's wig sail through the air.

Now Augusta smiled at Nellie, who was putting the cane and the rest of her treasures back into the box. "I'll never forget that night. You were magnificent, Nellie. We expected Mother to punish you, and we were so surprised when she was actually proud of you instead."

"What was even more important was that you were proud of me," Nellie said. She looked at Augusta wistfully. "And that didn't happen very often once you had entered puberty. One day I was simply cast out of your life. You wouldn't let me take a shower with you anymore, you wouldn't let me in your room, I went from being your best pal to the dust under your feet. I would have pushed that old battle-ax into the fountain if it would have gotten you back."

"As I remember, it was *you* who wouldn't have anything to

do with *me*," Augusta said, recalling how Nellie suddenly
began to attach herself to their mother. From the age of eleven
on, her home life had been agony: Lydia berating her, nagging
her, Nellie behind her mother's skirts echoing her like a little
Igor. Her father drinking and disappearing and philandering.
She could have used a good sister.

"Nellie, I wonder what was really happening back then.
Maybe we'll never know. I only know I was miserable. And
things changed between us forever. They certainly haven't ever
been the same since."

But Nellie wasn't listening. She was thinking of her early
relationship with Augusta, so tender and exciting that it ran
through her memory like a clear stream. A love affair, really.

Augusta would take Nellie around everywhere. They would
sit in the shower stall, brown tiles all around. It was like being
inside a tall box. Augusta would say they were orphans lost in
the woods. She would fill the cavernous shower with images of
trees and ferns, the water slurping and spilling off the leaves
onto their skin. She would put a finger to her lips and whisper,
it's a bear and we have to be as still as glass because he is so
near his breath ruffles up the bottom of the curtain and we can
feel it on our legs. We are so wet and cold and we have to
huddle together but it's hard to hold on because our hands are
soapy and they slip all over each other.

"Mother certainly left you the things that were sentimental
to her." Augusta's voice broke through Nellie's reverie. She was
giving Nellie's heirlooms a lingering look.

"Yes, aren't they wonderful?" Nellie said. "And you got so
many really valuable things," she added, noticing that in comparison, the contents of her own box were really rather shabby.
This fact, however, bothered Nellie not at all. "Mother knew
us. She knew what we would each appreciate most."

"Why would she leave you the wig?"

"Maybe because I was here to see her wear it," Nellie said.
She looked out the window. "You know, I almost feel Mother

is talking to me from the grave through these things. Telling me that I was important after all. Telling me how much I meant to her."

"Let's get going and get this room over with," Augusta said, suddenly feeling impatient. She opened the last item in her box. It was a manila envelope containing a silver baby bracelet, some tiny baby pearls on a gold chain, and a packet of watercolors signed by Coert Van Voorhees. Two of the watercolors showed a Renoir-like Lydia holding Augusta in her christening dress; another depicted Augusta as an apple-cheeked little girl, golden curls floating against a backdrop of blossoms.

She stared at the portraits, so romantic, so lovingly rendered, and fear slowly sliced down her back. And what, she thought, is Mother telling *me* from the grave? In a flash, that evening came back to her, that evening two years before when she had told her mother she was going to meet her father in Canada, and go fishing with him rather than come home from California to spend her vacation at Woolsey Orchards. Her mother had flown into a rage, and then gone to pieces. Accusations flew. The two of them resurrected every fight, every betrayal, every bitter disappointment of their relationship, and finally Lydia, shaking with fury, told Augusta that Henry was not in fact her father anyway. That Augusta was a mistake, the result of an illicit lapse by a lonely and foolish young woman. Her mother had said she had been so ashamed that she had nearly aborted her.

Later, Lydia retracted the words; she had taken out Augusta's birth certificate listing Henry Bean as the father, she had cajoled, she had persuaded. Too heartily. From then on, even in the face of Augusta's absence in her last days, Lydia had been completely accepting of Augusta. Too accepting.

Augusta had put the devastating suspicion that she was really illegitimate out of her mind, dismissed it as one of her mother's momentary hysterical fantasies. But now she realized, looking at the portraits, that it had been there all along, nagging at her, deriding her, filling her with a rage she could not even acknowledge, preventing her from getting on those planes when she should have come home to be with her dying mother.

Augusta fingered the paintings. This illicit lapse her mother had taunted her with, had it occurred with the milkman or a cosmetics salesman or a tax accountant . . . or the farm manager?

Why had Coert paid so much attention to her over the years? Why did they have this special bond?

"Are you all right?" Nellie asked. Her voice made Augusta jump. "You look a bit pale." Nellie was sitting on the bed, where she had spread the contents of her mother's jewelry boxes and drawers. "I've got two cartons to divide this stuff up into."

Augusta put the watercolors back and noticed a small sealed white envelope inside the manila envelope. It was addressed to her in her mother's writing. Her hands went cold, and she shoved it into her jeans pocket. Inside there might be an explanation of why she had been left the watercolors. And of why all of her mother's most beloved treasures had gone to Nellie.

Augusta looked down at herself: baggy jeans, her father's old shirt, unwashed hair; her dishevelment wasn't just to discourage William from pursuing her. She looked like a college sophomore hiding out during midterms. Having dramatically ended a life of illusion in Hollywood, she had entered another one here; it was impossible to avoid facing the tortured reality of her heritage. She had thought that getting rid of all this memorabilia would stop her nightmares, would allow her to let go of these two opposing mothers who had always haunted her. But why did she ever think she could skate over the past? How did she imagine she could avoid letting its pain close in on her, digging back down to find the truth? But would the truth free her? And would she even recognize it when she found it?

"All right," Nellie said, "I put the blue shawl in my carton, and her lovely new pink pearls in yours—I've tried them, they just make me look washed out. We're going to have to fight it out for the rest of the jewelry. I already know what I want, but I'm ready to negotiate. Of course, my favorite piece of all you already have—the Woolsey cameo."

"You can have the Woolsey cameo," Augusta said weakly. What right did Augusta have to it?

"But Augusta, it's worth a lot of money!" Nellie looked at her with surprise.

Augusta stared at the bed covered with scarves and bracelets, beads, evening bags, fans, stockings. What had seemed so important a while ago now seemed almost pointless. She had no interest in these possessions; this note growing damp beneath her fingers might indicate that her mother had in mind for her to inherit revelation instead.

"I thought we were going to be clawing and tugging over this stuff, dragging Daddy in to mediate," Nellie said, looking rather disappointed. She picked up a topaz ring the size of a walnut. "Maybe they aren't so incredible, after all, these Woolsey things. Every woman in this family was oversized, and we're not big enough to wear most of the family jewels. At least not yet.

"But where's the star ruby, and her diamond engagement ring?" Nellie asked suddenly, alarmed. "I've checked through all this stuff and haven't found them anywhere. You didn't take them, did you?"

"Of course not," Augusta said, noticing that Nellie was already suspicious of her disinterest in the rest of the heirlooms; no Woolsey ever took any pronouncement at face value. But right now all Augusta wanted to do was get rid of her sister and see what was in the envelope Lydia had left for her. "They must be upstairs in the master bedroom," she said. When her mother become too ill to climb the stairs, she had moved into the sickroom, but many of her belongings were still upstairs. "You go on up, I'll come in a minute."

As soon as Nellie had left, Augusta ripped open the envelope. The letter inside was dated a week before her mother's death: "Dear Augusta: In the big freezer in the cellar are the diaries I have kept from the time I was eighteen. They have been my salvation—the way I stayed sane. I wanted you to have them and I know your father and Nellie would never get around to going down there. I put them there for safekeeping. I have always loved you. Mother."

Augusta stared at the note. She had never thought of her mother as someone who would keep a diary. And, if she had kept diaries, why would she exclude Nellie and her father from reading them, yet want Augusta to? Could there be something there, such as the truth about Augusta's conception, something Lydia wanted only Augusta to know? Had the Good Mother left them to Augusta to favor her—or the Bad Mother to punish her?

Augusta's mind was reeling. All her life she had yearned to live in the moment, like others, and all her life she had been hiding instead inside the family secret: the whispers, the pretense of normality, the shame beneath. Nothing was discussed, and so the secret weighed heavily, often descending over her like humid air, suffocating her, slowing her down, keeping her from moving on with her life.

She put the note in her pocket and went up to join her sister. Her footsteps resounded heavily on the mahogany stairs. It reminded her of her mother's heavy tread up the stairs when she was depressed; it also reminded her of the sound of footsteps in the night thirty years ago, next door to her room, running, running, screams, thumps, waking her, propelling her out of her bed. Half-asleep but still aware of what she must do: she must stop her father from hitting her mother. Only when she had stopped him, only when he had left her bedroom, would her mother be safe, would Augusta's work have been done.

"Isn't it like a fairy tale in here?" Nellie asked when Augusta walked into the spacious, bay-windowed master bedroom. Nellie was circling the grand double bed, Lydia's pink satin robe swishing round her ankles. She was running her hands over the spiraling worlds of lace tatted into the spread, over the cherry-wood posts curving up like the outstretched women of Modigliani, holding up an arched canopy over the palace of love below. No one had slept in the bed for more than a year, no couple for more than three decades. "I think sometimes of how lucky you were," Nellie said. "By the time I could walk, Daddy had moved down the hall into the spare room. I think of you being in this bed with Mother and him, your beautiful yellow curls bobbing in and out of their arms."

"I was never in this bed," Augusta said.

"Yes you were. Mother told me. Don't you remember the family hugs? You know, you got to be the ham in the middle of the sandwich? I remember it and it didn't even happen to me!"

"Listen, Nellie. If I was in that bed at all, it was to separate Mother and Dad. There was no cuddling, no adoring three-some, only fights. When I was little, Daddy was already on his way out the bedroom door."

The hall radiators hissed on; the weather had turned raw and chill for April. The sound reminded Augusta of the signal Lydia had used to summon the toddler Nellie for a morning cuddle.

"You were the one who cuddled all the time in that bed. With Mother," Augusta went on. "I was always lying awake listening for noises, and I would hear her whisper 'psst' to signal you into her room. I knew that as long as you two were giggling in there, Mother wouldn't be in here yelling at me to get my lazy body out of bed." Nellie and her mother, wrapped together like praying mantises. Nellie and the Other Mother. Augusta would put her fingers in her ears to drown out those sounds.

"Oh Augusta," Nellie moaned. "You know Mommy enveloped us with love. I can see her now, the way she held us, so close, it was like we were just one big body."

"She held *you* close. I was out of favor by then," Augusta said. "I can see her watching me, constantly. I can hear her saying 'I own and operate you.' I can even remember that it felt like love. But I have no clear memories of her hugging me. Ever."

"Oh God," Nellie groaned. "Maybe she never really did hug me. She certainly never hugged Daddy. Why do I have this feeling that you're going to tell me something like Mom and Dad never had sex after I was born?"

Augusta sat down on the bed. "As a matter of fact," she said, "knowing whether they slept together used to be the most important thing in the world to me. Sometimes I would listen at their door to hear if they were fighting, but really hoping I might hear proof that they were still making love."

"Oh God, Augusta, eavesdropping at bedroom doors, listening for noises!"

"I was terrified the family was going to fall apart," Augusta said. "At one point, they suddenly started kissing each other good-bye in the morning, and of course I knew right away it was phony; I had overheard poor Mom telling Daddy to do it because it was important to me. I guess somewhere she knew how much I wanted them to love each other."

"But did they?" Nellie asked. "Do you think Daddy really loved Mother that way?"

"Of course I loved your mother." Henry's voice came from behind them. Both women jumped. Nellie cringed toward Augusta. "Daddy!" she said without turning around. "How long have you been here?"

"I just came up," he replied, putting his hand on Nellie's shoulder. "How beautiful you look in your mother's robe. I haven't seen that for years."

Augusta was struck by how much Nellie, in spite of her Woolsey chin and close-set eyes, looked like their father; she had his thin still lips. And Augusta also noticed, looking at their reflection in the elaborate oak dressing-table mirror, that she, Augusta, shared not one feature with him.

Henry put an arm around each of his daughters. "Love your mother? How could you even ask? The word itself is inadequate. She was my whole life. Then and now."

Henry had realized long ago that the other women were mainly a physical release, a physical warmth that she would never, could never, give him. If only he could have realized this when she was well. They had wasted years in a perversion of love. They had argued and teased; she had nagged, he had gotten drunk; she had needled, he had lost his temper. She had to get sick for them to know what they really meant to each other, and even then there hadn't been enough time left. Did his daughters realize how hard their mother had been on him, and how hard she was on him still? Life after Lydia was an eternal confession, uttered silently into a black space where only his own ghosts existed. A recollection, each time it came out of the caverns of the past, would come out dragging new kill. Some unremembered incident, some forgotten gesture could alter and alter again his vision of their life together.

Augusta felt her father's arm grip her shoulder more tightly. His physical power, his authoritative voice, his caressing baritone that always told her everything was going to be all right even when it wasn't—these had always masked his weakness and given him the illusion of strength. Augusta had loved these manly trappings, for her own weakness would flow out into his strength and she would be suffused with peace. Now, however, his arm felt heavy; she saw it rise up to abuse her mother and she began to wheeze under its weight.

"It's hot in here, the heat's up too high." Augusta slipped out from under her father's arm. How different he had become, this sweet bumbling man in mismatched clothes. And yet even in her childhood, he, like her mother, had been two people: the liquored-up husband and the sweet heroic father who rushed in to save her from the oncoming car or to shield her when a kilt she had unbuttoned in the restaurant came sliding down to her ankles as she got up.

"I don't think I've been up in this room for years, have I, Nellie?" Henry said. "I hope you kids are going through everything carefully. You think a box is full of junk, and then, lo and behold, up turns the Hope Diamond. Especially the way your mother hid things away."

"Daddy," Nellie said sharply, "we can't find Mommy's engagement ring or the star ruby. Do you know where they are?"

Henry looked at her blankly, then knitted his brow. "No . . . no, I don't." Then he turned and started for the door, trying to look casual. With his shoulder blades stuck out from his cardigan, he looked to Augusta like a man attached to the earth by a fragile thread. "I'll have a look downstairs."

"You mean you'll go have a pipe or fiddle with your bees," Nellie said under her breath to Augusta. She spoke out loud once he was gone. "Well, at least I got him to stop drinking. And I've kept hot meals in front of him. Otherwise he probably would have collapsed completely by now."

"Nellie, let's get the hell going here," Augusta said. "We haven't made any headway in cleaning things out."

Nellie went over to the mirror and stared at herself. "Imagine Daddy saying I looked beautiful," she said absently. "Mommy always used to complain that you could do no wrong in Daddy's eyes. She said you would always be 'Daddy's little girl.' But I think she was wrong." Nellie pressed her arms in so that her cleavage peeked up through the white feathers of the peignoir.

"That doesn't look like a pose for Daddy," Augusta said.

"No. This isn't for Daddy," Nellie smiled.

Augusta watched her sister raise her shoulders and pull the satin skirt tighter until it outlined her hips. She watched her glide her hands down her thighs, undoubtedly thinking of the moment when those hands would be William's hands. Augusta felt the letter in her pocket growing damp beneath her hands, and her heart began to hammer. It suddenly seemed strange to her, Nellie's constant chant that Augusta had gotten everything. Augusta felt now as if she had nothing; not her mother's early love, not her most cherished possessions, perhaps not even the right to her name. Perhaps, from the moment of her birth, Augusta Woolsey-Bean had been created out of lies. The mythology that she was the child with the advantages, the brains, the talent, that she was Daddy's little girl, perhaps it had all been an attempt by her mother to cover up the fact that Augusta was a colossal mistake; a sin she wanted to abort, a half-breed, an embarrassment to these gene-proud Woolseys.

Augusta had felt so guilty about her favored position that she often thought she would do anything to achieve redemption, to assuage Nellie. She had imagined over these past weeks that she could finally reach a state of grace by sacrificing William, by steering this gorgeous creature into her sister's arms. But now, standing there watching Nellie in the mirror, her hands suddenly felt empty of anything to give. Something primitive rose in her throat; all the cold lonely mornings listening to croons of love between her little sister and her mother, all the nights listening to love come apart between her parents, all the times that Nellie had stood behind Lydia, the two of them berating her. Berating her surely because something was fundamentally wrong about Augusta's existence on earth.

"I want that after all," Augusta said, going over to her sister and tugging at the collar of the satin robe. Augusta was surprised at how easily it slid off Nellie's shoulders. How ridiculous she looked standing there in her underwear, how much like the victim she had always rather profitably pretended to be. All these years, Nellie, the one who claimed not to have anything, had had it all. She was her father's daughter, the legitimate heir to the Woolsey estate.

"What the hell are you doing?" Nellie cried.

"And I want that four-leaf clover pin too," Augusta said, folding up the robe.

"Augusta, why are you suddenly doing this? You have dozens of lovely things like that," Nellie said, her voice rising. "You probably have robes that Myrna Loy wore on the set! This is a dreaming robe for me—it's not about you, it's about Mother and me. We're the dreamers in this house. You have no idea how all these things make me feel, how they help me to dream. Me, unsuccessful, unbeautiful—they give me love. You don't know what the familiar means. You have no reverence for it. You just want to destroy it, obliterate it."

"And you just want to obliterate me . . . take my money so you can live in this mausoleum to Mother . . . take away my right to success by making me feel I don't deserve it," Augusta said. "If she had meant you to have that robe, she would have left it to you."

"Well, take it then. You're just trying to kill Mother all over again," Nellie cried. "I thought you had matured, Augusta, but when all is said and done, you really are a bastard."

"What do you mean by that?" Augusta went rigid. Had her mother said something to Nellie? Surely, her mother would not, could not have been that cruel.

"Oh Augusta," Nellie sighed. "Let's stop. Let's just get through this stuff now. Look at all this mess we've made. Let's get through these things and put Mother's room back in shape."

CHAPTER 6

It had rained the night before, a torrential late April shower, and now the air was unseasonably warm. Conditions such as these were perfect for the outbreak of fungus. Coert, attaching the sprayer to the John Deere tractor, had enlisted Augusta, Nellie, and William to help him cover the orchards with the new fungicide. Otherwise, scab might spread through the trees like wildfire, killing the apple blossoms before they had a chance to bloom.

Down in the Christmas Orchard, William watched the big sprayer lumber like a dinosaur between two rows of Staymens, shooting the glistening spray up into the trees at a velocity of 115 miles per hour. Augusta and Nellie were following Coert in the much smaller supply tank, which they would use to refill the sprayer when it was empty.

Poison hovered in the atmosphere, but William put aside his aversion to chemical toxins long enough to take a deep satisfying breath; the sweet sharp smell of the air reminded him of the smell of sex. As it happened, poison and sex seemed to be all he thought about lately.

He had decided to go after the Apex Electronics Corporation, for he was sure that they were illegally dumping hazardous wastes with insidious abandon. Apex was not a multinational corporate octopus; it was in fact a small company manufacturing computers and other high-tech equipment. But its owners had high hopes for this relative newcomer to the burgeoning electronics market. William's sources told him the company was pouring all its resources into competition and expansion, while skimping on things like workers' benefits and compliance with federal laws passed the year before that regulated the disposal of toxic materials.

These last few months, with every landmark of his childhood he and Nellie had revisited, he had felt a strange stirring in himself, a giving way of ambition, of aspiration, and a deep, forgotten devotion to what he had grown up with. Crouching in meadows like his father before him, waiting for pheasants to clatter forth from their nests, stalking the woods with Nellie for mushrooms that grew big as platters, feeling his blood rush with the river as it carved its way through the farms below. This was where he belonged, this was where his own history resonated; it almost seemed like all his farflung environmental projects had been arrows directing him back here, to the place where his heart felt restful, where he was at one with the natural wonders of his past. He wanted to protect the meadows, the forgotten streams, these fragile wonders of the county, much as his father had wanted to protect the poor and unfortunate among its citizens. And he was going to start with Apex; he was going to find that dump if it was the last thing he did; he was going to stop them from perverting the land he loved with their toxic sewage.

Nellie would help him, that he knew; she had already begun collecting data on Apex. If Augusta was uninterested, even dismissive of William's theories on the effects of chemical toxins, Nellie had been instantly captivated. And this was where the sex crept in.

In spite of the almost overwhelming attraction that they had both felt when they first saw each other three weeks ago, Augusta had slammed the door on a physical relationship with William, exactly as she had two decades ago. In response, William had immersed himself in his land-preservation foundation. But then, after a while, he found he could not stay away any longer.

The Woolsey sisters were hypnotizing him. He loved watching them. They were so different, yet there was something so similar about them—an intensity, a sense of drama—that made him feel as if he were standing beneath two great chiming bells. Nellie might not be as commanding as her sister, who was now refilling the sprayer while Nellie helped her by steadying the hose that ran from the pump on the supply tank to the manhole on top of the sprayer. But beneath Nellie's rather unruly copper hair and her occasional buffoonery lay a placid brow. At the Hopestill Arms, she fielded the phones and the guests with witty aplomb: she was contained, not easily read, a person who had learned to wait her turn. Augusta, on the other hand, was everywhere, gesticulating, bossing, reacting, fixing Nellie with her azure-eyed stare, tossing her long cornsilk hair; her changing expressions so fascinated William that half the time he felt like a camera zooming in and training his lens on her dewy essence. All he had to do was recall that lusty kiss in the cellar, his very first introduction to lust—he whose adolescent hormones were like comets whistling through space. All he had to do was remember it, and this newer, greater lust would come on him so powerfully that for relief he would turn and look at Nellie.

Lately, however, he had found her countenance less than soothing. Was her color higher? Her cat-green eyes brighter? Her nose funnier, her chin that was hardly a chin more endearing? Had Augusta's return somehow impassioned her, so that beneath her heedlessness there now simmered a strange allure, a disturbing potency? Or was William losing his mind?

He could no longer deny it: the brotherly friendship that he and Nellie had so lovingly nurtured was dead. Now she clearly wanted a love affair, and he was in a growing heat of confusion. He had always been drawn to Woolsey Orchards the way a boy is drawn to Arthurian legends, with their locked doors and secret chambers and damsels pining within. But now his attraction threatened to spill over into everything. Every time he set foot on this soil, he felt a disturbance deep in his soul. He was becoming more and more attracted to two women at the same time, sisters no less, and he hadn't the faintest idea what to do about it.

This was entirely uncharacteristic of him. Though he had always had a strong libido, too strong at times, he had tried to keep tight control over his personal life, particularly since his parents had died. He doubted that he had ever satisfied his father, whose standards were merciless, and he surely seemed incapable of satisfying women, who always seemed to want something different, something more, something better, from him. He was deeply suspicious of himself, afraid that he would disappoint, or worse, hurt the ones he loved, and the pressure of this fear was so great that he would never stay with a woman long enough for it to happen. But lately, he had tired of resisting involvement: he wanted to really know a woman, to know her and to possess her—and to feel, at least for a while, the soft embrace of being possessed.

"Hold the hose up!" Augusta was scolding Nellie, who had let the spray nozzle from the supply tank fall and drip. Augusta had handed it down to her after she had finished filling the sprayer, but Nellie had been dreaming, watching William, who was at that moment trying to regain his own equilibrium by concentrating on the glittering apple branches. "Nellie, you know we can't afford to lose one drop. This spray is expensive."

"It looks as if the trees are sprouting coins, doesn't it, William? And don't we wish that it were so?" Nellie said cheerily, hoping to drown out the effect of Augusta's scolding. Since they had cleaned out their mother's room a few days before, Augusta had been irritable and strident. But was it Nellie's imagination, or had she become doubly so since William's reappearance?

"Stolen coins, I'd say," Augusta sighed, kneeling down to peer under the supply-tank tractor, where Coert was tinkering with a faulty brake mechanism. "If you can't fix it, Coert, we'll have to steal another spraying tractor someplace."

"Hmmph," Coert said before coming out from under the machine. "Brake should hold now. This old thing may or may not last out the planting season, but it'll do for today. Take her over to the barn and mix up some more spray, but don't take the shortcut up the hill and back down again. Go around on the perimeter paths. Even though they are windy, they're flat, and you shouldn't use that brake any more than necessary."

Augusta mounted the tractor, and William and Nellie squeezed behind her on the three-point hitch that attached the tractor to the supply tank. As they bumped along, Nellie fell against William, at first by accident, and then not. She was becoming slightly drunk with the nearness of him, and with his scent; it was like the rosemary in her kitchen window, rosemary and wet birch bark when you peeled it off the tree. Surely he felt something too! The way he looked at her now, the way he acted when the three of them were squeezed together in the front seat of the Imperial last night; surely he was not just tensing his leg for the gas pedal, but giving her a signal! Her experience with men was not great; she realized she was a twenty-nine-year-old with the nerve ends of a teenager. But was she foolish to think that maybe, just maybe, he had been attracted to her all along? Even though she had snuck into her sister's room and dabbed on her lavender toilet water, even though she must have smelled like Augusta, maybe that kiss in the cellar eighteen years ago really *had* been meant for Nellie.

If Nellie had learned one thing over the years, it was that

things are seldom what they seem. Woolseys wallowed in ambiguity, beginning with their great-great-grandfather Cornelius, who had made quarters appear and disappear from their ears. Perhaps William had seen Nellie being teased that day by the apple-picker kids, and Augusta had sent him down into the cellar to comfort her. Maybe William had been suddenly carried away! Had Nellie not fled, who was to say that the kiss would not have led to more kisses, would not have changed the course of both their lives?

Augusta drove the tractor into the barn, which was crammed with crates and chutes for apple grading, old tires, rusty tools, lengths of cable, coils of wire, empty paint cans; there were chairs with missing seats, rolls of pink insulation, a slashed tractor seat, and a large, vibrating furnace filled with fragrant burning applewood. Resident barn swallows swooped through the beams, filling the cobwebbed ceilings with their shrill music. Nellie jumped off the tractor hitch and took up a can of fungicide powder before Augusta could get to it. She grabbed the hose that was attached to the water tap, climbed atop the supply tank, straddled the spout, and prepared to mix the spray. She would show William that she was the one in charge, not Augusta.

She aimed a stream of water into the spout with one hand; with the other, she gingerly poured in the powder. She thought she felt William's eyes bore into her and she sucked in her stomach, but when she looked down, he was staring at Augusta. And Augusta was staring at him.

Was she imagining it, or could she feel the electricity between them? It seemed strong enough to light up the town. Augusta *wouldn't,* Nellie thought. She wouldn't take William out from under her own sister! Augusta had wept for weeks after William had ditched her back in high school; how could she take up with him again?

On Nellie's birthday in December, when William's breath, coming with the comical force of a hurricane, had joined hers in blowing out the candles, she had known that never in her life had she felt so sure of herself. He had given her a French silk scarf for her birthday. He had put his arms around her and held her for an instant. Didn't that mean something?

Nellie suddenly lost her grip on the can of the precious poisonous powder, and cried out in alarm as it tumbled down the side of the tank. She watched in horror as it bounced off Augusta's head and covered her hair, her face, her clothes, with fungicide.

Nellie scrambled down. "Oh Augusta! Oh dear! I'm so sorry! I don't know what happened, it just slipped out of my hands!" Augusta began to gasp through clouds of white grit. Nellie reached out to her, but Augusta pushed her away.

"Jesus, Nellie, are you trying to kill me? Can't you do anything right?"

"Please, Augusta, let me help you." Nellie wondered who would faint first—Augusta of poison inhalation or Nellie of embarrassment. "Don't breathe in, try not to breathe at all."

Just then, Henry Bean came into the barn. He had interrupted his melancholy meandering through the house in order to move his bees farther away from the spraying, and he was looking for his daughters so they could praise him for this considerable effort of will. Now he was suddenly in the milieu which always mobilized his lethargic molecules: a crisis. When he saw his elder daughter coughing, covered with fungicide, he began frantically brushing her off; then, his face deepening in color, he looked around for someone to get angry at, and he seemed to fix on William. "Dad, it was an accident," Augusta said.

"Get out of those clothes, quick!" Henry said, and he began taking off his own jacket to cover his daughter.

"Oh Daddy," Augusta waved him away. "I'm not taking off my clothes." She shook her head, blew upward, and looked sharply at Nellie. "The damage is already done. What are you always saying about this stuff? That it causes miscarriages, liver trouble?"

"No," William said firmly, stepping in with his handkerchief and dabbing at Augusta's face. "This is only a fungicide, and we don't know if there's anything really harmful about them. You'll be fine. Nellie, get some water, will you?"

"Of course, yes," Nellie said. She picked up the hose, and, almost without thinking, aimed it at Augusta and squeezed the handle. A stream of freezing water shot forth and hit her sister square in the face. William and Henry leapt out of the way.

"Nellie!" Augusta spluttered through a sheet of water. "You ass! Coert was right, you don't know how to help. Stop it!"

"Well, at least we'll get this stuff off you nice and quick," Nellie cried, training the hose up and down Augusta's body. And as she did, she felt increasingly peaceful. Their mother used to say that Augusta would show her "true colors" if pushed to lose her temper. Her sister in a rage had always become incoherent, overcome with emotion, just like their father. But Nellie could control herself; Nellie could get even.

She noticed that William was looking shocked at the childish insults Augusta was hurling around; perhaps he would also notice how plain and worn Augusta's bra was, now that she finally took off her soaking T-shirt.

"There's not a bit of powder left on you now, thank God," Nellie said. Henry held up his jacket and put it around Augusta, glancing at Nellie doubtfully.

Augusta stood shivering; her face was red, her lips were blue, her eyes had gone black as onyx. "We don't need to look as far as Apex," she muttered, huddling inside her father's coat. "We have Nellie dumping chemicals on us."

"I think you should go over to the doctor, or the hospital, make sure you're all right, Augusta," Henry said with authority. "I'll take you." But Augusta was already halfway out the barn door. "I don't want anybody to do anything!" she said. "I'll take care of myself, myself."

． ． ．

Augusta hurried into the house, threw her father's jacket down, turned on the bath, and stepped into the tub, burning herself with the hot water and slipping on a bar of soap. She broke the soap in two and hurled it across the room, then let the tub fill, and lay back in thankfulness. Suddenly the plug that had been fitted into the bullet hole that Great-great-grandfather Cornelius had shot into the side of the tub during his senility popped out. Water began to spurt through the side of the old claw-foot tub. Augusta put her finger into the hole and began to sob.

An hour later, having knelt in an inch of water and scrubbed herself with pieces of broken soap, Augusta finally luxuriated in the warm cocoon of her bedquilt. Shame was replacing her anger. She had made a spectacle of herself down there in the barn. In a matter of seconds, Nellie had reduced her to a spoiled child. She could not remember behaving that way in years. William was heightening the already unbearable tension between them, pulling them even farther back into the behavioral patterns of the past. You wouldn't recognize how different I am with other people, Nellie had said, but in William's presence, Nellie became the very same prepubescent horror who had once made Augusta's life miserable. For days, Nellie had been looking at Augusta with that old look, their mother's look; that veiled contempt only Augusta could recognize, that malignant invitation, her mother's invitation, for Augusta to lose control. If the anger Nellie caused her was uncontainable, so was the guilt, predictable and unremitting, that followed it. Should she ever get free of her mother, she would never be free of Nellie: her sister lived unhatched beneath her, like an egg beneath a brood hen.

But William and Nellie were not the only reasons for Augusta's current unease. She had not yet dared to retrieve her mother's diaries; she had vowed to steep herself in the past, but she had not even been brave enough to open the freezer, only brave enough to imagine what revelations she would find, what judgments her mother would pass on her.

As Nellie and she relapsed farther and farther into childhood, as the diaries grew colder in the cellar, the Other Mother had begun to loom larger and larger. She saw her all the time now, her tall, heavy, magnificent presence filled the room as it had always filled any room she entered, her half-lidded eyes boring into Augusta with the message: "You will pay."

Augusta suddenly threw off the quilt; she would no longer indulge herself in the masochistic family fascination with the dreadful unknown. She marched downstairs and opened the door of the cellar.

As she descended the steep steps, she imagined her mother negotiating this last trip, stopping every few steps to rest her body that at last had become so bony. When Augusta opened the freezer, the frost was so thick that she had to chip and chisel with an icepick until she finally freed what looked like a leg of lamb left over from the days when her great-grandmother Mildred liked to make mutton curry with apple chutney. There, underneath, lay a large plastic bag. Her heart beating fast, Augusta took the bag up to her room, locked the door, and emptied it out.

There were dozens of journals, some covered in satin or pigskin or fancy Italian book paper, others simply in spiral notebooks. She stared in amazement; her mother, her all-pervasive mother, who flew about town helping the poor, learning everyone's secrets, trying fruitlessly to know her family's, had had a secret life of her own! After an hour of sorting, Augusta discovered that the diaries were chronological, and covered the last forty years of her mother's life; the entries were sometimes regular, sometimes sporadic. She separated the icy pages of the first one and read:

July 16, 1930

*E*ighteen years ago today, I came into this world—and God only knows why. The sun has set on all my birthdays with the same bittersweet light.

If Mama had truly wanted me, wouldn't she have wanted to be with me on at least some of those birthdays? If I had a best friend, I would be too mortified to tell her, it seems so shameful: my mother is never here, even on my birthday. She is off in the Orient or the Levant or wherever else half the blessed time. It's embarrassing, too, with times so hard and people starving. Each year, Grandma Millie takes my chin in her hand and says "never mind." She takes me to the store and lets me choose a cupcake, but it doesn't make up for the fact that Mother is never here. Does she hate me, is that why she goes?

And is that why everyone in this town stares at me? Could I secretly be an orphan? Was there something the doctors told her at my birth that I don't know and everyone else does? Something about the fact that Mama married her second cousin, Augustus Woolsey? Are they looking for signs that I am some dangerous product of intermarriage?

Maybe Mama can't stand to sit and wait for me to go berserk, a helpless victim of garbled heredity, so she races madly around the globe, avoiding me. If she wept with disappointment when she looked into the cradle, I will never know. Nobody discusses how anybody feels about anything in this family, and whenever I try, the words get stuck in my throat. We are a family of weather vanes, we just "indicate" the direction of the wind, no details supplied.

Great-grandpa does take something of an interest in what I think, but when I'm not on his mind, I might as well be dead. When he looks at me, it's like he's examining a Golden Delicious to decide whether it's good enough for him to enter in the county fair.

Grandma Millie, with her bib apron and her thick black shoes and her high pursed lips and her pink nose, she keeps looking out over the mountains, the light through the kitchen window making her abundant white hair look iridescent, like spun sugar. Wisps come loose from her bun like tiny children leaping from a haystack. I know she is looking for my grandfather Samuel Beaumont, who walked out one day and never came back; she is brooding over where her husband went, though she never talks of him. Grandma Millie keeps his photograph, secretly, in the back of the frame that holds Mama's baby pictures, and she sometimes slips it out. I know that even if she wanted to, she couldn't forget him. His glorious mustache and beard hid his receding chin, but nothing can hide Mama's. She is his spitting image, and maybe that is why the very presence of Mama has always seemed to irritate Grandma Millie, which may be why Mama is never around.

I know that Grandma Millie sometimes steams open Mama's mail when she is gone; maybe she thinks one of those letters might be from Sam Beaumont. Sometimes I dream that I will see him, lurking around the county fairgrounds in a dark fedora, romantic and handsome, anxious to catch a glimpse of the little girl, Mama, that he left behind. And especially the granddaughter he never knew. When he sees me, in my dream, he swoops me up and takes me away from this creaky old house.

Long ago, I used to dream Daddy would take me away in the flying machine he was working on in his invention shed. Oh, Daddy, with your brainstorms and your soft kind eyes. Everyone but me thinks you are loco. I have kept all your secrets, all those times I was your guinea pig,

2

the times I came crashing down from the shed roof, flapping in vain the rice-paper wings that didn't work. Daddy wants to be only with me—when he wants to be with anyone. I can feel Mama bristle at it. I think I am my father's only love.

Maybe that is why she sent me down south to college at the age of fifteen. I hate that school and I'm glad this will be my last year. The first two years, I spent crying in the shower. Each time I get bad grades, they make me stay there for the holidays, marooned in the library, without a friend, while everyone else goes home for turkey and love.

On this, my eighteenth birthday, I make this vow: I vow I will leave here. I will get away from the mighty magnet of my family. I will escape the smell of Mama's awful pea soup, the dark halls, and the old-fashioned clothes. I will marry a man who lives in a world I can go to. A man who will give me babies I can love and cherish, the way no one has ever cherished me, and never ever leave. I will make hand-embroidered dresses for them, I will put ribbons in their hair. Every birthday, they will have a homemade cake with three layers; they will have not one but a dozen presents; and most of all, they will have me.

Augusta put down the volume and stared at it.

They had had those cakes. Every birthday had been like a diamond jubilee: balloons, confetti, armfuls of presents throughout the day. How Augusta and Nellie had loved birthdays, the one day of the year when all tensions were dissolved, when Augusta could count on magically emerging from the doghouse to become a princess.

How could Augusta not have known that her mother, far from being fussed over as a child, had felt so desperately deprived? How could she have not known that Lydia once wanted to escape Woolsey Orchards as intensely as Augusta did!

She crept up to the attic and rummaged around until she found a carton of clothes. Yes, here they were: the matching little girl's dresses her mother had smocked in every color of the rainbow. When Augusta held them up, mouse droppings fell from their sleeves. Nellie's was perfectly in scale, but her own looked odd—short waist and overlong skirt. And then she remembered. Oh, the humiliation of wearing that dress out to dinner, a budding teenager looking like an overgrown Kewpie doll with puffed sleeves! Just the way Lydia must have felt in her own old-fashioned clothes. In her determination to do things differently, Lydia had forced her twelve-year-old daughter to wear a seven-year-old's dress. Lydia had vowed to dote where her mother had neglected, and in doting too much, she had ended up repeating history.

Augusta went back through the hall and picked up one of the pictures Nellie had put up. She wanted to locate an earlier mother: Lydia in her cap and gown, the wind blowing her hair, eager and unwearied by life, so startlingly different from the stern, reproving figure who haunted Augusta now.

Back upstairs, she locked the door again, and picked up the diary of this soft vulnerable girl she had never known.

August 4, 1930

*D*earest diary, you breathe. The world breathes. The paper I am writing on, my pen, they breathe. Until this very moment, I know, now, I was a mummy buried in a tomb.

He has a deliciously high forehead, he smokes a pipe that smells like cherries burning, and he is tall, tall, tall! Oh, to meet a man who finally makes huge old me feel practically dainty! He's an intellectual like Daddy, a maverick like Daddy, he looks at me over the top of his glasses just like Daddy does, sending something positively wonderful down my toes, and he seems to have much more horse sense than poor old Dad. He has a shy, funny smile and a timid way about him, but there is something wild and exciting in his eye. Daddy and I were pressed into a crowd at this entomological conference—or more plainly put, a *bug* conference—to get a glimpse of Albert Einstein, the great man himself, and my nose got sort of buried in this man's tweed jacket and then I noticed he had turned around and was not gazing at Einstein anymore, but at me.

His name is Henry Bean and he is from New Jersey. His family was a victim of the stock market panic and he had to leave Rutgers to help his father sell patent medicine made from frog glands. His family, he says, is wildly weird and he imagines mine to be splendidly down-to-earth and sane, ha! He thinks I look like a statue of Joan of Arc with my perfect posture, my raised chin (because I'm afraid it will recede like Mama's!), and my "strange and haunting eyes."

He is coming for the weekend and will feast on nature, which he loves: to do that in New Jersey, he has to go to a glass-littered vacant lot. Mother insists on doing my hair (yes, she's around these days). She won't let me shingle it the way everyone else does, because she says that with my large face I'd look like a mule; she is making a royal mess of it. She just keeps brushing and pomading it, as though she's trying to transform me from the ugly lummox she has to suffer into some lovely vision. I half think that if I could slip out from underneath my hair, she wouldn't notice that I was gone. I look the very vision of a greased poodle.

Oh dear, sometimes I want to swallow the whole universe in a gulp. Sometimes I have the feeling that I'm going to jump right out of my skin. At blossom time, when the whole barn smells like a giant apple, my body is a rumbling engine and I feel like I might take off at any moment. Sometimes I want things so badly. I see a horse and I want it. I watch its shiny red flanks rippling and I want it, I want it.

Henry, please, come quickly. Somehow I think that you are a man who will, at last, truly know me.

Turning the pages, Augusta read an entry from the following spring.

April 2, 1931

*F*or four years at this college I've been socially invisible, and suddenly this girl bursts into my room last night and says, "Grease your heels, Lydia, we're all going over to Duke for a costume ball." My folks would be shocked to know that this girl is a Jewess named Shulamith. And that I really like her. We all piled into Shullie's Studebaker and at the dance I met a darling French exchange student named Georges, who was dressed as a fried-egg sandwich and kissed my hand and asked me to come in under his bread. We gals laughed and sang all the way home. Shullie has a nose that belongs on Abraham Lincoln and a sense of humor that big too, not to mention a heart. She has brushed my hair forward in half moons and I've bought the latest helmet hat. Mama will die! To think that all the sorority girls had left me alone because they thought I was strange and stuck-up! Why didn't Mama teach me how to dress? She has been all over the world, though that never seemed to affect how frumpy she looked. Why didn't she urge me to go out and make friends, to be popular, why didn't she force me?

May 2, 1931

After getting almost no letters from home, now that I'm about to graduate, the mailman knows my face. They all want to come for graduation, even Great-grandmother Hopestill. Before she was stuck in a wheelchair, Great-grandma would go into Newberry's Five and Dime and just drop nail polish and candy and things into her purse. They had to call Great-grandfather to come pick her up. What if she comes here and gets caught trying to steal someone's cap and gown or something?

The thought of my whole family arrayed on the steps of the chapel for all to see makes me go cold. But I should be glad for the attention. And soon I will be free. Free to do anything I want. I can go anywhere, even to Europe and the Levant, like Mama.

July 1, 1931

I have been home barely two months and already I feel like I'm sleepwalking. My real life is a dream, a long sleep, and there are only brief interludes of waking.

Daddy is under a black cloud. With his latest venture—high fashion gold-flecked brick which, as it turns out, no one wants in a Depression—he has plunged us into near-bankruptcy. He has been giving money away to the destitute and has failed to evict people from our tenements who cannot pay their rent. Great-grandfather has taken responsibility for the major properties away from him. As long as I can remember, this family prided itself on family loyalty and protection. But everyone is being vile to Daddy and I just wonder whether it is because he is the wrong kind of Woolsey. Only I know the truth: Daddy is not stupid, he is a saint. How can I leave now that this has happened? Daddy needs me. I am all he's got.

August 4, 1931

Everyone hates outsiders here so much, it is a relief they are being so nice to Henry. Whenever we can, we sneak off to Candy Apple Ridge and kiss. The way Henry walks, moving with the long gait and awkward grace of an antelope, fills me with tenderness. The way he talks, like he knows everything about the world, fills me with hope. How can a man who takes out his rough black jackknife, slits open an apple, and explains so eloquently exactly why the seeds grow, how can a man like that ever fall prey to foolish visions of "papples" and gold bricks? We bend to look at the apple and all it takes is his cheek to accidentally brush mine and the breath goes out of me, I feel something flow through me that commands my body, my soul, to stand in willing obedience to his wishes. I yearn to give myself to him completely, but I can hear Grandma's warning: "Give yourself away before you marry, give yourself away for life."

Sometimes I think that to a Woolsey sex is a dirty secret, like a retarded child tied to the bedpost. Has the act really so rarely been committed in this house, or has there been some depraved incestuous coupling that still haunts us all?

August 10, 1931

A few short hours ago, I was almost made a woman. Now I have been yanked back into miserable childhood. Henry has been sent home.

I still don't understand how Great-grandma Hopestill

got her wheelchair all the way up to Candy Apple Ridge alone, unless she grew wings, but how else would she know every tiny detail of our day together, even down to the fact that my brassiere dangled from the branch of a McIntosh? She has convinced everybody that it was all against my will, and now even Mama believes that I'm covering up for Henry. As for Grandma Millie, the only thing that bothers her is that this occurred in broad daylight when we should have been having our tea. I have assured Mama I can still wear white at my wedding, but she thinks Henry has ruined me.

Do you know what I think? I think that Great-grandma Hopestill has perpetrated a gigantic fraud. I think that she can walk.

August 30, 1931

*H*enry and I are betrothed. Now no one can touch us. He can kiss me anywhere, anyplace, from here to eternity. He kisses me in the orchard, he kisses me in the barn, in the garden, even in the house. If anyone walks in on us, they walk right out again. They can disapprove, but they cannot stop us. I do not belong to them anymore. I belong to someone else now.

What delights lie in store for Henry and me! Romantic tête-à-têtes over candlelight, scrambling our own eggs, half-naked breakfasts, and my very own bathroom! My own house, my own husband, my own life!

October 1, 1931

*H*enry broke the news to me this morning. The savings he had planned to use to take us away from here was lost by his father on the stock market.

Henry is not even speaking to his parents, he is so angry. And so we must live here until we accumulate enough capital to move away and be on our own.

Great-grandfather is giving Henry management of the properties not lost by Daddy, and he can keep some of the profits he makes. Henry is sick about disappointing me this way, but secretly, I know, he loves Woolsey Orchards. Ever since he could remember, he has yearned to escape the asphalt and smog of New Jersey; he has longed for green and growing things, for an end to the screaming of cars on the highway under his bedroom window, for the sounds of crickets and leaves twirling in the breeze, for things that fly and crawl. His dream is to have an apiary. He wants to be a farmer. He wants, has always wanted, to be exactly what my family is.

October 10, 1931

*H*ave I made a terrible mistake? How can we make a marriage, how can we find peace and solitude here in this batty house? How can I face daily the humiliation in Daddy's eyes as Henry does the family job he used to do?

How can I resist doing exactly what Henry wants? He turns my bones to chalk. I become the tide rippling and rocking against his mighty hull. He puts his arm tight around me and his eyes take me in and I know that from this time on I will be the source that nourishes him; he will need me to flow through him always. How can I even know my own wishes when his very presence is my wish fulfilled? All the trees I grew up with, he has replanted them, recreated them in my imagination with his knowledge, his tenderness. He covers me with kisses, promises me a lifetime of kisses. He casts his silhouette everywhere.

And Mother? Dear, absent mother is suddenly giving me parts of her as fast as I can take them, me the miserable, bottomless child. She has ordered the walls torn down in the servants' hall to create the grandest bedroom in the house. The newlyweds' room will overlook the Victory Orchards. It will have dollhouse eaves and a dressing room for me. She has already selected the wallpaper, and she managed to locate the pattern of my beloved childhood bedspread: tiny violets surrounded by a halo of baby's breath.

Augusta closed the volume. She walked downstairs slowly, went into the library, and stared at the portrait of her mother's mother, Amenia Woolsey, that peripatetic grandmother with her exceedingly benevolent eyes that now appeared to have just a glint of malice. Augusta closed her eyes and suddenly felt located beneath the angry ivory brush of this woman, who was pomading the life out of her poor hair. Involuntarily, Augusta's hand rose and knocked the heavy gold frame to one side, making Amenia look as if she were in a drunken tilt.

Augusta went out the front door. She could hear the sprayer down in the orchards below. They had not yet sprayed the Newtown Pippins here at the edge of the yard, and the perfume of the first apple blossoms filled her nostrils. And there was Auntie Mame, already wearing an incongruous bonnet of pink; each year she bloomed a good week before any other tree.

Augusta had somehow imagined her mother as being beyond erotic love, yet her diary revealed her yearning for it. For love, and for sex.

She imagined her father, if he *was* her father, young and

handsome, bending over her mother, filling her body with lust, filling her heart, her mouth, with kisses. And her mother had sacrificed her liberation for love. Dying to leave home, just like Augusta, her mother had stayed for love, for sex. There had been no one to help her, to support her, to urge her forward, the way Augusta had been helped, in the end, by *her* mother.

Lydia's diary voice now filled Augusta's head; her breathless sensuality, her happy desire for Henry Bean . . . and perhaps for other men as well.

Did her mother realize that what she felt for Henry Bean was utterly molten sexual desire? Her mother! A sexual person? As long as Augusta could remember, Lydia had been as straight-laced, as prudish as any Woolsey grandmother, loving but never sensual. What had happened to that desire? Had it shriveled into some hard hurt that lay waiting like a cancer to explode in her breast?

Augusta's hands were damp. Wasn't this just how she herself was, in so many ways? She carried the Woolsey legacy; sexual lust weighted down with sexual guilt; sexual fear that paralyzed her. More than once she had been accused of being tense and standoffish—including by William Hurley, way back then—when in reality she was aching to be touched, to be loved. She might attach herself helplessly to one man after another, but she had never been able to enjoy helplessness in bed. She had always wondered how people could so misinterpret her, but she was beginning to think that she had been simply imitating her mother; her sexual self was like water trapped behind a dam, unseen but pressing to be released. Had she given the wrong signals to the scriptwriter last January, when she lay motionless, hopeful, in her desert sleeping bag? Was she squandering her youth, her sexuality, as Lydia had?

She saw William emerging from the trees. He was striding up the lawn, the swollen buds of the Pippins grazing his dark hair. He was carrying his tweed jacket over his shoulder and his muscles strained the buttons of his shirt. Or was she imagining that? She wasn't imagining the adorable smudge in the middle of one of his dimples. A feeling like that of warm chocolate suddenly flowed through her, and she went quickly down the hill toward him.

CHAPTER 7

"Are you all right?" William asked, peering intently at Augusta. "I thought you'd come back down to join us in the orchards. I was worried."

Augusta blushed. "In the movies, that's just the tone of voice they use with mental patients." She raised her eyebrows sheepishly. "I'm fine except that I'm hoarse from screaming at my sister and I'm not very proud of myself."

William waved his hand dismissively. "Oh look, you were showered with poison and then hit with a jet of freezing water! Ask my roommate about the time I took off a pair of new boots that leaked and threw them into the Potomac. Or the performance I gave on the Senate floor when they filibustered my clean-water bill."

"You mean you feel right at home with raving banshees?"

"Oh yes." William smiled. "I do. I trust people who show feeling. Sometimes I fall in love with them." And sometimes, he thought, it's my mouth that leaks, not my boots.

Why did he have to say something like that to a woman who had repeatedly rejected him? Whom he was not even sure he wanted more than he wanted her sister—a woman who *did* seem to want him. Step back and control yourself, he thought, pick some nice, neutral subject to talk about.

But this woman beside him was transfixing him—how could her skin be so white and so smooth, exactly as smooth, he thought, as the petal that was brushing her cheek?

He found himself ambling over to the gigantic Newtown Pippin they called "Auntie Mame"; he found himself spreading out his jacket on the ground, which was still damp from last night's rain, and motioning for her to sit down. And he found himself saying, "You *do* have an impressive temper. It's rather exciting to see."

"It's rather a handicap, at least that's what Mother always said." Her mother had also said no man would marry Augusta if he found out about that temper.

She had an urge to run back up to the house, to shut the door on William and the confusion he represented. Plunge into the mountains of diaries that were even now thawing out on her bed. She sat down on his jacket instead.

She studied him as he settled himself beside her. In her struggle to avoid him, she had not fully realized how much he had changed; how in little ways he had become older, gentler, less threatening. Gone was the smooth, sleek skin, the peach-fuzz, the odd angry pimple, the flashing eyes, the nervous tapping of his fingers; the restless energy that had kept him moving, turning, touching; the thrust-out chest of the football hero. Instead, his vulnerability now seemed to define him: a furrow of crow's feet, a ruggedness around the eyes, a dryness at the corners of his still-sensual mouth. The old William, the one who had hurt her, had always been poised to leap. This one was calmer, more earthbound, his body poised to hold.

"Your mother and my father, we can't seem to get away from them," William said. He was suddenly feeling hungry, though he had eaten an enormous breakfast. He was always hungry, but he suspected that at this particular moment it wasn't really food his body wanted. "You know why Dad insisted I join his practice after law school? He talked the liberal talk, but secretly he hated my radical politics. He wanted to keep me under his thumb. He was afraid I would disgrace him. I wasn't just his child, you see, I was his mirror. I think he thought I would turn out to be his worst self, foolish, rash, and penniless."

"I know what you mean," Augusta said. "You always thought my mother was so warm, so accepting, but you never saw her go cold, you never saw her suddenly put me in the dock and appoint herself judge and jury. If you were a mirror, I was a kind of hat. But I never fit quite right on her head."

William laughed and nodded. "I did see it. She had poor Nellie running around at the end, forever wanting her to do things just a little differently." Nellie. She was waiting right now for him to come back, William thought guiltily. They should go now, back down to the barn to help Nellie, who had such a crick in her back after having dropped the poison on Augusta that William had to massage it out.

"Even after I left home, I felt Mother watching me," Augusta said, unable to take her eyes off William's feet. She had never realized that men's thin socks, revealing the outline of their bony ankles, could elicit such a feeling of tenderness. "The first time I made love, I really thought she would come bursting into the dorm any second." And men's belts, the way the long leather strip strained at the loops, the gold buckle glinting in the sun.

Made love! How dare she have first made love with anyone but me, William thought irrationally. But he said, "I wonder that you could have enjoyed it at all."

Augusta smiled. "You know you were the only beau of mine that mother really liked. Sometimes I got the feeling *she* was dating you, not me. When you broke up with me, she took it very hard."

William wished he had kept his jacket on his lap so that he could hide the event that was taking place there now. "Your back," he said, "when you took off your shirt in the barn, it was so sleek and beautiful, it made me fall in love with you all over again."

Augusta looked away, out into the trees. She saw her mother standing on Candy Apple Ridge drinking down Henry Bean's promises, feverish with desire, and Augusta suddenly felt that she too had bones that were going to chalk; her body a river flowing forward to its end, this man beside her with his sexy eyes, his mouth, his arms a rapids pulling her around and around, threatening to open the gates out of which would flow her most cherished self, the self she had fought to keep from her mother, to preserve unharmed from the chaos of her child-hood.

William also looked away. He thought of Nellie, but the stab of pain he felt receded before his attraction to Augusta. The sun was filtering through the branch she was holding, and drops of diamond light were caressing her arms. When he cupped her chin in his hand, for once she did not retreat from his touch. He had not fully realized until this moment how long he had been without a woman, how many months he had simply avoided them, and how lonely he had been.

"This is wrong," Augusta said. "I don't want to get in-volved. I don't want to get distracted. I have plans." But the words meant nothing. Meant nothing before the pressure of this desire that had been thwarted over and over, had been beaten down just when it surfaced, had left her suddenly cold and capable of only the most pitiful shadow of sexual enjoy-ment: fizzling orgasms, skin rendered insensitive, waterfalls of kisses that became puddles of oblivion. When would she be able to completely let go, to stay in the moment of passion, to break free of that hereditary hook that pulled her back into the icy world of retribution? "Now," Augusta found her-self saying. "Now."

William looked at her in surprise. Her round cheeks were the color of roses, roses floating in fresh cream. And she had an expression he had never seen before. "It's as though you've taken off your mask. I've never seen you look like this, so kind of naked."

"That's exactly the way I want to be," she said, slipping her hands beneath his shirt, caressing him until he fairly dragged her under the thick, stretching branches of Auntie Mame.

"Do you know that Nature never forgave you for not making love to me?" he said, unbuttoning her blouse. "That our desire has been ticking away like a time bomb for twenty years?"

"According to that theory," Augusta laughed, "if we make love, we'll explode. And I think I'm going to like that."

But as the clouds, moving like puffs of white across a nursery wall, disappeared from sight, Augusta felt herself stiffen in the darkness beneath the tree. The damp earthy smell brought back Nellie's childish voice, her little arms around Augusta's neck, holding on for dear life. "Oh God, I can't do this. My sister and I, when Mother got into one of her moods, this is where we would hide. We would—"

William put his hand over her lips, kissed her face. Her pulse was like gunshot.

"Isn't that Nellie's voice? Do you hear that?" Augusta asked. William listened and shook his head. "I thought I heard a distant calling. If she's trying to find me, she might look under here."

"Oh, of course she won't," William said. "You'd think it were still twenty years ago."

"What if she needs me?" Augusta asked. She saw her sister running across the fields, weeping, running from the bullies who picked the apples.

"I need you more," William replied.

The sun broke into a million pieces, swam like a school of fish over William's face beneath her. Augusta thought of herself during those days in the desert, longing for a lover while, unbeknownst to her, her mother lay dying. William's arms enveloped her, turned her over, and the twine of blossoms above him was bluish white, like a dead woman's fingers. She heard her mother saying, "Kiss me, Henry, kiss me," and felt the pain her mother must have felt when Henry had finally stopped kissing and holding and touching her forever. The moist sweet smell of William sent a shiver down her back, but she saw suddenly his naked form in a dream, soft and shiny in the desert moonlight, so innocent and yet endowed with the power to impart such guilt, such unsolicited pain.

His tongue felt suddenly hard, shooting forth like the drawer of a cash register, and she recoiled. It was happening again: the thing that was terribly wrong with her was manifesting itself— the lid was shutting just like it had shut on generations of Woolsey women. She tried to transform William back to his desirable self, but all she could feel was his callused, groping fingers, his noisy breathing; it embarrassed her. And he would know it; soon he would sense the chill.

She hated herself, Augusta hated herself for following her mother, and her grandmother, and her grandmother's mother: for condemning herself to watch her desire shrivel, become a silent howl in the wind, a pinched, cold, frightened ghost of her youthful dreams. Augusta hated herself so much that she suddenly threw herself on William. She was tired of giving off mixed signals. If lust eluded her, she would go after it with a vengeance. She would be a lion pacing in the zoo, she would exaggerate herself just as her mother had exaggerated her accomplishments. William would be lucky if he escaped with his life.

As she ran her fingernails down his back, as she sucked his neck, she suddenly realized one reason for her sexual fear: she was afraid of drowning, afraid of becoming completely enslaved to those addictive men whom she could never leave.

But right now, right here, she was not drowning; on the contrary, her active role seemed to be giving her a sense of power. And she was beginning to feel something else. Lust was rushing, foaming inside her, and suddenly she knew that to keep from being washed away, to keep from losing passion, she had to break through and let go, let it take her, let her body ride the crest of the wave.

Augusta opened her shirt, slipped off her bra, and ran William's hands roughly down her breasts. He was unprepared. He had wanted her, but had not known how badly until she had shown him. The hardness of her nipples, the hair that slid off his fingers like strands of silk, could he have dreamt these things? Out of the corner of his eye he saw the white blossoms fluttering above, as pure and fresh as her skin. But there was nothing virginal to be found in the kiss, so hot and salty, that she was giving him now. Who was this woman? Not the prim little girl in Peter Pan collars who had held herself like a glass statue, who had let him steal just one kiss in the dark cellar. Not Augusta, the aloof and guarded thirty-four-year-old woman. She was growing stronger under his embrace, filling up all the space. When she twirled her tongue around his mouth and pressed her fingers into his back, he felt himself rising, higher and higher in her hands, until it seemed as if he was snatched away from himself. No woman he had known had ever kissed him like this.

If he was uncomfortable with her sudden, uncharacteristic boldness, he was powerless to change it. He was lost. In the tangle of hair and tongues and moist skin, he could not find the substance of himself, nor of her; she was as elusive as a cloud, and yet she was able to throw bolt after bolt of lightning through him and in his confusion, he had no idea that she had taken over his role as the actor so that she no longer had to be the one acted upon.

All at once, Augusta sat up and pushed William away. She quickly pulled on her shirt and told him to do the same. The sound of the tractor, and of distant yelling, was unmistakable. "It's Nellie," Augusta said.

"Yes. Oh, Augusta," William said, kissing her back and her blue jeans, and reaching to kiss her bare feet before they slid out from under the tree.

. . .

Nellie was maneuvering the supply tank up the ridge, ignoring Coert's instructions to avoid the hills because of the tractor's slipping brake; as far as Nellie was concerned, he was always exaggerating the danger of a situation. This route would take her up from the barn to Candy Apple Ridge and down the other side of the hill directly to the South Orchards, where Coert was finishing up the spraying. She would not have to waste a half-hour going all the way around the flat perimeter of the property. And maybe she would run into William. He would be so impressed when she revealed her plan to sell the Christmas Orchard to this French apple-growing expert. Augusta and Coert kept saying the trees in that orchard were shot, producing a sparse crop, and then there was the worry of the toxic seepage. But the buyer didn't seem to care: he did business with a French agricultural concern that wanted to test various new fertilizers and sprays in this country. The sprays, made from mostly natural substances, were designed to produce a larger, tastier apple; the quantity of the crop did not matter, and there were still many perfectly fine trees in that orchard.

What Nellie really wanted was for William to come across the yard and see how elegantly she handled this behemoth of a supply tank down the slopes, and perhaps to hop on the tractor beside her. She had come to feel vaguely panicked when she was away from him, when she did not know where he was. He had left her in the barn to go up to the house to check on Augusta, but it had been an awfully long check. Nellie wondered whether they were enjoying a nice cozy cup of the coffee Nellie had brewed and left on the stove.

After the accident with the insecticide, she and William had talked and talked. She had felt guilty about hosing down Augusta and he had soothed her, sympathized with her anger at this sister who had abandoned their mother and then come home to take over everything as though she was a feudal lord.

William had said the incident could clear the way for a better understanding between herself and Augusta, a working out of their resentments. This surely was a hopeful sign for Nellie. If he had even contemplated choosing Augusta over Nellie, wouldn't he know that their resentments, their broken sisterhood, could never be healed?

Nellie could still feel William's fingers going deep into the muscles of her rock-hard shoulders while the barn swallows fluttered romantically above; she had been seized with the back spasm just as he was leaving to go see about Augusta, and he had been there behind her immediately, his fingernails grazing her neck, sending ribbons of joy down her spine.

The smell of the orchards was sweet and pungent as Nellie drove the supply tank through fountains of pink-budded Romes, the branches on either side of the row brushing her gently. It was the steamy, deep apple smell of the air after you took a bath, the fluffy, tickling feel of the towel going round your small body, wriggling, giggling with the pleasure of just being inside a towel.

When she emerged at the top of the ridge, the clean line of the road cresting over the hill evoked an unpleasant memory. She saw the old armies, the swarms of boys and girls her father had hired to pick the apples, coming out of the trees at harvest time and closing in on her like a posse. As a child, Nellie had been perfect bait; she was shy, she was homely, she cried at the drop of a hat. Even her own family called her Calamity Jane because of all the accidents that she had, bumping into things, breaking her toys by mistake. And she had a head too small for her body. She tried to make it look bigger by wearing a beanie, but the beanie only called more attention to it; she was a pinhead.

In her isolation, Nellie had turned to her menagerie—birds, turtles, gerbils, cats—and they brought even more ridicule down upon her. Inspired by Nellie's mother, whom they had overheard threatening to throw out the guinea pigs unless

Nellie cleaned their cages, the kids would taunt: "Smelly Nell, Smelly Nell/ Drown your piggies in the well."

The picker kids were Italian, Irish, brought up in the street-smart poverty of the tenements once owned by the Woolseys; and in spite of the famous family philanthropy, in spite of Lydia's charitable work inside the tenements, they resented the Woolseys with a historic resentment. Their grandparents had had to go hungry during the Depression because everything they had went into rent: their unyielding landlord, Cornelius Woolsey, might have made a show of helping the poor, but when it came to Woolsey business, he would throw a "rent cheat" out of his home without a second thought.

These kids were clever, and they always made sure no grown-up was around when they went after Nellie. But Augusta knew, Augusta saw. When Nellie came home with bumps and scratches, Augusta knew that it wasn't just Nellie's clumsiness. Augusta had pleaded with her parents to get rid of the picker kids, but the farm was still reeling from Grandfather Augustus's disastrous losses and could not afford professional help. Her parents needed their youngest daughter's tormentors in order to survive.

"Tell them, 'Sticks and stones will break my bones, but words will never hurt me,' " her father said. She followed his advice, and they threw sticks and stones at her.

Nellie remembered crouching in the trees, vowing over and over that someday the orchards would be returned to her; if she had to wait twenty-five years, the day would come when she would not feel hunted on her own land. And, of course, that day did come; Nellie had gotten a turn running the Woolsey estate.

But now Apex was harassing them with offers to buy out the orchards and Augusta was scheming to sell even the rugs they walked on. Nellie was being put to the test. She supposed she should thank those young apple-picking bullies, for they had given her the hide of a rhinoceros. While Augusta got flustered and furious when mistreated, Nellie had learned to get even.

At dawn one morning last week, before anyone else was awake, she had brought her prospective buyer to survey and map out the fifty acres by the river that made up the Christmas Orchard. Even if she had to sell some of it out from under the family, Nellie would never again lose control of this land.

William Hurley had helped her learn how to fight back. From the time Nellie was eight or nine, he had loved to hunt and birdwatch on the property, and he would often come upon the pickers preparing to ambush Nellie. When they saw him they would freeze in midattack. It wasn't his rifle that intimidated them, for he put that down on the ground. It wasn't his size, for he was just a couple of years older than most of them. It was the way he could transform Nellie, shoot her through with courage, make her look into their eyes. He made her walk right toward them, even though she was quaking inside; he taught her to set her mouth and squint her eyes until they backed off. Then off he would go, searching out some nest of pheasants with his binoculars, or heading down into the woods to hunt. Sometimes she would wait in the Christmas Orchard until she saw him emerge. But often he would have a woodchuck or rabbit swinging from his belt and then she would run away in horror, unable to stay and thank him; Nellie had come to depend on animals for her emotional sustenance and could not bear to see them hurt.

Then, one November day two years later, the pickers collected their last pay of the season and snuck back down into the orchards to make a final grand foray against Nellie. Nellie lost her bravery; she ran up to the house and cowered in the cellar. Augusta had usually been the one to find her in one of her hiding places, to cheer her up and comfort her after an attack. The touch of her sister's fingers had been like the touch, the smile of a thousand mothers, like lamps flooding the darkness. But that afternoon the footsteps in the cellar were too heavy to be her sister's. Nellie's heart was throbbing, and tears of fright rolled down her cheek, and then suddenly there were these lips on hers, these arms enfolding her, like warm flannel.

It had been different from any kiss she was ever to receive again; different from Boots Korshak's slobbery smooches, different from Roderick Digby-Downes's dry, measured approaches. William Hurley's kiss on her eleven-year-old's lips had the warm, smooth, grown-up feel of lips coming to life from the cover of a movie magazine: smooth and cool like the skin of a plum, opening, succoring her, taking her away from her tormentors. No, it was not foolish to believe that William had known, had really known back then that he was kissing not Augusta but her little sister.

Nellie had brought the tractor almost all the way across the ridge and was near the house now. There was no sign of William.

How many times had Nellie dreamt of a man like William emerging out of the swollen trees that were now aching to burst into bloom? When it came to men, the pickings in Stonekill Landing were very slim. Every time Augusta had come home from California, she had done Nellie's hair in the latest styles, brought her dramatic, way-out clothes from the coast. "You're too pale," she would say. "You look like you live in the ground. You need to glow, to appear succulent," then she would fuss with blush and mascara to make Nellie over. But it all seemed wasted on the likes of Sam Purnick, who worked at Newbury's Five and Dime and still had terminal acne, or Gustav, the Vassar German professor whom Nellie had dated until he told her he was leaving the wife she didn't know he had for one of his students named Jeffrey.

Nellie had not exactly planned to find herself at nearly thirty still living in her mother's house. She had had her own modest ambitions. A place of her own. An interesting job, in organic gardening perhaps. Romance. She did not know exactly when it began to be expected that she would remain at home. All she knew was that when Augusta left for California, her status in the family underwent a dramatic change.

After Augusta went raging into adolescence, Nellie became

her mother's adoring sidekick; but still, she often felt taken for granted, even used, by Lydia. She was like a vestigial tail that her mother used to beat Augusta with. Once, when they were playing charades (they liked to pretend they were household items), Lydia had written on Augusta's instructions: "Act out the gold Haviland china. Breakable. Fine. Heavily remarked upon." On Nellie's she wrote: "You are the plain flatware: durable, can last forever. We eat on you every day."

But when Augusta went away, her mother suddenly began to shine onto Nellie the light she had always reserved for Augusta. She shifted her obsession with Augusta to a preoccupation with Nellie. It was a new and enticing sensation for Nellie, to feel that she, the afterthought, the second fiddle, might have some amazing importance of her own. Gradually, however, it came to seem like everything her mother wanted her to do was a test for Nellie, a test to see whether she was suited for the outside world; and Nellie began to fail every one of them.

The tests themselves were almost wired for failure, because the more she messed up, the more her mother lavished on her the attention that had been so meager when Augusta was living at home.

Though Nellie got into Vassar (she studied maniacally, for she could not suffer rejection from the college her sister had attended), her grades there were poor. Money burned a hole in her pocket, and her mother had to parcel out her allowance on a weekly instead of a monthly basis. She could not seem to get in with any popular crowd, and what friends she did make, made her mother livid; she complained that they were "goofs and oddballs."

And then, in February of her freshman year, along came Boots.

Boots was a big gorilla of a senior who had gotten into Vassar on a rugby scholarship with the first wave of men admitted to the hitherto all-girl school. He and Nellie had met, quite literally, over a biology quiz. Nellie had sensed a shadow at her back and turned around to find the towering Boots copying her answers. From then on, he followed her around campus. Wherever she looked he would be gazing at her; it gave her the willies. It reminded her of the picker kids lying in wait. Then, one day, Boots disappeared from class. She looked in the gym, on the playing field, but he was nowhere to be found. Finally she found him in the infirmary, where he was in bed with mononucleosis. She went up to his ward, stood in the door, and just stared at him while he stared at her. When she turned to go, she heard his boots clopping right behind her (he got his nickname from his feet, which were the size of box turtles). She found herself running down flight after flight of stairs. But instead of going out the door, she ran right on down to the basement laundry room. To her shock, when he came toward her, her hands refused to obey her, refused to push him away, and it was then that she remembered William Hurley and the kiss in the cellar. She realized she wanted it again; she wanted to have again that anonymous experience that had gathered such importance in her memory.

She let his giant paws rest on her shoulders. The muscles rose up at the base of his neck like a bull's, but his fingers were astonishingly shy. Nellie's own hands, however, seemed to have a life of their own, sliding down his back, parting his thin cotton johnny, feeling the cool, hairy curve of his spine, moving down into a valley whose hills she took by the handful. Finally she unleashed the animal in him, and it was with difficulty that she made him understand that he did not have to rip off her dress, he could slip it right over her head.

Afterwards, they lay on a bed of plump laundry bags and exchanged names. Then they started up all over again. Actually, all they achieved was some heavy petting, but what petting! It turned out that Nellie had a maidenhead that must have been given to her by Great-grandmother Mildred— strong as Firestone rubber, and to this very day, to Nellie's secret anguish and embarrassment, absolutely impenetrable. But then it had hardly made any difference, for Nellie had discovered an unbridled side to herself she never knew she had. She found she was capable of venturing out of her everyday existence; she could come crashing and tumbling out of the china cabinet if she wished. If her mother, her grandmothers, had always created an ethos of degradation and guilt around sex, Nellie had somehow escaped being infiltrated: she positively, without reservation, thought making love was smashing.

For the rest of the school year, Nellie and Boots repeated the rituals of their introduction at thirty-six different campus sites, including the E–F stacks of the library, the bell tower, and the orchestra pit in the music building. In between times, they ate Vassar Devils—chocolate ice cream cake sundaes—and did Boots's homework. Even Boots did not really care that they did not actually achieve intercourse, for they achieved most everything else. Nellie's grades improved dramatically that year; coaching Boots made her realize she was smarter than she thought, and Boots himself, to the astonishment of his Polish immigrant father, who thought he would never get a diploma, graduated with honors in his major. Boots went off to the Midwest to play pro football. They gradually lost touch, but their relationship had been so magnificently sensual that Nellie delighted herself for a long time to come by darkening her room and tuning her memory into the Boots Korshak Show.

Lydia was not unhappy about Boots's departure from Nellie's life; the one time he had lunched at the estate, he had blown his nose on a hand-tatted lace napkin and proved himself to be just another symptom of her daughter's social waywardness. Lydia set about cultivating her high-class friends in Gristbrook so an introduction to a more suitable prospect for Nellie could be made, and finally a weekend was arranged for Nellie with one Roderick Digby-Downes II, a senior in the Yale class of 1969, grandson of the former ambassador to the Court of St. James. Lydia was so nervous about the date that she paid for a crash course at a New York charm school for Nellie, who subsequently arrived in New Haven with her cheeks sucked in, her toes touching the ground before her heels, and her voice pitched so low that the Digby-Downes boy could hardly hear her.

Even in the fall of 1968, the shadow of the oppressive fifties still lingered on Ivy League campuses, and coolness was the preferred state of being; the tall, arrogant Roderick was taken, even slightly challenged, by Nellie's pronounced cool, and her enigmatic smile was appreciated at his rather self-conscious literary fraternity, St. Anthony's. She was as cool as a frosty gin and tonic, as sharp as the taunting faces that had peeked out at her in the orchards. She was a walking credit card, her value carefully coded and laminated. Her mother had been right; she knew the secret of being loved, and it was so very simple: don't let anyone see who you really are. Even after the traumatic end of their relationship, the persona she developed for Roderick stuck; she had internalized the trick of containing herself.

"I've gotten into Yeats," Roderick would remark, unfastening her buttons. "I love 'The Second Coming.' "

" 'The best lack all conviction,' " Nellie yawned, having previously memorized the poem after being tipped off about Digby-Downes's latest interest, " 'while the worst are full of passionate intensity.' "

For several weeks Nellie kept Roderick on the fringes of her life; she was really only seeing him to please her mother. But then the ever-growing tide of the weekends began to wash right over into both sides of the week. He moved through her life like a silver shark, and the rest—her classes, her friends— blurred into a murky sea.

Roderick became the only one who could give or withdraw her self-esteem. And when he did withdraw it, which he did more and more frequently, it seemed to confirm her mother's view that Nellie was unfit for the real world. She took to staying in her room in case he called, to haunting the mailbox for his handmade cartoon postcards, which were once adoring but had now become insulting, like the one that showed Nellie climbing a mountain that wore Roderick's shirt. The cartoon bore the caption, "Rod finds a little something itching at his back." She would dream and dream about a nice moment that had happened between them, endowing it with elaborate meaning; yet the more value she put on these moments the less they came, and in turn the more time she dwelt on them, until the cycle became vicious.

The lamination that Nellie had so carefully developed began to crack. What she dreaded had begun to happen: her true nature was laid bare. She was a masochist, a rug under the feet of her boyfriend, her sister, her whole family. She wanted to go to bed with Roderick constantly, just for the reassurance of it, yet the more she wanted reassurance, the less Roderick gave it.

She knew he had once had a girlfriend named Sally, a tall blonde with an ironing-board figure and a clever mouth—and probably a maidenhead that had yielded like Jell-O. He kept her picture in his top drawer and would sometimes mention her. At the annual St. Anthony's spring literary weekend, Nellie had spent days preparing her costume, which she thought was a daring coup: a quill pen with a stiletto heel that emitted real ink, and a plume rising dramatically from her head. Rod came as a book of his own poems, and the high point of the evening was when he read one of them, "A Sally into Paradise," which rhapsodized on a flaxen-haired woman he had loved and forsaken. Nellie proceeded to drink seven glasses of tequila punch, and ended up in a tangled, ink-covered heap in the ladies' room downstairs. The next morning, Roderick was looking at her when she opened her bleary eyes in the motel room. "You're thinking about Sally, aren't you?" Nellie asked. "You wish I was her, don't you?"

"Sally fit in better," he said rather simply.

That day Nellie clung to him like a wet leaf to a pane of glass. His shoulders, when she reached for him, would stiffen. By the end of the weekend, they were walking separately. Nellie refused to believe he was dumping her, and when she returned to Vassar, she wrote him and called him. Finally, he let her know it was over with deadly effectiveness. He arrived on campus in his red Saab and drove around from dorm to dorm visiting their friends, who duly reported his appearance to Nellie. She herself spotted the car several times. Once, it almost ran over her at a campus crosswalk, and then gunned right past her. Two weeks later, he graduated and sailed for Africa. With Sally.

"Do you know how hard I try to make things happen for you?" her mother had said, when she came home to be comforted. Her mother was in the kitchen peeling a Paula Red, circling the apple so expertly that Nellie noticed only the thinnest layer of skin was detached. Nellie remembered now how statuesque her mother had looked on that occasion; she had lost weight, and her hair was arranged in soft youthful curls around her head.

"I don't want to discuss it," Nellie had snapped, but inside she was dying of humiliation. The rejection by Roderick did not compare to the feeling of having once more failed her mother.

"Did you cling?" her mother asked. "Did you get too emotional? Let's analyze it, and then we'll know where to go from here."

"I didn't do anything wrong."

"You must have done something! Men don't just walk away for no reason."

"It doesn't matter. I didn't like him anyway. It's not important!"

Her mother put down the knife and took her daughter by the shoulders. Tears were running down Lydia's cheeks. "It *is* important. You *are* important. To me you are the most important person in the world. And don't ever forget it."

After she graduated from Vassar in 1970, Nellie came back

to help at Woolsey Orchards. She felt she was needed there. It wasn't until two years later, when Augusta nagged her so much about not leaving home, that she finally worked up the courage to try living in New York. With Augusta's help, she got a job designing needlepoint canvases at a shop on Madison Avenue; she took a room at the East Side Hotel for Women. Everyone was always running everywhere in New York, even when they did not have to hurry, and Nellie began to run as well; looking up at the skyscrapers, she had the feeling that she had fallen through a crack in the universe. Lingering in the moment would mean falling further away. The traffic, the noise, the smog, the slap of soles on concrete, all impelled her forward, and the only thing that stopped her were the city's bag people. They seemed to be as foreign to the rhythm of New York as she was. Coming upon them on her way to work in the lovely cold sunlight, Nellie would pause, fascinated. A woman beneath a carved cornice, tossed there like a lump of clay, carefully swaddling her toes in scraps of cloth; a man with the hair of a prophet, his skin colored a ruddy plum, displaying his sores like battle wounds valiantly earned in some different century. Amid the slim silky legs and ivory faces of Madison Avenue, their rags and ruddy complexions, their bright, burning eyes, seemed ripped from forgotten time. Wolfmen from the paleolithic era or pilgrims at the Mount of Olives, all they could do was stand and sway, time-warped, stunned, bewildered.

One day, Nellie was crossing the street as she watched one of them, and a bus suddenly charged directly for her. She panicked and began to run not across the street but down it; she hallucinated that the bus somehow had obtained free will and could chase her anywhere, up a sidewalk or into a store. This big, belching tyrannosaurus of a vehicle pursued her for what seemed like forever until she froze in her tracks, sobbing. Then the bus stopped too, at a bus stop.

After that, it was downhill for Nellie and New York. A

flasher exposed himself and she fought back, pummeling him
with her purse; she ended up being charged with assault. She
was almost evicted from the hotel for leaving the bath running
until it overflowed all the way down to the rooms below. Meanwhile, her mother informed her that she and her father had
stopped speaking to each other and were near divorce. It was
clear to Nellie that with their children gone, her parents' marriage had lost its point. Afraid that the family would break up,
that her father might just pick up and leave, Nellie quit her job
and went home, back to Woolsey Orchards, back to the
kitchen to take her place on the shelf with the everyday china.

Since then she had not been entirely unhappy living at
home. She was devoted to the orchards, to the house. But her
love life had been agonizingly dull. She had begun to despair
that she would ever meet anyone worth loving, until William
Hurley appeared, as if by magic, to ease the pain of her
mother's passing.

From the start, William had encouraged her to be herself.
He had liked her whether she was cool or not, whether she was
clumsy or emotional or smart or dumb; anything she did was
fine by him. Yet he was certainly no goof; he was everything
that her mother had valued.

Nellie was starting downhill from the ridge now. The wind
began to cool her cheeks.

You could not be a moth, flying toward a lighted room and
crashing into glass forever. Sometime the window had to open,
or you died.

They had been so close to kissing down there in the barn,
so close. Could this be the moment for which she had been
practicing through a thousand dreamy nights? Could this be
the ultimate redress for every sorrow she had suffered?
Couldn't a new life emerge for her out of the shell of the old?
Nellie was barreling along now, down the long decline that led
to the South Orchards. She tried to slow the tractor by pump-
ing the brake, but it didn't seem to be catching. She was going

faster and faster, ten, fifteen, now twenty miles an hour, with several tons of heavy metal at her back, heading straight for a solid line of Red Delicious trees.

Nellie yelled for help. She screamed. Then, by some miracle, she was able to swerve onto a wide path to the right and miss the trees—but that path also went downward. She leaned forward and pushed the brakes as hard as she could, but they seemed powerless against the lumbering forward motion of the heavy Massey-Ferguson tractor. It seemed to have a life of its own beneath her, like that New York bus, like the flood of bathwater she had forgotten to turn off, like her family, like her failures, gathering power, outdistancing her.

She tried to slow her descent by swerving from one path to another, zigzagging down the hill; but how long could she keep it up, how long before she skidded out of control?

How fitting, Nellie thought bitterly, as the branches whipped her face raw, that on the eve of being joined to her Dream Man, that at this very fateful crossroads of her life, she, Calamity Jane, stupid and foolish to the last, ignoring sure danger for a glimpse of her beloved, should get her comeuppance. Now she was approaching a dead end. She could turn neither right nor left. The red stone pump house was coming at her like a toreador's cape, larger and faster, lunging, waving. And Nellie knew that in a few seconds she would be hurled pitilessly into the air, that as hard as she held onto this steering wheel, the impact of the crash would send her sailing over a stadium of apple trees like a doomed zeppelin.

CHAPTER 8

From the ridge, William and Augusta could see the supply-tank tractor careening wildly down through the trees; clearly, Nellie was out of control.

The two of them raced down the hill and reached Nellie just as the tractor was a few yards from the pump house. As she lumbered by, William grabbed at her, trying to get hold of her arms, but she was gripping the steering wheel, rigid with fear, her eyes squeezed shut. William tried to jump onto the three-point hitch, but tumbled to the ground and just missed being run over.

With a boom that echoed through the valley, the tractor and supply tank, a combined weight of several tons, crashed at an angle into the pump house. As the building's concrete blocks gave way and crumbled like sand, Nellie went hurtling into the air straight toward the spiked branches of a Golden Delicious tree.

Augusta's reaction was instinctive. She moved a few inches to the right, swiveled to the side, covered her face, and fell backwards a millisecond before Nellie, breaking her sister's fall.

Nellie's body jammed into Augusta like a battering ram, like the hand of a giant. It slammed the air out of her, whacked her on one ear, assaulted every cell in her body. The two landed in a bruised, intimate tangle, and lay there too dazed to move. As Nellie's breath blew warm on Augusta's neck, as her legs straddled her sister's waist, Augusta's mind was dominated by a discovery of intense clarity: people are born with a scent they keep for life. She had not been this close to Nellie for years, but her sister's smell, suddenly so strong, brought back to memory the child who once had giggled and squirmed upon her lap.

Nellie, groping through a miasma of pain, barely knew that this soft cushion beneath her was Augusta. Then she became aware of William, of his hands as they turned her over, of the smell of his rosemary shaving cream as he lifted her up. She realized, vaguely, that he was being careful not to bump her arm, which was twisted back grotesquely. She heard Augusta's voice saying that Nellie's shoulder must be dislocated; she heard Augusta tell William to hurry, to carry Nellie quickly up to the house.

Nellie fought to close her mouth. More than anything else right now, she wanted to look graceful in William's arms. Clearly, he had saved her life. The pain in her arm was sharper with his every step, yet it and the commotion of Augusta yelling for Coert, her father bellowing from beyond—all receded before the intimate experience of being pressed against the beating heart of her Dream Man. Unobtrusively, half conscious of what she was doing, she unfastened his shirt button with her teeth, tasting the hair on his chest; she raised the top of her head to his lips each time he leaned forward in his climb up the hill. Did he return the pressure, give her hair a kind of automatic kiss, the way a father might kiss the head of a child? Nellie opened her eyes and willed herself to gain control of her facial muscles. She felt strength begin to flow through her. She knew then how true were the claims for love's secret powers; why it had enabled mothers to ignore their wounds and lift whole cars, or fathers to endure raging flames, or nonswimmers to swim rivers to save the ones they loved.

Henry Bean had happened to have been looking out his bedroom window when the accident happened. He met William at the top of the hill and accompanied them up to the house, holding Nellie's hand, cursing the damn tractor, and trying to control the panic he always felt when one of his daughters was threatened.

As they came into the front hall, the big old-fashioned telephone, which had been amplified by generations of deaf Woolsey grandparents, rang its bone-crushing ring, rattling the glass table and penetrating through Nellie's euphoria. "That'll be the doctor. I called him soon as I saw the crash," Henry said, running to the phone. "Hello, Erastus? We're falling apart up here. One of my daughters just crashed into the pump house, and this morning the other one got a load full of insecticide. Can you come right away?"

Erastus promised to come, and William carried Nellie up to her room, where he laid her on the bed. Nellie hoped that William might actually undress her, but then a bedraggled Augusta swept into the room, followed not long after by Dr. Erastus Weatherbee II.

Erastus was the only doctor in the region who still made house calls, and the only one that Nellie trusted. His family had been friends of the Woolseys for generations, and Erastus had put himself through medical school pruning unwanted limbs off Cornelius Woolsey's fruit trees. Now eighty years old, he still kept faithfully to the old ways. With shriveled but steady fingers, he applied herbal plasters to Nellie's cuts and bruises, set her shoulder, and gave her a dark syrup that he promised would put her to sleep. Then he examined Augusta, marveling that she hadn't suffered from either the spray or the assault by Nellie. He gave her agitated father a thimbleful of the dark syrup too, and told him to go to bed.

Augusta suggested that William leave with Erastus. She

suddenly felt exhausted, unnerved. Her desire for William had crumbled along with the pump house wall. The only person she wanted to hold now was her poor injured sister. She sat down beside Nellie's bed.

"Where's William?" Nellie murmured groggily. "Is he all right?"

"William went home," Augusta said. "Why wouldn't William be all right? All he did was carry you up here. I'm the one who might not be all right—you fell on *me.*"

"On *you?*" Nellie asked, raising her head. Her sister's face looked so far away, as if it were at the end of a tunnel. "That was *you?* You saved my life?"

"Why do you sound so surprised?"

Nellie stared at Augusta's fingers, which lay over hers; the loose skin on her otherwise slim youthful hands, the ridged nails—Woolsey hands; Great-grandmother Mildred had fingernails like that, but hers had grown yellow and furrowed like a field of corn. In a few years, Nellie's hands would probably look like that too. Augusta was the only soul on earth with whom she would ever share these little oddities.

As Nellie gazed at Augusta's protective loving eyes, a picture of their mother, one that she had not recalled for years and years, flashed through her mind. Lydia was moving quickly, jerkily, she seemed to be shifting inside her clothes, to be looking about for something or someone upon whom to discharge the sudden anger that was spreading over her like red heat. Yes, Nellie had not remembered this picture until now, had not wanted to remember things that would confirm Augusta's ugly images of their mother.

And Nellie remembered Augusta: Augusta watching for Lydia's danger symptoms, and then quickly leading Nellie away to shelter to their hiding place beneath the safe skirts of Auntie Mame. Augusta would make Nellie her slave; Nellie would have to swallow her fear and sneak back into the house for cookies, she would have to sit on the wettest spot, to yield the nice dry place beneath Auntie Mame to Augusta. But it was all worth it, because Augusta would turn the blossoms into fairies, could make their lacy dresses rustle in the wind, their wands of sunlight touch her eyes with dizziness. Augusta was the one who knew how to make an imperfect world perfect.

Why indeed should Nellie be surprised that once again Augusta had saved her life? And why should Nellie hate her for it?

"Nellie, put your head down, go to sleep." Augusta's voice came indistinctly to her ears. Her eyelids fluttered; they felt like captive birds. In the half-light of her stupor, Nellie saw her ankles growing thick and protruding from orthopedic shoes; they were the ankles of her Woolsey grandmothers. She imagined the skin on her hands becoming loose, veined, brown-spotted. She tried to scream, "Don't! Augusta, don't make me take your hands!" and then she fell asleep.

When she was sure Nellie was asleep, Augusta went to get her mother's diaries and brought them back to Nellie's room. She held a clothbound volume, staring at its cover, until her hands grew damp. She felt like some invisible reverse magnet was pushing her away, preventing her from opening the book. If William had referred to the unfulfilled attraction between Augusta and himself as a time bomb set long ago, these particular chronicles had also been ticking away, just waiting to explode in Augusta's face. Once read, they could irrevocably alter her life. It wasn't just her mother's feelings toward her that she feared, it was the facts: if it turned out that Augusta was another family secret, a horrible mistake, could she ever feel truly legitimate again? What if it turned out that Augusta had committed some terrible crime as a child that would account for her mother's mistreatment of her? And what if this diary was designed to somehow manipulate her into throwing up her own life and devoting herself to the orchards?

Augusta slapped the volume down. She was angry at herself for her cowardice, and she knew that if she kept sitting here staring at the covers of these diaries, Nellie would wake up and catch her in the act. She had to get on with it, and so she opened the next volume and began to read:

October 31, 1931

I am writing by moonlight, sitting on the window seat behind the curtain so that I will not disturb this man who today was made my husband. I love him more than my life, and I wonder if he will ever forgive me.

How I have treasured the anticipation of this night; imagined his long arms and legs wrapping themselves around me! How I have imagined merging into him, our souls and minds melting together like butter! How I have dreamt of this, our wedding night; of Henry filling me up, taking away all the hunger I have felt for so long. Oh, I prayed it would be different for me, that I could find a secret pleasure none of them had found before. I listened to their warnings, I listened to Mama say marital relations were a cross a woman has to bear but not enjoy. I eavesdropped when Gran Millie said you had to squeeze hard down there to protect yourself from your husband's excesses. I raised my nose when Mama declared my thighs, visible in my daring new bathing dress, an insult to human eyes. I listened and laughed, pitying their pursed lips, their hard faces, the way the light of desire only came into Gran Millie's eyes when she saw some delectable bit of food. I felt superior to them all. I would be different! No wonder Gran Millie hates sex, I thought—her husband filled her with Mama and then disappeared! How I laughed and pitied them. And now, if they could see me—they would be doing the laughing.

When Henry did it, I felt repulsed. I hated him. He became like a shadow, a stranger. Something, some elemental force inside me appeared and took me away, far away from him, as though on a cold sea where the terrible prow of a ship was slicing me in two. I sobbed, I screamed; Henry didn't know what to do. And so he stopped, abruptly; he put his head in his hands. He apologized. And then he held me. But I only wanted to get away from him.

Now I sit here, listening to his gentle snoring, and I wonder whether they in the other bedrooms heard my screams and thought them screams of pleasure. It serves me right, to dare such heresy, to have the effrontery to think myself better than my mother, my grandmother, that I could escape their fate. They were right, sex *is* horrible, this way God has of us letting us love each other. I feel reviled, dirty. I wish I had left myself pure, untouched, like snow, like ice. As shimmering and mysterious as polished stone. I have no more mystery; I have been opened and can never close myself up again.

Do you know what the worst of it is? I cannot help but believe that Henry, having spent his first bullet of love, will now feel nothing for me but lust; secretly he must know he has killed off this virgin love and be shamed by what he has done.

January 2, 1932

Great-grandma Hopestill is dead.

Mama had to pry open her hand to remove the locket, which held the most beautiful picture of her ever taken. It was when she was the dream of every young bachelor in the county. She had masses of curls all around her face, and her eyes were wide and luminous.

I saw her after she died. Those lidded eyes seemed so small, then, after eighty-one years, like stones sunk into the sand. She was a vain and rather selfish woman, but her husband, Great-grandfather Cornelius, has always said that she was the flame that inspired him to his great works; though she sat senile and small as a doll in her wheelchair, he still held ivory mirrors to her face, still thought her the most beautiful woman on earth.

Grandma Millie stood like a pole in the receiving line at the funeral, and to expressions of sympathy for the loss of her mother, she let forth a tart, "Well, we all have to go sometime." How typical of this family; no sign of emotion in the face of the complete and utter extinction of human life. Everyone calls the death a blessing, but what is so blessed about being wiped off the face of the earth, poof, as though all your struggles and tears and joys and plans mean absolutely nothing? It is appalling, death.

Poor Great-grandma Hopestill, she had planned for a trip with Cornelius to their honeymoon spot in the Adirondacks; she had even begun to rise from her wheelchair and say to her daughter, "Now, Millie, I'm going to walk again. After twenty years of saving my strength, I ought to be able to do it." Gran Millie says Hopestill originally willed her legs to quit because she liked the attention that being an invalid got her; and then when she wanted them to work again, it was too late.

March 27, 1932

Many years from now, I want my children to know what the Woolsey family stands for. Great-grandfather Cornelius is so stingy he rolls his own cigarettes, but he is not too mean to help those who cannot even afford tobacco. He curses the "damned Democrats" and agrees with Herbert Hoover that what the unemployed need is some inspirational poem to lift them out of their sloth and fear, but he is also sacrificing our woodland to create jobs for men whom he will pay out of his own pocket. He is going to hire the jobless to chop down our three hundred acres of oak and locust north of the orchards to make firewood, which he will then give to the poor. And he has vowed that no man in Stonekill Landing will go hungry at harvest time as long as we have apples on our trees.

Old Man Depression has dragged his chains up the length of the Hudson River. Tarpaper shacks go up daily along the river at the edge of our property. Children beg leftovers from motormen in stalled trains. Men who yesterday sold scrub-brushes today jump the freight cars. Each day we take kettles of soup down to the "Hoovervilles." Gran Millie has been layering fine old wools into warm clothes for the poor.

Sometimes I feel that the eyes of my family are always upon Henry and me, that we are in an eternal dress rehearsal, waiting for the directors to come forward and approve our performance so that we can once and for all begin our marriage. Every time I start to pity myself, to brood over the fact that I am still a captive in this house I swore I'd escape, I think of all the people who are really suffering, the suicides, the losses, the human worlds falling apart. I think of us, four generations huddled here together, protecting each other, gathered round singing "Rock of Ages," Gran Millie's brilliant contralto soaring over the piano. I think of how instead of hoarding our wealth we are sharing it, refusing to ignore the needy masses outside. And I am proud that I'm a Woolsey.

July 16, 1932

*T*wenty years old today, and though I'm still living in the Woolsey household, at least I've brought my hair into the twentieth century. Grandma Millie can wear braids atop her head, Mama can imprison hers with a million combs and pins, but mine I have cut it all off and shingled it to boot. My husband says the new "do" gives me sex appeal!

Poor Henry has been so patient with me. He says that I am very young, that in time I will learn to enjoy sex, that he will teach me about my body as he has taught me about my orchards. But his hands feel like warm fish! And his breath, as it comes heavy in my ear, suffocates me. I cannot bear to let him think his "tender ministrations" are not working, so I pretend to be aroused, a little more each time, even as I am plotting ways to evade him.

If Henry knew how lonely I am lying beside him; if he knew the hunger that I always feel, he might throw up his hands and walk out the door. Thank God for this diary, thank God for a place to confide.

I have a new plan to help things. I have gotten rid of my woolies, bought new satin nightwear, and I hope the satin will feel so nice to my husband that he will let me stay clothed in bed—because the problem begins when I take off my clothes. Naked I feel ugly, and nothing but nothing can persuade me I am otherwise. Henry is the only man tall enough to make me feel really petite, but I cannot stop imagining that Henry must be seeing me with Mama's eyes. I cannot stop thinking that he sees me as too big, too ungainly. I cannot stop seeing Mama's expression whenever she saw me half-dressed or in a bathing suit: that contempt, that repulsion, that horror of having created this sorry specimen.

Augusta set down the diary. That look, that suspicious appraising scornful stare, Augusta had seen it too, in her own mother's eyes. It had been there to greet Augusta as she modeled her first miniskirt; it had prevented her from ever mustering the courage to wear it out of the house. It had been there to stop Augusta cold when she was twirling around the kitchen in a burst of youthful energy. "Oh Mom, I'm in a world of my own!" she exclaimed, and her mother had sneered, "You'd like that, wouldn't you?"

Now, Augusta felt pity for her mother, pity and understanding. When Lydia had belittled Augusta, she had only been imitating her own mother, Amenia, who undoubtedly had been repeating the contemptuous treatment of *her* mother, the abandoned Mildred.

Relief traveled down Augusta's body, right down to her fingertips. Perhaps it had never actually been Augusta herself who had elicited Lydia's anger and disgust; perhaps it had been some broader, more congenital disgust passed down from mother to daughter through the generations. And Augusta suspected that Amenia was repulsed not by Lydia's body, but by the sight and thought of any body that was ripe and seductive and emanating the sexuality that had been forbidden to Amenia herself.

William had said that he was a kind of mirror to his father, who was always searching him for his own worst flaws. The metaphor fitted the Woolsey women perfectly: perhaps it had not been Augusta who her mother had seen twirling about, or parading in a miniskirt, but the specter of her own younger self, the one that Lydia's mother had hated and that Lydia had come to hate as well.

Augusta picked up a volume dated almost a year later, and began again to read:

April 20, 1933

Great-grandfather has reopened the brick factory that was run into bankruptcy by Daddy. He has put aside our own hardships and poured all our capital into an enterprise designed to save the town of Stonekill Landing. I think it's a very idealistic thing to do. In a ceremony at the town bandshell, with the crowds going wild, threatening to carry him off on their shoulders, Great-grandfather announced a plan whereby the profits of the brick factory will be divided up among all the workers. Mama says that we will be the only township in the state where nearly every man who wants one will have a job, thanks to Cornelius Woolsey. And Gran Millie is going to hold a Poverty Ball at the house to raise money to put washing facilities into the tarpaper shacks. Isn't that terrific? Perhaps I am just trying to make myself feel better for staying here, but I can't help thinking, what a family the Woolseys are!

October 1, 1933

I have learned a devastating secret that has turned my world on its head. Everything I have believed in is a lie.

Daddy and Great-grandfather have had a colossal blow-up and Daddy told me why, on the condition that I never breathe a word to anyone.

Cornelius Woolsey is a fraud. He is a cunning, greedy man who has committed crimes that, were Daddy to reveal them, would put him, our revered family founder, in jail.

It turns out that Cornelius got a grant under F.D.R.'s New Deal work projects to reopen the brick factory—he didn't spend family money to do it. And even though he has been doling out profits to the workers, he has been pocketing plenty himself, by illegally padding his expenses to the government. And he sold half the firewood from the clearing and reforestation project instead of giving it away as he promised he would. And, he ordered Pieter and Coert to patch up the holes in the fence around the orchard, even though he had publicly invited the poor to come and pick all the apples they wanted.

This afternoon, Daddy and I defied him. We went down with wirecutters and cut man-size openings into the fence. Daddy snapped the wire with such determined force, I wonder whether he was imagining that he was snapping Great-grandfather in two.

It seems that Great-grandpa has been keeping two sets of books. The second set, the one that records the proceeds from cheating the government and selling the wood, shows that the Woolsey enterprises have had their best years during the Depression, profiting from the despair of others. And Daddy told me that just before the banks closed earlier this year, Great-grandpa took all our money out and then used it to make more, by offering high interest rates to suffering farmers upstate.

I suppose some people would say that Great-grandpa, in spite of taking care of himself, still helped the jobless, still saved the town. I suppose they would say he had to make up for Daddy's losses or we would have been ruined. But the thought that Great-grandpa's famed "self-reliance" was really naked opportunism, fake philanthropy riding on the backs of others, makes me sick. He has lowered himself in my eyes. And I feel smaller too.

I've urged Daddy to demand his responsibilities back from Great-grandfather. But Daddy is selfless, and I wonder sometimes if Great-grandfather is not correct, that selfless men often lack a self. He refuses to threaten to expose Great-grandfather because of the heartache that a rift in the family would cause. He is refusing because Grandma Millie is right, he is not a grade-A Woolsey. He is not half mean enough.

August 23, 1934

*H*allelujah. At last we are going to have our own house, down near the river at the end of the orchards. Now that Roosevelt is bringing prosperity back, we won't have Hoovervilles in our backyard anymore. Henry sunk the foundations of our house with his own two hands. He built the scaffolding. He worked nights through the summer with only Coert and Daddy to help. Dearest Henry, I think it was the fuel of forbidden sex that urged him on. We both hope I will change when I am in my own house. He thinks that I'll become a wanton woman, and oh God, I pray he is right.

February 4, 1935

I am sitting here in this hospital of a kitchen, in one of Gran Millie's old seersucker robes. She is taking care of me. She has turned the steam heat up so high even the wallpaper looks as if it's going to wilt.

Since our half-built house burned down, I have sat here day in and day out. Henry can no longer stomach my depression and he is out in the orchards, working among the trees he has grown to love. I think about that fire and how no one knows how it started. Sometimes I imagine that my mother set it to frustrate me. Or perhaps Great-grandfather, possessive soul that he is, engineered this to keep me in my—his—place. In any case, who knows when we will be able to save enough to build or buy another one? When we do, one thing is sure: it will be as far away from Woolsey Orchards as we can get.

My joints feel stuck together; I feel that I am a child stuffed into an old woman's wrapper. I have been eating endlessly, in spite of (or perhaps because of!) Mama's disapproval. Around her, I feel made of glass. I imagine she can see inside me, see the extra doughnut I have secretly eaten. I sit here long after everyone has left the house, sinking back into myself until I am a flash of light, diving and flying and soaring through the trees, so quick I can never be caught. Sometimes, I am so far away, it does not even feel that it is my hand that moves so clumsily, that overturns the mug, that causes the coffee to spill in milky streaks down the table leg; it feels like the arm of another that reaches in vain to touch Henry as he goes out the door, while I, long gone, gaze down pityingly from my forest of blinding light.

Augusta went to the window for some air. Too much information was rebounding in her head, and she felt dizzy. The early disintegration of her parents' marriage was moving across her eyes like an action movie, a movie in which, strangely, she felt like a participant; reading each entry with a rising sense of panic, wanting to scream at her mother to do it, just do it! Make Daddy move you out of the house! Relax and make love to him!

If indeed, Daddy was in fact Daddy.

If indeed, her "father" was not just another family illusion: another entity masquerading as something other than the person he was.

Her mother, the warm and gracious Lydia Woolsey-Bean, had been, it turns out, not only publicly puritanical, but privately and pathologically frigid.

And her great-great-grandfather, the great patriarch, the illustrious Cornelius Woolsey, had actually been a fake, a liar, an exploiter, a cheat.

And her mother, brought up in an atmosphere of deceit, had created her own web of lies, partly to cover up and perpetuate the lies of her ancestors. As long as Augusta could remember,

Lydia had embellished Cornelius Woolsey's mythic reputation. How could she have done this when she knew the truth to be otherwise? And when she herself had, in this diary, categorically refused to forgive him for it?

Nellie was tossing restlessly, and Augusta sponged her forehead gently without waking her. Then she picked up the diary again and resumed reading:

April 14, 1935

*H*enry has clearly forsaken me for a greater love: the sunlit meadows of his daydreams are what sets his heart racing now. How can I blame him when I see him standing there, proud as Johnny Appleseed, looking east, looking west, and wherever he looks, acres of McIntosh and Red Delicious and a blue sky wider than he ever dreamed, all those years ago in the alleys of Newark?

He has become a deeper part of this family than I ever wanted him to. He even loves Gran Millie's eggs—dreadful things cooked by spooning grease over them! He listens raptly as Great-grandfather teaches him how to graft a new tree; he seems happy, even grateful, at the noisy dinner table, for the opinions, the piano, the acres of crop. Mama says I am selfish the way I complain that my family has appropriated my husband, invented him almost. And she is right; my aloneness is a wall of my own making. So many people have so little and I have so much. I am protected, loved, cared for. And no one need have a moment's worry any longer about the orchards, and whether I could run them one day. I must swallow my growing fear that Henry will never leave this farm. My purpose is now pure and direct. I must pray that God blesses my poor womb with a Woolsey heir.

June 16, 1935

*T*his morning I went looking for Daddy, hoping that he could help me save my marriage, help me convince Henry and Great-grandfather that we should take an apartment in one of the family tenements across town. There were strange noises coming from Daddy's invention shed, so I peeked through a crack in the boards and there was Daddy with a bottle of applejack in his hand at ten o'clock in the morning, dancing around and singing "Flat-Foot Floogey with the Floy Floy."

Daddy and Henry have taken to making bootleg liquor from apple mash in the cellar; they come up to dinner with red eyes and powerful breath, even though they know they will have to endure Mama and Grandma's locked, angry jaws. When I saw Daddy jiggling around like a minstrel amid his soldering irons and his electric saws, when I saw him there in his succulent world of inebriation, I suddenly understood how he had survived our family, these redoubtable Woolseys who had so charitably taken him in and entrapped him. I have always known that he loved me best of anyone, but now I understand why he held me away. His bottle was a jealous mistress; its oceans of love and happiness gave him so much more than I could give.

I remember sitting on Daddy's knee as he lit a pipe, the clink of the big silver lighter as he flicked the top off, the blue flame, his clean, soft hands cupped around it, his heavenly smile, the smell of shaving cream, his chin, nubbly as a washcloth. And the way he blew smoke into my ear when I had an earache. I loved him so much, but he never really did love me—not as much as he loves the lonely ecstasy he has found in the shed of his inventions.

August 20, 1935.
Lake Greenwood, New Jersey

I have disgraced myself. We are visiting Henry's parents, and his mother, with her fuchsia dresses and her collection of china bulldogs, already thinks I am a snob: now she knows I am a stupid one. We are here at the Beans's rented cabin, surrounded by a hundred other dreadful little cabins arrayed around this pitiful little lake. This morning Henry took me out in his father's sailboat. He was showing off for his family, who were watching on shore. He was zigzagging all over the place, barking these commands at me. I have been yachting on the Hudson, of course, but have never sailed a little boat. I was holding the jib rope (or rather the "line," as Henry corrects me) and he shouts "Hardy Lee" or some name like that. I hold tight to the rope, and I'm sure he didn't make it clear that I was supposed to shift my weight and let go until after we had already hit the rock and tipped over. Henry's father was the favorite to win the local cup race tomorrow, but now he won't be competing. His boat sank to the bottom of the lake.

Oh, the humiliation! I would not have cared how cold the water was, as we held tight to the overturned boat, I would not have cared about those angry obscenities which even here I cannot repeat, I would not have cared if only he had not looked at me that way; his face sent a chill through my heart. It was the face of a man who has just discovered that he does not love his wife.

November 16, 1935

*N*ow, Henry, finally *your* honeymoon with *my* family is over. At last you no longer think it quaint to bump into people on the way to the bathroom, to shave in a garden of elderly ladies' underwear, of metal eyelets and bone stays; to shower under a canopy of laddered hose; to breathe the aroma of pine tar and starch and Spirella corset yellowed and stretched from one decade into the next. Yes, I too have longed for another bathroom upstairs.

And as for your quarrel with Great-grandfather, I think he might serve you the carving knife the wrong way round if you memorialize our ex-President as a feather-headed ostrich one more time. And I'd mind your p's and q's around Gran Millie. And do leave your muddy boots, and the boots of your fishing pals, outside, or you might find yourself cuddled up with them in the toolshed all night long. Or worse, you may be forced to leave this temple of tolerance and build your wife her own bathroom within her very own house.

January 10, 1936

Our bedroom has become a hell. Henry goes to sleep unsatisfied; in spite of his tutoring, I am still about as lively in bed as a stick of wood. And then, I cannot go to sleep because of his horrible snoring that drives me to get up and go downstairs, where I eat. Henry's snoring is like being inside the zoo, a soft cooing that builds up to an explosive snorting that shakes the bed. I cannot help imagining that he is doing it on purpose, to spite me.

Henry says that the ghosts of my family are in our bedroom with us. He says that Gran Millie is here, Mama is here, the whole damn crowd floats in and drapes themselves around the bedposts, and now even *he* is getting self-conscious. He says my horror of sex has perverted its beauty, made it as cheap as something you find in brothels. I am terrified that his manhood is being compromised; Daddy is living testimony that when a person's manhood goes, everything else goes too.

Augusta shivered. And what happens, Mother, when your womanhood goes?

Her mother must have inwardly suffered for her frigidity—not just repressed sexual hunger, but also the loss of her femininity. To be unable to make your man happy, to live without his endearments, his reassurances, his touches, to be powerless to transform him through love, to lie miserable on one side of the bed while your husband lies on the other. No amount of satin nightwear, no amount of pretending, could ever make up for that spiritual vacuum.

Augusta went over to the window again and saw her father down in the yard blowing smoke from a metal smoker into a beehive he had brought over from the fields; the smoke was to calm the bees so they would not sting when he worked on their honeycomb frames; if they looked like they were going to sting, Henry had repeatedly taught his girls how to very slowly, very gently, brush them away.

Henry could take care of his bees, and take care of them meticulously, but he couldn't take care of himself. As loud as his voice might boom, as gallantly as he might pull out your chair, as sagely masculine as he might look puffing his pipe, he could not do what men do, and that is take care of business. *Had* his manhood been compromised by Lydia's frigidity, by the suffocating Woolseys? If so, he had chosen his own fate. He had become a slave to alcohol, he had become weak and dependent, he had looked to others to support him—just like his father-in-law, Augustus, who was his spiritual twin, even though they shared not one drop of the same blood. Perhaps, Augusta mused, heredity was less about genes and more about character traits slowly observed, copied, absorbed.

Augusta picked up the volume again and turned to an entry
dated two months later:

March 11, 1936

*H*enry at times seems savage to me, yet under the con-
tinuous burden of our nearly celibate marriage, I have
become no better than an animal myself. I reject his
feverish search for release, but I have my own brand of
desire that has flowered in the desert of our chastity. His
love is not enough. He does not touch me enough. No
matter what I do or say, he cannot stop himself from
rushing headlong into the part I hate.

What I want is for him to stroke me endlessly. I want
him to devour me with kisses, to hold me so tight I can
barely breathe. I feel as though I have never in my life,
even as a baby, been held closely enough. I want Henry
to tell me, to show me he loves me better than anything
in the world, to tell me endlessly until finally I believe
him. I hate it when he comes home and looks for his pipe
and smoking jacket before he looks for me; I want him
to fall through the door into my arms. I hate it when he
pores over seed catalogs as if they are the blossoming of
his day. I want him to think of me for half of every minute
of every hour.

But I cannot stand to have sex with him. Oh Lord,
Mama is probably right—who knows half the time what
it is I want?

Augusta had to stop reading. She felt as though Lydia were
right there, sitting beside her, finally telling her the truth. And
telling her, "I can help you. You can learn from my mistakes."
If only her mother had confided in her face to face! If only they

could have shared, and overcome together, this unfathomable inhibition!

But in spite of the great sadness Augusta felt for her mother, she also felt a growing sense of well-being about herself. Her body ached as though she had done a very long and a very hard day's work. For the first time in her life, she did not feel so abjectly alone. Lydia was with her, holding her, pushing her on to conquer what Lydia herself could not conquer. Augusta had inherited the Woolsey self-denial, but it had been imposed upon her and she could shake it off. She had already begun to do so under Auntie Mame this morning. With William, she had fought hard against her frigidity, she had broken through as she had never broken through before.

But then Augusta felt her heart sink. Yes, she had broken through, but any further breaking through would have to be done with someone other than William Hurley. She looked at her sleeping sister, her face white, red curls stuck, childlike, to her damp forehead. Years ago, Augusta had done to William exactly what Lydia had done to Henry—she had excited him and then pushed him away. Augusta had repeated the same pattern, this morning under Mame, and she would not, she could not tease William any longer. She had had her chance long ago with him; now Nellie deserved a try.

Augusta stretched her legs and gazed at Nellie's needlepoint pillows piled at the end of her bed. Each one was decorated with the name of a Woolsey. Augusta put "Mildred" and "Hopestill" behind her head and picked up the diary again. As she skimmed through the next entries, she noted details of the family during the war years—how Henry had received a deferment from military service because of asthma (a condition Augusta had inherited), how the family had gathered around the radio and heard with horror the raspy screaming voice of Hitler, the chorus of *Sieg heils*, which Amenia, refusing to believe these were the lovely German people she had met on her travels, said had to be some acoustical trick. Throughout, there were notations about how the farm continued to struggle and barely to survive under what the Republican Woolseys were now calling the "Roosevelt Depression." There was a hilarious account of a trip to the 1939 World's Fair, where Augustus displayed his corn-husking machine (to everyone's shock, Cornelius had moved mountains to get his grandson-in-law a booth), and where, at the opening, Grandma Millie sang "Nearer My God to Thee."

And then there was a new theme: Lydia, aglow with maternal desire, overcame her phobia about sex in her determination to try to have a child with Henry. They kept failing to conceive. Augusta began to read more slowly.

May 12, 1940

*M*onth after month, year after year goes by, and still no baby. Henry feels less and less a man, I less and less a woman. Yet, oddly enough, our sex life has improved somewhat because of our barrenness. Knowing that the sex has a purpose seems somehow to have given my body permission to relax. Henry and I have been drawn together in our misery, like prisoners of war.

The family has actually been unbelievably supportive. I have never received so much attention. Perhaps it is because they are all desperate at the thought of the Woolsey line ending with me. I know Mama and Grandma blame Henry's drinking for our childlessness, and they've taken to secretly watering down his applejack.

September 13, 1940

*W*ell, we really have tried everything. Exercise, vitamins, Mrs. Carson's Tonic, douching, counting, positioning. Praying, lying in bed, concentrating, not concentrating. Trying to enjoy it, trying not to enjoy it. Applying ointment of aloe, avoiding hot baths, avoiding cold baths, refusing candy, asking for backrubs. And on and on. Shulamith writes that I should eat oysters daily, and two cups of turnips, and raise my legs like I was riding a bicycle. I'll eat the oysters and the turnips.

January 30, 1941

*T*here is a raging blizzard outside my bedroom window, and I am bleeding again. And this time I had really believed that the curse would not come. Surely, I thought, my womb had finally managed to blossom.

When oh when will God deem me fit enough to produce a child? Does God think I don't really want one? Oh but this yearning I have for a baby is like nothing I have felt in my life. I want to teach her and dress her and hug her and hold her, as I was never held. I want to bake cakes and hang balloons and go galloping through the orchards. She will be the most beautiful, the most perfect human being alive. And the love I will feel for her will be a pure love, it will be the Ideal Love I thought I would find in marriage but didn't. She will be someone, the first one, who will belong to me and me alone. She will exist for me, and I will exist for her. Nothing will sully our relationship. I will raise her, not the Woolsey way, but my way. She will be like me, the secret me that lives only on these pages.

March 10, 1941

*A*t last we have enough money to live in a place of our own, but I cannot bear to move because every doctor I have consulted says that the strain of a move would lessen my chances of getting pregnant.

Sex between Henry and me is now a matter of life and death. At the right day, the right hour, we must lock together in an anatomically perfect clutch, remain so for as long as we can, and then I must lie motionless at a slant on my mountain of pillows for what seems like forever. One lazy thrust, an inadvertent sneeze—would any of these things prove fatal to our child? If poor Henry should have trouble, then I know what I must do, no matter how much I hate doing it. And how will I ever know whether I would still hate it if I did not have to do it?

August 6, 1941

*T*he cycle of our marriage now mimics my monthly cycle: hope, exhilaration, disappointment, depression, and then on around to hope once more. We are on a roller coaster. After we think that this time our lovemaking simply must have born fruit, Henry and I are so tender with each other, even holding hands under the breakfast table. Then my time of month draws near and we begin to get tense with anticipation. I nag him about his socks, which he tosses about at random as though they will sprout wings and fly into the Gainaday Electric Washer-Wringer. Then I am late, I get excited, and then, when we are fairly flying, I crash: there is the telltale spot on my underwear. We drift apart again, bicker, and I think we both blame each other, though we never say so. The days go by, my anger at Henry turns to humor, we make jokes and it dissolves the tensions. Then my fertile time comes around again and we begin the cycle once more. It reminds me of being a child, never knowing whether the roller coaster would be going up or down. Motherless one day, full of mother the next.

Augusta swallowed; there was a lump in her throat that wouldn't go away. She had always thought the story about her being a "gift-child" was just that—a story. She had never dreamed her mother had suffered to conceive her. How happy she must have been when Augusta, this gift, had finally materialized to ease her terrible burden of infertility. To make her feel like a woman again.

Augusta longed for her mother now, longed to show to her her own words, written so long ago on these pages, and to ask, "Mother, what happened? You wanted me so much, you needed me so much, you planned to be so different from your own mother. What happened?"

Lydia had vowed not to reject her children as she had been rejected, but that is exactly what she had done to Augusta. Lydia had not been hugged; she was so hug-deprived that not even her young, lusty husband could hug her enough. She craved to touch and be touched, to hold and be held—so why did she stop hugging Augusta? Why did she end up pushing her away? Why did she end up retreating inside herself, afraid of touch? Afraid of Augusta's touch? What made her become that which she most despised: an impenetrable Woolsey woman?

Augusta sifted through the pages of the volume she was holding. She wondered just why her parents could not conceive. Was it Henry's fault? How did they succeed in finally getting pregnant? Or did they? Her attention was arrested by one entry in particular:

August 15, 1941

I have done something unspeakable.

Daddy and Henry went up north to fish the Canadian streams, and Mama is in Mongolia, no less. It's only Gran Millie and me here. It was the dreams, really, that started it.

I began waking before dawn with visions of long arms stretching out across great chasms, trying to reach me. I would get up and walk through the orchards before day-break. It was lovely the way the pink satin of my robe turned sparkling silver in the moonlight, as though the Milky Way had descended upon me and the moon was a pearl that I had thrown up in the sky. Oh, those minutes before dawn, when the birds would alert me to the coming flood of light, when the trees would shiver like great hands ready to receive the day!

It must have been this unearthly and romantic atmosphere that made me talk to Him at all. And then made me stand there, simply stand there, hushed, while He touched the sparkling satin of my robe. I will never reveal his name anywhere, and my pen, heedless of the blasphemy, will capitalize the pronouns I use for him, for He came to me in my loneliness, in my starvation, as if He were a god.

Never in my life have I done anything so reckless. Fine Woolsey stock, with a straight back and moral heart, that's Lydia Woolsey-Bean. I married a solid man, and I never left home. An arrow among all the other Woolsey arrows pointing straight to heaven.

How little they know of me. Erastus tells me I have lost my young easy ways and have grown inscrutable. He says I am becoming a perfect Woolsey, a haughty and elusive Victorian. But long ago, I learned that to tell my family what I really felt is as dangerous as soaring off the barn wearing one of Daddy's flying contraptions. Erastus would be shocked to see these journals, these pages that save my life by bearing witness to my secrets and my hidden longings. To the fact that I have a self; a life.

After I let Him touch the sleeves of my robe, he

touched my face, then my neck. Oh so delicately. And then his hands were all over me, everywhere, as gentle as feathers, and nothing else mattered. It did not matter what sin I was committing, what mattered was that for the first time in my life—at last—I was touched in the way I longed to be touched; that I knew, finally, what it was to have my body set on fire.

CHAPTER 9

Coert was in a state of agitation. He moved through the aisles of Romes and Cortlands, Empires and Tidemans, like a priest through his parish. It was the first of May, two days after Nellie's tractor accident, and some of the trees were in bloom now. For Coert, walking through the orchards at this time of year had no peace to it.

It should have been a hopeful time—from these little flowers would grow a bounty of fruit, and perhaps this year God would make it bountiful enough to save the farm. But the blossoms always made Coert think of the people who had died: his mother, his father, Pieter, friends, and girlfriends, and now Lydia. The petals of each blossom huddled together like a choir of six-day angels looking upon him with doomed faces. Scattered among them on the branches were the buds yet to open—fat and swollen with promise, and such a deep and delicate pink, they made you lose your balance. Their loveliness was not only of itself, but called forth streams of memory; the tight cluster of buds, like the fingers of a baby's hand, had opened slowly, and soon every bud would bloom, and then the five petals of the flower, still silky and tender, would suddenly darken and fall prematurely to the ground. Their beauty was quick and soon dead; to gaze upon them was to feel an ache rising up in you, for like innocence, they perished before you could be sure they had ever really existed at all.

Up at the house, Augusta sat in Lydia's bedroom, less aware of the bloom than of her sister, who lay dozing in the big four-poster bed. Since the accident Augusta had not left Nellie's bedside, and she had barely been able to look William in the eye. The sight of Nellie's bruised face, her bandaged arm, filled Augusta with remorse for having had a sexual encounter with the man her sister wanted. Augusta could not keep at bay the terror of having almost lost her sister; Nellie could have fallen under the wheels of that tractor, she could have been impaled on a branch, she could have cracked open her head or snapped her neck, had Augusta not been there to break her fall.

Augusta reached inside her pocket and felt the pigskin diary, smooth, cool, reassuring. It evoked images of the sensuous First Mother, the good mother. It was much nicer, much safer, to just sit here feeling the book, rather than opening it and finding out what had happened between the time of Lydia's moonlight liaison with "Him" and Augusta's birth thirteen months later.

Augusta gazed at Nellie, plumped up in a profusion of pillows and white peignoir feathers. Her sister had wanted to move into this more spacious bedroom; she had wanted to wear Lydia's pink satin robe. She had received roses from William, and comic books from her father, who remembered that they were what she had loved when she was sick as a child. Nellie was exquisitely happy being fussed over, and she did look rather like a princess, in spite of the tea stain that trickled down her sleeve; Augusta had brought her a nice lemon drink with Woolsey-made honey, and Nellie had promptly spilled it all over herself.

The more Augusta stared at her sleeping sister, the more Nellie looked less coddled and pampered than imprisoned. Trapped in this bedroom, this house, just like Lydia had been.

If only Augusta could show her the diaries! But no, not yet. She wanted to work through the revelations in these chronicles first, to resolve her own conflicts with Lydia. And she would not show them to anyone, Augusta thought uneasily, until she had found out just what had caused their mother to leave them to Augusta alone.

But wouldn't Nellie go through the roof when she found out that the family founder was a conniving devil, Augusta thought with just a little relish. Nellie's whole existence in this house was built on the family illusions. But if Nellie could see how she had been seduced by the Woolsey propaganda, how she was just one link in a long chain of women who were belittled, devalued, overpowered by the previous generation, yet so inextricably bound up with them that they could not escape—perhaps Nellie would be able to leave and start her own life.

Through reading the diaries, Augusta had begun to form a picture of the way each generation of Woolseys had greeted the next: like a lion tamer with whip and shield, warily welcoming the new arrival into the cage. As long as Augusta could remember, her great-grandmother had shrunk from touching her daughter, who had shrunk from touching her daughter, who had stopped touching Augusta in midchildhood. Mildred had sniped at Amenia and Amenia had sniped at Lydia and Lydia had sniped at Augusta. In the beginning, Augusta had believed that Lydia had tried to break the cycle, but then the family gene had asserted itself and she had fallen into the Woolsey way of childrearing: treat your daughter as completely indispensable yet lucky to be alive; a potentially dangerous creature who might be corrupted if surrounded too frequently by two cuddling arms.

She must help Nellie see that they were part of this pattern; she must find a way to impart the information, the insights she was gleaning from these documents of her mother's. They would both have to find a way to break free of the pattern, otherwise one day they too might end up wandering in the moonlight, searching for love yet afraid to take it, craving what they couldn't tolerate, like alcoholics on Antabuse.

Augusta's heartbeat grew more rapid as she thought about her mother having a moonlight rendezvous with some man down in the orchards. After reading that entry, she had put down the volume and been unable to read any more. Augusta felt her chin to see if perhaps there was a hint of her father's dimple there. She could hardly believe that Lydia herself had actually committed adultery! Her mother! It made Augusta glad, frightened, and angry all at once. But had she really had an affair? Or was this "He" just a religious vision, a fantasy? Did they make love then? Later? Was He the one who had ended her mother's infertility?

She caught sight of Coert through the window, going down to the Christmas Orchard with a chainsaw; her throat tightened; she could see him painting those watercolors her mother had left her in that envelope, sweeping the brush lovingly down the paper.

Augusta opened the pigskin book, bracing herself. She perused the next entries, but there was no reference at all to the moonlight stranger, only to Lydia's pregnancy, and the joy both she and Henry felt.

March 15, 1942

At last I am full of new life, blooming like the big old Newtown Pippin at the end of the yard. Everyone is beside themselves; and Henry cannot keep his hands off me! I feel like an entire orchard is in my belly, and I am down on my knees every day thanking Him. I don't think I'll ever doubt Him again, now that He has given me my baby.

October 25, 1942

A ugusta Mildred Woolsey-Bean was born at two in the morning on September 25. She is absolutely ravishing, and her besotted father goes about telling the most appalling fibs about her perfect smiling face looking up from the sea of squawking babies in the nursery and actually nodding at him.

Great-grandfather asked for the hyphen, as he had with my name. Horrible if we allowed "Woolsey" to miss a generation. The Augusta is for Daddy, who keeps looking at her and sighing and saying, "Well, well, well. Well, well, well!"

How could there have ever been a time when she was not here? Haven't I always smelled her deep, sweet smell, sweeter than the first cider and sharper than the last? I can measure her miraculous purity by comparing her to myself. I bring my cheek to hers in front of the mirror; my skin seems like sandpaper, my pores are put there by pins, the backs of my hands are elephant hide. Her fingernails take my breath away. They are so tiny and fine, like little crystal buds.

Shulamith writes that I must breast-feed her if we are to be close later in life (she studied under this Viennese alienist, Sigmund Freud, before he took refuge from the Nazis in London), but I tried and had to stop. It made me feel strange all over, and I couldn't stop feeling like a cow being milked.

October 30, 1942

I'm so blue. Whatever have you to be blue about, Mama asks. But Grandma looks at me as if she knows. She pats my hand and nods her head. I look at little Augusta and begin to cry. I cry for her coming into this rough world. I cry at her innocence. I cry that she wasn't born to a better mother.

November 13, 1942

*A*ugusta cries constantly. If she's not crying, she's bothering me for something else. I feed, I burp, I diaper, I bathe, I launder diapers, I sterilize bottles, and then it's time to feed again. And not even a little smile. She is the Queen and I am the throne she sits upon. I'm ashamed to admit how much I resent the attention my infant daughter gets.

She bawls to be held throughout the night until I am a tattered rag of a woman. Mama says I should let her cry; that is what she did with me.

February 15, 1943

*M*y body has fallen apart. I have diarrhea, hives; I've had surgery to remove a benign tumor from my breast. For two months, shingles have kept me from holding Augusta.

And I long for, I ache for Him. For his hands, for his mouth. I long to be touched. But that can never happen again. I am a mother now, a mother who has prayed and waited years for this child. It is appropriate that the flame this Man lit in me must swerve, change directions, must move to her and grow into a blaze of passion; I can love only Augusta now. In fact, I don't think I'll love anything again as much as I love her.

For Henry, she is a narcotic, she turns him into the young boy I fell in love with. He rushes up from the orchards early for lunch, just so he can play with her.

May 11, 1943

I cannot believe I created this magnificent child. Of course, there is just one perfect baby in the world and every mother has it. But the belly button of *this* baby is like a little acorn, and her ears are so delicate that they filter the light. She fits into my body perfectly; I brush her skin with my lips and can feel her cheek rising in a smile; I chew her earlobes and she bubbles with laughter. No one has ever found me so entertaining. When I hold her, it is as though I am being held. In my identification with Augusta, I almost feel that I am being my own mother, vicariously getting the care that Mama was always too busy to give me!

Henry, Augusta, and I create our own orchard in our bedroom. The rain sliding down the windowpanes cannot touch us, and even when Henry's gaze inevitably drifts to the window, when he gets up, puts on his boots, and goes down to the orchards, for the first time I do not feel left alone. The baby is beside me always. My whole life I have waited for Augusta, yearned for someone who was there always, who could love me and receive my limitless love. So sweet are our moments together that their inevitable loss tinges them with melancholy. I want to freeze her in time, stop her before she reaches eight months old, I want it to be this way forever. I dread the day when she walks— when she walks away from me.

October 2, 1943

*A*ugusta has passed her first birthday and thinks the world is a three-ring circus. When she tires of bouncing on one knee, another can easily be found. She is learning to play her audience like Shirley Temple, and the family lavishes more attention on her than is good for *any* child. Sometimes she calls my mother "Mama," and it puts a dagger through my heart. My mother is constantly criticizing my skills as a mother: the baby can't behave, make her drink her milk, make her sit on the john, stop spoiling her. When I needed Mama most, she went on trips. Now that I don't need her at all, she won't go away.

Augusta threw a glass of milk at Mama yesterday, and I would have laughed had I not been so humiliated at my daughter proving my mother right. I could feel Mama's Mother Superior eyes boring into me while I sponged up the mess.

March 10, 1944

"*M*a'am, do you consider your marriage a bad or a good one?" asked the telephone-survey caller. How could I answer? I had just flushed my husband's socks down the toilet.

Clearly, my marriage is better than my parents' marriage. But sometimes I am so enraged at Henry's messy disregard for me, the scads of toothpicks and pennies and socks socks socks he tosses about everywhere, that it is exhilarating to watch them swirl around in the toilet bowl, to see them swallowed in one loud, guttural gulp, to watch Henry's bewilderment at his dwindling sock supply.

Sometimes we are so happy, Henry and I. Filled with poignant love for our daughter, teasing each other with affectionate banter. *He* never frosts me over for weeks, he does not pierce me with sarcasm, he does not talk through others in order to avoid speaking to me; he has none of these iron-willed Woolsey ways of expressing displeasure. Although his impassivity sometimes drives me to greater and greater measures, in the end, what use is it to chip away at Mount Everest? I am forced to curl up inside myself and protect what little is left of my pride.

A voice inside me says that my marital misery is my own doing. For when I least expect it, I will look at Henry and it will be as though John Wayne just rode into town. He will give me the smile I married him for, the one where his mouth goes up like a slivered moon shining just for me. And I will feel such a stirring down in my lower stomach that I'm too embarrassed to be near him for a time.

November 7, 1944

Augusta has become my passion. We are as intertwined as Siamese twins. If she has a cold, I get it immediately. If I am thirsty, she also wants a drink. We finish each other's sentences. We cannot bear to be apart. At breakfast, she sits on my lap and we never know into which mouth I will put the next bite of Gran Millie's fried apples and coddled eggs. Even when she flirts with Henry, I think she does it for my benefit. I am the springboard off which she makes her leaps into the world. I am the center of gravity; she spins back to me always. She mimics my phrases, my voice. I catch myself mimicking her funny, lilting accent. In the morning, I hear her toddling down the hall into the space in my bed that Henry has vacated, and we tell each other how much we love each other. More than the moon and the stars, more than the apples on the trees.

January 30, 1945

All my life I have been lonely. I never thought anyone could take away my loneliness, but Augusta has. She has made everything different for me. I really don't think I knew what love was before now. She has wiped away all the bad that has ever happened to me. This two-year-old lifts something out of me, something that has been driven down deep inside me. I am the one who is supposed to provide her with care, but her care for me, her devotion, has brought me out of my cocoon, made me soar like a butterfly.

The only one who has come close to giving me such feelings is Him. Should this make me uneasy? It is almost as though God took this Man and transplanted him in Augusta. But then, it may not be God that has done this, isn't that right? The thought that it is not God turns my blood to ice.

It's the dreams that make me worry. They come to me like a message, a warning. Horrible dreams, carnal dreams. I dream that I am doing something awful to my daughter, that I am putting my lips between her legs. Oh Lord, for weeks and weeks, months and months, I have had these dreams. Sometimes I am fondling her, touching her with my tongue in a horrible way; I come into these dreams with spit dripping from my teeth like a dog.

I have to take a deep breath, a cool bath, walk around the orchard, before I can face her again, before I can even go to pick her up. Then the dreams go away and we are free again, free to cuddle and nuzzle and kiss and hug.

Sometimes I pretend she is an ear of corn, and I nibble her from head to toe. We wrap ourselves around each other and I bury my face in her sweet, silky hair; I am transported back, back, until I feel like a baby myself. Oh, never ever have I enjoyed this luxurious sea of sensation, never ever has anybody touched, stroked, tickled, kissed me endlessly, endlessly, until finally all my yearnings are gone.

And then, sometimes, just at the moment of pure

happiness, all these good innocent sensations seem to gather up in a ball, travel down, down, until they stop where they should not stop. Until the happiness becomes urgent, a dark, evil, disgusting urgency, an overwhelming sensation like the one that plagued me when I tried to breast-feed Augusta, like that feeling I got with Him, that feeling which, at least at first, made me flee from him. And I feel so ashamed, I cannot bear even to be close to this poor child any longer.

I struggle to get hold of myself. I tell myself that it is all in my imagination, all this is just in my head. How could anything that gives both Augusta and me so much pleasure, how could it be wrong? I have never felt so suffused with warmth, so alive, in my whole life, so how could that be a sin?

May 15, 1945

Augusta and I were forming O's with our lips and we were pressing them together and we were yelling into each other's mouth, and our voices made muffled echoes that were swallowed up by the cavemen hiding under our tongues. We thought it was so funny; we were yelling and laughing. It was just a game, just an innocent game.

Then, suddenly, a shadow fell over us. I looked up and there was Mama's long, tall body. She was looking down at me as if I were a slug covered with dirt. Her eyes were full of disgust, full of hatred. My heart froze. She didn't say a word, not at that moment, anyway. She didn't need to.

I knew then that she had found me out, that she was forcing me to take a good hard look at my behavior. The dreams hadn't been dreams at all. They had been mirrors.

Mirrors that had only slightly exaggerated the distorted way I have been loving Augusta. I should have known it was all too good to be true. I should have known that if it was good and I felt it, something was bound to be wrong with it.

"Can't you keep your hands off her, sister?" Mama asked afterwards. "You're always pawing her, clinging to her, mauling her, it's repulsive. It's indecent. What's the matter with you?"

Mama is a hard person. The lids of her eyes are hard and heavy, and her mouth is like a shriveled lemon rind set in her doughy chin. But Mama is right. I have been indulging myself at Augusta's expense; our sweet secret joy has really been secret sin. And who but Mama could know better? She never did love me properly, so it should come as no surprise to her that I don't know how to love properly either.

June 15, 1945

I feel dead inside, I can barely stand to look at myself. Augusta tugs at me, I give her a brief hug and then move away; she climbs in bed with me, I get out the other side. I don't trust myself anymore. I know Mama is extreme, I know that anything that smacks of sex is a perversion to Mama. But still, I cannot help believing that I went too far. My need for love, for my daughter's love, was too great. When I think of those dreams, when I think of what I felt with her, the ways I touched her, I am horrified. I am too poor a person for love. I cannot be trusted with it.

Sometimes I think that, at worst, I'm no better than a criminal; at best, I'm abnormal.

Oh God, it is so hard to restrain myself from loving this

poor child too much, this child who surely feels my retreat so acutely. I want to gather her up and hug her to death. But haven't I damaged her enough?

Sometimes I actually hate her for all of this. I blame her for being so beautiful, for tempting me, for giving me a taste of what can never be mine. She made me mistake my twisted feelings for normal ones. She somehow unleashed this devil in me, caused it to disguise itself as innocence.

She cries for me to hold her, but I can't trust myself more than a few seconds.

The sky looks as if it has lowered down on Mount Freedom today. Whispery, ghostly fog everywhere, webbing the forest with disease. Then it suddenly clears. Not a wisp of vapor anywhere. The orchards below look glazed, magical, like a dream of life, not life itself, but then all at once the fog is back, rising through the trees, filling the sky with smoke, settling over the highlands like an old, disintegrating wedding veil. Fingers of fog slip in between the mountains, stroking the crevices, insidious, beautiful, everywhere. It reminds me of love, the way people wrap themselves around each other, and then before you know it they have sidled off, like ghosts, like fingers of fog you cannot hold.

The words that Lydia had written suddenly melted and ran down the page. Augusta patted the paper with her sleeve, before the inked words dribbled into oblivion, before Nellie awoke and caught Augusta in the act of stealing their mother's secrets and of expunging them with her tears.

Augusta's memory of her early years had always been a kaleidoscopic blur. But if she had never clearly remembered being held by her mother, she remembered it now, or at least she remembered its abrupt cessation. She saw it: a white bed sheet, empty and wrinkled; her mother's nightgown disappearing out the door. She had pried Augusta's fingers from around her arms and left her sitting on the bed all alone. Her whole being was a hazy rainbow of pain, the sun flooding through the window, making the dust dance, the sensation that she was falling, that the bottom had fallen out of her. She felt as if her body was vanishing, disappearing like the dust; she felt she wasn't there, without her mother she wasn't even there; there wasn't anyone sitting in the space she occupied on the white sheets of the four-poster bed.

She only knew that she had done something terribly wrong; she had been so bad that she had caused her mother to hate her forever but she didn't know what it was she had done.

Augusta's tears fell again on the already smeared page. So this was why her mother had withdrawn from her: the fear that she was being sexual, that she was being seductive with her baby daughter. But couldn't Lydia have told Augusta about this, instead of telling her damn diary? Why, before her life had ended, in some quiet moment, had she not taken Augusta aside and given her this knowledge, released Augusta from the anguish of thinking it had all been her own fault? Was it because Augusta had not let her, had deserted her, had retreated herself, particularly this past year? Was this why her mother had left her the diaries? Was she telling her in death what she somehow could never tell her in life?

Augusta suddenly felt as though she were back in 1945, inside her mother's skin, feeling her uneasiness, feeling the loss of her special bond with Augusta. After Amenia had confirmed her fears about loving Augusta, after she had reawakened the self-hate Amenia had put there in the first place, how could Lydia ever feel the same again about Augusta? The voice of that one woman, Amenia, was too powerful—both the maternal voice within, represented by Lydia's carnal dreams, as well as the maternal voice without, embodied by the Amenia who caught Lydia in the act of simple yet needy mother love. How ironic, Augusta thought, that this is what Lydia and Augusta had in common: the mother within each of them spoke so loudly that it drowned out their own voices.

Augusta could see now how it all had happened: how Lydia had increasingly held her first daughter off, year after year, until, by the time Augusta entered puberty, they no longer touched at all. Lydia must have felt so many things for her "gift-child"—love and guilt and anger and need all rolled up in one. Just as Augusta had ended up feeling this same mixture of emotions toward Lydia.

Nellie, when she was born three years later, must have been a great outlet for Lydia. A safe haven: another baby. You *had* to cuddle a baby, no one could disapprove of you for that. You were expected to do and feel all those things for a baby that smacked of perversity when you felt them for a child.

Augusta had always sensed that she embodied some sym bolic center of her mother's life, even when her mother had gravitated toward Nellie; but she had not until this moment known that she was supposed to give Lydia the love she had never gotten, that she was supposed to be a kind of savior. What a fall Augusta had taken—from savior, from bestower of self-worth, to temptress, elicitor of perversity.

Augusta suddenly threw the diary across the room; the binding cracked, and several pages fell out. She picked up the pillow bearing Amenia's name and punched it several times. She was so angry at them all, at her grandmother, at her mother. Would she carry that anger around the rest of her life?

She searched her memory for recollections of that time before her mother's withdrawal, but she could not remember concrete details. Only feelings. Had Amenia's accusations been just another piece of sexual hysteria? Had Lydia's self-accusations been nonsense? Or *had* her mother been sexually seductive with her? Even sexually abusive? Augusta recognized that in addition to the positive feelings she felt about her very early years with her mother—feelings of sensuous warmth and light and laughter—she also had some uncomfortable ones; a vague sense of recoil. And from puberty on, if Lydia did not come near her daughter, Augusta also shrank from Lydia's touch. Even when her mother was ill, Augusta had been unable to do anything more than give her mother a peck on the cheek.

Perhaps she would never know the real truth; and perhaps it didn't matter. What mattered right now was that, in spite of the anger she felt, this diary entry had lifted a tremendous burden. For years and years she had thought it was some flaw in herself that had driven her mother away. Now she was freed from that. Now, finally, she knew that she had been just a helpless child who had fallen through the cracks of her mother's distressed psyche. She felt almost happy as she picked up the diary from the floor. She sat down, put it back together, and found the next entry. Her mother, she learned, had responded to the loss of her closeness with Augusta by going out and getting a job.

August 3, 1945

I am officially a wartime woman munitions worker! Every morning I report to work at the Hudson Valley Gunpowder factory wearing an unbleached white muslin coverall. I take my place on the assembly line mixing explosives. Daddy helped me get the job and he helped convince the family that I should take it, because I have been so morose lately.

Every night, all of us gals must wash our uniforms because of the risk of infection from gunpowder. I also had to replace the metal clasps on my corset on account of the danger of flying sparks heating the metal. The plant is hot and dark and dingy and absolutely glorious. I feel I am part of history, joining thousands of women taking the place of the men away at the front. And oh, how glad I am to be away from that house! The women working in the factory have a tremendous bond; I had not realized how much I missed the friendship of women, how isolated I had been. I hope eventually to save up enough money for that long awaited home of our own. I *will* have one, with or without Henry.

September 20, 1945

Grandma Millie has had a stroke. I have had to quit work and take charge of the house: all the men are out in the orchards every minute with the harvest, and Mama does the bookkeeping and helps with Augusta. I polish the stairs (not like a mirror, as Gran Millie did) and I listen for Gran's gravelly whisper to come through the speaking tube in the kitchen from her bedroom upstairs. Her mouth has fallen to one side and the hair on her chin looks suddenly endearing, like the fuzz on the small of a baby's back. I bring up her broth, the broth she has brought so many times to all of us.

We have long talks. She told me that Mama, in spite of her neglect of me, would always stand by me. We are a family that has something very rare, she said; we are a pyramid, one generation supporting the next, each standing by the other. A long time ago, she said, she was like me, yearning to leave the farm for greater adventure. "But what good would a life of adventure be to me now?" she said. "Adventure cannot hold my hand, nurse me, make me feel worthy in my hour of need. If I had left, I never would have had you here, my dear Lydia."

October 11, 1945

*T*he Woolsey ruby is a fake! What mystery is going to be exposed next in this house! Apparently Great-great-grandma Hopestill bought the ring at a bazaar because she thought it was pretty; she didn't care a hoot that it was glass. She wore it to the fanciest balls and everyone assumed it was real, and she never disabused them of the notion. It was passed on to every new generation of Woolsey women with great ceremony and telling of anecdotes, including how it had been admired by the Duchess of Windsor. Mama said she never bothered to tell me it was glass when she passed it to me on my wedding day, because she thought it was irrelevant, considering the ruby's illustrious history!

November 20, 1945

I cannot stop thinking about the newsreels of the liberated concentration camps in Europe. I have not stopped weeping for days. I just can't believe what these German Nazis have done. People piled up like broken wood, thousands of men, women, and children hardly more than bones, like some strange form of animal just discovered in the wilderness. The world is in shock. People keep saying there has to be some mistake, but the camera doesn't lie. How can we live with this truth, that an entire race of people were walking around, going to work, putting by their preserves, powdering their babies, and then suddenly, for no reason, other human beings get the notion to herd them up, put them into ovens like bread, and turn what's left of them into these strange starving skeletons? Even animals do not behave like this!

I feel that I never want to think of leaving these orchards again. Gran Millie was right; the world has become a harsh and ugly, unpredictable place. How can people wake up day after day and think things will ever be the same after this nightmare?

Daddy and I have decided we are going to secretly divert some of this year's crop profits to a Mr. Abraham Rosensteil of Albany, who is trying to bring over as many Jewish war refugees as he can. Lo and behold, Mama the bookkeeper is going to help us, and we will just not mention it to Great-grandfather. This horror in Europe has united us all.

Somehow, it now matters so much less if every one of the Woolsey jewels are glass, or if Great-grandfather is not the picture of generous goodwill that he seems. I have a sudden new appreciation of everyone under this roof, as we sit in the kitchen and roll bandages, as we sit at the old table with its wood, soft and rich as velvet. Mama has taken to singing "Indian Love Call" after dinner, and she sings it so beautifully I see tears in Daddy's eyes. I realize that even they, across what I had thought were loveless years, have been, perhaps secretly, fond of each other.

January 13, 1946

Augusta is suddenly exhibiting strange behavior. She defies me constantly. If I choose a lace pinafore for her to wear, she howls until I say she can wear what she wants, and then she chooses, more often than not, the very same pinafore! She turns away from my outstretched arms, and instead follows Henry everywhere. She has taken to running her hand down his cheek, batting her little eyelashes and lowering her head. Shullie says Augusta's sudden love affair with Henry is the "Oedipal complex," and is natural and healthy. For everyone except me, that is.

March 9, 1946

*I*t is just Henry, Augusta, and me; we have the house to ourselves. The rest of the family have taken Gran Millie on a convalescent trip to Florida. At first we were exhilarated, like kids let loose in an empty museum. But now it has become a little like taking off your clothes down by the stream; you love the feel of it for a minute, but you would not under any circumstances wish to go about naked forever. Perhaps that is really why we have remained here all these years; we are too used to having others around.

Nothing I do pleases Augusta, and sometimes I just want to kill her. It still takes such courage for me to trust myself to embrace her, but now she just wriggles away from me and runs to her father's legs. It becomes worse when Henry goes down to the barn, because then there is just Augusta and me, and this feeling of emptiness gathering in the air, so strong and palpable it is like a third person in this big empty house. I wish the rest of the family would hurry home.

June 19, 1946

I went away to a college reunion, and when I returned, Henry and Augusta and Mama and Daddy and Gran Millie and Great-grandpa with his shrunken body greeted me as if I had been gone a year. How I wish that I did not feel as though it is another person they love, someone they expect, someone they have created, who is part of their picture, like moss that will always grow in the damp forests. I wish that they could know the real me, the person who appears on these pages.

June 24, 1946

Augusta seems to hate the sight of me, and yet she follows me everywhere. I don't have a minute's peace. She seems to follow me in order to tell me how terrible I am. I tell her she cannot have candy and she says, "Oh yes I can, Grandma will give it to me." Before I know it, Mama has taken a butterscotch out and given it to her. When I see the look on this child's face, of pure unadulterated defiance, she is the image of my mother.

Augusta flipped quickly through the entries for the next year. She was impatient with her mother now, tired of her self-involvement. The entries showed Lydia increasingly troubled by Augusta's attachment to her father; and increasingly, she personalized what seemed like the normal behavior of a four-year-old, feeling that every accident, every naughtiness committed by Augusta was done to spite Lydia.

Then Augusta's attention was caught by the two next entries:

July 10, 1947

I may not have been able to escape this house through war work, but at last I see another avenue out. Augusta has been accepted at Miss Frayter's Kindergarten in Gristbrook Corners, the most exclusive school in the county. Gristbrook is, of course, the fanciest town in the county, full of Connecticut Yankees and horse farms. I'm starting to become part of a "crowd" that includes two lovely Frayter mothers, Peggy Steptoe, and Betsey Blanquette. Of course, the fact that the Steptoes are Mayflower descendants delights my name-proud family. Woolseys, while being leading members of society, have always stood apart, or rather above, the fray, and becoming part of a clique is "not done." Still, I bet Mama and Gran Millie are saying thank heavens I chose Gristbrook over the gun factory.

Not one Jew lives in Gristbrook, and this rankles Daddy and me. Henry also complains about the insensitivity of the Gristbrook WASPs. But he seems to have quite a good time sitting in their Frank Lloyd Wright homes, around their baronial fires, drinking down their fifty-year-old bourbon.

September 21, 1947

*F*or the fourth straight day, Augusta sat down on Miss Frayter's floor and would not budge, until they called me to come and take her home. Betsey Blanquette was giving me a luncheon so that the ladies of the Gristbrook Country Club could meet me; she had already postponed it three times because of Augusta's refusal to stay at nursery school. And now, today, just as we had finished rolling the cream-cheese balls in nuts, Mama called to tell me Miss Frayter had called; Augusta was doing it again. The ladies arrived as I rushed out. Of course, now there is little chance that they will vote me into the club.

And it is such a lovely school! The dollhouse is hand-made, and even the doll dresses are imported from France. Why couldn't Augusta for once be happy with what I chose for her?

I wanted that Gristbrook group. I don't care if I'm a rotten mother, I wanted them. For all the lonely days of my childhood, I wanted them!

These were now incidents that Augusta remembered with clarity. Her mother had neglected, for some odd reason, to mention that, at the time of this last entry, she was pregnant with Nellie.

In fact, Augusta remembered kneeling down by the four-poster bed to pray that God would bring them a healthy new baby. And then, suddenly, without explanation, Augusta was sent off to this strange "nursery" school, which she had sus-pected was so named because it was a nursery and she was going to be traded for a new baby. She remembered sobbing for her mother day after day, and she remembered Miss Frayter standing her up on a chair in the corner with her face to the wall because she wouldn't stop crying.

That fourth and last time her mother had come to fetch her, apparently from the luncheon party, Lydia had gotten Augusta in the car, yanked closed her checked car coat, and shook her finger in Augusta's face: "I won't do this anymore! I have my own life and you're not going to take it away from me." Augusta remembered thinking that this was it, the final word: her mother was going to send her away. She definitely did not love her anymore, because now she had her own life and that life was no longer Augusta.

She picked up the diary again and read the last two entries in the volume:

December 5, 1947

*T*his pregnancy has gone beautifully. It will be a fine baby, I know. I am sitting on the window seat in my bedroom, imagining being a child, the sky filled with snow, whirling, twinkling snowflakes melting on my mittens, stinging my tongue, frosting my eyelashes. I hear the sleighbells and the reindeer hooves on the roof. Daddy used to climb up on top of my room in his red velvet suit and beard, and stamp and shake the sleighbells outside my window. Then he would put presents under the tree so that I could see them when I peeked through the stair railing. Now, this winter, we will begin it all over again, for Augusta's benefit. Gran Millie is letting out the suit to accommodate Henry's paunch. Henry hates Christmas. I am sure he won't be as graceful, or as convincing, as Daddy.

December 8, 1947

*H*ow do you hug a child? I know how you hug a baby, but now Augusta is four and a half years old. Isn't it strange that, with all these relatives around hugging the very life out of my daughter, I cannot remember any of them hugging me? And I still get confused about what is proper and improper. What is the difference between the way Mama hugs Augusta, for instance, and the wrong way that I hold her? You can't quite cuddle a child up like a puppy because her legs dangle down. And when she tries to wiggle away, do you hug tighter? Is it wrong if you kind of rock her? Do you stroke her hair? How many hugs are healthy, and at what point will I be either spoiling or perverting her?

203 ☙

December 16, 1947

I am due in just a few days, thank God. How strange it will seem to be in my beloved delivery room, not as a volunteer aide but as a patient! This baby will come just in time. I've never been so lonely.

CHAPTER 10

Augusta, having put away the diaries, slipped out of the house by the back door, hoping to avoid William. He was supposed to have delivered a bundle of Paulared scions down to the barn this morning, and she had waited until she thought he had come and gone. She could not wait any longer, however, for Nellie was still asleep and she wanted her sister to remain asleep—and out of the way—while they destroyed her beloved Christmas Orchard.

Actually, its old, mice-girdled McIntoshes were history by now. Coert had cut them down this morning, and they had already been hauled away by a firewood company. Now Augusta was going down there to help Coert graft the scions onto the stumps, which they hoped would grow into new Paulared trees with remarkable speed. Nellie had kept delaying the project—hoping, perhaps, it would never happen—and then the accident had provided an irresistible opportunity for Augusta just to go ahead and do it. She didn't like going behind Nellie's back—oh, she wanted to stop the family pattern of lies and deceptions once and for all!—but if they did not move ahead now, it would be too late for the new grafts to take this season.

Augusta breathed in the fresh, fragrant air of early May, and started down through the orchards. And then she felt his hands on her shoulders. She stood there for a moment, frozen, while he kissed her neck and his arms slid around to encompass her shoulders, pulling her back tight against him. She wasn't even surprised; somehow she knew he would find her. "No," she finally said, trying to shake him off. "Absolutely no. Let go of me."

His arms remained tight around her. He buried his face in her neck.

"I don't want this," she said. "Can't you understand? My sister loves you. I love my sister. She thinks I've taken everything she's ever wanted. And I'm not going to take you!"

William's voice was muffled. "I can't sleep. I can't eat." His hands were moving down, he was breathing fast. His fingers brought goosebumps to her belly.

"I'm already cutting down her goddamn orchard!" Augusta said. She didn't know which was stronger, her shame and anger at William or this desire that was again awakening within her, moving down into her very fingertips, making her hands shake, her voice shake, her whole body tremble. It had been so long that she was starved for it, as starved as her mother had been. His hands were cupped over her breasts, which were firm and large and fit exactly beneath his fingers. He circled them with his thumb, and her knees gave way.

"Stop it," Augusta whispered.

"I can't." William's voice sounded strange, as if it were forced way down into his throat, as if he were a child mumbling in his sleep. But there was nothing childlike about what was happening to him. Augusta could feel him swelling, rising against the small of her back. She could feel the beat of the blood in his fingertips as he turned her around and lifted her face, as his tongue thrust inside her mouth, reaching.

"Come, under here," William said, leading her back toward Auntie Mame.

"Oh no, not again!" she said, and went slack under his grip.

But he picked her up and carried her beneath the tree's dipping, lacy cover. She thought she might start wheezing, she thought her childhood asthma might come to the rescue, but her bronchial tubes remained stubbornly clear. Across her mind flashed the sudden vision of her unmarried mother, caught making love in the orchards with the man she craved, caught half-dressed like this by Great-great-grandmother Hopestill, caught, punished, humiliated, her craving for Augusta's father perhaps forever thwarted. When, Augusta wondered, when will I be able to stop thinking of my mother whenever I am about to have sex!

She sat up suddenly and pried William's hands from around her. "Get hold of yourself!" she said.

"Get hold of myself!" William was angry now. "Look. Three days ago, we kiss passionately, you act like you're crazy for me, and then you abruptly turn me off! I've been here before, Augusta. We were at exactly this place nearly twenty years ago. Me feeling desperate for you, you holding me off, teasing me, sending my hormones raging out of control. I would just look at you and get an erection. It was terrible to be sixteen and in such a state that you knew each day you'd end up embarrassing yourself at least once. It was like having a disease, or owning a dog that bit."

Augusta began to laugh.

"And then, when we were together, I was in this constant state of anxiety and discomfort," William said, feeling again that old frustration, the reawakened sting of her rejection after they had shared that wonderful kiss in the cellar. When his frustration had finally brought him to ask her for his football cleat back, her reaction had both horrified and thrilled him: she pretended she didn't care. Then, for days afterward, he would see her puffy red face everywhere, in the cafeteria line, on the bleachers at Glee Club rehearsal, pedaling past his window on her bicycle. "I was always wondering how you could claim to love me but not want even to kiss me twice."

As Augusta recalled, they had not kissed even once.

"Funny about the past, right in the middle of a riveting present, it just suddenly comes charging up like an unruly child," she said and sat up. "Sometimes, if the past did not happen the way we think it should have happened, we weave little circles, little stories round it. Take our past, William; I admit, I was scared of sex. But I also remember waiting for you to get the better of me, for you to make a *real* move."

"Augusta, I tried everything, but you knew a million ways to dodge me. You were so subtle, so clever. When I lowered my head to kiss you, you would bring yours even lower!"

"I didn't want to appear too forward," Augusta said, remembering her mother's warning: don't paw your men, don't cling. Walk with your head high. Well, she had. After William had broken up with her, she certainly had. Her chin leading her down the gray linoleum corridors, the whole school watching, knowing that his football cleat no longer bumped against her cashmere sweater. "If you really wanted to kiss me, you would have kissed me."

"Well, here's for all the ones I missed," William said, and kissed her. He slipped off her sweater and she let him. He took her nipples in his mouth and she let him. It was useless to fight it any longer. She was falling, and this time she would allow herself to fall, to fall as far as she could.

Oh, how different this was than when she was very young, when she ungrumblingly endured the fevered ministrations of clumsy boys, or later when she gave way a bit more beneath the male sexual acrobatics but still remained safely locked up, suspended somewhere above, observing the proceedings. Time must bring out in a woman some ancient instinct for the carnal, for at the age of nearly thirty-five, with this luscious man looming over her, the ground was opening up beneath Augusta for the first time.

It was as if she had been without water for 100 years and just now came to drink; and how she drank—as her skirt became twisted around her waist and his bare toes slid the panties down her leg and his belt buckle was cold on her flesh and then wasn't and she was reaching up with her legs like a woman waiting for the ship to come to port, and he came into her hard as a rocket, a submarine swimming shooting parting the waters and she was tide, all tide surging heaving moaning splashing lapping over the dock, then gently, quietly . . . bobbing in his wake.

They lay in silence for a time, but it was not for long. Soon they began to stir again, kissing, exploring every detail of each other's bodies as if they were in a dream. They ignored the noontime whistle and they ignored the breezes and the chilly dankness under the tree, for the heat of love kept them warm. They ignored Coert's voice calling for Augusta, as it got closer and closer and then faded away; they ignored the raindrops that slid through the branches; they ignored the mud that the early afternoon shower created beneath them, around them. They couldn't get enough. They couldn't stop. At one point, they became aware of the mud sticking to their skin and began to laugh, but their laughter was drowned out by the darker, more urgent tide of desire they had unleashed and seemed unable to satisfy. This time Augusta became something so sensate, so primal, she was pure feeling, pure forbidden feeling, it rose from her like steam, rushing toward a pinnacle of light, her body racked with waves of preorgasmic ecstacy. What is happening to me, she thought suddenly and with alarm, am I drugged, am I hallucinating, am I dreaming, have I died? As he moved inside her, she was filled to overflowing, and then finally she was gathered up, shrunk, compressed tight into a fist of unbearable desire, as though the gods were making an example of her, igniting every cell of her body, preparing to send her up into the sky for the grand finale. The pressure then became too great; she could not rise, instead she was going down, down, beneath the surface, heading toward something terrible, a body of water pressing onto the boulders of the dam until suddenly it burst and flooded forth and the stones went tumbling, shattering down through the air, and Augusta barely heard herself giving forth the cries of the fallen, delivering herself of generations upon generations of muffled whimpers, ancestral cries, her screams echoing through the empty paths between the trees, curling up through the branches and disappearing unheard into the air.

They lay still, finally, Augusta curled in his arms. To hell with Nellie, she sighed: to hell with everyone. This was the way life was supposed to be. It was the way her poor mother's life should have been. Just like this. Free of remorse, free of constraint. Free of twists and knots. As crystalline and intense as the moment of orgasm. As perfect and pure and simple as an apple blossom.

Her voice finally found its way out of her throat. Looking at the blurry dark underside of Auntie Mame's branches, at the bars of light filtering through, she said, "We are in a cave. There are lions outside."

"Yes," William murmured, draping his shirt over her back. "We have to stay here forever."

"This is a different cave from the one I was in several hours ago," she said groggily, "I'm a flower that has opened . . ." She twirled her hand up in the air, touching a blossom ". . . a butterfly that has burst its cocoon, an ostrich shaking sand from its ears."

William kissed her eyes, her nose, her forehead. "Is your name really Augusta? Did I do this to you? With you? How did you keep that wild animal inside you secret for so long?"

"Do you know," Augusta said suddenly, "that I am probably the first Woolsey woman ever to enjoy a sexual experience."

And what about Nellie, Augusta thought, her heart sinking. Sexually eager Nellie, who, had it not been for Augusta, might have been lying in this very spot enjoying the sensation of William's fingers gliding down her back. Augusta felt pricks of shame, remorse, those old and sickeningly familiar emotions, but she fought to keep them subservient to this new sense she was experiencing of power, of pride. By this act of love, she had broken the cycle. On this day, she had altered the course of Woolsey history. No wonder, as she lay here, that she felt no fear of annihilation, none of the characteristic uneasiness that she would again lose her self, her will to the will of a man. After a lifetime of being sexually closed, she had made love, fully and without inhibition, to the person she had once loved but had been unable even to kiss. It had been the diaries that had given Augusta back her sexual self. By revealing her own sexual shame, Lydia had altered her legacy to her daughter. Dead, she had given her daughter the mothering she had been unable to give while she was alive.

Augusta explored William's face, the rough skin, the dimple chiseled into his chin—the feature of William's that Nellie so loved. Nellie with her funny little chin, who had persuaded William not to hide his beautiful strong Michelangelo face behind a beard.

What would her mother say if she could see Augusta now? Even if Lydia could applaud her daughter's new sexual self, she would never condone such cruelty to one's sister. How could Augusta share with Nellie the knowledge of the destructive secrets of their family while continuing to keep her own secret about William? Yet how could she possibly tell her? Everything between them, every hope of change and growth, would be destroyed. How sad it was, how paradoxical, that even life's positive transmutations so often carried the seeds of sin and betrayal. How ironic that a dramatic life-change for Augusta should by coincidence so deeply affect Nellie. And how eerie that just when the truth about the Woolseys was replacing the old myths and fairy tales, the family's fantastical, magical way of looking at the world should be resurrected: if one sister was happy, the other must reap misery. Augusta's freedom would not be without cost. In rising out of the ashes of her family's morbid constraint, she was going to break her sister's heart.

"What are you thinking about?" he asked her.

"I'm thinking about you," Augusta said, imagining how William, the same man who had absolutely exhausted himself under this tree, might summon up the energy to be the lover of two sex-starved Woolsey women.

"We have to go," Augusta said. "I don't want to, but I have to. Coert's looking for me. I have to help him graft."

"We're never leaving here, we've already decided," William said. "We could just stay here, settle down under this tree. Raise a family here."

"Everything will be ruined if I don't get down there. The Christmas Orchard has to be replanted fast, while Nellie's asleep, because if she catches me in the act now, I think I might cave in and let her to turn the whole orchard into a birdwatching preserve."

William smiled. "That reminds me of my dad. Do you remember when he used to come here early in the morning with his binoculars, even before the sun came up, just so he could catch a glimpse of those purple orioles? He was a devoted birder." William turned and pulled Augusta back down. He kissed her breasts.

"Come down to the orchard and help me," she said, sounding stern, trying to get up. "Come on." But William had no intention of leaving: he kissed her long and deeply and finally she gave up and they were lost again.

Augusta emerged an hour later, muddy and disheveled, from beneath the big Newtown Pippin at the end of the yard. In case they were observed, William was to emerge sometime afterwards. Augusta went up to her room, washed and changed, and made her way down toward the Christmas Orchard. She tried to arrange her facial muscles normally, but she was unsure how successful this was, since everything about her body felt far from normal. She had the sensation, in fact, that she was on wheels, or more exactly, flying along on someone else's feet, fluttering like a blossom somewhere above, laughing at her own progress down the hill. She felt as if she had taken a drug, as if she had mainlined love: she had absorbed it into her pores, she had swallowed William and made herself whole. She found it hard to focus.

As she got closer to the Christmas Orchard, however, she had a vision of Coert, bending and squatting, cutting and grafting, gently, expertly planting new life in the Woolsey orchards. She remembered the language in the first diary entry she had read this morning, the choice of words that could be taken more than one way, just as her mother in life often meant something other than what she said. Her mother, when she found herself pregnant with Augusta, had written how she had thanked "Him" for filling her with a child after years of her infertility with Henry. But which Him did she mean? God? Or the Mystery Man in the moonlight? Lydia had written that the flame the Man had lit within her must change directions, must become a burning passion for her child. Was that also a way of saying that the Man, and not Henry, was really Augusta's father? That her parentage was as fake as Cornelius's philanthropy or the Woolsey ruby? That her real father was of the orchards, a man of the trees who painted angelic watercolors of the child he could not claim?

Augusta came to the end of a row of Tydemans, rounded the corner, and the butterflies in her stomach suddenly flew up into her throat. Where just yesterday there had risen densely planted silver-budded trees, each shimmering in the sun like a giant candelabra, there was now a long gash in the land. The Christmas Orchard was gone. All that was left of the McIntoshes that Cornelius had planted in 1948 to celebrate Nellie's birth were rows of sawed-off little stumps. They looked uncannily like heads. They looked like the heads of people who had been buried up to their necks in the sand and then stoned to death. They seemed to be shrieking the news of the orchards' demise, the plastic and concrete destiny that awaited them if the Woolseys failed to save their heritage.

"Looks different, doesn't it, Missy?" Coert said. He was wearing a carpenter's apron filled with grafting tools, and in his hand he held a wet burlap bag full of the Paulared branches.

"I never dreamed it would look like this! This field is so small! And I never realized the railroad tracks were so close!" Augusta was looking at the brush that barely hid the abandoned tracks and the river beyond.

"Rows of apple trees are like that," Coert said. "They're lush and the branches grow out toward each other until they almost touch. You can sit and rest in 'em and they give you the feeling of privacy even when you're not private at all."

"Oh God, Great-grandma Millie!" Augusta said, drawing in her breath. "Coert, did you remember that Mildred Woolsey's ashes are scattered here? I was so busy thinking about what this orchard meant to Nellie. How could we have forgotten about Great-grandma!"

"I didn't forget, but I was hoping you would. Now she has a better view of the river." Then, when Augusta stared at him coldly, Coert reddened. "I didn't mean to be flip, Miss Augusta. But if you want to save the farm, we got to get rid of the orchards that are producing fruit that ain't even fit for cattle feed. You know we're already a month late for grafting, and we'll be lucky if we catch it before the sap rises. You know that, Miss Augusta."

"Just Augusta, Coert. Once and for all, just call me Augusta." Suddenly, it seemed all wrong to her, Coert standing there with his arms still tan from last summer, the veins snaking over his muscles as he moved, his neck and shoulders strong as a bull's, calling her "Miss Augusta."

"Grafting on these Paulareds will start the farm down the road of producing salable apples again. We can only hope that all this cool weather will have kept the sap down so's the grafts will take, no thanks to your sister if it does, Missy."

"Augusta," she said. She wondered if Coert would look different without sideburns, in a vest. With a pipe.

"Don't think I can get used to that, Missy. Now, if we get these grafted today, I can have the Newton Pippins up by the house cut down in a day," Coert said eagerly, and then he paused. "What's the matter, Miss Augusta? You look a little strange. A little peaked. You okay?"

"Oh, I'm fine." She waved Coert off. "A lot has happened today, that's all," Augusta said, suddenly thinking that what had happened to her was a kind of collision of past, present, and future, all transformed. A new past revealed in her mother's diaries, a new present forged under Auntie Mame, and the future—her future could at any minute be altered by a bit of information from this farmer who had been so loyal for so long to the Woolsey family. Coert was looking at her with concern, and . . . was there something else? She had always known she was Coert's favorite, though she had tended to try to deny it, even to herself, because of Nellie's feelings. But she had never noticed before how tenderly he looked at her. How much he seemed to worry about her, cater to her. Or was she imagining things?

"It's all this Woolsey family sentiment, that's what's affecting you," Coert said. "Your ancestors are reaching up out of the ground and pulling you down. And it's not healthy, you girls taking so long to go through your mother's things. She wouldn't have wanted that. She lived in the here and now, your mother did. Ran this orchard in a businesslike fashion. She liked everything to be as clear as day."

"Did she, Coert?" Augusta looked at her hands. She noticed how big her knuckles were: big and red just like Coert's. She ran her hands down her waist. No one in her family had such a long waist. Augusta noticed that Coert did.

"I think she liked dreams and moonlight," Augusta said. "I think she liked taking moonlight walks in the orchards. I think she liked getting up before dawn and chasing down her dreams."

"Well," Coert smiled, scratching his sideburns, "your family's always had something of an eccentric streak. And she was a Woolsey, after all."

"And so am I," Augusta said. "I'm a Woolsey-Bean. Or am I?" Her hands were growing cold inside her pockets. She suddenly had an image of hardy Dutch sperm, fording miles of Woolsey vaginal canal, crossing into the valley of the cervix, moving through the vast uterine ocean, shooting into the dark, menacing fallopian tunnels where the phlegmatic Bean polliwogs feared to go, making a direct hit on the shimmering egg that would be Augusta.

Coert stared at her thoughtfully.

Augusta stared back. How far would she have to go? Would she have to come right out and say: and where were you, Coert Van Voorhees, on a certain moonlit night nine months before I was born?

Just then, William appeared out of the trees. He seemed not even to see the changed surroundings, but instead simply stared at Augusta, drinking her in; she looked almost quaint in clothes, for it seemed as if he had known her, forever and uniquely, in her fully, luscious nakedness. Augusta let out the breath she had been holding in anticipation of Coert's reply and looked at William with dismay.

Coert strode up, handed William a grafting tool. "I found the scions you left in the barn. Now you can pitch in and see what it is we do with them."

"Oh," William said, suddenly noticing the empty, stump-covered orchard. He took in the open field and then pointed to the state-owned woodland that divided the Woolsey orchards from the Apex land. "What a clear view of the woods! That's the very woods where Apex is probably dumping."

William put his hand on Augusta's shoulder and kept it there rather awkwardly. "I just talked to my source over at Apex's administration building," he said. "Some of the workers are complaining of headaches and fatigue, and word is beginning to filter out about a dump. See how the woodland gradually slopes upward? If toxic wastes *are* being dumped nearby, they could have been washed down here by rainwater, been dispersed by the stream, and conceivably seeped into your water supply."

"You mean we could be drinking the stuff?" Augusta asked. "It could be in our well?"

"Do you know exactly where this dump is yet?" Coert asked.

"No," William said. "But I'm going to find out. Even if I have to lie in wait all night at the factory and catch them in the act."

"You need someone to dig into their files, get documents," Augusta said. "There must be some record. One of my screen-writers, a client, has sold a script about a reporter in Louisville who found evidence that the government was illegally testing biological warfare weapons. He posed as a janitor and got into the files. It was all there in black and white."

"Do you want to pose as a janitor for me?" William asked, hoping that Augusta actually would offer to help him. Even now, at this very moment, Augusta was making his spent body stir. How in good conscience could he continue to involve Nellie in his work on Apex when he was so crazy about her sister?

"You know, I don't think I realized until now just how serious this toxic dumping was. If I didn't have to worry about making the farm profitable, I *would* help you," Augusta said. She realized with surprise that she was already separating her-self firmly from William's work, in spite of the fact that it might turn out the dump was affecting her own family's health. In the past, as soon as she had slept with a man, he might as well have owned her, her own concerns so dwindled in compar-ison to the responsibility she felt for his life.

"You folks going to just stand around and chat, or are you going to get busy and graft?" Coert grumbled. "Sun will be down in an hour or two."

Augusta knelt down in front of a stump and began to show

William how to graft. She clipped two short lengths from one of the Paulared branches in the wet burlap bag, making sure that each scion had at least two leaf buds. Then, taking the grafting tool in one hand and a small mallet in the other, she made a split in the stump and clamped it open with the other end of the tool. She held William's hand to show him how to fit the scion vertically into one side of the cleft so that the bark was flush with the bark of the stump. "You have to make sure the barks are crossed so the sap of the two can meet and flow together," Augusta said.

"Like us," William mumbled, holding onto Augusta's fingers, pressing his knee against hers. "Come away. Back under the tree. I want you. Now. Forever."

Augusta smiled and squeezed his hand, but inside she felt the stirrings of alarm. A sensation of weakening, an old feeling brought on by the sight of his flat belly and strong shoulder with the hollow where her head belonged; they made her feel like wax softened to receive a stamp. They made her feel like throwing herself down and saying that from now on she wanted only to assist William. To belong, to be owned and operated by this man who knew how to be kind to her, who would, in a sense, mother her. Augusta moved a few inches away, breathed deeply, and attacked a stump with her grafting tool.

"Now what would you be doing here, Missy?" Coert said, staring at Augusta's graft. "You only grafted in one scion. You need two, in case one doesn't take. Have you forgotten everything you knew?"

Coert knelt down, and with callused hands made two sharp, sloping cuts at one end of the budwood so that a triangular wedge was formed. His knife shone in the sunlight and his hands looked like rawhide. He fitted the second scion into the stump and smiled up at Augusta. "Don't you remember what your mother taught you? She was a fine teacher."

Yes, I remember, thought Augusta. She went to the opposite end of the row from William, knowing that she could not concentrate on the grafting if she stayed near him. Yes, she remembered that cold, bright April morning, her mother's large hands on hers, guiding her, teaching her the lessons that were forgotten but always came back to her again like buried treasure. Augusta had made a mess of the grafting, cutting the scions to shreds, but her mother had not ridiculed her; she had smiled, and gently corrected. She had been the Good Mother that day, with the daughter who was, magically, not bad, even though she was doing a bad job. The sun of her mother's smile, the love in her touch, had blinded Augusta to the thought that Lydia ever was any different. Augusta would have given anything if only this Good Mother would stay, even for just a little longer.

Now, Augusta breathed in the warm, sweet smell of the new grass. As she bent and squatted, bent and squatted, the image of William receded before the draw of her own history. My grandmother and grandfather, my great-grandmother, my great-great-grandfather—all of them are dead and gone, Augusta thought. None of them remains, and yet here I am doing what they did all of their lives. I sleep in their beds, I am farming the land which they farmed down through the decades.

"How long will it take for the new tree to grow?" William asked. He was grafting quickly now and had proceeded rapidly down his row. He was only three trees away from Augusta.

"In two years, it will be a nice full-grown Paulared," Augusta said, painting a stump and its graft with gooey black tree coat. "Eventually, you won't know where the old McIntosh tree stops and the new Paulared begins, unless you look closely down at the girdle line."

"How long would a Paulared take to grow from seed?" William asked.

"It couldn't," Augusta said. "To get an established variety, you have to graft the branches onto a rootstock."

"You mean apple trees cannot produce their own off-spring?" William asked.

"That's right," Augusta replied. "That's what's so fascinating about them. If you planted a seed from a Paulared or a McIntosh or a Red Delicious or any variety, you wouldn't get a tree that produced the same kind of apple. It would be a wild sprout with a completely different genetic makeup. You'd end up with a wild apple."

A wild apple. That was what Augusta's mother had called her once. "It's too early for you to be leaving home," she had said when Augusta had announced, in her first year of college, that she did not intend to spend another summer working in the orchards. "Listen to me. Every once in a while we find a wild apple tree that has sprouted up from seed," her mother had said. "Sometimes we find them among the McIntoshes or the Romes. They are not bred, they don't produce, they don't even grow properly. No matter where they take seed, we don't bother them, but they never, ever survive."

At that moment, Augusta had feared she would be crushed by Lydia, but she had fought back. Don't try to compare me to an apple tree, Mother, Augusta had said. Maybe apple trees can't endure without being bred from rootstock, but human beings can. Human beings, Mother, don't have to be one of a breed to last. They are individuals, they can't be grafted and regrafted. If a mother, like an apple tree, were meant to perpetuate herself, the Lord would have given her power to lop off her arm and watch her double grow. I am not your arm, Mother. And Augusta had gone to work as a chambermaid in a resort hotel in Cape Cod.

"Augusta!" A shrill voice cut through Augusta's reverie; she and William and Coert all turned around.

There, at the end of the cleared field, stood Nellie, her arm in a sling, her face a sickly gray. "Oh Augusta, what have you done? What have you done?"

"Nellie," Augusta said, dropping her tools, "I didn't want to upset you. The Christmas Orchard was finished. The apples were no good. We've started all over. It had to be done."

Nellie looked around in disbelief. "But, but," she sputtered,

"I had someone who was going to *buy* this orchard. He was going to use it for an organic farming experiment! He's from Normandy, he makes natural cider, he wanted to test this company's organic pesticides and fertilizers!" Nellie said, her chest heaving. "He didn't *care* about the condition of the trees, he didn't *care* about how many apples they produced, he didn't *care* about the mouse damage! He *preferred* to experiment with weak trees! And it was money, a lot of money, and it was almost in the bank."

"But you never said a word about a buyer!"

"Augusta, why did you have to go behind my back?"

Augusta tried to speak but could not. Finally, she said, "But if you were selling this field, you were going behind *my* back too."

"Oh, Augusta, you've always been jealous of the fact that Great-great-grandfather planted this orchard for me," Nellie said. She was shaking. "You know that the family albums are all full of pictures of you growing up. The attic is full of Augusta's First Watercolor, the remains of Augusta's First Sandwich, Augusta's First Diaper. And how many baby pictures of me are there? One? Two? There are no little locks of hair or bronzed shoes, but this orchard was the one thing that indicated the family was glad that I was born!"

"Nellie," William said, going over and putting his arm around her. He felt protective of this bruised and hurt young woman. This was the woman who had helped him, befriended him when he needed a friend. If Augusta had gone behind Nellie's back, so had William; he also had cut her down. He felt the hurt he had done to her. No matter how intense his feelings were for Augusta right now, he could not desert his friend when she clearly needed his comfort. He took out his handkerchief and handed it to her.

"I messed up the farm. I cracked up the tractor," Nellie said, tears streaming down her face. "This was the only thing I had going for me, this deal to sell my orchard."

"Oh look now, what about Apex?" William said. "What about all the work you've been doing to expose those bastards?"

Nellie blew her nose.

"Look, why don't you go up to the house? You shouldn't be out of bed yet." Then, seeing the stricken look on her face, he said, "Come on, I'll walk you back and fill you in on Apex. I have a lot to tell you. You were absolutely right. That company is even worse than we thought. We have our work cut out for us."

CHAPTER II

Overdue but abundant, the bloom had fully come. Every bud on every tree throughout Woolsey Orchards had broken into blossom, bringing the orchard alive with song and fantasy. The birds had given the signal at dawn and their sounds woke Coert, who opened his tiny loft window in the barn, halted Henry, who was feverishly looking inside his socks for his wife's rings, answered the dreamy wishes of Nellie, and rang sweetly in the ears of even Augusta, who had spent a wakeful night. After the early blooming of Auntie Mame, the buds on a scattering of trees had opened over the following twelve days, but the cold had slowed most of them. And then, last night, swollen to the bursting point and warmed by seasonable breezes, the rest of the orchard acted in concert to declare the advent of spring. Swallows, geese, nut-hatches, cardinals, red-winged blackbirds, sparrows, bluejays soared over the trees. They hopped like high-wire artists from branch to branch, chirping and chattering, flying straight for windows and then veering off at the last moment. The mood was infectious.

Henry brought the last of his bees down into the orchards from the field across the road; he watched with satisfaction as they streamed out of their boxes and into the branches. His normally frail purchase on life seemed to vanish beneath a new forthrightness. From Coert's collection of baseball caps which hung on hooks in the barn, Henry had donned the cap of the winning Yankees. He handled the red, yellow, and green crates of bees with the importance and care of a star manager, which in a way he was, for the bees would have to run the pollen from tree to tree, hitting every blossom, if there was to be a good crop of apples.

The feeling of abundance was not only in the bloom but in the bustle of activity around the orchard: the sound of power-saws razing old trees, of tractors turning over ground, backhoes digging deep into the earth and taking out stumps whose roots had burrowed downward for nearly a century. Seeds were being dropped into the plump mounds of earth made ready to receive them: pumpkins and zucchini, squash and cantaloupe, rows and rows of corn. In the South Orchards, spindly saplings of the popular Golden and Red Delicious varieties stood bravely in the furrowed soil, bending with the breezes; in the North Orchards, rows of Macoun branches had been grafted onto old stumps. Although the Macoun apple bruised easily and did not keep well, it was so tasty and well loved that Augusta and Coert had decided to risk large-scale planting of the variety. They had hired three itinerant farm laborers, and everyone was pitching in, even Nellie on the days she didn't work at the Hopestill Arms. After exacting a promise from her sister to spare the Newton Pippins that bordered the lawn, she had reconciled herself to the razing of the Christmas Orchard; she had even planted several acres of lettuce that she planned to grow organically.

The money from the DeCarlo auction, along with some funds from Augusta's savings, had paid for the sprays, the seeds, and the laborers' wages. Starting with the lettuce in June, the sale of the vegetables as they ripened throughout the summer was supposed to provide enough revenue to keep the farm going until the apple harvest in September.

As she gazed down from her window upon the replanting of

Woolsey Orchards, Augusta felt an abiding sense of release. The recovery that she had set in motion was now moving on its own—Coert, once given permission, and her father and Nellie, once given impetus, had turned out to be eager and industrious. Could her family really begin to survive on its own?

Augusta stared at the diaries that lay arranged on her bed. There were leatherbound ones, there were books covered in cool, peach-tinted satin with little gold locks, one bound in marbled swirls of color, another, a homemade book tied with silk ribbon. Sprigs of lavender and rue, yielding up a sharp sweet smell, had come tumbling out of that one. But every volume had its own particular scent, its own soft, palpable feel. As Augusta turned their pages, it was as though her fingers magically gave way to the fingers of another, as though she were being uplifted by her mother's hands, strong and confident hands she had always yearned for and never found; they were moving her gently, slowly, from one place to another.

When she had first come home, before she had found the diaries, she had woken up each morning with a feeling of unbearable heaviness. She would never be free, she thought. She would forever awaken this way, her sister standing over her with reproachful eyes just as her mother had done, her father shuffling aimlessly below, Augusta having failed to lift their misery. Wherever she went, whatever she did, she would always hear her family's silent recriminations.

But with the diaries had come a shift in her understanding. She began to see herself as part of a whole rather than as the center of her mother's universe, as the fount of all good and evil, the person upon whom everything depended. Her family's troubles had begun long before Augusta was born; she was just another small pattern in the large design, another human being upon whom Lydia Woolsey-Bean had pinned her hopes, the hopes that had never been fulfilled by Lydia's own mother. She was no more responsible for Lydia's misery, for her parents' rupture, than she was for her sister's life.

Augusta put the diaries back in their hiding place under her bed; while they had thrown her life into confusion, shattered its structure, turned its assumptions inside out, they were also healing her, and she had been returning to them hungrily whenever she got the chance. She was still afraid they might reveal something dreadful; why else had Lydia left them to Augusta alone? And she felt increasingly guilty about keeping them from Nellie, particularly since she had shared their existence with William. But opening their vellum pages had become addictive; even the dread had become addictive. She could not be away from them for long, she was as eager as a junkie to be swept back between their seductive covers. They were hospital-warm, soft as a psychiatrist's couch, a cottony cocoon like the one she had shared with her mother before Nellie had come screeching into their lives. It had been ages since she had owned her mother exclusively, and she liked it just fine this way.

Augusta drenched her body in lily-of-the-valley cologne, dabbing it under her arms, on her neck, on the inside of her thighs, imagining the little white flowers bending their necks, their bells freshly opened. She put makeup under her eyes to hide the evidence of the night's wakefulness.

She had, of course, developed more than one addiction. She was obsessed with William, even as she was obsessed with the diaries. When she wasn't searching for the meaning of her mother's life, she was searching for the meaning of William's body. When she wasn't soaking up the past, she was compelled to devour the present, to lie down with this wonderful man on the crisp-sheeted featherbeds of the Hopestill Arms, on the soft grass in the woods near the stream, on any surface that would indulge their passion for each other.

Most addictions, she mused, plunge the addict downward into stagnant illusion, but hers seemed to be serving just the opposite function; she was being enlightened, freed, shaken from her axis and forced to consider life from another angle of the prism.

Each time she and William made love, she seemed to shed

another layer of her past. As she allowed herself to experience greater and greater sexual pleasure, as she became more and more confident that her mother's judgmental presence was fading away, she found a part of herself that hitherto she had always lost in the process of loving another. Instead of becoming helpless, she was becoming stronger, more sure of herself. The sexual longing, the overwhelming frustration that her mother had revealed in the diaries had seemed to unleash Augusta's own, and to urge her on to free herself by pursuing what her mother had lost. And as her sexual guilt faded, so did her old, inevitable slide into worthlessness; she no longer felt so needy for the love of the one with whom she had sinned.

But the latest diary was not without its disturbing revelations—it was pulling her back toward her mother. She had learned that Lydia had managed to connect herself to the young William Hurley through, of all things, sexual drama.

Late last night, Augusta had been skimming through the later volumes, looking for lines that would give her a clue to the mystery of her legitimacy, when she had come across William's name. Lydia, in an entry dated the fall of 1959, had written that among her many good samaritan cases was a poor family named Casey, who lived across town in the seedy tenements that had once belonged to the Woolseys. At the beginning of Augusta's senior year, shortly after William had broken up with her, William had taken up with the Caseys' fifteen-year-old daughter Arlene, and Arlene had gotten pregnant. According to the diary, Arlene had come to Lydia for help, and Lydia had not only helped the two find a doctor at the hospital where she volunteered who would perform a clandestine abortion—she had promised to keep it a secret.

Augusta closed the volume in anger and alarm. But she didn't know at whom she should be angry. At William for something that had happened two decades ago and that was essentially none of her business? At her mother, for making such an enlightened and courageously kind gesture? For not telling Augusta about it?

Augusta could not sleep. At first, the information had dragged her back down into the old quagmire; here was more evidence of her mother invading even the parts of her life that Augusta had tried to keep so separate. Her mother, who had jokingly said, "I own and operate you" when Nellie and she were little, had first monopolized William and then had spread her tentacles to connect him to her for life.

Augusta recalled with distaste how much her mother had always doted on William, engaging him in conversation, enlisting Amenia to ply him with food. Why? What was William to her? After several hours of tossing and turning, Augusta had fallen into a dream.

She was on a beach and she was being carried on her mother's back. Suddenly her mother was torn from her by a gigantic wave that carried her away to another shore. Augusta was all alone, looking at her mother from a distance, admiring her, smiling at her. They smiled at each other, and all of Augusta's resentment had gone. When she awoke, it was with a sense of peace, of separation from Lydia. If William and her mother had a connection to each other, it did not necessarily have to involve Augusta, or exclude her from William. It did not have to plug into old constructs, be scrutinized for meanings that would confirm old convictions.

Augusta dressed quickly, in a rose silk blouse and trim slacks. She was meeting William at Newbury's Five and Dime, that quirky enterprise which was part coffee shop, part dime store, part general store, and part outlet for designer seconds trucked up from New York's garment center. With the orchard abustle and Nellie working at the Hopestill Arms, it was a place where they could at least talk privately.

When she arrived, William sat waiting for her in a booth, the top of his head nearly grazing an overhanging rack of false eyelashes. The store was almost empty, and smelled of cheap chocolate and the first coffee of the day.

Augusta slipped into the booth and told him about her

discovery of the diary entry that revealed his affair with Arlene, Lydia's involvement, and the abortion.

William looked down into his coffee cup. "I was afraid you'd find out before I could tell you. I thought your mother might have put it in there. I wanted to tell you, but I just didn't have the guts."

"I suppose I should be glad that it happened to Arlene instead of to me," Augusta said, closing her eyes and feeling the steam rise up from her tea. "It does give a certain metaphysical justice to what you call my pathological prudishness as an adolescent, doesn't it?"

"I never would have compromised you," William sighed. "I just wanted to hold you, kiss you, not destroy you. But you were untouchable. You treated me like I was part leper, part lecher, and I suppose that's what I became."

Augusta held up her hand. "Don't say it. Don't say, 'Arlene made me feel like a man again.' "

William stirred his coffee.

"Don't you think you could have exercised some little bit of self-control? Waited a decent interval after dumping me before you went catting off to the tenements to take advantage of some poor fast child? My God, she had orange hair!" Augusta said, fixing her gaze on a tree of matching black and red Dior garter belts and bras: there used to be shelves of long aprons there, the kind her grandmothers wore. "You don't love me," she mumbled, unable to stifle the words she had always ended up uttering to the parade of withholding men she got involved with. "You never did really love me. You don't now."

William threw his napkin down on the chipped Formica table. "Oh look, do you think I enjoyed hurting Arlene? Do you think that the experience of making her pregnant was a casual one for me? Am I at all casual about anything? No, wait a minute. I *am* casual. I am casual with women. But do you know that it's an act to cover up the fact that I'm not casual at all? It's a hard, tiring disguise meant to hide the utter seriousness with which I take every woman I date. It's meant to protect the female race from pinning its hopes on me. And you know something? I'm tired of all this studied casualness in my life. I'm tired of paying for my mistakes. Would you by any chance marry me?"

Augusta nearly spit out a mouthful of tea. She certainly had not expected this—or wanted it. "Let's take one subject at a time," she said. "Let's take the fact that you brought my mother in to help you. My puritanical, Victorian mother! The mother of the girl you had just jilted! How on earth could you have chosen her to turn to?"

"Arlene turned to her. Your mother had helped birth her little brother in the delivery room. She had helped the whole family. Arlene was scared, and desperate. She saw your mother as her family's friend."

"My mother," Augusta said through closed teeth. "My mother was the one who instilled in me the sexual rigidity that landed you in the lap of Arlene! Up until I was twenty-five, I still was afraid I would end up as one of those bizarre cases who got pregnant through heavy petting!" Augusta sighed. "I suppose my mother was so glad it wasn't me that was knocked up, she helped you out of sheer relief."

William looked at her. "No, Augusta. Your mother helped us because she cared about other people and she liked to help them. She may have been the worst possible mother to you, but to me she was the perfect surrogate. If I had told my parents I had gotten a girl pregnant, my father would have never survived his disappointment in me. But your mother never once condemned me. The situation was too serious for condemnation, and then, after all, I wasn't her child."

Augusta clattered down her cup. "You know, I wondered at the time why you never came back to talk to me after we broke up, how you could witness the pathetic way I was flooding the school with tears and still be unmoved. But I guess you had other things on your mind."

William put his hand on hers. "You weren't pathetic. But Arlene really was the only thing on my mind then. It was awful, Augusta. I'll never forget the look on her face, and the little gold cross around her neck, and the rosary she was clutching when she went into that office, how white and hunched she was when she came out. Thank God for your mother and her hospital contacts, thank God she was able to get a real doctor to do it! You know, I don't think Arlene ever got over the abortion. She dropped out of school after that. She was so ashamed. It killed something in her soul. We had created sacred life and then we had murdered it, and no one could convince her otherwise."

"And what about you, William?" Augusta asked, her face softening. She returned the pressure on his fingers. "What did it do to you? Why have you avoided getting seriously involved? Why does a man of thirty-five still play the field like a college kid?"

William pushed his plate away. "The first sign of someone falling for me, and I feel like bolting. I used to think it was because of the suddenness of my parents' death. That I just hadn't dealt with it, that I was kind of keeping myself on hold. But you know, I think it's more that I'm always afraid I'm about to hurt someone, that they are going to want something from me I can't give them. That I'll turn around one day, and I'll have ruined someone else's life. Arlene wanted to have the baby, you know. Your mother talked her out of it. If she hadn't, I would have given up going to Columbia and married her. Your mother saved me for my Dad's law practice. Thanks to her, I didn't even have to bear the consequences of my father's wrath, and he could die happily deluded that I had not been the moral fuck-up he'd always feared."

"But instead you've had to bear the consequences of your anger at yourself, which has to be worse," Augusta said. "Poor William. You are probably the most moral soul I've ever known. You know that we've only been together two weeks and already I trust you, and I never trust anyone."

"And I feel worthy of it," he said, stroking Augusta's cheek. "I don't think I've ever felt so liberated in a relationship. If I've released your sexuality, you've released my capacity for love—and for commitment."

Augusta averted her eyes. She knew that look; hopeful, shy; it was the look she had given one man after another, their impassiveness fueling her desperation. "William," she said gently. "Please don't get any ideas about me. You know my plans. You know that I'm leaving, and nothing can change that. I would be miserable living here.

"I want to tell you something," Augusta added, anxious to change the subject. "Something that will release you even more from the past. William, your father knew about Arlene. It's there in the diaries. Mother told him. And he had no wrath, only forgiveness. He understood. He felt badly for you."

William stared at her incredulously, then he looked down at his cup, circling its rim with his finger. "That wily bastard . . . why the hell didn't he tell me he knew? Now that I think back, he was extra nice to me during that period, really talkative and involved, which made me feel even lousier. I thought, if he only knew what the son of Stonekill Landing's revered attorney has done! My Dad could send you to hell with his silences. The person was never born who could achieve his high grade of character."

"That sounds like a description of my mother. They really were kindred spirits," Augusta said thoughtfully. "Whenever your father came birding on our property, he'd stop up at the house. They would talk. About charity work, mostly."

"You look beautiful when you put your finger to your chin that way," William said. "And I think I'm falling in love with you yet again. Do you suppose it's the fact that we had our first argument, or is it that I've never seen you in that shade of pink before?"

"Maybe," Augusta smiled, "it's because I helped take away some of the weight of your secret about Arlene, and the abortion, and my mother, and the debt you owed her all these years."

William brushed his face against her hair as they got out of the booth, ran his hand down the silk of her back, then unobtrusively slipped it inside her belt.

Augusta reached back to stop him. She was thinking that if she looked at some later diary entries, they might explain more about why her mother treated William with such acceptance, seemed to be so attached to him. "I have to go back home," she said.

"Don't even think about it. We're going back to my room. To bed," William said, and with uncharacteristic boldness he pushed her forward. "We'll have to sneak in the back door of the inn, because Nellie will be up front at the reception desk by now. Hurry up. God, I want you. Do you think we can get there quickly enough?"

Nellie left the house early to walk the two miles to the inn. There was something she wanted to do before she took up her post at the reception desk. She snapped off several small branches from the Newtown Pippins that she had saved from Coert's chainsaw. The blossoms looked languorous, alive; they looked like lovestruck mermaids lolling lazily on the seabed, their petals quivering like skin lightly touched. If only Augusta would go on a trip, Nellie would take William swimming, one thing would lead to another and Nellie would slip off her bathing suit so William could view her naked underwater, where all bodies look smooth, firm, the fat lifted and toned by the weight of the water. But Augusta was not going anywhere, not yet. Nellie would have to walk with dignity, like generations of women who suffered under the sweet, cutting burden of unrequited love, who lived in states of constant ambiguity, hoping that the one they loved would ultimately choose them. She would be fueled not only by her passion but by the belief that one day he would see that it was she, Nellie, whose love was truest.

The last unplowed field north of the orchards was heavy with dandelion. It looked as if it had been spread with mustard. She picked some stalks of hardy orchard grass and a few flowering weeds to complete her bouquet of apple-blossoms. The blossoms were terribly beautiful, each one a stab in her heart. She went down through the trees, stopping to watch the bees descend on them. She had always loved to watch the bees working. Some of them floated from one blossom to another, burrowing their black snouts deep into the pistil and then delicately wiping their feet on the petal, depositing enough pollen from a neighboring tree to pollinate the flower. These bees reminded her of herself. Other bees behaved differently, moving crazily from petal to petal, sucking at the pistils. Those bees reminded her of Augusta. They were the kind that would turn on a passer-by, for the getting of pollen was such an urgent instinct, anything that threatened this achievement drove them wild.

Nellie began to run. Two of them were descending on her and she ran faster; one of them tangled itself in her hair, but she was able to bat it away. The other luckily lost its stinger in her jacket sleeve.

Why, oh why, couldn't Augusta have just given William to her, the way she had handed over the rest of her hand-me-downs? Augusta could have any man she wanted without lifting a finger, but William might be Nellie's only chance. And he was, he really *was* interested in her! The way he sat close to her when they were working on the Apex data, reaching over her to point to something, his arm brushing her arm; Nellie could tell.

Nellie looked the other way as she passed the razed Christmas Orchard—the memory of that day when she had come down to find her trees gone was too painful. But the trees were the least of it—it's what she had sensed between William and

Augusta, standing there next to each other, grafting knives in their hands, looking guilty. Something was happening, or was going to happen, between the two of them: the air was reeking of it. Would Augusta stop it before it began? Would William? Could Nellie prevent it?

It was strange, Nellie thought, walking along the Hudson River, its muddy waters coursing like an artery through the valley: it was odd, but her lovelorn state did not bring forth the old misery, the hopeless feelings of once again being passed over and belittled. Far from being bitter and immobilized, she actually felt buoyant, as though rising to some challenge. She watched herself move toward town, a spring in her step, her jacket flapping against her back, a ray of sun revealing the peach-fuzz on the curve of her cheek. Down through the years, she had watched women like this enviously, imagining lives for them that were full of adventure. But today, she felt like one of those confident strangers. She would invent her own life. She had been emptied and had only to reimagine herself.

And who, to her astonishment, was responsible for Nellie's new outlook? Augusta, that's who. By some miracle, her sister suddenly seemed to be a changed woman, and she was helping Nellie to change too. What a paradox: the person who had brought about her loveless plight, who had swept down and mesmerized William at the very moment he was about to fall in love with Nellie, had also begun to make Nellie see how lovable she really was. Augusta had grown wise and less selfish, and in spite of the tension over William, who was seldom overtly discussed but who was always present between them, the sisters had grown closer. Augusta had helped Nellie to see more clearly how their mother had foisted the role of ne'er-do-well on Nellie, and how really, Nellie was—what had Augusta called it?—"a powerhouse within." Augusta had helped her to see that as long as she held fast to her grievances (and it was true, Nellie did spend most of her life nursing a gigantic griev-ance against Augusta), she would never get out and seize her own life.

Augusta was not dressing sloppily anymore; she looked neat even when it was only for the benefit of Nellie and their father. Most important, she was treating Nellie with a new respect and tolerance . . . even tenderness. The old cynical Nellie would have suspected this behavior, would have concluded that Augusta had probably gone ahead and stolen William out from under her; but the new Nellie saw that Augusta could not have been such a snake. No, perhaps the reason for the change in Augusta was Nellie herself!

After all, her sister must have been impressed with Nellie's competence in arranging the sale of the Christmas Orchard. And then, after Augusta had cut it right out from under her, who could not have admired the way Nellie, with little rancor, stepped aside, involving herself in the Apex project, so Augusta could have the freedom to overhaul the farm the way she wanted?

Nellie smiled at the waiters as she walked into the Hopestill Arms. No, I don't think I *will* sit back and nurse a grievance about William, she thought; I'll get out there and fight for what I want. And let Augusta's advice come back to haunt her!

She took the passkeys from behind the reception desk and, clutching the flowers she intended to put in his room, hurried up and let herself into William's room. Her eyes went immediately to his unmade bed. She knew it. He was a mangler of sheets, a twister of blankets, a puncher of pillows, just like her; he tossed and turned. Behind the most placid and cool exteriors, the heart simmered. His tweed jacket lay folded over a chair, his pants were hanging over the antique valet, the belt still in them; a snakeskin belt, with a big silver buckle that was cold to the touch. He liked big buckles; he had one in brass and two different silver ones. Nellie shivered. He had deposited the contents of his pockets—pennies, collar stays, toothpicks— inside the big bowl on his marble washstand.

On the Sheraton desk were piles of material about Apex and toxic wastes that she had helped him gather and collate. They had made exciting progress. Nellie had canvassed orchards up north in Columbia County and found that no one was having the severe problems of mottling and poor coloration that Woolsey Orchards had suffered the past few years. Nellie had unearthed a UCLA study that showed fruit trees could definitely be affected by benzenes. They had ascertained that underground veins of water that ran downhill from abandoned wells on Apex property, beneath the stream and into Woolsey orchards, could carry toxic chemicals into the Woolsey well and into the soil that nourished the trees. Nellie had taken samples of the Woolsey well water to be tested, and even though the tests were inconclusive so far, she had stocked the cold storage with bottled water and ordered the family not to use any from the tap. The next step was for Nellie and William to find out if toxic wastes were being dumped into the abandoned Apex wells or nearby sites, to obtain documents from their Apex sources about the dumping, and (the most exciting plan of all) to catch the dumpers in the act.

They made a brilliant team. William said Nellie was a crack researcher, a born snoop. Nellie hoped that when they had gathered proof of Apex's illegal acts, they would write an article together, an article that might land Nellie a reporting job, or something else that would get her out of Woolsey Orchards, that would start her on a new life.

Nellie went into the bathroom to fill a vase with water, and her heart sped up at the sight of his razor and shaving cream. He used the old-fashioned mug and brush, just like her grandfather had. She could see him, stirring up a soft creamy lather, patting it onto his cheeks, taking up the sleek, silvery blade, and sliding it cleanly down the side of his face. She could nip the attraction between William and Augusta in the bud, she knew she could! She had the power. She was a powerhouse.

Watch out, you're cutting yourself! She takes a washcloth and dabs at the cut on his chin, applies a bit of Kleenex to staunch it. Some of the blood falls on her bare shoulder. He looks at her lovingly, gratefully. I should have known you were the one all

*along, he says, and he kisses that spot on her forehead which
he likes to kiss so often.*

There was suddenly the sound of a key turning in the lock.
Nellie froze, then dropped the vase of flowers onto a stand and
ran to the large closet on the opposite side of the room. She
closed the door behind her just as the room door opened and
William and her sister came in.

William threw down the key and took Augusta in his arms.
He kissed her roughly and his hands reached under her blouse.
All he had to do these days was kiss her, and Augusta floated
up onto a plane of pure, excruciating pleasure. Every cell in her
body was alerted, every nerve was erect. The feel of his fingertips traveling down her back made her spine shiver, his lips
brushing her ear was felt down in her toes, and when his
thumbs began to rub her nipples it was so unbearable that her
breath caught in little childlike heaves.

William stopped, alarmed. "Is it your asthma?" he asked.

"No, no, it's you! It's getting worse and worse," Augusta
said, herself somewhat alarmed. "This can't be normal. I mean,
I know you've brought out my buried sexuality and all that, but
this is ridiculous! Even the tips of the hairs on my arms are
sensitive. I feel dizzy."

"Maybe it's those flowers," William said with concern. "Oh,
look, why would the maid put these weeds in the vase?" He
dumped the flowers into the toilet and flushed it, then came
back and took Augusta in his arms.

"What's that noise?" Augusta said. "It came from over
there. In the wall."

"Mice, maybe," William murmured and began to kiss her
again.

Augusta, in the last week, had been in a state of nearly
perpetual arousal. She no longer had control over her body.
William could instantly plunge it into turmoil. She looked
almost longingly back on the days of her life before William's
reappearance, when she would go through the motions of mak-

ing love, enjoying it mildly but really half-numb, barricaded against the annoyance of bodily intrusion. Sex, clearly, was mostly in the mind, and right now her mind had left its house and taken her down into a tunnel, where William's tongue raced down through the darkness, a train careening, pointing, reaching toward a dazzling spot of light in the center of her being.

William broke away from her, gasping. "Now it's me who forgot to breathe," he laughed. "God, kissing you is unbelievable. Back when we were sixteen, it was that kiss, that one kiss down in your cellar that I remember better than anything else we did. I hated you for teasing me that way, for giving me a kiss that you never gave me again, but now I'm glad you did. It was a map that brought me back to you."

"What kiss are you talking about?" Augusta asked, puzzled. "I never kissed you."

"Have you forgotten? I ran down after you through the bulkhead and into your cellar. After we had one of our fights about petting. You were against the wall. We kissed. We certainly kissed. A French kiss. Again and again."

"William, you're daft. I'd remember it, I know I would. As much as I hate to tell you, I do remember my first kiss, and it was not with you."

William looked at her. "Then who did I kiss?" he said. "I didn't imagine it. I kissed someone down in your cellar!"

William glanced at the pile of manila folders on the table and felt a sinking sensation in his stomach. Who else but Augusta could have been down in that basement? What other little girl might have stood silently in the darkness and enjoyed the embrace of her big sister's boyfriend? Who else but the person who years later came running whenever he wanted her, whose passionate green eyes gazed at him with such rapt attention?

"Oh God. Nellie," he said. "It wasn't you at all, Augusta. It must have been Nellie who I kissed all those years ago."

"Nellie?" Augusta said. "How could it have been Nellie?"

William paced in front of the closet, banged his hand against it. "All these years, remembering that incident! Thinking that you had responded physically to me and then shut me out. God, how could I have made such a stupid mistake? How could I have broken up with you for a rejection that never even happened! How could we have had such a miscommunication! I built this elaborate myth about you and me, out of nothing, nothing at all."

"It wasn't nothing if you kissed her! There was a kiss," Augusta said, sitting down on the bed. "I just can't believe it. Why didn't she ever tell me that my boyfriend had kissed her? She couldn't have been more than eleven, she must have been freaked out. She should have come running to me and—oh God, unless . . . unless she secretly liked it. Unless she secretly loved you or something." Augusta got up from the bed. "All this time I've thought her attraction to you was so tied up with Mother's death, and with our sibling rivalry. I really do live in a world of my own. It didn't occur to me that she might have always felt something for you independent of me."

William picked up an Apex folder. "She's done all this work for me. Even when I haven't been here, even when I've been with you, she has sat down there at the reception desk, poring over data on toxic wastes. Have I led her on? God, I hope not. Since you and I got together, I've tried my best to be like a big brother to her."

"I wonder if you've tried hard enough," Augusta said. "How could you possibly keep it business all those hours you spend working together? Are you sure you kissed her only once? Are you sure you didn't share more than just Apex this time?"

"It's absurd for you to be jealous, Augusta," William said, suddenly realizing what it was that had been hovering at the edge of his consciousness, bothering him. Augusta wanted him exclusively—she was jealous of Arlene, of Nellie—but did she truly want *him*? Or was her jealousy in a kind of vacuum, a vacuum filled with past hurts? William was feeling himself uncharacteristically ready for involvement, for settling down even, yet there was something in Augusta that seemed to resist this. They didn't talk very much, or very well; this morning's conversation at Newbury's was the most substantive conversation they had had. William wondered whether they were communicating any better now than they had twenty years ago. Nellie, for instance, acted more interested in William than Augusta did; Augusta seemed to be mainly interested in him for sex.

"Nellie is very fragile, you know," William said, wondering whether Nellie remembered that fabulous kiss in as much detail as he did. "And she damn well shouldn't be hurt by the likes of us. We should have told her about us. We've been foolish, stupid, insensitive."

"You didn't want to tell her, William. You didn't want to because you are attracted to her. You always have been. Maybe you're so attracted that you've been blind to how you've been using her, taking advantage of her feelings for you."

William had not shaved that morning, and his beard was dark against the pallor of his face. "That was needless, Augusta, considering our conversation about trust and how I feel about hurting people," William said quietly. "You're the one who's kept so many things from Nellie. After we first made love, you were determined not to tell her about us, you said we couldn't lay another trip on her after the Christmas Orchard. She was already in the midst of helping me on the Apex project. How could I tell her to stop helping me? She cares about the valley, she cares that Apex is poisoning the farm. I couldn't have stopped that in her if I tried."

"I wonder what it's like," Augusta sank down on the bed again. "To have a sexual experience when you're still a child and never tell anyone? How could I have been so foolish as to think I really knew Nellie?"

William sat down on the bed next to her. He kissed her

gently, and his hands moved almost involuntarily over the silk covering her breasts. Whenever he was close to her, he forgot everything but his overwhelming attraction to her.

She moved away. "I want to go. I feel sick. I can't think about sex."

"Sex is what we are," William murmured. "You can't leave now, you know you can't."

And he was right. Augusta could not find the strength to get up and walk out the door. Her heart was heavy but her nipples were erect and soon she was breathing fast. She did not stop him when he unzipped her trousers, buried his head in the satin of her panties, when he pinned her back on the bed. She was limp, she was submissive. There was a kind of remorseful darkness to their lovemaking this time. Something had changed.

William reacted with defiance. He took her up, imagined his fire bringing her feeble flame into his belly. Then he came into her harshly, angrily, like an automobile careening, crashing from side to side. His eyelids went red, he saw blood; he saw his parents, glass and steel and blood, he saw Arlene and the blood that gushed from her. He saw Nellie, her red hair, hot to the touch, her heart, hot, broken. He wanted to obliterate himself, his low, mean self, and when he thrust inside Augusta he felt himself thrusting out over the edge of his own being until he felt only Augusta. He *was* Augusta. He was her warm, moist skin, he was her delicate, innocent self, he was the hard protrusion of her breastbone, he was the jungle between her legs. He was blood brought back up from the pavement, from the doctor's table, poured back into the strong cylindrical tubes of the veins that pulsed in her temple like a baby's. He was her hands kneading his back, her white nails scraping his spine, her legs entwining him, pushing him, he was her whole body rising to the touch of his fingers, rolling him over, sucking him up in her essence.

Augusta, moving on top of him, fought against a sensation

of extinction: the old feelings were back, now that Augusta had taken something that was clearly Nellie's. She was losing the wholeness of herself; it was fracturing into those collection of sorry little selves that she saw in the eyes of her family, in mirrors, in scrapbooks, each reflection desperately full of self and yet so pathetically absent of it. She fought to reclaim what she had gained. She pressed her molecules into a dense mass, a tight primitive ball of sensation, focusing on a tiny drop of light at the edge of her eyelash. She moved William up and down inside her, slowly, too slowly. He tried to lift her, to twist her back down so that he was on top, but she had the leverage, she would not let go until she had broken his will. Suddenly she moved quickly, she brought him to the edge of ecstasy, then she abruptly stopped. Then she did it all over again. And again. Only when she felt strong and separate, beyond shame, beyond conscience, beyond need, matter faithful unto itself, did she take William where he desperately wanted to go.

Nellie sat in the dark closet, her fingers in her ears, her eyes shut, William's clothes hanging all around her. She felt as she had when she had been thrown from her bicycle as a child— stunned, groggy, a lump of wood.

The closet was open a crack, but Nellie did not look out. She had to hum softly to herself to drown out the sounds of their lovemaking. She was ashamed for Augusta, whose entire life had been spent appearing perfect. Augusta would die if she knew her sister had seen her like this: as naked and as exposed as a dog.

CHAPTER 12

February 7, 1948

*M*y poor Nellie. The family loves the idea of a second heir to the dazzling Woolsey heritage, but the reality—this homely little sprite with an oversize nose and a tiny corkscrew mouth that quivers and screams from morning till night—is too much for them. Great-grandpa is happy about finally sending even more of his name down into history, but even he is uncomfortable when he pokes his head into the cradle. Her odd red hair is found nowhere on the family tree, and Mama looks at me suspiciously, as though I had set out deliberately to insult the family.

Were it not for Augusta, they would be as enchanted by Cornelia as I am. Augusta has spoiled them. She was exactly what you dream a baby is going to be but almost never is: pink, placid, perfect; she inherited my widely spaced eyes, my full mouth, but God drew them more finely, colored her more boldly. Cornelia doesn't have much of me—her close-set eyes are pure Woolsey, her weak chin seems to be Mama's exactly, and she has her father's little rubber-band mouth—but what she does have of me, the prominent cheekbones and large nose, are grossly exaggerated. As though the sculptor had thrown on the head of clay, but left before he was really finished.

May 20, 1948

I am in a howl of exhaustion; a mothering machine with no other purpose. Poor Cornelia and I are confined to a spare room in the servants' quarters so Henry and everyone else can sleep through the night. Grandma Millie thinks the baby's wakeful crying will affect Great-grandpa's weak blood vessels.

Mama recommends that I just let her scream through the night. Self-reliance cannot be taught too early, Mama says, but all I can think about is Cornelia's panic as she rattles the bars of that dungeon of a crib in which she is trapped. I see it so clearly that it must be a memory of my own.

July 25, 1948

*W*e took pictures of the girls under the Newtown Pippins, and even the photographer remarked how sweet and motherly Augusta was to Nellie. Then, when our backs were turned, Augusta began hugging Nellie so tightly around the neck that she was choking her. I am so afraid Augusta will hurt her that I've forbidden her to be alone with Nellie.

I've felt Augusta's every ache as though it's been my own, but now it is only poor Cornelia's pain that I feel. The family continues to lavish little gifts on Augusta while her seven-month-old sister gazes on wide-eyed. I vow that I will never be so unfair: what one girl gets from me the other will receive its equal.

March 5, 1949

I grew up in a shroud of camphor and enforced quiet, and now that I have children I can finally have a childhood. I throw open the halls to light and laughter, and I take the girls on imaginary excursions. For all the years that I was essential to no one's happiness, I am now indispensable to these two children, who must depend on me for everything.

Augusta continues to pick on Nellie, and I get beside myself with anger. I think it's because I know what it feels like to be so small and cowed and lonely, the world a frightening forest of unyielding oak trees.

Nellie still does not climb very steadily, and she had made her way painstakingly up to the top of a little slide Pieter had built for the children when Augusta came along and blithely pushed her down to the bottom again. I felt like thrashing Augusta three ways from Sunday. A little later, Augusta accidentally shut herself in the linen closet, and I would not open it. I wanted her to suffer, I wanted her to know that for every bad deed you do, the bad comes back to you. So I listened to her wails for several minutes, knowing how helpless she was, how little it takes to crush her, but knowing too that she got the gifts, she got the popularity, and she will always have the power to hold Nellie's reins. Like my mother, in her lovelessness, held mine.

Augusta sat staring at the ink-stained pages that she had just read. Then she took the load of shirts out of the washer and, one by one, pitched them in hard wet balls into the small, creaky top-loading dryer that had miraculously survived thirty years. She felt like pitching the diaries in too, then watching their pages come loose, shrivel up, disintegrate.

Now that Coert had the farm operations well in hand and Nellie was working hard on the Apex project, Augusta had taken over responsibility for the laundry, a chore whose novelty she rather enjoyed—especially since William, along with his sexy shirts and striped boxers, had moved into the house. Ironically, it was Nellie who had insisted William save money and stay with them instead of at the inn, and she had done so even *after* Augusta and William had told her they were in love.

It was a fine morning for the middle of June, and Augusta, while waiting for the wash cycle to be done, had succumbed to the diaries again. Several weeks ago, she had reached her bottom: control of her life had slipped away and she was at the mercy of this mother resurrected on vellum, swinging her back and forth with her endless surprises, sending her up with praise, then sinking her with condemnation. She had gone cold turkey and let the bag of old journals gather dust under her bed.

But lately, Augusta's guilt over Nellie had bitten like a wire into her love for William, and even more so because her sister had taken the news of their affair with completely uncharacteristic grace. Though Nellie seemed oddly ready for the blow, she did not express anger, she did not express bitterness or self-pity. And her friendly aloofness since then had been chilling: was there a gleam of malice in her eye, or was Augusta's morbid imagination putting it there? Nellie's inscrutable attitude was haunting her, clouding the first healthy, purely joyful relationship she had ever had. So Augusta had taken out the diaries once again, hoping to find something that would ease her burden of guilt.

She had been skimming the diaries selectively, holding them at arm's length, determined that she would make them work for her, not the other way around. Surely she would be able to find evidence that Nellie had woven this myth about how Augusta had taken the riches, leaving the younger Nellie empty-handed. Lydia might have later encouraged Nellie's failures in order to keep one daughter at home, but surely she gave them the same love and regard when they were little.

And here, in those ink-stained pages lying on the ironing board, was ample proof: Nellie had been absolutely right. Lydia had decided that Nellie was second-best before she had even left infancy. And instead of feeling sheepish about this discovery, Augusta was angry.

Augusta, the gift-child, might have had it all, but she had it no better than Nellie; they had both suffered under Lydia's tormented psyche. It was as though Lydia's two children represented the two halves of her own fractured self, the child who had nothing and the child who had too much. And while she could not bear to let the child who had less even cry in her crib, she set out to punish the other one for her privileges, much as her own mother had punished her.

From the first, Lydia had defined who her children were going to be, condemning them to prearranged roles, pitting them against each other. Her mother had actually blamed Augusta for being so perfect that Nellie really couldn't get a fair chance in the Woolsey household! Augusta shook out Nellie's childhood bedsheet from the wet laundry. Covered with a pattern of little trains, it was worn, tattered. Augusta put her finger in a hole and the sheet ripped easily in half.

The sacred credo her mother had lived by, that everything comes back to you, bad and good, yin and yang, give to one what you give to the other, suddenly seemed disgusting, spurious to Augusta. For every ounce of attention Augusta got from her grandparents, Lydia had undoubtedly withdrawn an ounce of her own. Just to keep things even. Just to heat up the sibling rivalry. In truth, the arrival of Nellie had probably given Lydia an excuse to vent her own jealousy at Augusta's popularity.

Augusta's primitive fears, the ones she was too embarrassed

to admit even to William, were coming forth now as quickly as the water that spurted into the second load of wash: she had always had this little feeling that behind all the orchestrated hoopla about Augusta the Chosen, there lurked a nasty truth: that she, not Nellie, was actually the scorned child, the one that Lydia had found wanting. Perhaps the diary was part of a gigantic effort to cover up the fact that Augusta was a seed unwanted.

Oh, how Augusta hated these feelings. She was nearly thirty-five, with a career, a future, and her whole well-being seemed to hinge on whether, decades ago, she had lost her mother's love to her little sister! And oh, now, for the first time, she remembered her mother's arms; she was three, she was two, she was bound belly to belly by those mother-arms that brought her closer, closer, pressing her body like a sponge into soft earth, pressing her flesh like a button into clay; a swarm of exciting sounds and smells—oatmeal, lipstick, cold juice trickling into the cup, talcum powder—and then her mother's stomach growing bigger and bigger, until it was no longer soft and pillowy but hard and mean like a rock. And Augusta was ripped up by the roots, lifted and deposited down on the cold, hard floor of the place called Nursery School.

Augusta remembered it with razor-sharpness: Lydia, skirts rustling, swooping down to take Nellie away from Augusta's eager grasp, looking at Augusta coldly while she cuddled this soft little thing that fit just right in her arms, her parents feeding the baby late at night, Augusta trying to join them, and her father bellowing for her to go upstairs to bed. Exclusion, rejection, creeping wormlike down her spine, settling hard and heavy in her gut, for days on end. A picture: sharing a bed with Nellie in a motel room, hearing her mother stir in the bed nearby, Augusta crunching her body up tiny, making herself small so that her mother will cuddle with her, but it is Nellie her mother picks up, always Nellie; she hardly ever hugs Augusta anymore.

. . .

Augusta heard the sound of her sister's footsteps on the stairs and quickly thrust the diary into her pocket. She only had time to throw a shirt over the stack of other diaries on the washing machine before her sister strolled in.

Nellie leaned against the wall and gave her sister one of those mild but appraising looks that she knew unnerved Augusta. It had been more than a month since she had hid in the closet at the inn, but Nellie was still marveling at how you could never quite look at someone the same way once you've seen them in the act of sexual intercourse.

"I can't believe I'm actually watching you lift an iron," Nellie said, gazing at Augusta's yellow hair, which was pulled back into a careless but elegant twist, with wisps of it sticking to her damp face. "Love transforms even the hardest cases." She walked over to the washing machine and lifted up William's shirt by its sleeve, exposing the diaries. Augusta dumped a pile of sheets over them a second before Nellie looked down.

"William has brought out the submissive and the domestic in you, sis," Nellie smiled, running her hands over the sleek black hose connecting the washing machine to the water supply, "but you don't submit to him, do you? I mean, he's not like all those other men in your dark past, the ones you said could shake you like a hose, making you slither and sputter out of control. You should marry him, you know, you're so much alike. Professional, successful, gorgeous."

"Your sheet fell apart in the wash. I put it in the ragbag," Augusta said, surprised at the acidity in her voice. She held up the pathetic pieces of sheet. She wanted to shake her sister's clear unwavering glance, to bring back the old resentful Nellie.

"Oh," Nellie cried. "How could it have fallen apart? I've had that since I was little! Oh well, it's a sign of sorts," she added. "I once had plans that included things like that sheet and this house, a man, maybe, but I have new plans, better plans now."

"I know, and you won't tell a soul about them. I wish you'd just get mad over William and despise us openly, Nellie," Augusta said. "You're killing me with your maturity."

"I'm not trying to," Nellie replied, seriously. "What makes you think I despise you at all? And if I despised William, would I be working on Apex with him? I spend more time with him than you do, because of Apex."

Suddenly Nellie, beneath her impassive stare, looked so much like a crestfallen child that Augusta felt ashamed. When would Nellie and she stop blaming each other for what their mother had started so long ago? Here Augusta had been helping Nellie let go of their mother, had, through her own growth upon reading the diaries, been showing her sister she was not condemned to molder in the past. Now she was baiting her, trying to keep her from moving forward.

"I wish," Nellie said wistfully, "I could get my hair to look like yours. I wish I could get my makeup to look like yours."

Augusta put down the iron and studied Nellie's face. "Let's get you to look like yourself," she said, and went over to her purse and extracted her makeup bag. "First off, you shouldn't wear your hair skinned back in barrettes. Less eyeshadow, and not blue—bronze, and bronze on the cheekbones too. Don't bother trying to bring out the blue in your eyes, they're green, they'll always be green—your big feature is your smashing copper hair, and you should try to get the most mileage out of it, let it work for you all down your face." Augusta fluffed out Nellie's hair, put blusher on her cheeks, wet her finger and smoothed out the shadow caked on her eyelids. "Look at you," Augusta said, when she was finished. "You could get any man you wanted looking like this!"

"Even William?" Nellie smiled sweetly. "I'm not serious," she added.

"Do you know what is serious?" Augusta said, slowly and carefully lifting the laundry, and the diaries beneath, off the washing machine. "I've always envied you."

"*You* envied *me?*" Nellie said, reaching to help Augusta,

who whisked the laundry away from her and onto a chair tucked in the corner.

"I've always thought you were smarter, and funnier," Augusta said. "You hardly studied and yet you ended up with B+'s at Vassar. I had to work double time, and I still do, to get anywhere at all. I have a mind that leaks."

"Just because I've stopped knocking myself doesn't mean you have to start knocking yourself."

"You know you have better legs than I do," Augusta said.

"You have the beautiful skin, and eyes," Nellie said. "They don't resemble a mole's."

"You have an excellent figure, better teeth, and better hands," Augusta said.

"Too bad," said Nellie, gazing at her while Augusta shook out one of William's shirts, "they didn't make just one of us." Nellie took a letter out of her pocket. "Well, you'll be glad to know I've been busy up there. I've just junked nearly the whole lot of the stuff Mother had me store in the spare room. Old opera programs and Christmas cards and letters, letters, letters. Boring letters, hundreds of them. I can't believe I ever thought all this clutter was worth saving."

"Hey, good for you," Augusta said. "You didn't toss out anything I would be interested in, did you?"

Nellie handed the letter to Augusta. "I thought you'd like to see this."

It was postmarked Florence. Augusta opened it; it was a letter written by Amenia to Lydia. It went on about the Italian mosaics, the bunions on her feet, how tired she was from walking through museums, and then it congratulated Lydia on Augusta's promotion to senior agent at Celebrities International: "You must be proud, Lydia, though I know that it will never make up for all the suffering Augusta caused you when she was an adolescent. The verbal abuse, the scatological vocabulary she subjected you to, nothing can ever make up for that." Augusta sat down.

"Augusta, I was going to destroy this letter, but I couldn't do that to you," Nellie said, coming close to her sister. "You have a right to know. And it confirms you were accurate. Amenia Woolsey-Woolsey really was a pluperfect bitch."

Augusta swallowed. "She was always such a wonderful grandmother. I really loved her. I never dreamt she felt this way." Augusta looked at Nellie. "Did you have to show me this letter?"

"Augusta, you've been telling me for weeks how terrible Grandma was to Mother, that she made her feel like an abnormal misfit—well, here's the evidence! It's not you she hated, Augusta, she hated Mother. Imagine, spoiling Mom's enjoyment of your success with a crack like that. I'm glad for this letter, I'm glad for anything that can help us demystify the Woolseys."

The kitchen door slammed and William came into the laundry room. He stared at Nellie. "Hey, you look great! You look different, your hair and everything." Then he crossed to Augusta and embraced her a little stiffly before turning to Nellie with barely repressed excitement.

"I've never seen anything like your organic wild strawberries, Nellie," William said. "They're all loaded up in the truck. They're so plump and red, and perfectly formed. And the taste! Juicy, fragrant."

"Hmm," Nellie smiled. "You make them sound like Playboy bunnies. You see," she looked at Augusta, "you can grow things very nicely without spraying them to death."

"Then you should be able to get a top price from the wholesaler. Don't forget we still have to pay for hormone spray," Augusta said.

Nellie and William were taking strawberries, radishes, and lettuce from Nellie's organic garden to a wholesaler. Everyone was excited at the sale of the orchard's first cash crop. The farm-renewal operation had been going along well. The tiny marble-sized apples that had set after the bloom were unusually plenteous, though that was a mixed blessing. Coert was afraid the normal June drop wouldn't be adequate, and that a hormone spray would be needed so that some apples would fall, allowing the rest to grow into large tasty fruit. The other crops—corn, zucchini, summer squash, tomatoes—were sprouting up green and healthy and looked as if they would be ready for harvesting by July and early August. There were some causes for concern: the mice still seemed to be proliferating around the orchard, in spite of vole poisons; and strangely, a whole block of trees near the old Christmas Orchard had not set at all. But generally, hopes were high that Woolsey Orchards would make a major recovery.

Nellie turned to William. "I phoned up for the latest tests on our well water and typed them up for you. The tetrachloride levels are getting slightly higher. I don't think we should even use the tapwater to brush our teeth. I put a bottle of mineral water in your bathroom, Augusta."

"Thanks," her sister replied. "Golly, I hope you nail those Apex bastards."

"Everytime I look down on that belching megalith," Nellie said, "I feel my blood boil. I feel like we're locked in a struggle to the death. Either they go or we go."

"Just remember to forget your emotions when we get inside the administration building," William said to Nellie. "We have to act like we belong inside those long shiny corridors." After delivering the vegetables, William and Nellie were going to the main Apex building to become familiar with it and to meet their source, a female worker whom they hoped would obtain some documents pinpointing the place where Apex was dumping industrial wastes.

William gave Augusta a peck good-bye, then he and Nellie left by the kitchen door. As he passed the laundry room window outside, he winked at Augusta, but it was an odd wink. There was something there she couldn't place. Regret? Longing? Confusion?

Augusta brought the iron down on William's shirt. The

steam hissed deliciously, rising in little bursts from the collar. She had never in her life ironed a man's shirt before. It was a kind of forbidden pleasure, like refusing to iron your man's shirts had been at the beginning of the women's movement. Outside, it was darkening. Soon rain would come, nourishing the roots of all things growing on Woolsey soil so they in turn could nourish the Woolseys. The rain would drench Nellie and William; Nellie's newly puffed hair would go flat; they would have to take cover somewhere. Augusta was glad she was here, inside, watching the lazy drip of rain on the window, feeling the steam settle under her chin; she liked the smell of the spray starch; she liked the way the cuffs perked up with a simple gesture of her arm. Moving the iron back and forth, watching the apples grow rounder and bigger every day, she understood the generations of housewives secretly loving to lose themselves in this hot steamy dreaminess.

The June wildflowers were everywhere now; she liked to watch them clutch and rock together, back and forth, on the hills beyond. At this moment she felt she belonged right here, that this was her eternal place; laying out shirts lovingly over the ironing board, breathing deeply the smell of the flowers and steam and old wood; making smooth a man's wrinkles, sleeping soundly after a day of doing small tasks well. How simple life was, really, and how complicated we make it; it should be as natural as breathing in and out, a lovely rhythm of being and letting be, of sowing and harvesting, of shaping order from chaos.

The look of her father's shirts suddenly saddened her. His polyester-mix shirts were thin and pilling; they cringed next to William's 100 percent oxford cloth. How her father would hate to see the comparison as she did! Her proud father, she felt embarrassed for him, his mustard checks and grayish whites that bleach could not lighten, lying in undefended piles, shown up by William's snappy pinstripes and snowy cuffs . . . cuffs that could still send a thrill down Augusta's belly.

Over the last weeks, something had crept into her relationship with William, something fragile and reverberating, something beyond even the uneasiness about Nellie, or the worries of the real world—Apex, the farm, her father's helplessness. It permeated their harmony; it entered every room, every bed, with them; it whispered through the empty spaces of their embraces, was felt like a cold draft in the corners. It was as though their union had been borne like pollen on the wind and was fated to darken and fall like the tender blossom of the apple.

For some reason, William's kiss just then, before he had gone off with Nellie, had brought with it the cold hand of ancient memory, reminding her of her unfaithful father's obligatory embracing of his wife. How the currents of past and present must be jumbled about in her unconscious, Augusta thought. But she couldn't deny it, there was something so sickeningly familiar about the triangle that had been created by Nellie, William, and herself. It was as though they were the living Doppelgängers of her mother, her father, and her father's mistress. While reading the diaries this morning, Augusta had quickly passed over a section about Henry's first extramarital affair: when he came back to his wife's bedroom, Lydia had written, he did not come alone, but brought for all time the palpable presence of his mistress.

Augusta put down the iron. That was it; she had not realized it, but she felt like the mistress in her own love triangle: she was sleeping with the man who rightfully belonged to her sister.

Augusta extracted the diaries, and after some hesitation took up the volume that told the story of Henry's first venture into adultery.

March 16, 1949

*H*enry is getting restless; I cannot plead postpartum difficulties any longer. They have machines for everything now, Daddy has even made one for polishing boots (though, as usual, it doesn't quite work), so why can't they make a machine to satisfy a man's lust?

I am terrified he will leave us. If it weren't for the dirt, I would be tempted to send him to one of those red-light houses in the city.

I'm so tired at night, I just can't bear to do the things he wants me to do. I was shocked at my own daydream the other day: I imagined that I asked Henry's secretary, a rather plain young woman who comes in part-time to help him with the real estate ledgers, to help Henry in another way, and thereby me as well.

July 1, 1949

I don't know whether it was the starry nights, or the way the crickets sound so sweet this summer, or just that I had not seen my lovely Man for so very long. We met down in the orchards for the first time in years and years, and though we barely touched, only talked, he made me want sex. Like I have not wanted it since he last touched me seven years ago. I am a mother, and to have a liaison with Him would be unfair to my children. What I want to do is to make love to Henry again.

For the last several nights, I have been feeling it strongly. My toes crawl up Henry's pant legs beneath the dinner table, and Henry looks at me dumbfounded. My breasts are throbbing. What on earth has come over me? I know the family sees my lack of restraint and that they are confused. Is it that I am approaching forty, and my hormones have begun to rush? Can I suddenly feel the cold shadow of death? Or has that lock on my body finally rusted through and broken, that pearl of moral righteousness that I clasped to my bosom finally rolled away? This purity, this secret chastity, I thought it was my sustenance, my salvation, what made the loneliness bearable. But it was as much a chimera as Hopestill's priceless ruby; a false comfort that brought me nothing but needless sorrow. Now, something in me has burst forth indelicately. I have stopped hovering and fussing over the children; I race the car on back roads. I yearn to feel Henry's weight upon me, to entwine myself round him all night. Last night, I had what I think, what we both think, was my first orgasm. He lay smoking afterward and shook his head and said, "Why did it have to happen now?" He was right. All those years wasted trying to keep my body as pure as polished agate.

August 20, 1949

*H*enry has been at an apiary conference for two weeks, but I know that he is not in the pines of New Jersey. I know it because of how his skin smelled, like violets, like some woman's violet toilet water. I know it because the whiskey has been so strong on his breath that even the cloves couldn't hide it. I know it because the night before he left, when he thought I was asleep, he untangled me from his body and pushed me to the other side of the bed.

It is so quiet in this house, there is a quietness that seems loud. Grandfather glides round noiselessly in his wheelchair and looks at me with concern. My heart goes cold when the telephone rings, but it is not Henry, it is never Henry.

August 25, 1949

*A*pple crisp, warm from the oven, dripping with brown sugar, plump raisins popping in your mouth, and spoonful after spoonful of fresh whipped cream . . . each time the cream melts into the cake, you put another spoonful on. When you put maple syrup and honey on too, it has a sweetness so intense, it wraps you like a bandage.

September 1, 1949

I've invented a marvelous dish—mashed potatoes, drizzled with melted butter, stirred up with bacon and deep-fried onion rings and slathered with gravy.

Gran Millie found seventeen candy wrappers hidden underneath my bed, and I couldn't even bring myself to feel ashamed.

September 6, 1949

I have gained twenty-five pounds. I cling to Augusta. Without her I would have no one, for I cannot bear to let anyone else know anything is wrong. Poor Augusta knows plenty is wrong. She knows how her father has betrayed me. She invents these stories to make me feel better. She says a letter came from New Jersey telling about the bees he has seen but that she lost it.

It is terrible to be seven and have no father. I took her to the drive-in to cheer her up, but she was so upset when I ate four pepperburgers that she began to cry.

September 8, 1949

*S*ometimes I think I have acquired so much adipose tissue so that I have a nice cushion to lie back on, safely removed from the hurt of the world. It is easy for a fat person to hide emotions. The layers disguise the trembling of the heart. I can hold the fat on either side of my rib cage; "love handles," they are called, but I think of them as arms which have slipped gently round me from behind.

September 13, 1949

*A*fter Henry was spotted on a street in the backwaters of Albany, my family apparently decided Henry Bean was not going to escape the way Sam Beaumont had. With Henry gone, Daddy and Mama have worked overtime on the harvest, but they dropped everything and went and hauled him back home. He had been on a frightful bender with that secretary, or rather that former secretary, but since his audience with Great-grandfather, he has been slinking about like a whipped animal.

I try to feel sorry for him, but every time I do, his distance, his reticence, his refusal to do what he should— throw himself at my feet and beg forgiveness—makes me go cold. He is a dipsomaniac. He takes medicine to help him stay off liquor. His hands shake so, his chin is covered with shaving nicks, and his breath is foul on my cheek. His face is dead white. Like my own father, Henry's only real mistress is a cool, smooth, glistening bottle of booze. As far as he's concerned, everything else could be wiped off the face of the earth.

September 20, 1949

*T*he agony won't stop. I keep thinking about those little things of Henry's that were once my province alone: the funny cowlick in his pubic hair, the scar on his thigh. I cannot bear that her perspiration, her perfume, the infinitesimal traces of her makeup, have been between my sheets.

In bed, I am stone again, I have gone back inside myself. He showers, he scrubs, but still I smell that perfume . . . that cheap revolting scent of violets.

October 1, 1949

*E*verything about Henry sends me into a rage. I suddenly see how unpleasantly he eats—looking down at his plate, taking an eternity to assess, cut, and lift three bites of food to his mouth. And instead of being perfect, as he should be after what he has done, he still throws around his clothes, not caring where they land. His silence in the face of my nagging infuriates me, makes me believe he's even guiltier than I think.

October 8, 1949

*T*he gaskets finally blew. Henry and I had such a terrible fight, I don't know that we'll ever get over it. He threw books at the wall. He put his hand through the window; blood and glass were everywhere. Then he started banging my head against the wall until Augusta came in screaming. She crouched in the corner and screamed and screamed until he left the room. He has moved into the spare room and I will never let him back.

He tried to blame me, said I hinted he should have carnal relations with his secretary and then, when he did, that I staged a sudden seizure of desire for him. As if I could help that! He said he would have left me if it weren't for the children. He says all I do is belittle him, make him sink lower and lower, make him feel like half a man.

That is because he is. He used to be able to make my heart flutter, he used to be my tall, gallant cowboy. He can make me sob, he can make me furious, but he cannot make me respect him ever again. John Wayne has fallen off his horse and into his own spittoon.

The family is excruciatingly polite to Henry, and goes to great pretentious lengths to pretend what happened never happened. At the dinner table, Mama and Grandma chirp like a couple of telephone operators about the interesting shades of nail varnish at Newbury's. The only sign that anyone thinks something amiss is that Gran Millie has taken to carrying silk handkerchiefs from her wedding trousseau and sitting down at the piano to play "Nearer My God to Thee" until I want to scream.

He said he did not love me anymore. He said he had stopped loving me. He said it very quietly, and when he did, my world fell apart. I think that I could have borne his adultery, I think that I could have borne anything if he had not said that.

Sweat was coming up on Augusta's forehead. She put down the volume, left the heat of the laundry room, went outside, gulped fresh air. But nothing would stop the rush of her memory. She heard her parents teasing each other, the teasing suddenly shifting into a darker tone, the tension growing brittler by the minute—when will her father erupt, when will her bitter, berating mother suddenly turn into a scared rabbit under its force? Augusta, age seven, chattering away, trying to drown out the icy silence, trying to keep the volcano from erupting. It is late on a dark night now. She is watching out her window, listening for the sound of wheels on the gravel, running downstairs when she sees her father reel around the front of the car and rip the skirt of her mother's satin dress, shining pearly in the headlights. Another night—this time Augusta has a friend over and they are telling ghost stories in the dark. Suddenly the sounds of thumping, muffled yells, it's only my parents' television, don't be afraid, don't go! Augusta, crouching against her parents' closed door, praying for the fighting to subside, and then, when it only worsens, the sickening approach of the final action, the only one that will unfailingly quiet her father. Augusta bursts in, throws her arms around his waist, her nose jammed against his belt buckle, his stomach going up and down, squeezing him tightly so his breathing will slow, telling him to stop, she loves him, she loves him, when actually, at that moment, she hates him more than anything.

Augusta surveyed the lush lawn, such a peaceful pastoral backdrop for such dramas of repression and violence. On the night of the bedroom fight described in the diary, Augusta must have learned that she was essential to their marriage, that only she could stop her father's violence. To see her parents reunited in the canopied bed, to hear her father say he loved her mother after all, it had become her most passionate childhood wish, a wish that came true only at the end of her mother's life, when Henry came back to give her love, not through sex, but through sickness.

As Augusta grew older, her role as peacemaker became more intricate. She became deceptive, clever as a snake-oil salesman. She would hide behind corners, gather information, and work to sabotage their fights. She would secretly clean up her father's messes, his jars of insects left in the bathroom. She got her father to write "I love you" on a little card, ostensibly as a keepsake for Augusta, but instead she put it on a little box of Valentine's Day chocolates under her mother's pillow. That was so successful that every Christmas since, Augusta bought lingerie or jewelry for her father to give her mother. The one year she did not, Henry gave Lydia a last-minute pair of cheap gloves bought at the drugstore, and the look on Lydia's face was so heart-wrenching that Augusta never fell down on the job again.

She told outrageous lies. She told her mother that her father had said she was the most beautiful woman alive; she told her father that her mother had fixed her hair, bought new clothes, done her nails, especially for him. Augusta hung mistletoe in hopes they would go under it. When they miraculously started kissing good-bye in the morning, Augusta's heart thrilled— until she learned her mother had asked him to do it for Augusta's sake.

Augusta went back into the house and began to press a shirt of her father's. The most difficult times had been when her father was having an affair. That required her to be doubly vigilant, to see that the illusion that he was not having extramarital affairs was not endangered. The illusion, it seemed to her, kept the family from falling apart. In these periods, when her father was drinking heavily, when he came home late night after night, or feigned an out-of-town bee or farming conference, her mother retreated from the outside world. She did not seem to have the confidence, or the independence from her anxiety about Henry, even to volunteer at the hospital.

Augusta would hide liquor from her father. She would sometimes steal the money from his wallet when he was in the shower, because she thought if he didn't have it, he couldn't spend it on anyone else. Once, she found a pack of condoms in his pocket and she cut them to bits and flushed them down the toilet.

Even in college, when her mother would come to her weeping, "I think your father is having an affair," Augusta would reassure her that no, no, she was sure he wasn't. And in fact she needed to believe her own propaganda, even in the face of the phone calls from women and hard facts to the contrary. The illusion was for herself too. She could never bear to abandon hope, to face the fact that her mission had failed.

Even now, with her mother dead and buried, the thought of her father coming home with another woman on his arm made her stomach twist up in knots. Sometimes Augusta would wake with the same dream, always a deep dream, as if she had been dragged out of a well: somewhere in the world, she would discover some hidden shred of evidence, some testimonial that would allow her to utter the truth that would bring her mother back to life, "Look! He loves you after all, Daddy does love you!"

"You're ironing my shirts?" Henry's voice made Augusta jump and she burned herself on the iron. Henry immediately took her over to the laundry sink and put her hand under the tap. "The secret to treating burns is put them right under the cold water. No butter or grease, that would be like frying an egg on a griddle. . . . Gosh, nobody's ironed my shirts for ages. What a wonderful treat. It makes me want to wear them." Henry was, as usual, in his pajamas, though it was past noon. "You'll never know what a difference your coming home has made," he added, putting his arm around Augusta.

His voice was so deep and soothing that Augusta, her finger throbbing, felt her eyes fill with tears. Through her parents' battles, through her own struggles with her mother, that voice had weaved a soft, iridescent path of comfort, allowing her to forgive him for his temper, his violence against her mother. Though Augusta had often taken comfort with Coert, it was her father's simple ministrations that she remembered: whispering in the dark, bringing her a glass of water, lifting it to her lips, tucking the blanket right up to her chin.

Standing here, allowing him to hold her fingers beneath cool water, she remembered how much she had adored him when she was five or six: she had wanted only that he be hers forever. But it had frightened her: would her mother find out that her father really loved Augusta best? The fights between her parents filled her with shame and terror, those naked looks of hate! Was she the cause, had her mother discovered the truth? But then it turned out that he did not want Augusta after all. He chose other women altogether and betrayed them both.

Augusta turned off the tap and pulled her hand away.

"Daddy, don't you think you should get dressed and go down and help out in the orchards?" Augusta said, realizing that since her mother's death, his daughters had taken up Lydia's nagging chant—a tone that meant he could ignore them.

He tapped his dead pipe in a wicker wastebasket whose holes were bigger than the flakes of tobacco ash.

"Oh Dad, look what you did," Augusta said crossly, pointing to the mess on the floor. Henry seemed not to hear her.

"I've been looking for things," he said. "In spite of all your work, this house is a nightmare. I feel like a rabbit at the bottom of a landslide."

"So do I," Augusta said irritably. She gazed at his unshaven face, his fine hair sticking up all over the place, and she suddenly remembered an earlier father, a tall, chivalrous gentleman who would race several yards to open a door for her college friends, or make them swoon by giving them his shy little "half-moon" smile and saying, "My, you look nice." He would come into her room and, unable to talk about important things, about feelings, he would look around for something to fix—a stuck window, a shelf that needed leveling, an unsafe scatter rug that needed tacking to the floor, any concrete little thing he could do to show his love. He had been protective, heroic: if outlaws stormed a room, you could be sure he would be the first one to lunge at their guns.

But now he had become so much less than a hero: dependent, deceptive, a shirker, disappearing into his own sullen depressions. He would cry over someone else's tragedy, but pretend his own had never happened.

"Dad," Augusta said. "What are you going to do when I have to leave here? Both Nellie and I can't stay here forever. Who is going to iron your clothes and nag you into taking care of yourself?"

"I'll manage just fine," Henry said gruffly. "I always have."

"No," Augusta said, knowing that his "just fine" was the overt part of the message, while his pajamas were the covert part; he was wearing them in order to keep her at home. "You just pretend to be a self-sufficient hermit, but really you want to be taken care of. *You* could learn to iron, or make a bed, or hire a maid, or farm this farm, for Pete's sake. Or sell this house and get another job!" Now that all the Woolsey grand-parents were dead, now that her mother was gone, Augusta realized that it was her father who had replaced them, making Augusta fear that he would pull her in, prevent her escape.

Henry stared at her, at the steam coming up from the iron under Augusta's chin, and he thought of Lydia on their honey-moon, immersed in the hot bath, her lovely hair tied up. While searching for her engagement ring, Henry had been remember-ing the fresh, eager girl who had once been his wife, who had sent a ribbon of love down his back, that wide-eyed, magnifi-cent female who had not yet begun to level him with a cold penetrating stare, who did not try to control him the way she later did. Could they ever have been the same person? When had that girl died, when had she given way to the woman who perished as his wife?

Henry looked at Augusta. "Sometimes I don't get dressed because I don't know how. I wear a plaid shirt with checked pants, and to me the colors match perfectly, but you laugh at me. You don't realize what your mother did for me: she told me how to behave at parties, what to say. She told me when I was making a fool of myself, when to stop drinking."

"Dad, I'm leaving right after my birthday," Augusta said. "Nellie will probably move out on her own soon too. And you can't even take out the garbage!"

"I didn't know you were leaving that soon," Henry said. "Can't you stay at least till the end of the harvest? I've been doing the best I can, Augusta," he added, wobbling over to a chair. "It's hard for me to do much with this hip."

Augusta closed her eyes. Here it came—he could swing her around like a child through the air; he could move her with such rapidity from rage to pity, from self-righteous indignation to crippling guilt. "Dad, will you please see a doctor? For the last time—please?"

"I don't want to spend the money," Henry said. "And we don't have it. My hip is fine."

Who was this man anyway? Not for the first time, the question crossed Augusta's mind. Just like her mother, he was two people in one; Janus-faced, ever-changing. As soon as she decided one thing about him, he seemed to prove her wrong. Was he a manipulative, deceitful alcoholic, or a kind, martyred father, picked on, belittled, and sexually starved?

Henry looked at Augusta and smiled. "You were the most beautiful baby. Did I ever tell you what the nurses at the hospital said? They put these little pink ribbons in your—"

"I know, Dad," Augusta said. "Don't tell me again." Guilt was weaving a web all around her. She had so much, he had so little. She had life, while his was dwindling away. She was the only thing he had left. If she went, he would probably never get dressed, let alone get out of bed. Then again, if she stayed, he might not either.

"I never did feel the same way about Nellie," Henry went on, ignoring Augusta's protests. "I've never had the same relationship with her that I've had with you."

"Please stop," Augusta said, and looked down to see she had scorched the collar of his shirt. "Don't worry," she sighed. "Maybe I can stay through the harvest."

"And maybe for Christmas?" Henry asked, brushing the ashes from his chest.

CHAPTER 13

The exultation that had accompanied the sale of the first Woolsey crop three weeks ago had been washed away in a torrent of rain that had fallen unremittingly, drenching the crops and giving rise to fungi and pests even Coert had never seen before. Some of the tomatoes, so carefully planted and tended through May and June, were rotting on the ground, literally drowned to death; others, starved of sun, had not even flowered and set. Today was the first dry day in the month of July, and Coert and Augusta were touring the peach trees, which had been hit with a fungus whose spores had spread like a plague from tree to tree.

"Just incredible, this weather," Coert said, wiping his hands on his pockets. "Everything's turned around. First it was too cold to plant and now it's too wet for anything to grow. And they're predicting a nice surprise for August—a lovely drought!"

Augusta reached up to touch a bough on one of the peach trees. Its leaves were curling up with fungus, and the peaches had swollen so big with water that they had split. She pulled one off, broke it open, and sucked the flesh. "It's delicious, in fact. It's *very* sweet. Coert, we can't sell these for produce, but maybe the wholesaler who buys Daddy's honey could find us a nice homemade jam manufacturer. We could turn them into jam and jelly!"

"No one makes homemade jam anymore, Missy," Coert said, throwing down a split peach in disgust. "And what about the tomatoes? The patch looks like the field at Bunker Hill after the charge of the redcoats. The zucchini and squash will be the next to blacken, and that will be a nice state of affairs, seeing as how we counted on them to produce revenue the rest of the summer."

"Not all the tomatoes are ruined," Augusta said as they came into the sown fields. She squatted, picked up a stick, and wound a vine of tiny, unsplit tomatoes around it. "We can stake the survivors so they're protected from the wet ground."

"What about the corn? Every other one is bent over by stalk bore. And the apples! Scab's all over the Romes. The spray schedule's gone to hell in a handbasket. Soon as I cover 'em, rain comes and washes the stuff right off. Now I'm out of spray. It's a losing battle. We can't keep going the way we are, Miss Augusta."

"We'll buy more fungicide, Coert. We'll get more pesticides. And we'll keep on trying until we beat the odds. We've come too far to stop now."

"Huh. Then Apex'll have nothing on us—this whole place will be swimming in poison. Maybe William and Nellie *are* on to something about them industrial wastes affecting the trees." Coert spat out a wad of tobacco. "Maybe we got some wild new breeds of pests raised on a diet of chemicals. Maybe they're resistant to all known pesticides. Maybe they can outwit even old-time farmers like me."

"Coert." Augusta put her arm around him. What a typical valley farmer he was, she thought, with his nay-aying and his obsession with doom and disaster. It was easy now to stand away and appreciate him for what he was—now that she knew he was not her father.

"I've finally figured you out. You put the worst face on

things for a reason. Because people don't blame you if it turns out you're right and things go bad on the farm, and they feel everlasting gratitude to you if it turns out you're wrong and things are just fine."

Coert looked at her sideways, then pointed to the sky. "Hear that? That ain't Henry Hudson bowling. That's thunder, coming out of the highlands."

"Not more rain," Augusta groaned.

"Worse than rain. Sounds like the beginnings of a major storm, kind that tears the branches off the trees. I can feel it on my ankles, low winds, kind of rustling the grass."

"I don't feel anything," Augusta said, looking down at her sneakers.

"When my grandmother was a child in Utrecht, they'd get these low winds crawling like moles along the ground. Called them gusts of doom. She told about how they would get stronger through the day till the house shook and the cooking utensils would rattle on their hooks. Meat cleaver jumped right down off its peg once and sliced off the tip of her thumb. There was so much blood it soaked the tomcat and the cat went tearing out of the house and was shot by my grandfather, who was running home in the storm and thought it was a red fox."

Augusta stared at Coert and suddenly started to laugh. Coert, after a few seconds, began to laugh himself, and they were still chuckling when Augusta left him to deal with the rotting tomato plants.

Augusta went down the path and into the rows of Red Delicious, where her mother had loved to walk. She felt the heaviness come over her again. She had had to pretend cheery optimism to keep up everyone's spirits, but inside, she had a fear whose pressure was building as sure as Coert's storm clouds. Two days ago, she had come across a diary entry of July 1952, in which her mother had identified the Mystery Man whom she had met intermittently in the orchards. The name made her sick at heart.

And it made her close Lydia's diaries again in despair. Nellie and William were exhausting themselves in vain trying to locate the Apex toxic-waste dump, her father was behaving strangely, everyone was depressed about the weather, and Augusta had to concentrate in order to hold things together. The last thing she needed was the long arm of the past to once again come up and clutch her. The fact that her mother had put a name to the Man had once and for all eliminated the possibility that he was a fantasy, and increased the possibility that he had ended Lydia's infertility and sired Augusta.

But it was the name itself that had shocked Augusta, and overwhelmed her with its implications for her life now. It had returned her to an old place of childhood terror—a darkened room, the shades ominously flapping, the shaft of moonlight playing over her toys while her nightgown grew wet with panic, something oozing its way along her floor, crouching by her bedside, ready to rip the tattered baby blanket from her arms, tear her away from her shiny bicycles and her embroidered dresses and all the little artifacts that made her the daughter of Lydia and Henry Bean; ready to rip her away from herself.

She could tell herself a hundred times that it did not matter whether or not she had come from the seed of her father, whether or not she was a bastard under the law: her parents were her parents, they had raised her. She could tell herself that a thousand times, but she still knew that it mattered, it mattered terribly to that bogeyman who still lay waiting inside her. It was ready at a moment's notice to show her that her mother's rages at her—the way she gazed at her with hatred and said "Who do you think you are?"—her parents' bloody fights, her father's affairs, they sprang, all of them, from that dirty secret: Augusta was the living evidence of her mother's original sin. She had grown unwanted inside Lydia, a scarlet letter, a stigma put on this earth to forever remind the Woolseys that their moral foundations were a sham; she was an alien lump of clay, an accident of lust, a creation dirty and suspect.

Augusta had rifled the diaries for anything that would settle her parentage once and for all, but found nothing. Even proof of her illegitimacy would have been easier to accept than this frozen hinterland of dread, the agony of not knowing. She had to know, even though she would rather have the Man be anyone else—Coert, an apple picker, a milkman, even a criminal—anyone on earth but the person her mother had named.

Things had been too busy, and Augusta had been too ashamed to tell William about the discovery, but she knew now, seeing him come down the hill through a row of Empires, that she could delay it no longer.

When they were a few inches from each other, William leaned forward, put his hands on her shoulders, and brought his forehead against hers. He sighed heavily. "Don't tell me we're actually alone. How long do we have before Coert or your father or Nellie will pop out of the trees?"

Augusta brought a comforting hand to his neck. He smelled so good, he felt so good. Almost automatically, her hand slipped underneath his shirt, and as she felt the hard muscles of his stomach contract, felt the goosebumps come up like soft sandpaper, she felt lust sweep over her. They had not made love in three days.

She could not tell him, not right now. Sex would wipe it out, would, for a time, wipe out this fear which kept poking up like a shard of glass. Sex had become her new ally, her new narcotic; at least she was no longer using unworthy men to obliterate herself, at least she was using her own resources, the power of her newfound sexuality.

She led him over to a grove of locusts near the stream. "Don't talk," she said, "don't say a single word." She hooked her thumbs around his belt buckle; he lifted her T-shirt, took her breasts in his mouth. He ran his lips down her belly and between her legs, then slipped off her shorts. She cried out, fell over his shoulder, twisted him around on top of her, caught his wavy dark-olive hair in her toes, brought her toenails down his back, hugged him tight with her thighs, wondered if she was slowing the flow of blood through his carotid artery, hugged him tighter still while the rest of her body was rendered limp, shot through with a drug that subjected it to spasms of terrible pleasure, severing every last thread of control. Her ego, her superego had fled. She was all id. And she was at his mercy.

The sky between the tall locusts was blackening; she was sinking down into a starry well of blackness, of black and white sensation rippling like the Milky Way, streaking up through her solar plexus, stars flashing, blinding her as his tongue reached way up inside her, up up into her inner universe, edging toward extinction, hurtling through the air, swimming, gasping, lost amid shattering waves, all legs, arms, rubbery, boneless, vibrating, shaking, an octopus whose tentacles were fluted with buds of feeling, his tongue playing on her, his very breath blowing shrill notes of conclusion upon her many limbs.

When she lay exhausted, nearly dead, he rose, looking like a muscular fisherman, his skin shiny in the half-light before the storm, illuminated by a bolt of lightning, raising his spear above her, sinking it into the soft flesh of her body. But now, she suddenly felt nothing. Her attention became fixed elsewhere, upon the trees bending above, upon Coert's gusts of doom; leaves whirling down like babies from their cradle. It was as though the William she knew were no longer there; it was as though this were some stranger shivering inside her like a pupa struggling to be born. As she felt him shed himself inside her, she was touched, but strangely, it did not touch her; she was as detached as if she had been sitting at table watching him pluck his way to the heart of an artichoke.

This must have been how her mother had felt with Henry Bean, the man who called himself Augusta's father; like a fallen comet, a stone left dead and cold on the ground. But how had it been with the Mystery Man? Had Lydia once lain here at dawn, her back pressed against the warm bed of leaves, her cheek next to His, her long, taut, agonized body burst asunder, flying apart in bright soft sparks that lasted a lifetime? Had her mother been filled with love and with life by the father of the man who shuddered with ecstasy on top of Augusta right now?

"Where are you?" William asked. They were watching raindrops come through the trees. "Not here with me."

Augusta turned to face him. "You remember me telling you my mother had this man, this mysterious Man she wrote about, the one who was probably her lover? Well, he was real, she named him. In a diary entry. William, it was your father."

He sat up, blinked. "My father?" he said. "My *father?*"

Augusta nodded. "The look on your face is exactly the look that might be on my mother's and your father's faces if they could see us now."

"Your mother and my father?" William gazed at her dumbly. "Oh, God."

"No matter how you try to get away from it, every damn thing comes right back to the family!" Augusta said. "Even our attraction is probably inherited. They're beating us from the grave with their genes! Lord, I never dreamed your father and my mother were anything more than friends. I get this eerie sense that we're completing the cycle or something—that we're finishing what they started."

"How long did it go on?"

"I don't know." Augusta sighed heavily. "But I'm afraid that what matters is when it started. It only needed to happen once. They began their affair about thirteen months before I was born. William, you could be my brother. My half-brother."

William stared at her. "That's crazy," he said softly, pulling his shirt over his lap. "That's absolutely crazy."

"Listen. There's something I haven't told you—a little like your not getting around to telling me that you made Arlene Casey pregnant," Augusta said. "A couple of years ago, Mother and I were fighting about my leaving her one vacation so I could go on a trip with Dad. She was livid, she was hysterical, and she implied that Daddy wasn't really my father. Oh, afterwards she took it back, showed me my birth certificate and other stuff. But since then I've never really felt sure about who my father really is."

William hastily pulled on his pants. He handed Augusta her clothes. "That must have been incredibly hard for you." He did not take his eyes off her.

"Mother filled diary after diary with the anguish of her infertility. She tried everything, but she just couldn't conceive. Then one night she couldn't sleep, so she went for a walk in the orchards. Then, Geronimo, she met Mystery Man who turned her on like she hadn't ever been turned on. And then, a few months later, she was pregnant."

"It must have been just before dawn," William frowned. "That's when he would come to the orchards . . . so he could see the birds come out to feed at sunrise."

William stared at Augusta. The drizzle was separating his curls. He looked primitive, prehistoric almost. His hair was shiny and black, and his face deathly pale.

"She never said that they actually had intercourse," Augusta said quickly. "Maybe my worries are unfounded. Maybe this moonlight infatuation only involved a few stolen kisses. Maybe it excited her hormones or relaxed her enough to conceive a child."

"We don't look anything alike," William said. "Not even a freckle in common. You're fair, I'm dark."

"My mother was fair, your father was dark," Augusta said absently.

William suddenly rose and pulled Augusta up. "I don't believe it, I just don't believe it at all. That my father is your father. And neither do you. Otherwise you couldn't possibly have wanted to make love just now."

"Do you think that's why Mother filled me full of sexual fear, because she knew I was dating my own sibling?" Augusta asked, slipping on her shorts and shirt. "Remember how she was always hovering around us?"

"In that case, she wouldn't have hated it so much when we broke up. For Christ's sake, Augusta, if my father were your father we'd know by now. My father never would have died without telling me."

"Maybe my mother didn't tell *him*. I'm scared, William. Don't be impatient with me. I'm worried. And you're worried too, don't try to deny it. You keep looking at my stomach. I'm not pregnant, I haven't missed a day of the pill, so that's one thing we don't need to worry about. Oh God, thinking about this is a nightmare."

The rain was coming fast now. "Let's get out of here," William said. His clothes were becoming heavy with moisture. "Can I tell you about my nightmare? I keep thinking that all this rain is bringing in a wash of toxic wastes from over there, into the water supply, into the fragile new one-year whips, the vegetables, everything. The stream has been overflowing, and I keep seeing that toxic dump flooding, that is if there is a dump. Nellie and I have combed the whole woods next to the Apex property, and we can't find anything. We've even stood up on the tractor from every vantage point, to try to see down into the woodland next to the Christmas Orchard. Nothing, nothing at all. Maybe it's a chimera, maybe it's a gigantic rumor with no foundation."

Augusta huddled closer to William as they emerged from the woods and went up the hill toward the house. "Do you know the worst thing about this, for me anyway?" she asked. "Everything looks different, everything I've struggled to understand and put in place about my past is suddenly atilt; it all takes on a different meaning if I'm illegitimate."

William stopped her. It was raining harder. "Listen to me, listen to me closely, Augusta. Your mother might have been a troubled woman, but she was not a maniac. She knew we might one day find each other again, and she would have warned you if we had the same father. She would not have left you a million words, she would not have left you all these explanations, all these answers, these truths, these secrets, without telling you the biggest truth of all."

"You know," Augusta said wistfully, "there's a part of me, just a little part, that was excited when I found out it was your father. He was a great character, strong, energetic. I'd be kind of proud to think I was his daughter."

William stopped. "You'd rather have him as your father than me as your lover?"

"Oh William, really!"

He wiped the rain off his forehead and shook it violently off his hand. "I guess I always knew Dad was never as righteous as he seemed. I'm not surprised he had something on the side. I suppose that's why he couldn't get too upset when your mother told him about me knocking up Arlene."

"You don't have to make it sound so sordid," Augusta said. "He didn't intend to seduce Mother. You should read what she wrote. She painted this picture, this beautiful picture, of a woman in a pink satin robe walking through the moonlit orchards, suddenly coming upon this shy, unsuspecting man."

"Who then cheated on his wife so he could take her to church and drown out the rest of his pew with his booming words about the righteous inheriting the earth."

"It *wasn't* that way. It was romantic, it was as romantic as what happened to us."

William looked at her. "And what did happen to us, Augusta? Has it really been so romantic? Or has our affair been about something else?"

"What do you mean?"

"Oh look, why don't you just come right out and admit that you basically want me for my body."

Augusta laughed. "That's exactly what I used to say to you! A long time ago."

"What's so romantic about the fact we have sex without

talk? What's romantic about the fact that we don't even talk
about dreams or plans, or what we really care about? Oh look,
sometimes you tell me about what's in your mother's diaries,
but today has been the first time you've told me how they make
you feel, what's going through your mind and all. And yes, I
tell you about my latest Apex adventure, but I know that you
couldn't care less. I don't get out two sentences before you've
got me in bed and so excited I've forgotten about it."

"Oh, and I suppose you're an innocent victim of my lust?
I don't notice you keeping your hands to your sides, William
Hurley!"

"I know. I can't be near you without wanting you. But it
takes up too much space, this passion; it eats up everything
else."

"And what are we supposed to do about it? Sit across the
room and have Socratic intercourse? Don't you want to make
love to me anymore?"

"Yes, yes, yes. Oh look, it's just that you seem to be going
down one track and I'm going down another and all we have
in common is that when we get within two feet of each other,
we slap together like steel and a magnet."

Augusta turned away from him. The rain had suddenly
stopped. "You know I don't want to live here in the valley."

He took her arm, turned her around to face him. "Augusta,
I'm sick of being alone, of bouncing around. When I found you
again, I thought that things could change. In these past weeks,
we've helped each other grow up, grow out of the emotional
ruts that have made us so unhappy. We've freed each other up,
but for what? Augusta, you're not in this relationship for the
long haul, are you?"

"I've been telling you that, or trying to!" Augusta said.
"William, you already know yourself, you know what you want
and what you want is right here in this town."

"Stonekill Landing is just a place on a map. Places aren't
people. If you love someone, it doesn't matter where you live.
That's secondary."

"But it's not, William. Places reflect people, what people are. You fit into this town, you want the kind of life it offers. I don't want it, I want to get away from it. I want to travel and see different people and places. Five generations of my family have been chained to this bloody land. You know that I have to leave, you know I can't ever find a way to feel free until I do!"

"Nellie seems to be finding a way," William said quietly.

"I'm not Nellie," Augusta said. "Though maybe you wish I was."

Augusta yanked a rotten tomato plant up by its roots and threw it down. "I'm not my sister," she sighed. "But I can never forget the fact that I could be yours.

"You want to know more about my feelings," Augusta went on. "I'll tell you. I feel disgusted with myself. You're right. I'm an uncontrolled animal. And, let's face it, our sex has gotten more and more carnal. Even the possibility of our sharing the same father couldn't dampen me. I've gone from being a prude to a nymphomaniac!"

"Maybe you've outgrown our relationship," William said. "Maybe you're saying that you've had your coming out party, your sexual debutante fling, and it's over and your only regret is that you let yourself go quite so wild."

Augusta saw the plaintive expression on his face, his brown, beagle eyes, the curls falling on his forehead; she felt a stirring again in her belly and she was afraid. What she had celebrated, rejoiced in, she now feared. What if her lust overtook her, prevented her from leaving: what if her sexual liberation sabotaged her much more important liberation from her past?

William returned Augusta's gaze. Her skin looked magically beautiful to him; soft and translucent, like a still-life covered with drops of glistening rain. "I don't want to lose you," he said.

She rested her head against his chest. "I wish I were different. I wish life were different. When I'm close to you this way, it does feel different. If I could just stay this way long enough . . . "

He kissed hot tears from the corners of her eyes. As their lips met, as she became lost in the hot, roiling sea of his kiss, she thought she would love nothing better than to marry this kind, handsome, voluptuous man. And then, as the mud came up around her feet, another less-welcome thought came to her: they had had a wonderful love affair that had broken ground for both of them; it had begun and would end in the soft slippery rain-soaked earth.

Nellie carefully closed the door of William's empty bedroom, smiling to herself. Then she went up to Augusta's room and cautiously slipped inside. She was being very careful these days, careful and calculating and thoroughly different. Never in her life had she been able to so skillfully take charge of events, execute a plan, and carry through with it. Everything was unfolding as she had hoped. For the last ten days, she had checked both of their rooms daily, their pillows, their sheets, the rugs, and there was no evidence that they had been in each other's beds. Moreover, she was quite sure she sensed a growing distance between them.

And, meanwhile, she and William had been slogging through wet woodland, shivering in factory basements, waiting on damp corners for documents to be delivered, sprawling knee to knee on couches poring over data. They had a mission, a passion, and each discovery they made, each failure they endured, brought them closer. People fell in love, people stayed together because of this. Sartre and de Beauvoir . . . Tracy and Hepburn . . . Pierre and Marie Curie. And the literature of love was full of scenes in which the doctor suddenly looked at the nurse, the teacher noticed his student assistant for the first time, the man took off his glasses after the applause had died and suddenly he knew he loved the woman who had made it all possible.

William did not know it yet, but she had been showing him, slowly, by increments, how well suited to each other they were. How easy and humorous their banter was, how excited they both became about the town and the environment. The ideas just cascaded when they began to talk. When the three of them were together, it was plain as day: Augusta and William were linked through sexual electricity, but had very little to say to each other; it was between Nellie and William that the conversation crackled.

She loved that man just the way he was; she would not change a thing about him, and what man could say that about the woman he loved?

It was so close. She could feel it. She thought of how often she had stood at the perimeters of life, watching her mother and Augusta, the family's centrifugal forces. If the two sisters were standing in a room, people always gravitated toward Augusta first, like nails to a magnet. And Augusta didn't even know it; she stood there among the starving as bewildered as Marie Antoinette. Even Great-great-grandfather Cornelius, who had wanted so much to celebrate Nellie, his namesake, could not help, even at the age of a hundred, being entranced by Augusta. Her eyelids excited him: "Best lids I've seen yet in the family, most like mine." Nellie had worked on stretching the folds of her own eyelids after that, but no one had ever even noticed them.

Nellie used to have a theory that sisters are like electrons and protons encased in the atom of the family, each one endowed with a positive or negative force without which the atom could not exist. She thought nothing could ever change for her; her effect was preordained, she was fated to be on the outer edge while Augusta's positive force was centered in the nucleus. Good old faithful Nellie, waiting in the wings until she could make herself useful, lock up the liquor, catch her mother's vomit in a basin, balance the books, manage the farm manager, clean the house, fix her father's meals, paste her sister's awards and pictures with movie stars into her mother's scrapbook.

But then her mother had died, Augusta had come back, and Nellie had changed after all. She felt as if she had grown so much in the last six months, as though she had grown right out of her hand-me-down identity, grown right out of herself.

Nellie looked at the little blue book made of construction paper and yarn that she had been holding. Its pages were full of the crayoned scrawl of a child, and it was labeled, "My Prayerbook, by Augusta Woolsey-Bean, age 9." It was just one more thing, one more discovered remnant of the past, that had helped Nellie to change her view of herself. The makeup of the atom had shifted. Nellie had finally had to admit that Augusta had not had it so good, and in some mystical fashion, that meant that Nellie had not had it so bad.

The door opened suddenly and a bedraggled Augusta walked in.

"Don't panic, it's only me," Nellie said, emerging from behind her sister's door. "I came in to give you something," she added. "But you're soaked! Here." She got a towel and a robe for her sister, helped her shed her wet clothes, then hung them up.

Afterwards she handed Augusta the homemade book. "I was dismantling my old crib in the spare room and I found this tucked in the mattress."

Augusta sat down and turned the pages; each one bore a different prayer: "Please God, I promise that I will be very good if you will stop the fights; Dear Jesus, I won't yell anymore, I won't take sweets, I won't cry ever again if you make Mommy and Daddy not get a divorce; Our Father who art in heven, Im sorry for talking back to my mother, Im sorry for lying, Im sorry for hiding from her, Im sorry for waking Gram, Im sorry for leaving on the bathwater so grandpa had a stroke, forgive me for breaking the lamp and for spitting out Mommy's pea soup and making her cry. Please let her love me again; Dear God, Ill do anything, take all my stuffed animals, even my white furrie cat, I wont even take great granny's hunny drops when she comes to comfort me, but please please make Mommy stop hating me and make Daddy come home."

Augusta looked up at Nellie. "I was so afraid Mother would find this. I guess I hid it too well!"

"I'm flattered you thought of hiding it under me, under my crib mattress," Nellie said, smiling. "Those words are so sad, Augusta; that prayerbook says it all. I'm beginning to understand things I never understood before."

Augusta put down the little book. It was time now. Time for an end to secrets, to all the secrets. She pulled out the bag bulging with the diaries from underneath her bed. "Sit down, Nellie, I want to show you something that will make you understand even more."

CHAPTER 14

Nellie sat cross-legged on her sister's white bedspread, her lap covered in a cascade of her mother's diaries. For a long time she had simply been looking at them, trying to absorb the astonishing fact of their existence. The soft pigskin, the cool smooth silk of them, the brittleness of the paper in the volumes dating from the thirties.

The hours were ticking by, but Nellie did not notice them. She did not want her dinner. She did not want to talk to her sister. She did not even want to see William. She wanted only to be left alone with her mother; to pore over the key volumes that Augusta had separated out from the mound of memories she had found in the freezer.

Nellie turned the books over in her hands, imagined her mother lifting her bold blue fountain pen, confiding in them like you would in a friend, in a priest, in a shrink; holding them like vessels into which she could discharge the secret anguish that she deemed unfit for human ears. How much larger and happier her mother's handwriting was when she was first married, when she was first a mother, and then, when things turned sour, how crabbed and small her words became.

Nellie thought of the pages, icy and stuck together, Augusta warming them between her hands. And she thought of the last day of her mother's life, when she, Nellie, had tried to rub warmth, rub life back into Lydia's hands, which were growing so cool, so blue.

Nellie ran her fingernail down a leather volume, leaving a crooked trail of white. Why, why had her mother emptied her soul and left it to the daughter who was not there, whose hands did not smooth her head, whose presence she clawed the air for in her dreams?

Nellie read, and when she read of her grandmother Amenia's abandonment of Lydia, tears came without warning, smearing the page, making her feel much as she'd always felt, much as she now knew that her mother had once felt—like the oaf who always made the mess. Hadn't her mother seen how alike they were, hadn't she known it was Nellie who should have had the diaries?

At times, Nellie read passages over and over with astonished disgust—the details of her father's adultery and alcoholism, pages and pages about her mother's erotic, narcotic relationship with food, the pervasive unhappiness of the family during Augusta's early childhood. More than once she had to leave and go for a walk. She was having trouble digesting all the news; she felt like a computer rejecting information, spewing forth printouts that it could not commit to memory.

One thing was certain: the diaries had once and for all proved Augusta right, and dashed any last illusions Nellie might have had about the Woolseys. The skirts had been lifted, the warts exposed; Cornelius had been a cheat and a conniver, and the "priceless" ruby was just a piece of glass. Nellie had thought that as soon as they located the missing ring, they might sell it to save the farm, but that dream had now gone the way of the razed Christmas Orchard.

Nellie wondered whether her mother had left the diaries to Augusta so that Nellie wouldn't see the morbid way Lydia dwelt on Nellie's inadequacies as a baby, her ghastly prophecy that she would never match Augusta. But far from wounding Nellie, this knowledge only filled her with rebellion. She looked at herself in Augusta's full-length mirror. She was *not* ugly! No! But a sense of ugliness had been planted and cultivated within her. Had her mother laid her plans from the first moment she saw this homely second child? Somewhere deep in her unconscious, had she said, this child is the mirror of my wounded self, the one I can keep at home, the one who will still be there holding my hand the day I die?

Nellie was a Woolsey, and Woolseys died hard. But she would die before she proved her mother's prophecy right. Proving it wrong could come sooner than she thought, Nellie smiled, fingering the name on the page that would always set her heart racing. William Hurley . . . the father. Her mother's lover! She read the entries about their meetings in the trees over and over. No wonder Nellie had found herself begging for that satin peignoir; it had spoken out to her, had almost beckoned her with its strange, secret connection to her ordinarily unfrilled and practical mother. Lydia would appreciate the magical symmetry of all this. Her revelation that Mr. Hurley was her secret love had brought Nellie one step closer to her own true love, his son. And one day, perhaps, Nellie would greet William in the same robe that Lydia had greeted his father in.

Nellie might not be beautiful, but Augusta was right—she wasn't dumb. She could see the dates, she could see that Augusta did not in the least resemble Henry Bean. How could it be proven, beyond the ghost of a suspicion, that William Hurley Sr. did not end Lydia's barrenness one night in 1942? That William and Augusta were not, in fact, committing incest? Less potent ghosts than this one had come between people who thought they were in love.

Just before midnight, after she had read all the entries

Augusta had marked for her up through the middle of 1952, suddenly she wanted her sister. She went to the stairs and called for Augusta to come up and join her. In spite of her wooziness and the late hour, she only wanted to read more, and she prevailed upon Augusta to come and read along with her.

Augusta sat cross-legged on the bed beside Nellie, their legs touching. It felt warm, comforting to Nellie; perhaps it was the late hour, the excitement of the diaries, but she did not feel embarrassed, did not instinctively move away. There was a lump in her throat. "I've only gotten up to my fourth birthday, but I see it already. Augusta, Mom was a troubled lady. All this time I thought we were the ones in trouble. I was so stupid—I never really wanted to see it. I didn't want to listen to you. What was wrong with me!"

"Nothing's wrong with you, " Augusta said. "Maybe you just needed to hear it from Mother herself."

"Augusta, we spent our whole lives trying to read Mother, anticipate her moods, figure out her erratic behavior, and here it all is, clear as day, as though spotlights were being shined on all the dark corners."

"I know." Augusta pulled the quilt over them. Were she and Nellie finally coming together, transcending the gulf that had separated them? She wanted to hug her, to give her a big un-Woolsey-like hug, and she imagined that, in time, she would be able to.

"I used to have a fantasy," Augusta said. "I used to think that one day she would come into my room in a sparkling dress, sit down on my bed, and say she was sorry, that I was the best kid in the world and everything that had gone wrong, it hadn't been my fault."

"And now she's done it," Nellie said. "Now she's explained everything that never made any sense. Her sparkling dress turned out to be these little books."

"I couldn't go on reading these without you," Augusta said. "They're her greatest legacy to both of us. Maybe we can really understand the craziness we grew up with. Maybe we can finally get rid of the past."

"All these words," Nellie mused, taking up the stack of diaries that she had not yet read and that were marked with strips of paper Augusta had inserted each time she came across revealing entries. "Frozen for all time. I can just see her getting the idea of putting them in the old freezer, where they'd be safe from fire and flood. She wanted so badly not to die, Augusta, and she finally found a way."

Nellie took up a diary volume and put one side on Augusta's knee and the other on her own. Together the sisters read on.

June 2, 1952

*A*ugusta and Nellie have made a tent from a blanket and have been under it, whispering and plotting all afternoon. Thick as thieves they are. It makes my pulse skip. I'm headed for a stroke, just like Gran Millie's. Is it them or is it the curse coming on? Bile comes up in my mouth, I'm drowning, I can't get to the surface for air. Sometimes they disappear for nearly an hour, and I am frightened. Perhaps they have fallen under Coert's tractor, perhaps they have run away, maybe they despise me . . . maybe they will defy me, reduce me to pulp under Mama's feet.

They jumped out of the cold storage to scare me yesterday, and I was so scared that I beat them with the wooden end of the broom. I was sweating and they were standing stock still and suddenly I realized it wasn't them screaming, they were too scared, it was me. I didn't know where

Mama was, but I knew she was there somewhere, I knew she had seen and I was so ashamed.

October 10, 1953

*T*he kids in Nellie's class are teasing her. They call her names, they run away from her. It tears at my heart, it distresses me so that I cannot sleep. Yesterday, I went to the school yard with dark glasses and a big hat and sat in the car, watching them play so I could find out why they do this to her. If I have to spy every day for weeks, I will find out. Then, I pray to God that I can help her, teach her better ways to be. What is wrong with her? Why is my daughter a little freak people can't wait to leave behind? This has all happened to me once already, when I was a child myself, why does it have to happen again! My anger is so great I have to hold myself back, but then I've had enough practice holding myself back, waiting at gangplanks for Mama to blithely wave good-bye.

January 4, 1954

*Y*ou cannot live through your children, or so they say, but I don't know if this is a lesson I can learn. With Henry off on one of his benders, Gran Millie wandering round the house in her wedding trousseau, Mama away and Great-grandfather so sick, my only refuge is Augusta and Nellie. They make me swell with pride and go sick at heart. Augusta's grades are terrible. She is disruptive. I want to help her, but she won't even let me feel sorry for her. Erastus says puberty is a form of temporary insanity, but this is too much to bear; I tried to put so much into my relationships with my children, for between my mother and me there was nothing, and now between Augusta and me there is only quarreling. She rubs up to her father like a revolting little kitten, but she has only venom for me. Oh, I know how she tries to protect me from Henry's affairs, his violent temper, but to tell you the truth, I think she hates me for it. I think secretly she blames me for driving Henry to this behavior. Why else would she treat me like dirt? Why else would she slouch around in public, making me want to pretend she's someone else's daughter, embarrassing me with her sullenness, her hunched shoulders, her rudely curious stares? Why else would she blow up and scream those terrible things at me? I long for the little girl I loved, the one that has died in this eleven-year-old horror. Oh, to feel her tiny arms go round my neck, to hear her say, "I love you so much, Mommy, I can hardly stand it."

March 10, 1954

*N*ow Augusta has taken Nellie away from me. Nellie doesn't want to ride to the store, she wants to go out and trail after her sister every minute. I got so sick of it that this morning I invited Nellie into my room and slammed the door in Augusta's face. That will teach her, as Mama used to say.

Later I felt guilty about it, so I told Henry to pay some special attention to Augusta, to take her off on a bike ride. He did, and when they went off down the driveway, you should have seen Nellie's face! "Why didn't Daddy take me too?" she cried. I told her that Augusta was Daddy's favorite, and always would be.

Perhaps I should not have said it, but when I did I felt strong, strong and impervious as steel . . . as light as a bird released from its cage. It is incomprehensible sometimes how Henry only has eyes for his darling Augusta. Nellie must have sensed it, and at least it has been put into words. As I stood there watching Augusta and Henry, I knew that I would always protect and defend Nellie, give her enough love to make up for all the love that she will miss in life. My strength flowed into her hand; in our lovelessness we would be united, in our loneliness we would create a bond that would outshine theirs.

"Oh, God, do I remember that!" Nellie groaned. "Mother held my hand so hard it hurt. It was horrible. You went off with Daddy, and I was stuck there at home with this woman who was telling me that he would never love me like he loved you. And I was convinced that *she* wouldn't either, because all she ever talked about was you."

"Oh, Nellie," Augusta said. "We were so vulnerable and helpless as children! If you had only known that her obsession with me was the dark side of love, not something to be envied! I may have been born first, but unfortunately for me, I wasn't born perfect. From the moment I was able to walk away from her, to talk back to her, I disappointed her. She hovered over my every fault."

Nellie nodded. "You did get the whole emotional waterfall—the blame and resentment and the burden of responsibility for her well-being."

"She was such a needy woman," Augusta said. "If she didn't have everyone's exclusive love, she collapsed inside. And by the way, I thought you were the one she really got along with, the one she really loved. When you tied yourself to her apron strings and the two of you ganged up against me, I was so jealous of you!"

"She used me to hurt you, Augusta," Nellie said quietly. "I was desperate for her love, and that was the only way I could get it."

Nellie looked thoughtfully at her sister. "It was kind of a system, wasn't it? It was kind of a circular family dance, everyone trying to grab crumbs of love and attention and no one getting enough. Mother would be jealous of you and Daddy or of you and me. She would go over to me to make you jealous, and then you would take refuge in Daddy, which would make her more jealous and around and around we'd go."

"And," Augusta said, "you and I learned the dance very early, going from parent to parent, making our own little concentric circles. Let's go on reading, you'll see how right you are."

The next entry was written after Cornelius Woolsey, frail but alert, had finally died at the age of 103:

November 17, 1954

*B*eloved Great-grandfather, sweet be your sleep. The house seems so different without you, oddly windy, vacant, endless, as if you'd taken the roof with you. How I remember you rocking on the porch, your eyes squinting with pleasure at the sight of your family. I don't think we disappointed you with our paltry gifts. You may have wanted a son in the Senate, a grandson on Wall Street, a fortune multiplied instead of dwindled. But could it be that you wanted something else even more? A family that would never leave you, never best you, always sit in adoration at your feet?

December 19, 1954

*I*t is snowing and so inexpressibly beautiful. As we unpack the felt ornaments that the Woolsey women have made over the decades, I hear the sleighbells of my childhood, I hear Daddy in his Santa outfit stamping his boots on the roof. It doesn't matter that Henry keeps putting rum in his mulled cider when he thinks no one is looking, it doesn't matter that the kids are fighting, that Mama restrings my cranberries and popcorn so they alternate properly, the only thing that matters is that it is Christmas and everything is perfect and even when it isn't, we can pretend that it is.

March 11, 1955

Gran Millie is dying. Hardening of the arteries has left her barely lucid and so thin that her heart beats through her rib cage like the heart of a small bird. Mama not only pretends to understand her garbled phrases, but behaves as though she has delivered the Gettysburg Address. As long as I can remember, Mama and Gran have had a language of their own—constantly snapping and bickering and trading dark, knowing looks. Their language is still unfathomable, but it is now clearly the language of love. The first time I have ever seen them touch was yesterday, when Mama rubbed rosewater into her thin arms. Mama, who has never wept, now weeps at something as small as Gran Millie raising her fingers and laying them over her own. Such a meager, tender, pathetic denouement between them—such a pity that they had to wait for death to reunite them.

What a shame Mama did not know this grandmother I had, this kind, abiding Gran Millie. I can still feel her presence filling Mama's absence: talcum and lavender, cold cameo bumpy on my cheek, her firm hands pulling rough long johns over my legs. She was as gentle to me as she was harsh to Mama; my existence was no comment on her own. Sometimes, when I am kinder than usual to myself, I think that perhaps Mama left home not to escape me but to escape her mother. Poor Gran Millie, I can hardly blame her for finding Mama's very face distasteful, staring at her as it did with Sam Beaumont's eyes, Sam Beaumont's chin, mocking her with the features of the man who had made her a closet widow without having the courtesy to die and confer on her the official status of widowhood.

January 16, 1956

I yearn for a gentler God, one who is constant, who will stay a while instead of soaring down only to reward or punish. Death and sickness haunt this house. First Great-grandpa, then Gran Millie, and now Daddy. Erastus says he has had a hemorrhage in his esophagus and a series of little strokes, like pistols firing in his head, or lights going out. The lights of his genius, too small to ever amount to anything but bright enough to have driven him to the bottle when his inventions failed. No more bottles for Daddy now, for Erastus says one drink could kill him. I have plumped the pillows behind him and spread out before him the children of his imagination—the corn shucker that shucked one kernel at a time, the see-saw-merry-go-round that gave me three unforgettable rides, the electric train that belched smoke. I play "You Are My Lucky Star" on the old gramophone like we used to do, and Bing's voice fills the musty sickroom while snow flies outside the window and the leftover apples grow soft on the trees.

Do we have to get sick in this family, or wait for weakness to overcome us, before two people can gather the strength to just sit and be intimate with each other? In between his broth and his medicine and his sponging down, our eyes meet and there is perfect understanding.

Sometimes the child in me wants to cry out, "If you had realized that it was I, only I, who understood you, would you have spent more time knowing me?"

It seems terrible to say, but I have never been so content, so happy, as I am here in this warm room nursing my father. When dusk falls over us like lavender silk, I almost wish we could stay this way forever.

May 5, 1956

I shall never forget the sight of what is left of our family, standing at Daddy's grave, their hatted heads bowed, their gloved hands folded, as lovely as a row of lilies. Love and death are woven together as tightly as a silk knotted rose. In the world I know, we are born with love and we die with it, but in between, we are destined to lose it.

I have lost not only the dead but the living. I lost my mother long ago. I have lost my husband. Now I feel I have lost my children. They do not care about my grief. I shower them with love but they turn round and defy me, mock me, frighten me, make me go so far away from them that they have to beg me to come back.

I walk alone through the orchards; He comes no more. I walk alone, drinking in the perfume, watching the buds uncurl. They are rather like pale, sickly children you desperately want to save with your kisses. But the more you feel your kisses are needed, the more they are not. The blossoms resist approach, turn brown when touched, seem to shun the advance of a nose.

Nature teaches you that you must stand apart, like treasure behind glass, for anyone to want you.

"Remember how dark and depressing this house was then?" Nellie said. "I remember wanting to stay outside the house all the time. Mother was a block of ice. For a whole year or so she never smiled."

Augusta shuddered. "You had to whisper, you felt like it was your fault that everybody was so sick, and if you dropped a book you were making them sicker. And then it was horrible, so quiet, after Great-grandma Millie died, and then Grandpa. I really missed them."

"But poor Mom," Nellie said thickly. She was having trouble swallowing. "Poor Mom. Everyone dying, all those losses, and no love anywhere. We failed her. We were miserable brats."

"No, I don't think so," Augusta said carefully. "I don't think anybody could have given her what she needed, because it was too late. She didn't get it from her mother, who hadn't gotten enough from her mother, and so on back and back. We were only children, we couldn't give it to her; we had our own grief, only she couldn't see it through her own."

"Behind all that decisive, polished outer stuff" Nellie said, wiping her eyes, "secretly she was completely controlled by her emotions. And she couldn't own up to them. She kind of twisted them all up. I mean, she really missed her father's love, she was dying for love, but instead of admitting that, instead of letting us in and just maybe getting love by giving it or something, she twisted it into some paranoid loneliness in which we were her attackers."

"You know what I think? I think that instead of being angry at her father for dying, she turned the anger on us!" Augusta said. "And didn't they all kind of do that? Amenia, Millie, they were engulfed in their own grievances and losses, and made the world around them mirrors of the people who had hurt them. They buried all these resentments and hurts, all the bitterness, and positioned themselves like stuffed hides in the natural history museum, posed separately, afraid to connect with each other. I think they were afraid that if they even touched one another, if one little hole penetrated the dam, they couldn't

stop the flood. But look, this is typical. A month later, when we bought that crystal apple, we were in favor again. Mark Twain's saying about New England weather should have been applied to Mother's moods: 'If you don't like your family, stick around a minute, it'll change.' "

July 2, 1956

*A*ugusta, Nellie, Henry—I love them to death. To cheer me up, they went out and bought me a Steuben glass apple. You can see yourself in a tiny droplet of it and in the droplet there's another apple, and another, and another, and on and on, just like our family, apples perfectly round, perfectly red, all bred alike. Not a wild or misshapen one anywhere.

May 13, 1957

I yearn for a man's comfort. I want Henry but Henry is drinking heavily. He hides the bottles in his fishing boots. With Mama in the Orient and the girls in their rooms doing homework, it is so quiet here at night. I got my courage up and put on that old pink peignoir and walked past Henry's open door several times, but he did not notice. How, short of bopping him with a club and dragging him away, do I let him know? I went again to his room late at night, but he was snoring away, tooting explosively; it sounded like the Hudson Valley Central Line coming through our house. So different from my father's snores, as sweet and gentle as the purr of a kitten.

I know now that Henry will not leave me. The slow,

punishing years of our marriage have sunk him like a post into the sand. The inertia of our union has created its own energy, a centrifugal force of alcohol and food and anger, sucking us down, down, down. I know he will never leave me, but will he ever make love to me again?

October 3, 1958

Nellie continues to get teased by the kids who pick apples, but we have our own private solace, a way to forget the cruel ones—we have our secret cache of candy bars. Unlike Augusta, who looks at me with disgust whenever I put the tiniest morsel in my mouth, little ten-year-old Nellie thinks it's fine as long as she gets some.

I hardly feel the extra seventy pounds I've put on since Daddy died. I'm the same inside, after all, and I need food to make me strong, to grieve with. Maybe people do not like fat people because they take up more space and more attention. Long legs, lots of hair, the world thinks that's fine. Why not flesh?

Sometimes I get so hungry, the hunger radiates down my shoulders and through my body. I feel like a starving dog. I run to the icebox, and I cannot even wait to butter the bread—I just take tiny bites of the loaf and the stick of butter, one after the other, until I feel better. Sometimes something like a Boston cream pie tastes so wonderful that I keep taking more and more to try to duplicate those first few bites, but it hardly ever works. That is partly why I like to eat alone, so I can concentrate on it. So I can float away in solitude on a cloud of repleteness. Hunger is the place where all my emotions go, the net that catches them, and food is the thing that hauls them away.

May 4, 1959

Augusta is going out with Bill Hurley's son. God works in mystical ways, but this takes my breath away. I've always liked the boy, but now that he does more than hunt in the orchards, now that he comes up to the house (the first friend Augusta has brought here for a long time), I see in his eyes his father's heart. He is so lovely, I am drawn to him as to the son I never had. And for now, he has brought peace to Augusta and me.

November 3, 1959

I never realized it before, but just before I get the curse, it feels like this wolf is inside me. A bird breaking into song can enrage me. I feel like lightning will strike me if I have an ounce of happiness. No wonder I gain and lose, gain and lose, no matter whether I report everything on Mama's diet chart or not. I cannot keep the weight off It is the fault of this lunar wolf.

I had a dream that my father was going to die—after he has been dead all these years! I dreamed we went to the hospital in the back of Henry's pickup and Daddy's head was in my lap, and I was trying to keep the life from being bounced out of him.

April 14, 1960

For many years, watching Augusta and her father has been a little like reading a dime novel: you hate it but you can't stop doing it. She still sits at his feet, he behind the newspaper. All Henry has to do is sneeze and Augusta thinks it is ever so interesting. She hates it when I walk between them. She still looks at me like a piece of furniture that happens to have blood flowing through it. She manages to eat a banana with one hand and play with his pant cuff with the other. He reaches down, finds her hair, pats it. She leans into his stroke. He brings his hand down over her forehead, her cheek. She puts her head on his knee, drops the banana peel on the rug, and hugs his leg, upon which he says, "Thank God, General Motors is up two points," and scratches her back.

Yesterday, we were all having a fine evening rocking and chatting on the porch, and it suddenly dropped upon me like a bomb: Henry had not only been looking at Augusta the whole time, he had been looking her *over*, and she was lapping it up!

It seemed obscene. I got up and I took Nellie and led her into the big white Imperial Great-grandpa left me, and we flew over the back roads with the windows open, sailing along, laughing and singing. We went so fast it was as though we had simply lost the asphalt, lost the car, it was gone, we were shooting along on our own in midspace. I looked over at Nellie and she was holding onto her seat. She looked both afraid and exhilarated, for she doesn't know what a superb driver I am. I am better than anyone in the family, and I assured her of that. Then we had sundaes. And then we came home. Augusta was watching from the porch and her eyes were green. We ignored her.

Augusta looked at Nellie. "Mother brought you into her addiction, she corrupted you. Kids took chunks out of you and Mother would stuff you with sweets—if anything it must have made your self-confidence worse."

"Another vicious circle. So many circles," Nellie mused.

"And triangles," Augusta added. "Our family was made up of triangles."

Nellie nodded. She took a piece of paper and drew two triangles. She wrote "Food" at the apex of one, and at its two bottom corners, "Mom" and "Nellie." At the apex of the other she wrote "Sex," with "Daddy" and "Augusta" at the two bottom angles. "Daddy committed adultery, you tried to stop him, you were oedipally attached to Daddy and Daddy to you, and Mother was jealous of you both."

"And you and Mom turned to food and that made me jealous of both of you. Whew," Augusta said, looking at the diagram. "No wonder we've been battling to stay thin all our lives, especially you. It's been a battle not only against fat but against ending up buried in layers of family behavior. Were you as embarrassed as I was by Mom's bulk? There was that trip she took to see me in L.A., after her first cancer operation. I remember she came to the Celebrities International offices and she was so glad to be alive and so proud of me, she acted like a lithe young girl, sitting on my secretary's desk, swinging her legs. It was so inappropriate and her legs were so fat, I almost died of embarrassment. I prayed that no one would come along and see her, and then I felt guilty about it. I almost felt as if she could read my thoughts, that I had spoiled this last tiny pleasure in her life."

"Guilt," Nellie groaned. "It's epidemic, it's everywhere. You don't even have to do anything bad to feel it."

They fell silent, and then they began again to read.

October 13, 1960

I went upstairs thinking of how nice it was going to be to massage my aching feet, and there was Nellie on my bed with my vibrator up between her legs. For a moment I didn't even know what she was doing, and then it was as though the earth had shifted and the daughter I knew was gone and some animal was left in her place. I can barely remember what happened, but I found myself screaming and pummeling her with the vibrator. I've read that this is what children do if they stay inside, in their rooms, in too much darkness, and so I grabbed her and took her over to the Gristbrook Country Club. Even though we do not belong, I just walked in as though we did and made her get a bathing suit on and go into the pool. She was sobbing, she didn't know anyone there, she said, but I left her there the whole day anyway. She had to walk home, ten miles.

October 16, 1961

I have thought and thought about it, but I cannot reconcile it. She is a stranger to me now, the freak that I feared. How could she think of putting to her privates a gadget that I use on my feet? I threw it in the trash—I certainly don't want to use it on my feet anymore.

If Mama knew about this, it would kill her.

April 3, 1961

*W*ith Augusta away at college, I've been trying so hard with Nellie, but it's no use. Miraculously, she got asked to the Junior Prom, and so we went to a discount store looking for a dress. This is what happened:

Nellie parades up and down the communal dressing room in a black crepe muumuu. It looks fine on her but I'm careful not to say a word. She can tell I like it, and she takes it off and returns it to the rack. Then she puts on an outrageous pink slinky number and asks my opinion. "Well . . . it's a nice color," I say. "But what do you *really* think?" she asks, her bottom nearly bursting the thing's seams. She knows very well what I think but I am careful to be noncommittal. Then she sticks out her bulging stomach and says, "Well, I think it's neat and I'm taking it." "Well, I'm not paying for it," I blurt out. "Ah-hah, Mother," she says, pointing a finger at me, "you *didn't* like it. You lie like a rug." By this time, of course, the entire room is furtively enjoying this scene. I ended up buying the dress for her, but Mama says that if it were her child, she'd simply get rid of it and then deny any knowledge of its whereabouts.

October 16, 1962

I am drawn to Vassar like a drunk to a sad song. I love my beloved Imperial with its giant headlights and double grate like a smiling shark in front and its eagle spreading its wings in back and I drive through the big stone gates, honking at the guard, who is now my best friend. Mama is right, I should stay away, but I seem to be under a spell. Sitting with Augusta's friends, I am a girl of twenty again, but a different girl, a popular, pretty, desirable one. Her friends love me, they love the way I "tune in" to their enthusiasm for the Kingston Trio and the adventures of the "Freedom Riders" down south. I gaze at Augusta, at the grown-up way she pours hot water into my cup from the hotplate I got her, and I want to cry. This is my daughter! The one who manicures her nails and goes over to Yale for mixers with boys from good families, this is *my* child who went behind my back and turned out just the way I wanted. As I watch the delicate way she answers her phone and asks the person to phone back, as she rubs cream into her face and brushes her hair up for the night, as I reluctantly get up to go, I think how very strange life is. I'm a little afraid of her and I'm careful, as careful as I would be with the president of the Gristbrook Country Club.

July 1, 1963

*T*his summer Henry and I began to turn on the radio and listen to the sounds of Tommy Dorsey's Big Band; we would cha-cha, tango, and even Charleston, which would bring the girls running in to see their old man make his knobby knees exchange places. I have worked diligently to coax out the best in Henry, to see his totem-pole face break forth into such light! I have discovered something that, unbelievably, I did not know all these years: Henry's aloofness, what I took to be his coldness, is really just shyness in disguise.

November 30, 1963

I've tried to protect and champion Nellie all my life, and this is the way she repays me. At least she doesn't swear, kick, and scream at me the way Augusta did, but I think her Woolsey habit of frosting me over is worse. Every week, without fail, she disappears into her father's little room where they lie on the bed and watch "The Beverly Hillbillies." Even Augusta, when she comes home, thinks it's highly strange, I mean a father and daughter slouched on top of a single bed eating greasy popcorn in front of a ten-inch Magnavox in the middle of a twenty-room mansion.

January 11, 1964

*T*his is what I found, word for word, in Augusta's drawer at school, written in her handwriting:

"She dreamt of a penis the size of the Empire State Building. A phallus big enough for all the women in her family, whose tight pockets of resistance no man had been able to open. She was destined for a difference. She had a libido as deep and wide as the Grand Canyon and it contained the unexpressed hunger of her cursed forebears. She desired a throng of gorillas inside her, and even if it took her years she would someday have them. When that day came she would roar with such hunger, nothing would be enough. Buildings, wild beasts, nothing could get to the end of her. Her vagina would swallow up all who ventured near. What she would need is the Empire State Building, oh yes, rising up under her, grinding through her like a rocket, emitting a primal scream. She wanted that monument in her mouth. She wanted it to pop its spire, to erupt and pour out its stairways, its floors and file cabinets, its men women and children, the whole world, into her body.

"My God, Augusta," exclaimed Nellie, feigning collapse from shock.

Augusta blushed. "You know, Mother acted absolutely scandalized by that little piece. We had a huge argument about it. But I now think some part of her rather liked it."

February 1, 1964

*A*ugusta has told me not to come back to Vassar, that I am stifling her, reading her writings, moving into her territory. She told me to leave her alone once and for all.

There is not a person in the world who is on my side. Last night, I started bleeding for the fourth time in two weeks, and I thought of the blood bursting in Daddy's body, one vessel after another. I lay down on my bed and slept and I dreamt that Daddy sent a boat for me and it came down a river of blood. I woke in a panic, sticky with menstrual flow, desperate not to die, not to get on that boat. I ran to Henry's room and stopped outside. The door was open a crack and I heard him and Nellie inside, talking, and just as I was about to open it, it slammed shut in my face. I don't know which of them did it, but it was like the slam of a coffin lid. I went to pieces. I dragged Nellie out and slapped her silly, told her I was going to take her to a psychiatrist, that she was sick, sick, sick. And then I heard her and she was sobbing, "Why, why, why?" How could I tell her I was hitting her for not loving me? I could not tell her. So I told her it was because she had left the kitchen a slovenly mess and had forgotten to run the dishwasher.

February 5, 1964

What a mess of things I've made. I wanted so much to be a good mother. Lord, how I vowed to be different from my own.

I vowed that I would never take a trip and leave my children.

I vowed that I would always welcome them home from wherever they went.

I vowed I would shoot myself before I missed their birthdays.

I vowed I would never lose sight of them, that I would be at the center of their lives always, that my life would be devoted to theirs. I vowed I would hang on their every word.

I vowed that if I ever felt uncomfortable about being physically affectionate with them, I would never show it.

When I was young, I imagined that the love of a proper mother was the love that passeth all understanding, a love so pure it would transcend petty jealousies, petty hurts. But the love I feel is unlike all other loves because it is reduced to an essence unbearably strong. It is like young passion in all its succulent pleasures as well as its dark rages, its intense desire for requital, for vengeance. Once you are a mother, you have divided yourself, broken off a piece which you can never retrieve, and you are constantly taken aback at the sight of it.

Nellie turned to Augusta. "Do you know that I hated *The Beverly Hillbillies?* I watched their show because it was a way of being with Daddy. I had to get away from her. And I was hungry for him. I wanted to know that I could be 'Daddy's Little Girl' too."

Augusta nodded sympathetically, then took out another volume dated almost four years later. "Of the rest of the volumes I've read, there are only two more entries I've marked. Let's read them and call it quits for the night."

November 3, 1967

I think this is the last time Henry commits violence upon me for a long, long time. Since Augusta left and Nellie went to college, his drinking and his temper have increased. He has a holiday with me. I try to stop him from drinking and he becomes enraged. Last night, at the hospital charity ball, he was slobbering over the women, filling his glass again and again, until finally I took it away from him and, in front of the whole table, told the waiter not to give him any more. He took off his nametag, wrote something on the back, and passed it to me. It said, "You are going to pay for this." The whole evening was spoiled for me, the biggest event of the year ruined. I was terrified, and I ate so many petits-fours that I went into a kind of stupor. Then I did what I always do to try to calm him: I became weak and conciliatory. When we got home I ran into the house and he ran after me, and I threw the Steuben glass apple at him and cut his head. Then he ran down and got his rifle, and I ran out of the house and he ran after me until I hid in the trees.

The next day, he was pale and shaking and absolutely astounded when I showed him the bullet holes in the fence. He insists that he only fired into the air, but I'm not so sure. I told him I was thinking of going to the police, and he took his rifles and all the other guns he owns and the ammunition and locked them up and gave me the key. And he says he will give up liquor for good. That will be the day.

January 15, 1969

*H*enry gave me a letter Augusta had written to him, and told me to deal with it. It was full of despair about the world, its hypocrisies, its avarice, its falseness. She wrote that she knew there was a side of her father that he had kept hidden; that he, like she, lived on a higher intellectual plane, that he had contempt for the frivolous world. She knew he could help her with this terrible ennui she felt as they all "marched toward death."

Maybe Augusta thinks her father hides copies of Kierkegaard under the pillow, but I'm the one who makes his pungent little bed and I know that it's cheap science fiction and cookie crumbs under the sheets.

I wonder how she will feel when the days and weeks

go by and she realizes her father is on too high a plane even to answer her letter.

"Enough," Augusta said, and clapped the volume closed. "I don't think I can take another word." She stared glassily at their bedraggled reflections in the windowpanes across the room. The roof creaked, reminding her of her father jingling Santa's bells at Christmastime, reminding her of the squeak of her mailbox each time she looked in vain for a letter from him.

Augusta looked so sad suddenly that Nellie felt a wave of sympathy and love for her. Nellie might not have been her father's favorite, but she knew by her resemblance to him that he *was* her father. And she felt ashamed that she had rejoiced when she read that William's father was probably Lydia's lover, and possibly Augusta's father. She wondered if that was what Augusta was thinking about, whether she was concerned about it. "Can I know what you are thinking?" she asked, putting her arm around Augusta.

"I'm thinking that it was typical of Mother to have left the diaries to only one of us," Augusta said.

"Listen, it's all right. I don't feel left out anymore. Not really. I don't really even feel bad about it."

"You know, Nellie," Augusta said, "maybe she couldn't stop herself from trying to divide us, even in death. Even as she was dying, maybe some part of her wanted us to stay divided, wanted us to be jealous, to crave her acceptance the way we did as children . . . so that she would still be first, and we would love her above anyone else. Leaving the diaries to only one of us—that might see to that."

Augusta got up and went to the window. The sky was beginning to lighten; she remembered how as a child she used to imagine the first dawn light swirling through the sky like cream through coffee. "Do you remember that we were inseparable when we were little? I remember crying once when you were gone for several hours, when Mother had to take you away somewhere."

Nellie got up and went over to Augusta. She hugged her. "We don't have to be so alone anymore."

"No," said Augusta, hugging her back. "We don't."

There was a clattering in the kitchen below. Nellie listened and sniffed. "I knew it—William. He's at the stove again! You'd think that someone who eats as much as he does would learn to cook. You should go make your poor starving man a midnight snack before he burns down the kitchen. Have you ever wondered how he can possibly stay so thin?"

Augusta watched the glow come into Nellie's eyes as she talked about William. How could Augusta ever have fooled herself into believing that Nellie did not really love him? She came to a decision right then and the decision, she knew, was final: inspiration warmed her—she had not felt so inspired since she was realizing her last film project. William was part of Nellie's world, not her own. She would right the imbalance, the only one that still divided her from her sister.

"You're the one who can cook around here. I think you'd better go down and help him," Augusta said casually. She bent over the bed to gather up the diaries. "He really *doesn't* know the sugar from the salt, and its time he had a good teacher."

CHAPTER 15

"Oh William, how could we have been so stupid?" Nellie cried as they hurried down the rocky, leaf-covered path.

"This has to be it," William said. "Look here, at either side of the path, where the leaf cover is blackened. This is where acids have spilled out of the dump truck Apex must be using."

"I *knew* it would turn out to be near the Christmas Orchard. Look at these tall brambles all around. That's what hid the dump, that's how we missed it."

It was the end of July, and for nearly three months Nellie and William had been scouring the several square miles of woods that ran from the Woolsey house down to the river and separated the orchards from Apex property. But they had found no clues as to where Apex might be illegally disposing of heat-transfer fluids and other toxic-waste products used in manufacturing electronic parts. Then, purely by chance, they had noticed some faint tire marks embedded in leaf cover on the floor of the forest a ways up the hill from the old Christmas Orchard. They had followed the treads over a winding, seemingly endless trail—marked as well by a blaze of broken branches where the truck had obviously forced its way through narrowly spaced trees—until it had finally put them onto the Apex service road. Then they had retraced their steps back into the woods, followed the tire marks down the trail, through an opening in a thicket of brambles, and down another path.

Gradually, they could hear the distant sounds of tugs on the Hudson River, then Coert's sprayer in the distance. They turned a corner and stopped in their tracks. There it was, spread out before them, at the end of a big clearing—an oozing, stinking, gelatinous pool.

The smell was like nothing they had ever smelled before, a sharp, sweet odor emanating from the copper-colored liquid glittering in the sun. Rusty drums were everywhere, their contents leaking out through corroded seams.

"Cover your eyes," William ordered. He gave Nellie his handkerchief. His own eyes seemed already to be tingling.

"At last, at bloody last, we've found it," Nellie said softly, then shook his arm. "William, we've really found it. *This* is what's been seeping in and poisoning our land."

William seemed unaware of her. He walked slowly toward the ditch, magnetized by it. "Trichloroethylenes, benzene, hydrocarbons, carbon tetrachlorides, cyanides, phenols, probably PCBs," he said dumbly. "PCBs have that sweetish smell."

"William," Nellie tugged at him. "Don't go any closer. You're scaring me. You sound like a robot."

"I thought we'd never find it. I was beginning to doubt myself," William said, looking at the flesh-colored deposits that had oozed into lifelike forms: misshapen hands, elongated heads, twisted spines. "Now I almost wish we hadn't."

He took out the old miniature Minox camera he kept in his pocket, and snapped some pictures; this was the first time since he began his investigation that he had had reason to use it. "I wish I had the big flash. We'll come back tomorrow and I'll get better pictures."

Nellie bent down to examine what looked like a battery.

"Don't touch it." William grabbed her hand. "It's an electronic capacitor. Look, they've dumped hundreds of them, they're all over here."

"The yellow translucent stuff, what's that? It looks like the Blob. You remember that horror film, when a ball of jelly rolls over the country, getting bigger with each person it swallows? See it? It's just the size of the Blob when the Blob started out on its binge . . . oh my God, look, it's moving!"

"Yes, probably is," William said absently, studying Nellie's face to see if she was having any adverse reaction to the toxins. He himself felt strange: cold and breathless without really being out of breath. "These chemicals just never die, they have perpetual life. They form and reform. That's why it's so hard to get rid of them. You just can't destroy them. Nellie, do you feel all right?"

Nellie shivered. "Only a chill down my spine. . . . William, the orchards couldn't even be half a mile away. I know we've both believed that Apex was dumping and that the dumping was affecting the farm, but let's be frank—we've been a little like children believing in magic. In fact, the less evidence we found that Apex was poisoning the environment, the more we believed it was! But it's all been theoretical, going through the data, staking out the factories, getting absolutely nowhere. Apex was the monster and we the tiny white knights. It's been like a dream. But I don't know that I ever really expected the dream to come true!"

William nodded. "The paltry apple crops could always be blamed on old trees and bad weather. The water tests have been equivocal at best. There's been nothing concrete to hold on to, nothing to really tell us that the monsters lived anywhere but in our minds."

"It's like Apex has called our bluff. I feel like we're back to square one. Do we now really believe all of our own propaganda? How can we? If we believe that this stuff is really leaching everywhere, into our soil, into our water, then how far do we take it? What do we do now? Do we believe that the

Apex workers are getting headaches and nausea and ingrown toenails and whatever because of the toxins—or because of the thought of the toxins? Do we assume our apples are full of poisons? Do we recall the vegetables we sold?"

"Take it easy," William said, leading Nellie away from the dump. Now he himself felt nauseous. "Some things we might never know for sure, but what we do know is that we have to proceed scientifically, in small, careful steps. We can't jump to conclusions. We can now get the Board of Health, the EPA, everyone. We're not alone anymore."

Nellie put her hand to her throat. "Do you remember those rashes you and Augusta got after the Christmas Orchard was cut down and regrafted? It was because you were working so close to the dump, wasn't it?"

"Possibly. Although Coert didn't get a rash," William said with slight discomfort. And because Coert had not gotten a rash, Augusta had assumed the skin irritations were the wages of sin: an allergic reaction, the consequence of wallowing naked beneath the pollen-laden bloom of Auntie Mame.

William traced a line with his shoe. "The whole scenario is just as we had imagined. The dump is located just enough uphill from the Christmas Orchard so that rain could have carried the poisons down into the stream, which could have distributed them into your orchard soil on the other side. They could also have seeped into veins of water that move underground, under the surface stream and into your well. These wastes could be lacing the water that feeds your crops, not to speak of the water that you drink up at the house. We'll have to mark a trail back to your property, and then look at Cornelius Woolsey's old water table maps."

"Look at the trees around here," Nellie said, pointing up to the straggly, pale yellow leaves of the locusts and maples in the area surrounding the dump. The sun streamed through them, making the area lighter than the rest of the forest. "They remind me of the straggly look of the old Macs that were cut down in the Christmas Orchard."

Nellie swallowed; she scratched her cheek. "Do I have a rash? Starting on my face?"

He took her chin in his hand, turned her face to the light, and smiled. "Not a spot." He put his hands on her shoulders: her bones seemed unusually small. He could encompass each of her shoulders with one hand. She always wore such big, blousy tops, he never thought her shoulders were so small and delicate. So much smaller than those of Augusta, the woman he was used to holding—or rather, not holding—in the last few weeks.

"Do you want to leave, are you frightened? I'll take you back."

"No, no," Nellie said, looking up at him happily. "I'll stay as long as you do. This is your pot of gold. You've worked so hard for this. You've worked so selflessly for us, for the good of selfish old hermits like the Woolseys. And you've been so stubborn! God, you've persevered!"

"And what about you?" William brushed a curl from her eye. She had lost weight and stopped wearing her hair pinned back in barrettes, and it now floated free around her head, a nimbus of fire against her bronzed cheeks, bronzed eyelids heavy over green eyes. She no longer projected herself as the ineffectual little sister; on the contrary, she had the strong and rather unnerving air of a woman in a Titian painting. It sent a ribbon of surprise down his spine. "Nellie, I've never worked with anyone like you. You've been at my side throughout this, ready with the right comment or the right document, the proper idea to move us forward. You've been marvelous."

"Now, William," Nellie said, her face deadpan. "If you keep that talk up, you'll ruin my hard-earned reputation. Pretty soon I'll get so efficient that people will beg for the old flapdoodle Nellie back."

"Flapdoodle Nellie! I don't know anyone like that. I think you must have dreamed that girl up."

"Not at all. I was the most famous flapdoodle in the whole

flapdoodle family. Did you know they couldn't even keep diapers on me? I unpinned every one of them, and you can
imagine what that was like. Everyone thought I would do very
well in life if I could get through it without stepping in front
of a car or setting fire to the house."

"Well, that girl," William said gently, "is gone."

And Nellie knew he was right. When William had first
come back to town, she had been stiff, coiled tight as a spring;
she could hardly speak, she was concentrating so hard on putting her best side forward, making sure her skirt covered her
pudgy knees. But now she could be herself, even laugh at
herself in front of him, for that was one of the things William
seemed to like best about her.

All at once, Nellie reached up and kissed him.

He knew he should move away but his shoes seemed nailed
to the ground. This close, her skin had the look of chalk and
copper and her eyes were deep, inviting. He felt the tight,
professional control he had carefully maintained in their relationship slipping away. Augusta had been avoiding him, she
had done everything but come right out and say their affair was
over; but now, as William looked at Nellie, he knew that it
really was. He took her in his arms.

Then suddenly they heard a diesel truck coming down the
path. They made for the brambles, William hurriedly clearing
a space for them, and they crouched, thorns scraping their
clothes, and waited. The truck was getting nearer. "Do you
think it's the dumper?" Nellie asked.

"How could it be the dumper in the middle of the day?
Although maybe . . . maybe they're on to us. Maybe they saw
us waiting near the factory after dark, maybe they shifted their
dumping schedule. It's a Saturday after all, and they wouldn't
be seen. They only have to travel down their own service road."

"I don't believe it!" Nellie said. "All those wasted midnight
vigils, and here they were doing it in the light of day!" All those
wonderful cozy vigils, Nellie actually thought, sitting next to

you in the car, drinking coffee, talking about ourselves and our pasts in the steamy warmth.

Just then the truck came rumbling into the clearing. It was hitched to a dented and dirty cylindrical tank. The trucker turned it around and backed up to the dump.

"They must have two independent truckers working for them!" William said. "Remember that letter on company stationery that our source copied? It's an agreement for a dump truck to dispose of sealed containers of waste. This is something different. This is a tankful of stuff that apparently hasn't even been stored and contained!"

The trucker got out of his cab, a stocky pale man with a straggly beard and red eyes. He moved slowly and looked unwell. "Poor guy, I feel sorry for him," Nellie whispered. "He looks like he lives on the outer edges."

"Don't," William said, "he gets paid plenty and by the ton. Cash up front before disposing of every load. Apex pays him three times as much to get rid of the chemicals as it pays a worker to make them."

The trucker went to the back of the tank, pulled a bandanna over his face, and opened a large spigot. The liquid flowed out, giving off vapors that sent him reeling backward. As he coughed and choked, William snapped picture after picture while Nellie held the thorns down so he could get a good view.

When the tank was empty, the trucker, still coughing, got in the vehicle and roared off. Toxic liquids leaked from the spigot as it bumped away. William and Nellie watched stupefied from their space in the bushes as the leaves sizzled and curled up under the liquid.

William took his last picture and then let out a whoop. "We've got them, darling, we've got them! Wait until the EPA sees these photographs! Wait till my friends in Washington get a look! This is history: the American dream becomes the American nightmare. The Apex Electronics Corporation, whose stock is listed on the New York Stock Exchange, caught in the act of breaking the law, of illegally dumping chemicals so toxic they can eat through steel drums. And doing it a mile from a landmark orchard that dates back to the last century. It will be on every television screen, in every newspaper and magazine; it will be written up as a cautionary tale in every environmental manual. We've got the bastards and they're going to find themselves in the middle of a national drama."

"I kind of like the little drama unfolding right here," Nellie said. "Just you and me and the dump."

William encircled her with his arms. "You believed in this project when nobody else could grasp its importance. Thank you for your faith in me."

The trust, oh the trust of this woman, William thought as he looked at her face. He loved being with her; being with her was being different, feeling different about himself. Never had he felt so comfortable with another person's devotion to him. Usually, when a woman began to show signs of depending on him, of expecting something from him, he would flee. But Nellie seemed to adore him without expecting a single thing in return. She was amazing. She had never even let on that William had hurt her by his affair with Augusta, though he knew he had. Augusta had told him that his influence was benign, positive; now Nellie was truly making him feel it. Augusta had helped him realize he was carrying too great a responsibility for Arlene's fate, for his parents' death, but Nellie made his shoulders feel light.

The day of his parents' accident was a movie that played regularly in his mind; how they had gone out the door, alive and full of worries and pleasures and love and complaints, full to the brim with all the tiny details of life, the intricately laid plans for the future. And then suddenly, in a matter of seconds, they were turned inside out, dead, canceled; they did not exist. He had been the one who took care of his father's station wagon; his father had no mechanical abilities. He had planned to take the car in for a checkup the next day. If only he had done it a day earlier, would the accident have been prevented?

Would the brakes have been found loose, and repaired? Would his father then have been able to stop just short of the car that had run the red light and sent both his parents crashing through the windshield on impact?

When he was with Nellie, those questions, those questions that had no answers, and which therefore he could not stop asking, faded, seemed like needless self-blame, survivor guilt. The person he saw mirrored in her eyes, that person was loyal and brave and responsible, a soul much less capable of causing hurt to others than the man he saw in the mirror each morning.

The sunlight coming through the trees, the strange satin colors of the deposits, they seemed to dapple Nellie with a bright beauty, a rich maturity he had not seen before. Her hair had gone deep red against the moist, darkening cover of the woods. In the dying light, the woods had become an other-worldly region: the thicker wastes spreading out like the hands of witches, the drums floating like water toys waiting for children to splash their way to oblivion. But the evil now seemed make-believe. He leaned down and brought his mouth to hers. Her smell was soapy lavender, her small lips seemed to grow large beneath his own, releasing a feeling that spread throughout his body; a flash of sheer joy went through him. He began to smile and, inexplicably, to laugh; laughter and delight and relief bubbled up in both of them. They stamped down the brambles, shook off the thorns to find each other's chests, to press their legs together, to cover each other with kisses. A delightful thought had flown into William's mind: there is a woman in this world who loves me not for what I can give, or what I can promise, but for what I already am.

"I didn't know it was possible to laugh and kiss at the same time," Nellie said, removing a thorn from his hair. The trees were dipping and rotating before her eyes.

"Of course, the first time we kissed, long ago in your basement, it wasn't a laughing matter," William said, looking at her wryly.

Nellie's face grew pink. She was there in that closet when

William had figured out that it was she, not Augusta, he had kissed, but should she express surprise that he knew? "I kept thinking maybe you really did know it was me back then," she said.

"Maybe I did," William smiled, kissing her nose. She looked so expectant; it was so poignant that she had kept the memory of that kiss all these years, that she had believed in his early attraction to her. How could he tell her the ironic truth: that the kiss not only fooled him, it had so aroused him that he had pushed the reluctant Augusta for more, which had caused such trouble between them, it had led to their breakup, which had, twenty years later, led to his rejection of Nellie in favor of his unfulfilled and feverishly reawakened desire for her sister.

"But you didn't," Nellie said firmly. "I know for a fact you thought it was Augusta."

"And how do you know that?"

"Maybe someday," Nellie said, afraid that her face was growing as red as William's shirt, "I'll even tell you."

William thought of how Nellie had been so patient, so content with the little that he had given her, the crumbs of friendship. He ran his fingers through her thick curls. She was softer, more yielding than Augusta. The thought of Augusta made him abruptly break away.

A week after he and Augusta had made love in the rain-soaked woods, William had found as much proof as he would probably ever find that they were not siblings, that Augusta was in fact Henry's biological daughter. He had dug back into his father's records and discovered that he had been on a trip abroad at the time Augusta must have been conceived. There was no evidence that William's mother had been on the trip and his father could have falsified his records, could have secretly met Lydia, but both Augusta and William doubted that. They were both profoundly relieved, although this did not seem to save their foundering relationship. Augusta had promptly become immersed in the crucial last years of her mother's diaries, too immersed to make love, too immersed to even talk to him about why they were not making love. It was clear that the urgency of their passion had been spent, but they simply did not have the tools of communication to admit it. In any case, William could not go further with Nellie before he talked to Augusta.

"Let's get out of here," William said, trying to disengage from Nellie, to cool himself down.

He made himself concentrate on the dump and the prospect that this was only the beginning, that by the end of the day he could have gathered enough evidence to blow Apex wide open. His source at the factory had reported rumors that the company was not only using the dump for waste but was also illegally discharging industrial solvents into the Hudson through old pipes left in the foundations from the days when the Woolsey brick factory occupied the space. He would have Nellie drop him off at the Apex hot-fuel lab. The complex would be practically empty on a Saturday, and he thought he knew a way to get into the lab's cellar.

Nellie was gazing up at him lovingly. "We have to go," he said gently.

"William," she said. She loved the way his sensuous name rolled off her lips like a honeydrop. "You've been wonderful to me. Tender and loyal, never withdrawing, never hurting me. I didn't even know you and Augusta were together until you told me, that's how careful of me you were."

"Hmm," William said uncomfortably. Behind Nellie's persistent and possibly disingenuous attempts to make him out to be a soul who couldn't hurt a flea, he suddenly saw the vision rise up of a man who played two sides against the middle. He put Nellie's hands down at her side. "You wouldn't want me to be disloyal to anybody now, would you?"

"You do know it was always meant to be us, don't you?" Nellie asked.

"That may be, but at the moment it is not us," William said, and turned and made his way out of the brambles. He reached back to help her, and all she could see was his outstretched arm, the tensed sinews, the reddened knuckles, the white wrists. The sight sent a sliver of heat down her legs; it was more devastating than the sight of his entire body. But she restrained herself. She did not mind William's reluctance. She did not mind even that she was hyperventilating on air laden with deadly poisons. She had never felt stronger, or braver.

How strange the world was. For the first time in her life, she was the winner, but the spoils of victory were not exactly the spoils that had tempted her when she had begun. It was not really her sister over which she had triumphed. Over the last months, they had worked to uproot their rivalry, like choke-weed from the garden bed; Nellie knew that Augusta could be happy without William. No, her triumph was over herself. She had dared to want something that seemed unattainable, she had gone after it, and she had gotten it. William might look nervous and guilty over this state of affairs, but that was destined to pass. Nellie knew that William would probably never want her as passionately as he had wanted Augusta, but she could live with that. They had so much else. Nellie knew, even if William did not yet know, that he was hers and he was hers for keeps.

As soon as she heard William and Nellie drive up, Augusta jumped out of her seat on the wrought-iron bench in the herb garden, grabbed her leather bag full of diaries, and fled down into the orchards. This little plan she had orchestrated to throw William and Nellie together had kept her on her toes, reminding her of her days plotting to bring her parents together. And this time, there should be a happier ending.

Augusta had had to swallow a great deal of primitive jealousy, of possessiveness over William, in order to pull away from him. But she knew it was the only way she could accomplish her present goals: to get away from Woolsey Orchards and to make her sister happy. She banked on William gradually coming to care for Nellie in the way Nellie obviously wanted him to; if everything went according to plan, after Augusta left in two months, her sister's friendship with William would blossom into something far more exciting.

Augusta felt such a tenderness and love for Nellie these days that she would do anything to make her happy, to make up for all the misery in her life. They had traveled a long road together these last months to escape from their past, and they would have to travel a long way still. But as much as they had grown out of their warped family roles, these roles, these feelings, would always thread through the fabric of their personalities. Augusta worried that if she seemed to discard William, hand him down, as it were, to her sister, it might spoil Nellie's happiness. Somewhere in Nellie's mind, an image might lurk of Nellie the victim, Nellie the second-best, William's consolation prize. No, Augusta wanted to bestow on her sister a gift unseen. Augusta imagined herself coming home to visit next Christmas, say, and taking the news gracefully: William's affections had shifted in Augusta's absence; Nellie had won him fair and square.

Augusta smiled to herself. Her confusing childhood had at least honed her talents for organizing, manipulating, rearranging, getting the unworkable to work. At the talent agency, they used to call her "the Great Orchestrator." In fact, just last week two friends of hers—a producer and a director who had made successes of themselves in Hollywood—had called to ask her to join them in starting a documentary-film company; no one, they said, could bring people together and fire them up about an idea the way she could.

Augusta settled herself under the dusky spreading limbs of a Red Delicious, closing her eyes to the disappointingly small, badly colored apples growing from its boughs. She spread out her old high school scrapbook, recently unearthed from the attic, some pictures of her mother, and the diaries she was reading. Her obsessive single-minded nature was showing itself right now: she was relieved to have a break from the sexual intensity of her relationship with William so that she could focus on those final years she had missed with Lydia; so that she could move toward a final resolution of her long love-hate relationship with her mother. Now that she was more certain that Henry was her real father, now that she didn't need to be afraid of what she would find in the diaries, she could plunge into them with something verging on pleasure. And the latest volumes revealed a much less depressed, resentful, and self-pitying Lydia. Here, at last, was the side of her mother that Augusta held most dear, that she wanted to remain part of herself: determined, strong, enthusiastic, a problem solver.

The diaries told how Lydia, in the years when Augusta was in California, had lifted the family out of its isolation and its gloominess by renewing her acquaintance with Peggy Steptoe and Betsey Blanquette. She was afraid that the dwindling of the old families, the arrival of the nearby Apex company, and the influx of the middle class would not benefit Nellie. So, instead, she exposed her to the society of the fancy Gristbrook set.

Augusta opened the latest volume:

May 13, 1970

We are still in a haze of happiness over Nellie's debutante party. Perhaps it is a sensation of pure relief after being in such a frazzle of worry all winter about the stained wallpaper and the brocade curtains which look like candidates for the Salvation Army. Living as we do at the mercy of the seasons, we again do not have the money to fix up the house, and we have entertained so infrequently in the past decade. How to make a nice party on next to nothing? Well, here is how:

Dress your farm manager up as a butler and set him to work. Then use the old barter system, trading bushels of apples for cases of champagne. Make the party start after sundown so the chips and scratches do not show. Decorate the house with the fruits of nature.

It turned out splendidly. Mama and I presided at the old silver tea service (both of us squeezed into our tightest old Spencer corsets!) and Nellie really did look lovely in Great-great-grandma Hopestill's Empire wedding dress made over by Mama. Henry disappeared from the receiving line three times, and I repeatedly introduced guests to an empty space. Mama drank too much champagne and went about talking like a tour director on a megaphone, but generally the evening, the first we have had since the grandparents were alive, was splendid. Here is what the *Wappappee Gazette* (once owned by the Woolseys) wrote:

"Just as the sun was sinking over the Hudson Highlands, staining the sky a slumberous pink, Mr. and Mrs. Henry Bean threw open the doors of their historic home yesterday to present their youngest daughter, Cornelia Woolsey-Bean, to Hudson Valley society.

"The old homestead was beautifully illuminated by dozens of candles which cast a lovely light over the priceless antiques. The evening took the form of a tea dance, and Mrs. Lydia Woolsey-Bean explained that although it was late to have tea, the hour was deliberately set as a symbolic homage to her great-grandfather Cornelius Woolsey, who built the Victorian mansion, and who never had his cup before six o'clock.

"Mrs. Woolsey-Bean said she was breaking tradition in another way; instead of the sweetheart roses customarily used in debutante parties, the decorations cascading from the marble urns were weaves of fern and wildflowers and apple blossoms from the blooming orchards, which incidentally provided a lush backdrop for the event."

October 31, 1970

I was walking in the orchards yesterday and suddenly I felt the presence of my father, stronger than I've ever felt it before. I looked up and saw a cloud all by itself in a sea of dazzling azure, sending out rays that seemed to reach over all the orchards. I felt hands on my cheek, Daddy's warm hands, and I fell backward on the grass. I opened my eyes in time to see the cloud dive forward and do a complete somersault like a child in a field. For a few seconds the sky was alight with silver, and then the cloud hung still, white and peaceful once more. When I returned to the house, no one else said they'd seen it, nor was it reported on the radio or in the newspaper.

January 14, 1971

I've been having nightmares and I've been having pain. Way deep down in my belly, so deep the pain sometimes seems to travel like hot light through a tunnel. Everyone says the pain's in my head. I am the only one left in this house. Nellie is finally trying her hand in the outside world, living in New York with a job at a needlepoint shop. Henry is away and Mama's on a cruise. The halls seem dark and as big as the inside of a planetarium. I imagine myself crouched in the attic, listening in fear to my own footsteps.

February 2, 1971

*T*he apples from last season are shriveled on the ground. Everything seems barren, mushy, even the branches of the trees. The natural world that we have worked so hard to control and harden into giving us our livelihood looks like it is turning to pudding.

I have begun talking to the pain. If Mama is right and the pain is just a bid for attention, then I should be able to get rid of it before the spring, when Erastus will surely needle me even more about getting those diagnostic tests.

Thank the Lord for Augusta in Hollywood, for her glorious, cheering successes! She is a bright movie in herself. I bring her out, I play her, she is a warrior against my pain. There doesn't seem to be any movie star she doesn't know, and so many of them are smitten with her that I wouldn't be surprised if she brings home Mr. Robert Redford himself!

March 10, 1971

Some days there is no pain at all and I am sure it is a thing of the past, a city conquered so long ago that the memory of it is dim. Then suddenly back it comes, a beam moving through dense clouds, intent on its target, a knife sinking into butter, a sensation so alive and familiar it reproaches me for ever thinking it gone.

I cannot rest easy in the moment, for even when I am purged sparkling white of pain, I am listening like an old lady for the intruder. My body is the most familiar friend I have; it used to be a warm, cushioned shelter for my tortured soul, but now even it has turned against me, a wilderness lurking with unpredictability.

The only thing that works is Augusta. She calls almost daily. She tells me every little detail of her life. It is as though I have the child back that I lost long ago, the one who ran home to tell me everything. Augusta gives me strength. She will not let me give in. A vision of her laughing with Mr. Redford, or a note of congratulations from her boss that she has sent on to me, I hold them close. They are like fingers reaching down and lifting out the pain. I think myself into a furious dance, a drowning song until the sickness is banished, for a time.

Augusta put down the diary. She wished she had written a dozen more letters, made a hundred more calls and visits, waged better war on her mother's cancer! She wished she had told even bigger and more exciting lies about Robert Redford and Cher and all the rest. But even as she thought this, a deep reservoir of remorse was breaking through, flowing out of her. She had wanted her mother to drive away that illness with the same passion that she had wanted her parents to reconcile when she was a child. But she realized now that nothing she could have done would have saved her mother, just as she could not, with all the games and the wishes in the world, have saved her parents' marriage.

Yet as long as she lived, Augusta need not wonder any longer whether she had failed her mother; the diaries revealed that she had done much more for her mother than she had thought. Augusta fingered the volume. She knew now, before reading any further, that her mother had forgiven her for withdrawing. And her mother, through the diaries, had given her the tools with which to forgive herself.

As Augusta had begun being easier on herself, she also began to be easier on her mother. She was beginning to understand Lydia more fully. She had always been repelled by her mother's glamorization of her successes, for instance, regarding it as yet another sign that Augusta was not good enough just being who she was. But now, suddenly, she understood that Lydia's capacity for invention was what had allowed her to survive her lonely childhood. Her ability to make the deadly and the drab into something magical, that was what had nourished Lydia, that was her heart and soul. She had not withdrawn or fled from motherhood the way her mother and grandmother had done, instead she had faced it head-on, giving her children lavish, if abusive, love. That love had pushed Augusta forward, and if Lydia herself had not succeeded in fully transcending the Woolsey habit of ferocious parenting, she had laid the groundwork for the next generation to do so.

Augusta had been so angry at her mother for so long—for dying, among other things—that most of her memories were seen through only one side of the prism. But that prism was slowly turning. Augusta leafed through the scrapbook full of pasted-in pictures of class athletes. When Augusta had looked at the scrapbook at other times, she had been disgusted at the clear fact that it was a scrapbook not for her but for her mother—it was full of pictures of pom-pom–waving cheerleaders looking like flushed, quivering begonias, of flattened corsages from occasions her mother said she would never forget and not one of which she remembered. There was not one thing in it that evoked the true state of the agonized adolescent known as Augusta Woolsey-Bean. What Augusta remembered about that year was not the dances or the football bleachers (she had actually never made the cheerleading team; her limbs flew out like a spider's), but standing alone on the catwalk around the tower, singing at the top of her lungs to an imaginary audience gone wild, or lying on her back looking at the stars and dreaming, not of boys, but of the titillating, mind-stretching idea of what nothingness looked like, of what lay beyond the outer edges of the universe.

But Augusta's popularity had seemed to take on an urgency for Lydia, just as Nellie's coming out had become a similar symbol. Augusta remembered how, with a single social triumph, she had been able to lift her mother from a depression, to make her break out into that warm smile, to make those hands rub together in delight. Augusta had always thought of Lydia as rather callously "working" on Augusta the way Michelangelo had worked on the Sistine Chapel, day after day, year after year, becoming enraged, for instance, when his angel would not blush properly. But now Augusta saw that, for Lydia, Augusta's being accepted by the outside world was all about Lydia not having had the courage to go into it. It was as though if Augusta cheered loudly enough, did backbends far enough, if Nellie dated the boys from Gristbrook often enough, Lydia's daughters would avoid her own fate. And it was almost as though Lydia, having felt inextricably different all her life, could only know that her daughter was not the same way if others told her so.

The plastic album cover reflected Augusta's image, reminding her that she no longer flinched at the sight of it. The negative image of herself that she had fought since she was a teenager did not overtake her so quickly now. Keeping that negative mirror image alive was a way of keeping her loving, abusive mother alive, and somehow she didn't need to do that any longer.

Augusta closed the scrapbook. She felt light and pleasantly weary, as though she had worked very hard for a long time. She was letting go of her self-loathing, her feeling of being either a martyr or a devil, as surely as she was letting go of the idea that her mother was either supernaturally evil or supernaturally good. The Other Mother was joining hands with the First Mother, and Augusta could see her now as a whole woman, someone who was, as Freud put it, more human than otherwise.

Augusta jumped. A soft voice was reaching down through her reverie. She looked up and there stood Nellie.

"Augusta," Nellie said. She sat down amid the diaries and the pictures. She looked tall and straight, statuesque almost, and her green eyes shone. "Augusta, we have to talk."

CHAPTER 16

Ignoring the knot that was forming in her stomach, Augusta took her sister's news with grace: Nellie and Augusta's lover William had found not only the ravine full of hazardous chemicals, but their own hearts, full of love.

Instead of proceeding in an orderly fashion, Augusta's plan had apparently taken on a life of its own. It had burst its boundaries.

It had blown up in her face.

Augusta fought down childish jealousy. The result had been inevitable; she would just have to accept the fact that it had happened much earlier than she intended.

The sisters discussed it calmly. Looked at from a distance, the whole situation had unfolded with Aristotelian symmetry: William had been a fount that had nourished the deep rivalry between them, a reservoir feeding old streams of joy and guilt, of excitement and betrayal. It had all been unspoken but palpable: this dazzlingly sensual figure from their childhood—good-hearted but known for never committing himself to one woman—had stumbled between them and become a stage on which they had reenacted their past. He had become a surrogate for their mother; a third party necessary for the triangular system so familiar to them. With childhood's lulling rhythms, they had moved in and out of William's heart, much as they had moved in and out of Lydia's. When Augusta had returned home six months ago, Nellie was in, and then she was out; now positions had shifted once again.

They agreed that Augusta, by holding William off lately, had all but pushed him into Nellie's arms. Yes, it was as inevitable and tidy as the smooth covers of the diaries that lay here on the grass around Augusta, the diaries that had helped Augusta to grow up and transcend the childish attitudes of the past, that challenged her this very minute to even higher levels of maturity.

"It's wonderful that we can both understand this so well," Nellie said with relief tempered by nervousness. "Can you believe we've come so far, Augusta?"

Augusta began to wheeze.

"Oh no," Nellie sympathized. "I'll go get your inhaler. You know, I wonder if it isn't these Apex chemicals in the air. You haven't wheezed so much since you were a kid."

"I don't think it's the chemicals," Augusta said.

"I wouldn't be too sure. William and I were both short of breath at the dump, although, come to think of it, I'm not so sure that was the fault of the chemicals! He was so sweet, he is so *sweet,* Augusta. The toxins were obviously making him queasy, but all he could do was worry about me."

"It's *not* the goddamn chemicals!" Augusta threw her scrapbook at Nellie's shoulder, and it bounced off, scattering programs and dried flowers all around them. Augusta grabbed them, stuffed everything into her leather bag, and started off toward the house. Then she turned back to the dumbfounded Nellie. "You lying, cheating little worm, you planned this, you plotted everything. All that blasé stuff about you not caring about William. That was bullshit!"

Augusta suddenly began trembling with a rage so primitive

that she had to turn away. She had always intended to make a show of protest when Nellie took up with William; she had even imagined her lines, full of martyred bewilderment. And even as she castigated Nellie now, she sensed that some of it was for Nellie's benefit. But much more came from deep down, from, among other things, that old sense of helpless frustration at trying to control her parents' lives but repeatedly failing. There was no denying it; somehow she had been blessed with the power—and the burden—to alter events, to steer people's lives in new directions, but she simply could not make them do it the way she wanted them to do it.

It came to her suddenly how much she would miss William: his hands, the warm, scratchy feel of his cheek, his tight, nestling hugs. A blade of panic cut through her, the same panic she felt when William had asked for his football cleat back twenty years ago. Had she made a terrible mistake? Maybe she could be happy living in Stonekill Landing after all.

"Augusta!" Nellie said, catching up to her. She was pulling frantically at her hair, dissaranging it, but it still looked becoming, worn in the new style her sister had created for her. "You must have known what William really means to me! It took everything I had to graciously defer to you after you took him from me, but you must have known how much it hurt!"

Augusta squinted at her sister. "I thought we had come so far, Nellie, but this act of yours has set us back years. It feels just like the old days. Don't turn your back on your smiling mother or your smiling sister, Augusta, or you'll feel a knife in your back."

"At least I told you right away!" Nellie said. "I didn't wait until three weeks afterwards. I didn't wait until we had made love a hundred times."

"Oh, thank you. I'm so grateful."

"You want William? You really want him? I'll give him back to you."

"What makes you think he's yours to give?" Augusta went

up the porch steps and sat down on a rocking chair. "A kiss is nothing. A kiss can be an accident. To read so much into one lousy kiss isn't realistic. It isn't even normal!"

"Whoever's making all that racket, stop it!" Henry's muffled yell came from the cellar. "My bees will be getting cross!"

"Oh Daddy," Augusta muttered. "He knows full well bees are deaf."

"So now I'm not normal!" Nellie said, sitting down on the chair next to her sister. "Maybe I've never had much of a sex life, but at least I give William someone to talk to. The poor man's starved for it. There's more to life than fucking."

"How would you know? Someone who professes a new era of sisterhood, who makes up with her sister and talks love and joy and then goes out and seduces her sister's boyfriend! You may see yourself as an innocent, but you don't even bother with the preliminaries before hurling yourself at the nearest man."

That did it. Nellie flew out of her rocking chair like a gunslinger out of a saloon. But she stopped in midflight, fascinated by the violent rocking of the empty chair. She had never remembered being able to get out of that narrow old rocker so easily; it had always seemed to hate to release her, her fat thighs pressing into the wicker sides like dough into a mold. Now, she ran her fingers down her shorts; diet and exercise had made the flesh firmer and trimmer. She looked at Augusta with as much contempt as she could muster.

Augusta's ribs were tightening like steel bands around a wet barrel. Behind Nellie's proud, defiant countenance, Augusta saw the Other Mother pointing her finger in retribution.

So now the piper had to be paid. The gift of knowledge from the diaries, her final separation from her mother, her taking of William out from under Nellie's nose, all these things had to be paid for.

The thought that Lydia's magical theory of reward and punishment, of unhappiness following happiness, had come back to haunt her made Augusta furious. "It will be hard for you, Nellie. He's used to having spectacular sex, better than he's ever had before."

"Maybe he's had too much," Nellie said. "I don't want him for the sex. Fucking is something any two people can do together. Animals do it; that's nearly all they do. Frankly, I sense he's bored with the whole thing."

Augusta was able to stop her fist just before it reached Nellie's face. She wanted to send her sister flying into the peonies. She wished she could put her back on the runaway tractor and stand and watch her crash. She was wheezing so much that she could hardly get the words out, while at the same time she felt as if she were watching herself curiously from a distance.

"Go ahead, sweet sister," Nellie said. "Hit me. Once and for all, do what you've wanted to do since I was born. Kill me."

Augusta stepped back and she reached into her pocket. She pulled out a little plastic gun, put it to her mouth, and took a long draw of her asthma medicine. Suddenly a swarm of bees came buzzing across the porch, heading straight for Nellie, who was so startled that she forgot to use the slow, relaxed movements that her father had taught her to swat them away. A bee stung her on the eye.

"Daddy and his damn bees!" she cried out, holding her face. Her eye was already swelling shut, and it flashed through her mind that this was a sign of defeat, a message from on high: put that doll back, it belongs to your sister. "Jesus, I'm not the one who deserves to be stung! Jesus, Augusta, I don't have any money. I don't have any nice clothes. I don't even have a real job. What do you want from me?"

"Oh Nellie," Augusta sighed, going into the house. "Don't start singing that old song again."

She went to the kitchen and wrapped ice cubes in a linen napkin, then came back out to the porch. The irony of Nellie being stung in the tender tissue of the eye—the absurdity of Nellie interpreting the bee sting as some magical force of unjust justice—at the very moment when Augusta was seized by the notion that the Great Mother in the Sky was exacting punishment from *her*, jolted her back into reality.

She handed the ice compress to Nellie. "We're both back-sliding," Augusta said. "Let's try to calm down and talk."

Nellie lifted her puffy face. "Augusta, if you would step out of yourself just once, you'd know that I can't live without William. I can't think of anything or anyone else. I never stop dreaming about him, in the morning, during the day, at night."

Henry came up through the bulkhead, carrying new beehive parts. "Oh Lord, someone has messed with the tape on this hive I was transporting!" he said, spotting the tape that had come loose on the entrance and ventilation holes. "Now I've probably got bees loose all over the place!" Ever since Henry had learned that the Woolsey ruby was a fake and that he had not misplaced a million dollars' worth of jewelry, he had been feeling his oats. Moreover, he had confessed to losing both the ruby and the diamond that Lydia had entrusted to him, and his daughters' reassuring forgiveness had further released him.

He went over to the hive he had brought up to the yard to work on, and which had yielded the bee that had stung Nellie. "Now where's my bee smoker . . . who took my smoker? Oh, here it is . . . Nellie, Augusta! I had five honeycomb frames here and now there's only four!"

Nellie and Augusta simultaneously ducked into the house to avoid their father, who looked around, then shrugged, picked up his beehive, and went down into the orchards.

As soon as he was gone, Augusta and Nellie came back out onto the porch. "Pain that he is, it's kind of nice to have the old Dad back, stomping about making himself heard," Nellie said. "It's hard to believe he's been dry since Mom died . . . over six months. I wonder if he'll really make it this time."

"Nellie," Augusta said. "If you had been clear from the beginning about your real feelings for William, instead of being so coy, I might have been able to stay away from him. I knew how you felt, I'm not as insensitive to you as you think, but all that secretiveness and ambiguity allowed me to deny how things really were. God, I agonized over it. I tried to resist William, I tried and tried, but I just couldn't. I know you needed him, but I needed him too."

"But you don't need him now, do you, Augusta?"

Augusta walked over to the end of the porch and looked down the sloping lawn to the Southeast Orchards, which led down into the vast Apex complex. Didn't she need him? "If Mother were alive, she would divide him up," she said. "Half for you, half for me. Then no one would be happy."

Nellie went over to Augusta. "Augusta, look at me. Are you in love with William? I mean, really in love? Answer me honestly."

Augusta knew the honest answer, but right now she was not going to give Nellie the satisfaction of hearing it. "And if I wasn't, that would make your actions all right?"

"It would only tell you why, down at the toxic dump, I didn't hold myself back any longer."

Augusta squinted down at the distant field near the Apex property. Two figures were running, one after the other, propelled along like scraps of paper. At first she thought they were deer, but then the first one did not try to jump the wire fence that separated Apex from the Southeast Orchards, but seemed to be scrambling up it. Then she recognized the red shirt she knew William had worn down to breakfast this morning. "Here comes your beloved," Augusta said. "And he seems to be running for his life."

Twenty minutes later, Augusta, Nellie, Henry, Coert, and the local sheriff stood in the kitchen of the Woolsey homestead, listening to the excited monologue of a guard in a blue uniform. The operations manager of the Apex Electronics Corporation, Harold Stubbs, punctuated the guard's account with sullen nods. The guard had surprised an intruder dressed in a red shirt skulking in the corridors of the hot fuel lab, and had chased the man for half a mile until he climbed a chainlink fence topped with barbed wire and disappeared into the Woolsey orchards. As fortune would have it, Mr. Stubbs happened to be in the lab on this Saturday afternoon.

Mr. Stubbs, a slight, narrow man who stood tensely, gave the impression that he could be snapped like a soda cracker. He moved out of a shaft of sunlight that his wife told him put his new hair implant in an unflattering light. He cleared his throat and pitched his voice in the low monotone he had so admired in Chuck Connors. "This same man, sometimes accompanied by a woman, has been seen loitering around the complex for weeks, questioning our employees. We have been watching him. He has also been seen entering and leaving this orchard at regular intervals."

Henry Bean, who was standing there chewing his pipe, began to cough, and took his time about it. When he had finished, he put his handkerchief slowly back into his pocket, folded his arms, and leveled his gaze at Harold Stubbs. "Now, who exactly did you say was doing all this prowling and spying? You folks or this red-shirted fellow?"

"There are people in your house who have been trespassing on our property!" Stubbs said, aware that he was losing the advantage. He was unsure of his ground. He was unsure of who this trespasser was, of why he was honing in on them asking questions about their waste-disposal systems, of how much he knew, of how much he had learned today. And he suspected, but did not know for certain, that the woman leaning against the oven was the one who had been accompanying him. "In fact, I think your whole family's involved!"

Nellie was trying to block the crimson cuff that was sticking out of the oven door. They had hurriedly stashed William's torn shirt there when they heard the sheriff at the back door; they had whisked William into the sickroom and closed the door. Nellie was grateful that William had insisted she hide under big hats whenever they went near Apex, for she did not think she was recognized. She tried not to look at the peephole in the wall; William, standing on the other side and exercising colossal nerve, had placed his gleaming brown eye to it.

The sheriff stood holding his hat, looking stolid and impassive. He had known Lydia Woolsey-Bean when she was still Lydia Woolsey. His family had always bought bushels of the orchard's first apples. "Anything to this, Henry? You know or seen anybody in a red shirt today?"

Henry hitched his trousers up and turned to Augusta, then Nellie. "You girls seen anybody like that?" They said no. "Then I guess I can't help you, sheriff."

"He's lying," Stubbs said, appealing to the sheriff.

The sheriff clapped his book shut. "Henry Bean's word is good enough for me," he said, and ushered Stubbs and the guard out the back door, glancing at the oven as he did.

"William!" Henry bellowed after the police car had gone down the driveway.

A bare-chested and vastly relieved William came into the kitchen and sat down. Nellie picked up the bottle of Mercurochrome she had been about to use on William when the sheriff arrived. He winced as Nellie swabbed the cuts where the barbed wire had bitten into his back and the palms of his hands. "I didn't even know they made this stuff anymore," he said, smiling up at her.

"And I didn't know that grown men broke into private property!" Henry said gruffly. He smacked his pipe against the sole of his shoe to loosen the burnt tobacco dregs. "The reason my word was good enough for the sheriff is that I've never broken it—until now."

William apologized to Henry. "Thank you for protecting me. I did break the law, I did break into that Apex building, and I know it's no excuse if I say that Apex itself is breaking the law."

"You're right there," Henry said. "Your father would have told you that. And I don't like you involving my daughter in this. You don't break the law under any circumstances."

"Oh look, that's not true," William said. "If Hitler opened an office on Main Street, I would guess you'd use every means you could to steal his plans for the annihilation of the Jews and expose them."

"That's hardly an apt analogy in this case," Augusta said. "We might not like what Apex is doing, but it's not exactly the Third Reich."

"But it is," William said, clearing his throat. "I think that Apex is deliberately trying to poison Woolsey Orchards."

Everyone stared at him.

"I don't think it's a question of corporate insensitivity anymore," he continued. "This dumping is not corporate negligence. It has more in common with premeditated murder."

"Harold Stubbs is trying to kill us?" Augusta asked.

"Apex is trying to drive you off your property. I'm almost sure of it. How many times have they offered to buy the orchards, Henry?"

"They were bugging us with offers right up until Lydia's death, and we gave them flat negatives. Then they stopped."

"Well, now they've decided to make you an offer you can't refuse. It's the new American way," William said. "The flip side of 'I can be anything I want to be' is 'I can do anything to get there.' If you can't lure your prey out of the lair, simply booby-trap them inside."

"Just a minute," Augusta said. "Have you noticed the smell coming from the pump house? I thought it was the fungicide we used, but this morning it was abnormally strong right by the well."

Coert shook his head. "If anyone was coming on this farm to tamper with the well, I'd be the first to know."

"They don't need to get anywhere *near* the property," William said. He described the chemicals in the dump that he and

Nellie had found, and voiced his suspicion that Apex was flushing wastes through the former brick factory's old clay pipes into the river. "I think they're dumping enough hazardous solvents to seep through every source of water in the area," William said.

"Gee," Nellie mused. "Stubbs himself looked like a human chemical depot, with his shiny polyesters and that ghastly rug."

"Talk about being refugees from a Charles Addams story!" Augusta said. "We're probably full of carcinogens. You know, nobody in the family ever died of cancer before Mother did. And she drank a quart of water a day."

"Calm down, Augusta," Henry said. "Don't you of all people succumb to the power of suggestion. Tell us the rest, William. What did you find today when you made the illegal entry to which I am now an accomplice?"

William stood up and paced. "When I was in the lab corridor, I heard Stubbs talking on the telephone in an office. He was talking about the load of pure unstored chemicals that Nellie and I just saw dumped. And he talked about your apple crop. He must have been talking to some higher-up. He said something like, 'Yes, sir, nothing on that farm is doing well. Looks like maybe our little operation has had benefits we never dreamed of.' Then he said he would step up the waste-disposal schedule. He finished with the words, 'By the end of the season, they will be begging us to buy them out at a nice price.' "

Henry put his head in his hands. Coert opened the back door and spat out a plug of tobacco.

"Apex is a small company, don't forget," William continued. "It's a newcomer to the electronics market, although a successful one. It wants to expand its operations. The only thing is, according to our information, it doesn't have the capital either to comply with the government's new industrial waste-disposal requirements or to pay top dollar for expansion land. It's found what it thinks is a perfect way to kill two birds with one stone. I plan to go to the authorities with all of this now. Thanks in part to Nellie, I have enough evidence to make a convincing case."

"Unbelievable. It's just unbelievable that folks nowadays'd do something like this," Coert said.

"It's so wild that if you hadn't such a good case, William, I would have sworn this was some fantasy about capitalism spread by the Communists," Henry said, getting up and going to the back door. "Come on, Coert, let's catch the last light of the day. Let's go back down to the bees, harvest a bit of honey, remind ourselves how things work in an orderly society. Bees do everything aboveboard, even killing."

"Nellie," Henry said as he went out, "I don't want you setting foot on Apex property. I don't want you getting anywhere near those characters. It's not safe, do you hear?"

Nellie stared at him. Then she nodded. "Yes, Dad," she said gently. "You're right. I won't."

"Don't worry," William said, feeling embarrassed in front of Henry that he had gotten his daughter mixed up in the mess. "Nellie is safe. I won't let anything happen to her."

Augusta abruptly pushed past William and went out the door.

William stared after her, then glanced questioningly at Nellie. She looked at him apprehensively. "I told her. She was upset."

"Oh look, I wish you had let me talk to her first."

"She's my sister, William."

William turned, and without a word followed Augusta down to the Newtown Pippins.

It was suddenly getting dark. Augusta lay down on the grass and looked up at the clouds scudding past a moon that was turning silver. William sat down beside her. He remembered how they used to watch the clouds endlessly, back when they were sixteen. They would lie there the whole afternoon, finding elephants and pianos and hunchbacks carrying televisions.

"See that woman up there?" he leaned over so Augusta could see where he was pointing. "She's stretching out in bed. See her arms?"

"I think she's writhing," Augusta said. "I think she's being screwed to within an inch of her life."

"Now that's a description I never would have imagined coming from your mouth when we used to watch the clouds," William said. "Although it *was* my favorite thing to do with you because I was hoping in vain it would lead to sex."

Augusta rolled over and looked at him. "Well, it did, didn't it? Twenty years later. Sex and more sex and more sex. Did you get tired of it?"

"What?" William said. He threw down the grass he was chewing. "I've been wanting to make love to you for three damn weeks! You've acted as though I was an old shoe."

"I suppose it was all the talking." Augusta leaned on her forearm and gazed up at him with her penetrating blue eyes. "You and Nellie talking, talking, getting to know each other better every minute. The sexual tension building, the sexual fantasies becoming more delectable, more forbidden. Nellie played it exactly the way my grandmother would have advised she play it, in fact the way I played it in high school. Only I got dumped and Nellie won."

"Augusta, stop it. I'm sorry, I'm really sorry." William could not bear to look at her, for her arm was pushing her creamy breasts half out of her shirt, and she looked devastating in the ripening twilight. It occurred to him that she was trying to seduce him, trying to spite Nellie, looking at him like that, but the thought made him feel shabby. After all, he was the one sitting there half-naked, talking about women stretching in bed. "God, I didn't want to hurt you, I didn't mean to hurt you. I didn't think I *could* hurt you, Augusta."

Augusta sat up and sighed. "Oh, it's all right. I've known for weeks that it was over."

"I didn't. Not really. I hardly know now."

"Well, if you haven't completely made up your mind between Nellie and me, let me save you the trouble."

"Look, Augusta, I've never had any regrets about choosing you. Even though we've grown apart, I didn't plan what happened between Nellie and me today. In fact, it happened so fast, I'm not sure I know what happened."

Augusta was tempted to remark on this lightning shift in his affections—after he had not long ago professed his love and commitment to Augusta—and what it said about his claim to have outgrown his old fickle self. But then she would have had to admit to him more than she cared to: that it was she who had conspired to push him into Nellie's arms. "We both knew about your attraction to Nellie. I just couldn't bring myself to force the topic out into the open."

"But I had no self-control!" William said. "And now I've hurt you. I've turned around and hurt and betrayed you just like I did twenty years ago."

"No, no, it's not the same, actually." Augusta got up. The sky was full of stars now, and the clouds had broken into a dozen little wisps dancing around a shimmering taffeta moon. She tried to close her eyes to William's shiny skin, the little nipples peeking out of his chest hair.

"The fact is," she said, "ever since you broke up with me in high school, I've had trouble leaving relationships. I just let them linger on, even when they're in shambles, even when I know I should leave. So I ended up always being left. Except this time. Maybe I couldn't come right out and say I was leaving you, but I left in my own way, didn't I?"

But William did not want her to; all at once he wanted her hair, her eyes, her mouth, that luscious body he knew so well. But he wanted Nellie too. He wanted someone devoted to him, someone peaceful. He felt sick with confusion.

"William." Augusta put her hand on his arm. "It's all right. We have to let go. I have never had a relationship like this, free of fear and worry and self-negation. I've broken my own sick pattern of getting mixed up with deadbeats and turning myself over to them. It got so that I knew I just couldn't get near men. They were like those toxins in the dump; they just altered my whole metabolism. I went from being animal to vegetable. And then you came along."

William laughed. "And you reversed the process! I swear I have never been with such an independent, self-willed woman. Not to speak of what you became in bed!"

Augusta blushed. "That is where it all began. Making love with you taught me that I could be fulfilled without losing myself; that I could get attached and not have to relinquish everything else I loved."

"Gee, it sounds as if I was something you broke your teeth on. A laboratory experiment, sort of. Did I have anything at all to do with it?"

"Of course," she said. She touched his shoulder, slid her hand slowly down his arm, feeling his muscles, feeling his wounds. He winced. She took his hand, kissed his fingers. She knew that as much as his earlier abandonment of her had fueled her longing for him, their rich sex life had allowed her to exorcise him. With each caress, each kiss, each orgasm, the power of the memory of the boy who had hurt her faded.

"I never did get over you the first time," Augusta said. "Until now, until I had you again."

"Until we finished what we started," William said, stroking her hair.

"So you're giving me up without a fight?" he asked. "Don't you think our relationship could grow if we gave it a chance?"

"William, the point is that we've grown inside it. It was like a greenhouse, it sheltered us while we grew. I've begun to learn that people who hurt me don't have to have eternal power over me, that I don't have to constantly search for love to feel lovable. You've been learning to love freely, without fear of hurting someone. We rewrote our own histories together. And now, instead of a symbol of our failures, our relationship stands as a symbol of our success."

"Oh look, that sounds like an awfully fancy way of saying I

don't love you anymore," William said. "You're so damn ana-
lytical. The next thing you'll say is that our little affair was just
preparing me for your sister."

"I'm just saying our relationship had a beginning and a
middle and an end, and Nellie came in at the end."

They stopped in front of Auntie Mame. William touched
Augusta's ivory cheek, her silky hair, traced her full, lovely lips.
"Auntie Mame's grown attached to us. How can you desert
her?"

Just then Nellie called from the porch. "Dinner, everybody!
Roast beef! Popovers piping hot!"

William and Augusta looked at each other and laughed.
"You're finally going to get enough to eat! You'll be fed within
an inch of your life . . . and my sister's popovers are sinfully
delicious."

They started up toward the house. "We're ending just where
we began," William said, putting his hand on Augusta's shoulder. He looked back wistfully at Auntie Mame. "With Nellie's
voice coming between us."

CHAPTER 17

"I'm a virgin," Nellie blurted out in the middle of Newbury's Five and Dime, her face approaching the shade of a cranberry negligee hanging on the rack.

Augusta turned away so that Nellie would not see her astonishment. "You are?" she asked, with as much emphasis as if Nellie had confessed she had never played pinochle before. "Oh, look, this is perfect," Augusta said, pulling out a snowy white gown with little blue ribbons dancing demurely round the bodice.

"Have you ever known anyone outside of an institution who was still a virgin at nearly thirty years of age?"

"Of course," Augusta said nonchalantly. But in fact she didn't, and she was flooded with tenderness for her sister; it was as though she had broken free from the net of their sibling enmeshment and was seeing Nellie, the woman, for the first time.

This feeling had come to her frequently since their confrontation two weeks ago over William. Nellie had predicted that Augusta would become reconciled quickly to the shift in their triangular relationship, and to her own amazement she had. In the final weeks of their relationship, Augusta's interest in William had dimmed, but now that William and Nellie were the couple, her attentions were recaptured. This time, it was with Nellie that her passion lay, for she felt an intense identification with her sister.

The day after Nellie and William had discovered the toxic dump, William had gone to Washington to alert his environmental contacts, get the dumping stopped, and set up meetings with government officials. He had left just in time, for the Northeast had been struck over the last several days with a brutal heat wave. The temperature had reached a hundred degrees, the vegetables were wilting, and so were the inhabitants of the Woolsey homestead, which, of course, had no air-conditioning. It was so humid that paper turned limp in their hands.

So no one would take an inadvertent sip of contaminated water or even wash a dish in it, Henry had gone up to the Catskills and filled jugs with water from mountain springs; he had tightened every faucet shut with a wrench. The heat was like a drug numbing them all, as was the growing evidence that they were sitting on a chemical time bomb. But beneath their stupor, each one of them felt a kind of inner excitement: the toxic seepage and the odd behavior of the mice had provided Henry with a crisis in which he could do a heroic turn or two; Nellie was anticipating William's return with terror and delight; Augusta was coming to the end of the diaries, reliving with her mother her last days. The family coexisted like marbles in a box, rolling and clattering against each other, each set on its own path but all coming together when the box was tilted by a unifying theme.

Nellie and Augusta had developed the habit of sitting by the fan in Augusta's room, talking late into the night about men and romance in general and William in particular. They had become like best friends, the older, more experienced Augusta preparing the younger Nellie in the ways of the world. But

Augusta, standing by the nightgowns in Newbury's Five and Dime, had not realized until this moment just how innocent Nellie really was.

"Nellie . . . um, I thought you had had full relationships with men," Augusta said. "There was that Boots guy and the famous Digby-Downes. How could you—"

"Augusta, I *have* had sex. I've had men, but nobody could . . . nobody's been able to, you know, crack the code, so to speak."

Augusta stared at her. "But Nellie, there are doctors who can do something about that! In fact, I remember reading that in the olden days women commonly had their hymens cut before their wedding."

"Oh Augusta, I'm not as worried about my hymen as I am about the fact that you're such a hard act to follow," Nellie said miserably. Augusta's casual acceptance of her virginity was enabling Nellie to share the cold wave of apprehensiveness that was coming over her once more. Newbury's had just gotten a shipment of seconds in silk lingerie, and Nellie had never in her life owned a fancy nightgown. "These are made for women like you. I'll look silly. He'll jump out of my bed and beg for you back. He may do that anyway, seeing that I don't know what I'm doing."

"Oh stop," Augusta said impatiently. She held the nightgown up to her sister. She fluffed up Nellie's hair. She felt a stab of regret. "Just look at you—a more gorgeous sight that mirror has never seen. William Hurley is going to be butter. His knees will fold before he can even get far enough to tear this gown from your shoulders."

Nellie blushed. "Shh!" she said, eyeing a saleslady hovering in the background.

"Anytime you begin to doubt yourself, just remember how you succeeded in getting your man," Augusta said wryly. She went over to the saleslady and handed her the gown. "We'll take this one."

"Augusta, I think you're getting a vicarious thrill out of this whole thing!"

Augusta took a blue satin robe from the rack and held it up; it deepened her eyes. "All right, I'll get something for myself then. For my next life, whatever it may be. Ooh, I look good, I really do."

"When didn't you look crushingly good?" Nellie said, examining her own profile doubtfully in the mirror, sucking in her stomach, thrusting out her chest. "Maybe he really will shrink with horror. Maybe he'll have to pretend he's making love to you."

"Wow, what an unusual feeling this is," Augusta mused, staring at the full-length mirror. "I've always faced the mirror as if I was facing an attacker. I've never known what it was like to look at yourself with all your flaws and to like even them. Not to love them, but just to accept them and kind of like them—to know you don't have to absolutely love the way you are, but just to mildly like it. It's so peaceful, it's so restful."

"Hmm." Nellie stared thoughtfully at her own reflection. "Yes, I'm beginning to see what you mean."

They lingered in the store, savoring the air-conditioned coolness, but finally Augusta began to feel anxious to get back home. Now she was at the point in the diaries when Lydia had had her first operation for ovarian cancer, and Augusta was pulled to her mother as strongly as she had been drawn away from her when it had actually happened. The world that had kept her occupied while her mother died now beckoned again: the Hollywood documentary women had been pursuing her, and she had been putting them off; they seemed like an intrusion, an irrelevancy when her mother was fighting for her life, when her anguish, her struggle came alive every time Augusta opened one of the little books that were arrayed in her room. She could only bear to spend a few hours at a time away from them. Nellie was not yet ready to read the final volumes, perhaps because she had lived those months with Lydia so closely. But for Augusta, it was a journey back, a second chance to be there for her mother, as though by holding the little books, absorbing them, she could reverse time, and prevent the death they chronicled.

"Let's go, let's get out of here," Augusta said, going up to the counter to pay.

"Augusta, you're being so good," Nellie said as they went out to the car. "Since we had the scene over William, you've been so wonderful. It's making me nervous. I keep wondering if it's real, but then I remember that this is the way we started out, so close, you so nice and protective of me when I was little."

Augusta fingered the fine, slippery fabric in the Newbury's bag as the car waited at the town stoplight. One day, long ago, Lydia must have gone shopping like this, fingered fine fabric, fingered the robe that became her dream-garment. Augusta felt suffused with a sense of loss, a longing for her mother, for the intimacy of the diaries.

"I'm scared I'll wake up and you'll decide you hate me again," Nellie was saying. "I know it's irrational."

"It's not irrational," Augusta said. "That's how we've been programmed. You would be blind to lose sight of the fact that I treated you like dirt."

"You're actually admitting that?"

"Nellie," Augusta said, "how could I have reconciled the two mothers that lived in my mind without recognizing the good mother and the bad mother in myself? Mother was unfair to you, and I was too. I treated you like you were nothing. You're a lot better than we made you think you were. You have to remember that."

Nellie put her hand on Augusta's arm. "If after everything we've been through you can see Mother's humanity, then surely you can see your own. And there's something I want *you* to remember: maybe we can't heal each other's wounds or fill up the holes created by the turmoil of our childhoods, but at least we have each other to know it really happened. We're the only ones on earth who bore witness to it. Thank God you were there."

Augusta and Nellie drove home in an aura of contentment, but their sense of well-being faded when they drove into the driveway and were faced with the specter of tired and ill-looking trees. Apex had halted the dumping and had been slapped with a heavy fine, but that would not remove the hydrocarbons and other harmful chemicals that had already leached into the Woolsey water, nor the heavy metals and the PCBs that had shown up in the latest tests of their soil samples. No one knew for sure what effect the chemicals had had on the delicate balance of the nitrogen and other soil nutrients that nourished the trees, but the leaves were pale and stunted, not lush as in previous summers, not as they would be if the unpredictable weather alone were the culprit. The newly grafted Paulared scions in the old Christmas Orchard had not budded, and adjacent rows of Empires and Golden Delicious downhill from the woods where the dump was located had deteriorated over the summer; more and more trees had been girdled by mice and were in various stages of dying, their sparsely leafed branches an iridescent bronze, dramatic as a death-rattle. The voles themselves were acting funny; it was almost unknown for mice to chew the bark off trees in summer, when there was plenty of fresh grass for them to eat. Moreover, these particular voles did not seem to have normal fear. They got up on their hind legs atop the apple crates scattered over the orchard, as defiant as convicts who had escaped their execution chambers. One of William's biologist friends had lent credence to Nellie's theory: it was at least possible that the toxins had altered the immunological mechanism of the mice, creating a new strain of survivors inured to strong chemicals, including phosphide-coated pellets of mice poison.

What was abundantly clear was the noxious effect of direct exposure to the chemical dump. Nellie and William had suffered rashes and nausea the day after their discovery; William had almost not made it onto the plane to Washington.

"Look at this," Nellie said as they passed several Romes. "The apples look like miniature hunchbacks of Notre Dame! God, when I think that I've been living in this house my whole life. I'm probably full of carcinogens. My stomach still feels like someone's rubbed it with sandpaper!"

"It's the heat, sweetie," Augusta said, feeling once again her own neck for the disconcerting lump she had felt there for the last week. "Apex hasn't been here that long, don't let yourself get so worried. It takes time for chemicals to make their way through the ground. They've probably only recently begun seeping over here."

"Oh Augusta, things are in such a mess," Nellie said. "The apple crop looks like it's going to be a bust. The house is so old the plaster's buckling. A big corporation is trying to poison us out. And look, we have a father who's gone from being a limp rag to a paranoid gun nut."

They drove by Henry Bean, who was sawing tires in half and putting them around the trees. He had the idea that the mice were rampant not because they were immune to the poison pellets, but because they were suspicious of these blue nuggets scattered in plain sight and were actually not eating them. His goal was to surround every surviving tree with tires, which would lure in the mice, who liked cozy, dark shelter. They would then eat the poison pellets and that would be that. Earlier in the day, Henry had been shooting at targets down by the Christmas Orchard. He had opened his gun cabinet for the first time since he had forsworn his gun hobby many years before. He was making ammunition, loading and reloading, and he had secreted several guns in spots throughout the house—he said you needed to be prepared for anything when you had neighbors who might be trying to poison you.

"It reminds me of the days of the Kennedy assassination, when he thought the Russians had already reached Cuba," Nellie sighed. "While you and Mom were collecting gun control petitions, Dad was rearming the Woolsey nation."

"Oh God, look up there, above the trees," Nellie said, getting out of the car. "The air is actually undulating. It's like bodies on a dance floor."

"It's moving all right," Augusta said, wiping her brow. "You can hear the molecules screaming as they get pressed closer and closer together. You go in and hug the fan. I'm going down and getting Daddy into the house."

Just then Henry started up the yard, so Augusta waited for him, stopping to pick some zucchini from the kitchen garden before they shriveled in the sun. For the last two days it had been so hot that Henry had been going around in his boxer shorts, an interesting variation on his pajamas, particularly since today he seemed to be wearing a pair that belonged to William. This was a fact of which no one seemed to be aware, except Augusta, who knew every pair of William's shorts by heart. They must have gotten mixed up in the laundry.

As she squatted in the garden, Henry's bare skinny legs walked through her field of vision and filled her with an overwhelming sadness: sadness for her father, old in young men's underwear, for her mother, who had told no one that she knew she was going to die, for herself, who was getting old, who should be cradling a baby instead of this zucchini in her arms.

"Oh, hi!" Henry said, suddenly noticing Augusta. The sweat was rolling down his forehead. "Don't say it, I know I shouldn't be working so hard in this heat. But it has to be done if this farm is going to have a chance."

Augusta felt her neck again. It was probably just the heat, swelling up her gland. "Daddy," she said suddenly, her throat tightening. Standing there in his shorts, dangling a piece of tire in one hand, a pistol in the other, he looked absurd. Absurd and infuriating. "You understand now that I have to leave here come fall. That's all settled, isn't it?"

"I understand," he said.

"All this, the underwear, the tires, the guns, all these things you're doing, are you trying to tell me something? Are you trying to tell me something you haven't told me directly? Are you trying to tell me that you're not ready for me to leave?"

Henry stared at her angrily. "I would have thought it obvious that I was telling you just the opposite."

"You promised Mother never to lift a gun again!" Augusta found herself almost shouting, remembering her mother's account of the fight during which he had shot up the fence, remembering her mother's pain, remembering her own. "All your drunken violence, your damned drink and your damned temper! Why are you taking up guns again, with all of that behind you?"

Pain showed itself in every muscle of his face. "Because it *is* behind me. I'm *not* drinking, Augusta. I'm not drinking. That's the main thing."

"Yes," Augusta said, ashamed of herself. And suddenly she let go of the old guilt; she let go of him. "Yes, of course. That *is* the main thing, Daddy."

A light, refreshing breeze cooled her. She watched his face clear, she saw how he had imbued her with the power to take away—and to restore—his self-esteem. And she knew the truth: she could not change him, and even if he wanted her to, she did not need to. Even though he might want her to think this, she did not have the power either to boost him or to crush him, only to be kind to him, to love him. He would be exactly what he was, he would continue just as he was, without her. "I'm sorry, Dad," she said.

Henry patted her arm. "Never mind," he said, taking the load of zucchini from her. "None of us is sane in this heat. Let's go inside."

Up in her room, Augusta took out the last two diary volumes, the ones her mother kept during her five-year battle with ovarian cancer. She settled herself on her bed and began to read:

January 30, 1972
The hospital

*H*ow ironic it is that I should end up with ovarian cancer. They were lazy, reluctant things, these ovaries of
mine, then they produced two beautiful human beings,
and now they are pouring bad seed into my body. When
I asked if the cancer would recur, the surgeon told me it
depended on a number of factors, which depended on a
number of others. Then he smiled beneficently and
walked out. He always does this when I ask a question
more complicated than the time of day.

Mama, who has practically never seen blood, and certainly not an open wound, regards me as though I had a
tarantula on my belly. She tried to change my dressing,
but when I looked up into her eyes I felt the ultimate
humiliation. Down through the years I have seen those
same eyes, catching sight of me getting undressed, watching me when I touched my children, eyes that are disgusted, pitiless. As she exposed the incision, her nose was
trembling with the effort not to smell. Then Henry came
in, slid his hands under hers, and said, "I'll do this,
Amenia."

Henry has turned out to be the silver lining behind the
cloud. He has forsaken his women, his whiskey, to linger
by my side. He is renewed; my old hero. And when the
fear starts coming up about two in the morning, when I
hear the lonely thud of the doctor's shoes along the corridor, the whispers of nurses huddling around the cancer
patient next to me, when I see the shadow of her I.V.,
the smell of disinfectant mixed with the warm, womblike
odor of this room, like the scent of pennies heating in the
sun, when my heart begins to race, that is when I think
of my husband. I see the top of his head, I see him bend
over me; he changes my bandage. As delicately as an altar

boy, he lifts the gauze, swabs the wound with a soaked cotton ball, applies the white pads as reverently as if he were nursing his bees. I have discovered that he is going bald on top. In the place of his hair is the most adorable fuzz, like the crown of a baby.

March 1, 1972

I am floating free, lying in luxury. It is now Mama who must live within the prison of household trivialities. It is she who must nag and organize and make sure the butcher sends the suet with the beef. The house smells horribly of pea soup, and Mama presides over the dinner table like a flagpole. Henry takes refuge in my room. Everyone, including me, seems to prefer me when I'm flat on my back.

May 3, 1972

*A*ugusta was so worried that I am not making better progress that she has come home for two weeks. Do you know that she has had symptoms similar to mine, at exactly the same time as mine? Hers turned out to be nervous colitis, thank God. If anything were to happen to her, I could not survive it.

Henry has perfected a new technique of bandaging the infected incision. He thinks I cannot manage it. He thinks he is indispensable to me, and I wouldn't dream of disillusioning him.

The apple blossoms seem to be coming right through my window; I close my eyes and the bedroom is papered with their delicate whiteness, it is snowing blossoms. I am reading the Bible, I am trying to dispel resentment, grudges, anger, so I can truly find God. I want Him to enter me so that I will have courage in the face of death.

Nellie says pointed things like, "When you are a grandma, Mom," and Erastus says my heart and lungs are so sound that I'll outlive them all. They are angry at me for not feeling better. They are afraid.

Betsey, Peggy, even Augusta and Nellie are astonished at my serenity, my uncomplaining peacefulness. They look at me like some fragile treasure whose worth they have misjudged. What they do not understand is that I have faced the ultimate catastrophe. I have a right to say, to feel any way I want, and no one can fault me. Not even Mama can dare to call me melodramatic, for she is past seventy-five and healthy as a horse and I am cursed and not yet old. And I know what none of them know. I am prepared for my destiny. I know that I will die of this disease.

July 26, 1972

At last I have left my bed. I do a little around the house each day. Augusta's frequent visits have done it, of course. How sad that it took illness to end my loneliness. All my life I have been empty of something, I knew not what, and now I am filled with something that no one can take away. If only I had given myself over to God earlier. If only I had stopped trying to make people love me, the love would just have come, the way it has now. God is everywhere, God is in Mama's comforting voice, Mama who in spite of her burning bunions climbs those stairs to bring me my tray three times a day. God is in Henry's fingers, God is in Nellie's hands as they rub my back. I look at all of them and whisper my gratitude for this

April 4, 1974
The hospital

Dr. Holman has strange and rather wonderful white skin. I suppose it's because there's not much sunshine in the operating room. He works so hard that I worry about him. He palpated me last week and gave me a gold star; the tumor has shrunk enough under the radiation treatment so that he can operate tomorrow.

I told him not to have a fight with his wife tonight, and that was my way of finding out whether or not he had a wife. But he only gave me a belly laugh. I wonder if he'll leave enough of my belly so I'll be able to laugh like that again.

When I think about Dr. Holman, I see his pale, pale skin, almost translucent, like an angel's wing.

April 6, 1974

I shall never forget Horace leaning over me as I awoke, saying I had such a cute belly button that he decided to leave it on. Fat old me with a navel stretched out like a rubber band! I wonder if that is the kind of thing he says to all his female patients. I rather think not. The belly button is just about all he did leave. Among other things, he removed my entire reproductive system.

May 17, 1974

Home again, at last. Dear Coert says the blossoms hung on the trees just for me. It seems like loneliness will never again be my lot. Every day, Peggy and Betsey arrive and shout some silvery silliness up through the old speaking

moment, this day, for days have an end, life a limit, and for me that limit is in sight.

Augusta put down the diary; tears blurred the pages. She looked out the window. The valley was in shadow now, dusk was settling over the trees, and her room grew cool. It seemed to echo with Lydia's voice. Augusta felt unconnected to her surroundings; she was situated elsewhere, disembodied, traveling through the valley of the shadow of death with her mother. Soon she would have to say good-bye.

Augusta read through the entries for the next seventeen months. Her mother had flourished under the concerned attentions of her family, but the more healthy she became, the more they took her for granted. And the more anxiety Lydia felt. As much as she wanted to, she could not translate her serenity in illness into serenity in health. Henry began staying out late. Augusta went to Europe with a boyfriend instead of taking her mother, a fact she had felt remorse about at the time. But now, reading about it in the context of Lydia's other disappointments, Augusta realized that Lydia's pain at her absence had less to do with Augusta than with Lydia and her unquenchable needs.

At the end of the year, Lydia's symptoms began to recur:

December 29, 1973

I didn't want to spoil everyone's Christmas, so I didn't tell them. I just sat in the corner of the parlor, concentrating not on the gifts but on this new pain, trying to drive it out. And today, at the doctor's office, I concentrated again, like you do when you are willing your airplane to stay up in the air, vainly trying to rearrange the words on the doctor's tongue in my favor. The worst thing about cancer is that you don't know where it is, when it will appear, what it is doing inside the dugout of your body. The nights are the worst. Last night I listened for Henry, hoping that he would again accidentally stumble into my bed, for even the blast of whiskey and perfume would be better than this dark empty terror.

I will spend New Year's Day in the hospital, and most likely will go under the knife. I had a dream that the whole family was watching the most beautiful sunset up in the Adirondacks. Suddenly a swarm of locusts descended and chose me as their target. Everyone in the family was grateful because they thought I would know how to handle them. But as soon as I swatted one group away, another came out of nowhere, until my muscles suddenly melted into defenseless blubber. Sometimes the locusts are wolves, sometimes spiders, but in all the dreams I am being eaten alive.

January 7, 1974
The hospital

*I*t is very quiet in the corridors tonight. The African violets Henry brought me look like the little paws of kittens swimming in the moonlight that streams through my window.

The cancer has spread too far. They opened and then closed me right up again. There is nothing they can do. I have six months at the outside. The family is so numb, they cannot even manage to get here when visiting hours begin. How can anyone expect me not to lose my faith? I want to go to the Orient! Mama has been twenty times. I want to see the next blossoms, I want to see my grandchildren. And I want to be beautiful. I want to be thin

and willowy. I suppose now that this last wish is the only one I'll get.

I won't forget who did this to me. Even though he dotes on me now, I won't betray my sense of his betrayals. My illness is the result of his adultery. My death will be the consequence of his infidelity. I will never tell him this. But he will know. For the rest of his life, he will know what I have known, and that is that the bad you do comes back to you.

I feel despised, pitied. My life hasn't amounted to much, really. I've never felt that anything I did lived on. I've made little impact on those I love. But after I die, they will have a surprise. For I will speak louder from the grave than I have ever spoken here.

February 1, 1974

*T*hank the Lord for Augusta. Tomorrow I go to
York to see a doctor who thinks he can opera
remove all the cancer. I tell everyone the story
proud. Augusta simply declared, "My mother i
to die." Augusta, my Augusta, you never
what you were told. You left your job ar
medical records and you went around to
cer centers until you found Horace Ho
who closed me up as "inoperable" sa
Holman proposes is "fruitless heroi
the heroics, thank you. I don't kn
but I believe in him and I thi

My beloved first child, hov
try to give me back my lif
of us both. All your life, I
and women who were
saved by the devotion
stories myself.

tube that dates back to when Great-grandma Hopestill was bedridden. Henry makes ever more perfect dressings with something close to, what can I say, rapture. When he swabs and anoints and cuts and measures my bandages with such precise Japanese beauty, it is as though we are making love. It is closer, in some ways, than we have ever come.

Nellie has always cared for her animals so tenderly, and now she cares for me with as much devotion. It doesn't even matter now that she gets talcum powder in my nose and never can arrange the flowers properly. She teases what's left of my hair after the chemotherapy into this dreadful beehive, and says I look wonderful. Horace says I must think of the chemo medicine as beauty pills. He is without shame—he says they may increase my bustline!

It melts my heart to hear Nellie bragging over the phone about how the nurses at the hospital loved me so much that they cried when I left. I did enjoy being a kind of Mother Superior, eliciting the stories of their lives, helping solve their problems.

June 23, 1975

What a character my surgeon is! He just sashays into the office, where I am shivering in a johnny. Without missing a beat, he winks, gives my cheek a little pinch, and swoops his hands down on my belly. As he proceeds to examine me, he keeps talking in this sexy monotone about how delicious my raspberry pies were and what a terrible cook his wife is and if it weren't for me, he would never get sweet, tasty things in his mouth. Oh, Dr. Horace Holman, I'll send you ten pies a week, fifty, I'll send you the entire summer harvest if you keep me alive that long.

October 4, 1975

I am immersed in volunteer work at the hospital. It is so good to get back to doing things for others. I work double shifts in the delivery room because they are shorthanded. And afterwards, I try to bring some hope to the men and women on the cancer floor. I like to hand out copies of *The Prophet.*

I miss Augusta, but last month Shulamith came, and did we giggle like schoolgirls! She took me to New York for my checkup. Horace was absolutely charming to her, though he reserves his most special smiles for me. She agrees that his extraordinarily long upper lip, and the way his mouth comes down in a kind of heart, is adorable. When he hears that Shulamith has invited me to France next summer, he suddenly shouts, "France!" so that all the patients in the waiting room must have heard him. "I love France! Can I come too?" I told him he could have anything he wanted if he put back my insides. "What?" he said. "But then you wouldn't have to see me anymore!"

January 25, 1976

*M*y doctor has again pronounced me "clean" of the disease. I am filled with peace, with love of God, of my family, of the land that has been ours for generations. Last weekend we all went to New York for my battery of medical tests—crowded into one hotel room, cots wall to wall—and even Mama was full of fun. Though I let them think that it was Fifth Avenue, Broadway, Sardi's, and my loyal family that had put the stars in my eyes, it was really Horace. I secreted myself in our one bathroom and put perfume on, head to toe, and of course he noticed the scent when I was lying on his table. He has let his hair grow, and it flops over his eye as he probes every inch of me. But the important thing about him is his hands—the hands of a sculptor fashioning a new woman from the shell of the old. The hands of a pianist, long-fingered, silkily playing over the surface, and then working deep, deeper, until they are familiar with every nook and cranny of me. He wants to know the details of my days. He wants to know what hurts and how to make it better. When he is finished with me, I feel known like I have never been known before.

July 22, 1976

I have had such a glorious year: barbecues in Gristbrook, bridge tournaments, charity balls at which for some reason I am the belle—maybe because I am so radiantly happy, happier than I've ever been in my life. I don't even mind that these lumps have appeared in my groin, beneath my arm. I am savoring every moment of life. The seashore at Betsey's house on Cape Cod was lovely, the waves coming up like white stallions, their manes falling forward. The skies were so lovely at night that you could cry—all those stars twinkling, thousands of galaxies lying untouched. It made me feel very small indeed, and yet also strong, as though I could close my eyes and zoom through this universe. I felt it all so intensely. Though I move very slowly over the sand, though my legs seem to be almost rusted, I don't think anyone enjoyed it as much as I.

August 26, 1976

*M*ama and I are alone in the house, and suddenly I have gotten so ill. I don't know which is worse, the white-hot pain or the groggy, sick feeling of being drugged with the opium drops. Old Mama has found the strength of an entire staff, and nurses me faithfully. The days are deep dreams stretching out endlessly, like an ocean of taffy. There is no time. Only the heat. And the pain. I count the days until Horace comes back from vacation.

September 4, 1976

I am a child abandoned, left alone with Mama. The days slither by like snakes under the sun. I am a baby, cuddled beneath this satin quilt, its feathers floating one by one into my nose. My nose is always filled with feathers and it's so warm in this quilt, in this womb of pain. Gran Millie used to bake lovely cakes. I remember that the frosting always stuck to my nose. Mama's hands do not glide over me, they move up and down in the air like drops of rain splashing. My head in the mirror across the room is all tucked up, shrunken, weird, like one of those nonsense animals in Dr. Seuss. The curtain blowing up in the window looks like a person. Branches knock against my window, trees crack like gunfire. My diary has always been my refuge, my best friend, its white, blank silence fully satisfying. But now I wish it could crawl beneath the covers, sprout arms, and hold me.

September 8, 1976

*H*orace is due any minute. I began to think Mama was keeping everyone away from me, monopolizing me like she monopolized Gran Millie at the end, but then when Augusta telephoned, she didn't like the sound of my voice. She ordered Henry and Nellie home and called Horace.

I have done what I could, but no amount of pancake makeup can hide the bags under my eyes or my drooping cheeks, no amount of spray can restore my wavy hair or make me look the way I imagine myself when I look into Horace's eyes. How cruel to feel youth and health rising up in you, only to have it cut off in its prime.

Later:

Horace swept up to my room, ignored the chair Nellie put out for him, and sat right beside me on the quilt. "Now, what's all this!" he said. After he examined me, he ordered me up (he didn't even leave the room while I dressed, though he turned his back and whistled!) and took me for a walk in the orchards. I was amazed I could keep up, but I did. He put his hand on my shoulder and pointed to the peaks of the Catskills, like he wanted me to understand them in some new way. He wants to start me on radiation and a stiffer course of chemotherapy. He said "stiffer" with such a positive thrust, as though I was the sort of woman who could handle "stiffer," that I felt myself get stronger on the spot. Perhaps, I thought, he doesn't see this ruined shell, but the devoted soul beneath. He wants me to forget about my illness, about the lumps, "Get out here and live!" he said, sweeping the sky with his arms. It was almost as though he wanted me to do it for him personally. Oh yes, Horace! I will live. I will live if you want me to.

October 4, 1976

*T*he new chemotherapy is making me desperately sick. Nellie went to a friend's house upstate and did not call us when she got there. I was so worried, imagining her broken and bloody on the highway, that I just rocked and moaned all night. Augusta came in for her birthday but flew right out again, and I was sure her plane would crash. There must be some good that will come of this hatcheting pain. God, just let me see the purpose—there must be a purpose. Can I see the rainbow? Can I just see it? Please let me see it! No rainbow—only pain and pain and more pain. My children! That is the reason for the pain. That is the good that will come out of this pain.

November 2, 1976

At last, I am thin. I can fit under the wings of men. I am willowy, and Henry and Horace tower over me. I can wear slacks, I can wear the trim little skirts Augusta sends. I will never have to go into the Oversize Dress Shoppe again.

December 7, 1976

It is so hard for me to climb the stairs now that I have moved into the sickroom downstairs. I can sit by the window and watch the last dead leaves float like dancers down to the ground. This bed is so grand; its ornate headboard is fit for a queen. And I feel like one, receiving my friends, receiving their gifts. There is a godly whisper that tells you the whole story of your life, why it began, what happened, how it will end; if you listen for it, you will know the truth, you will not be at the mercy of those who would surprise you with the news that you will soon die and they will not.

The family has been slow to accept the inevitable. Neither Nellie nor Henry wanted me to move down here to the sickroom where all the Woolseys have died. But now we can all be together. They have brought in the television, and they use my room as a sitting room. Every once in a while I have a good day, one without vomiting, which everyone is pretending is due to the chemotherapy.

I wished very much for Augusta to come home for Thanksgiving, but she did not, and that is all right. I understand. The shawl she sent is beautiful. I am tucked up inside it now, watching the leaves twirl and tumble like ballerinas doing a pas de deux.

December 12, 1976

I could have done things so differently—oh God, I see it now. Nellie was complaining about Augusta not coming home, and I defended her. Nellie said, almost offhandedly, "I guess it doesn't matter what she does, you'll always worship her." It is not that Nellie hasn't said this kind of thing before, but suddenly it was as though I was hearing it for the first time. I wanted to make both my children think they were the most special thing on earth, and I failed. I was neglected by my own mother, and so I smothered Augusta. I tried to make her mine forever, and when I didn't succeed, I thought Nellie would be the one. I should have encouraged Nellie to be independent. I could have bucked her up, but I did not. To see how low her self-confidence is, to be unable, to simply be unable to repair the damage, makes me sick at heart!

There is no time. There is no time to confess to Henry that I know what I did; I know that I pushed him into the arms of other women because of my own refusal to be a real wife. I whetted his taste for adultery, and then I could not stop him.

Time has run out on me. I cannot reach my children or my husband. They do not want to face reality; they do not want to talk reality, because I have never talked to them. They cannot even accept that very soon now I will no longer be here.

Mama comes in and out of my room. Sometimes she stoops over to pat my blanket, her pigeon-chest moving in and out, her breath tart and lemony, her elongated vowels billowing from her lips like little sails. Sometimes a large teardrop falls from her eye, and I watch it hit my hand, exploding and dispersing evenly in all directions, leaving the point of contact completely dry. I want to call out "Mama!" but I cannot; her tears give me some license, but not license enough for that.

Mama always embraced me as though she were hugging a bush of thorns. The only time I felt her hands was when she washed my hair with tar soap, her hard fingers rubbing into my scalp. All those hugs, all those years we missed, the cakes we didn't bake, the clothes we didn't swap! All those years I missed with Augusta, all those opportunities!

My mother was like the ships upon which she spent so much of her life, cutting through the waters, a vessel so sure and irreversible, so tight and self-contained, that nothing but an iceberg could stop it. We try so hard to be different from our parents—and then, just when we think ourselves safe, a word, a phrase, an attitude, even an emotion that we learned long ago comes bubbling up. My mother went off on ships. I went off in huffs. Once, after Augusta had been naughty and was trying to make up to me, I remember I pushed her away and said what Mama always said: "Don't try that on me, sister, I can see right through it." As soon as Augusta's arms fell to her sides, I wanted to take it back. But I could not. The words of my mother are indelible. They have passed to me and live on undiminished.

December 18, 1976

I wake at night thinking I smell a pipe smoldering. It rains and I'm afraid we will be struck by lightning. I fear we will be robbed. Last night, I took the diamond and ruby rings from the hall secretary where Henry put them and I hid them in the brass spittoon by my bed. No burglar would think of looking there.

Sleep is no longer a sweet interlude, it is dangerous, it can carry you off to death. I must fight it. I wake dozens of times and feel I must shake off death. Sometimes I'm afraid to close my eyes the whole night. Dawn comes and the terror fades. When death stands naked in the harsh light of day, it loses some of its power.

December 22, 1976

*B*etsey and Peggy have come in with armloads of holly to decorate the house. They knew I wanted it perfect for Augusta's homecoming. Betsey bought me a mono- grammed silk opera scarf to give to Horace, and the ingredients for the Woolsey grape and walnut overnight salad so I can make it from my bed

December 23, 1976

*A*ugusta is home and it is heaven. We are a perfect family, and everything is building up to the crescendo of Christmas. Last night the girls helped me out of bed and to the front door for the carolers. The snow fell lightly over the apple trees, their branches lit by the moon, and the sounds of "Silent Night" filled the cold air. I sang like I haven't sung for years, and so did Mama, who was standing behind me. We must have made some picture, Augusta supporting one side of me and Nellie the other, for tears sparkled on the carolers' cheeks, and they sang and sang and did not leave until I had to go back to bed.

December 24, 1976

*C*hristmas Eve, and I think I heard sleighbells. The girls very carefully brought in the grapes and walnuts and little marshmallows and the jar of mayonnaise and let me mix them together as I always have on this day, but the bowl just flew out of my hands.

I've been thinking of Daddy. I hear him tinkling those bells. Oh, how he loved me. "Don't worry, Lydia, my little silver bell," I hear him saying, "it's going to be all right. Soon it will be only you and me."

I keep thinking of the spoon slipping and the bowl falling and the mayonnaise and grapes spread across the rug, and the heartrending faces of my children.

December 26, 1976

*A*ugusta went back to California. Sometimes I think that I won't die after all. At the last minute the doors will fly open and Horace Holman will say, "Lydia, you've passed the test. Get up and look in the mirror." When Henry and Mama were lifting me into the bath, I thought of how Mama had lifted Gran Millie, and the irony of it made me laugh almost hysterically. Old Mama, that old fox Mama, with her heart like a hammer pounding a row of anvils, will outlive us all. "Sorry," I said, "sorry you have to do this lifting yet again." "Now, now," she said gently, "don't fret. You're so light now, it's no trouble at all."

January 2, 1977

Can't hold out any longer. I need the hospital and Horace now. When I tell the family, Henry will turn tail and run down to the cellar. Mama is the one I can count on. Tough, no-nonsense Mama will make them understand. I now must say good-bye to you, my faithful diary, for I do not want my words to fall twisted and bitter from the morphine. I know a place where you will be safe, and I just have the strength to put you there.

Everyone has been wonderful. It was a perfect Christmas. I would not change a moment of it, though I do regret not having been able to make the trip to New York to see the holiday window-display at Lord & Taylor. How the children loved those old-fashioned scenes of Yuletide in New York! I can almost see the scenes now: all the little dolls in their white fur muffs, the diamonds sparkling on their necks, the little men taking their arms and leading them into the little mansion where they will dance till dawn. Maybe on the way to the hospital, we can drive by it very slowly. Mama always took me there when I was very young. I used to press my nose up against the glass and stare and stare. I liked to pretend I could dissolve into that little scene, that I could think myself into that family bundled up in the sleigh with snow on their shoulders, and be glad with them that here, in this tiny, wondrous world, Christmas lasts forever.

CHAPTER 18

Something was descending on Augusta, something sweet and warm and spongy, and it felt good, oh so good. The air around her got warmer, windier, and then it became oppressive, until she couldn't catch her breath. Suddenly, she awoke with a start. She stared at her room—the cool blue walls, the sunlight pouring in the window. And she lay back down with relief. It had been a dream, just a dream.

She stretched luxuriously. It was September 25, 1977, her birthday. She was thirty-five, and on this day she was leaving Woolsey Orchards for good. Her work here was done.

She got up and went down to the landing and into the bathroom. She washed her face, brushed her teeth, and smiled at her eyes, puffy from sleep like a child's. She put on silver earrings in the shape of half-moons and then gathered up her hair and fastened it with the graceful Oriental combs given to her by her grandmother. She usually did not bother with makeup, but today she applied it with care and subtlety. She was, after all, reaching the age where she would need it to perform a few tricks of youthfulness. Her neck looked long and smooth; the alarming lump below her left ear had disappeared shortly after she finished reading the diaries.

Augusta sniffed as she went back up to her room. Could she smell cake baking? Then she realized what that morning dream had been about. It had been about her mother, her mother coming in, singing "Happy Birthday to You," blowing on her forehead, ruffling her bangs until she awoke. Augusta went over to the bed and sat down. Nellie was right. Her mother did live on here at Woolsey Orchards, but now she seemed to glide past with a gentle rustle.

Even in college, even when she was living thousands of miles away, it was a tradition that Augusta came home for her birthday. And on every birthday until this one, Augusta had opened her eyes to a cascade of treats, little sacks of marzipan, fruits, posies, a tray with fried apples and a sunny egg. And there was the smell of banana cake baking, always banana cake, Augusta's favorite, its icing so sweet that eating it hurt your ears. On birthdays, as well as on Christmas, Lydia was the perfect mother, and they were perfect children.

Augusta dressed, went to the window, and looked out at the milling scene down in the orchards. Nurses, doctors, society ladies, policemen, janitors, welfare families from the tenements—anyone who had ever felt the touch of her mother's generosity—were climbing trees, picking apples, filling burlap bags to help the Woolseys bring in the first fall harvest. They had come from Gristbrook, from the hospital, from all around the county to offer help. After the media had trumpeted the news that Woolsey Orchards was being polluted with illegally dumped chemical wastes, possibly on purpose, they had come by the dozen. It had been a story that had once and for all ended the insularity of the Woolseys, for it struck a chord in everyone who felt that the environment was out of control. The county's most historic family-run farm—the embodiment of what America was all about—was being threatened by the Orwellian specter of a sneaky, all-powerful technocracy that was trying to break its spirit. The pioneer, barn-raising response this elicited had not been seen in the valley for decades. Nellie and William, going on-camera with their David-and-Goliath tale of felling the giant Apex, made an earnest, touching, and handsome couple. They gave the story the sheen of myth.

The latest soil samples showed that toxic chemicals were still heavily present near and in the Woolsey well, and they were in a small area surrounding the regrafted Christmas Orchard. But the EPA had, as a precaution, sealed off the entire southwestern corner of the property bordered by the river and the woods next to the Apex property. The board of health had declared the apples in the rest of the orchard safe and free of all chemicals, and all the agricultural and environmental agencies that had become involved agreed that the poor condition of the trees outside the sealed area was due not to chemical contamination but to radical weather changes and mice damage. No one could agree, however, on whether or not these new poison-resistant mice were mutants created by the chemicals.

Augusta watched Coert's flatbed tractor, full of crates of apples that were bound for the cider-press, winding along the road to the barn. The Woolsey apples might be pure, but they were not beautiful enough to sell for eating. So Peggy Steptoe had bought the farm a used cider-press that William had found. She and Betsey Blanquette were leading the picking operation, passing out picking-poles and directing people to the rows of apples that were now ripe. Lustily singing harvest songs, their motley crew was tackling the trees with enthusiasm and emptying bag after bag of picked apples into crates.

Augusta marveled at the feeling for Lydia that was displayed out there in the orchard, motivating all those people to sacrifice their weekends to help the Woolseys. How her mother would have loved it, her mother who never had the emotional courage to change her own life, but who loved to pitch in and save others. The spectacle of people adoring her mother now gave Augusta nothing but pleasure. It was even hard to remember those days when this fact could have completely defeated her, when it seemed to be proof that Augusta must be a very bad seed indeed if everyone else in the world felt only the rays of her mother's beneficence.

Augusta watched Nellie confidently striding up the lawn. Her very gait had changed. No one could liken her hair to a rusty scouring pad anymore; it was shot through with light and air, its threads of copper-gold glinting in the sun.

Augusta went to the stairs and sniffed the air. Didn't she smell a cake? Maybe not. She went back and began to pack the rest of her belongings. She wanted to get this done before she went downstairs. She was leaving this afternoon for New York, and then would go on to Paris for a long vacation. After that, she would see: she was leaving her options open. She would travel around Europe for a while—having refused to pour all her savings into the farm, she had enough funds to support herself—and then maybe she would join the documentary women, or maybe consider an offer by her old boss at Celebrities International to head up their New York office. She had first worked for the agency because her mother wanted her to, and then she had used it as an excuse to escape from her. Now that Augusta had put to rest her own confusion of self, perhaps she could work there on her own terms, decide for herself if she liked being a talent agent. Then again, she might pass up the offer; she just might strike out on her own, take up an eight-millimeter camera, and see whether she had any film-making talent of her own.

Augusta sorted through a drawer of scarves, trying to decide what to take with her. She shook out a lovely old paisley scarf with black fringe that had accompanied her to college, and then to Los Angeles; it had first come into her life when she was six and was stricken with severe asthma. Her mother would put it over Augusta's head so that she could inhale concentrated steam from the humidifier. The noise that came from Augusta's bronchial tubes sounded like kittens mewing, she and her mother had decided. Her mother had named these kittens and gave each one its own story—all to keep Augusta from panicking, from making her wheeze worse. Augusta missed these kittens, which had comforted her, perhaps even saved her life. Nowadays there was no need for humidifiers, or for mothers monitoring their children's labored breathing through the night; an epinephrine inhaler did the job in a few seconds. She folded the scarf and stored it away in a drawer.

After packing her suitcases, Augusta turned to her final task—packing away the diaries. She bent over an empty carton and put them in, one by one, in chronological order. Augusta ran her fingers over her favorite diary cover, a soft pigskin one, then put it in the carton. Her mother's restless pen had blown the whistle, it had begun a process of toxic disposal as surely as the flushing machines would remove the toxins from Woolsey soil. Before reading the diaries, Augusta had only deluded herself into thinking that she had created herself anew; she had only imagined she had broken the spell that kept Woolseys anchored to their land. But in reality she had only aped separation. She had not felt it in her gut the way she felt it now: as a sad, painful, exhilarating release. And she had aped the behavior of her mother: outwardly competent and energetic, inwardly a coward. Augusta had so little sense of herself apart from her family that she had relinquished it to whatever man asked for it. Her mother's diaries had enabled her to extract her guilt and her unworthiness, to hold them up and see them as foreign matter pressed into a wax tablet, as toxic waste that had seeped down through the generations, like some tilted gene, some congenital defect of the heart.

Ironically, since their mother's death Augusta and Nellie had changed in opposite but symmetrical ways. Nellie, who had a decisive inner identity, mustered the confidence to be forceful in the world; Augusta, outwardly strong, had at last developed a new inward sense of self, a self that needed no mirrors.

Augusta taped up the carton, labeled it carefully, and put it away in her closet. Someday these diaries would be read by her children and Nellie's children, perhaps even by their children's children.

Augusta went down the freshly polished stairway, half-believing Nellie and William and her father would be waiting for her, would leap out from behind doors, tooting horns and throwing confetti. But only her father was in the hall. He was pointing a gun at the head of Jeeves, the newel post at the foot of the stairs.

"Good morning, Daddy."

"Augusta, I want you to watch where I put this." He loaded the revolver, removed the globe-shaped newel post, and wedged the small gun up into it. Augusta looked at him in disbelief.

"I hollowed Jeeves out," he said, with a twinkle of pride.

"You hollowed out that antique newel?"

"If an intruder comes, if an emergency happens, I want us to have protection at our fingertips. You can't do anything if you're caught unawares and unprotected."

"Dad, speaking of being unaware, do you know what day it is?"

"Saturday, and don't be smart," Henry said. "You don't know how swiftly an intruder could slip in and immobilize you." Mimicking the movements of one, he thrust Augusta, not violently, against the wall. "He's got you, you're powerless!" he cried. "You tell him you feel faint, you reach and grab the newel post, which you hold onto for dear life. And then, at the first opportunity you get, you lift it, pull out the gun like this, and bang, you start firing till he's on the ground."

"I see your point," Augusta said, slipping out from under her father. She left him and went into the kitchen.

"Well, I'm packed," Augusta said to William and Nellie, who were sitting at the old steel-topped pastry table. "It seems like I've been home longer than six months. I feel so much older."

William and Nellie didn't seem to hear her. They were bent over blueprints for solar homes; they wanted to build one of their own up on Mount Freedom. The publicity had brought them several offers to buy Woolsey Orchards. One environmental-research group wanted to purchase it to study the effects of toxic wastes; one group wanted to trap the unusual mice for scientific research; another, an antivivisectionist cult, wanted to save the mice. One promoter even came in with a proposal, which was flatly turned down, to make it an amusement park. Everyone agreed that the best offer had come from a rich Hudson Valley preservationist who wanted to underwrite William's plan to turn the downstairs of the homestead into a museum. Woolsey Orchards would remain a working farm, overseen by Coert, who would be given enough help to do it properly, and one part of it would be farmed organically by the farmer whom Nellie had interested in buying the Christmas Orchard.

The big hall telephone rang. It had not stopped ringing since Nellie and William's first television appearance, and Henry loved to answer it. They could hear him from the kitchen, authoritatively handling a request for an interview.

"It could be about our latest assault on the enemy, but I think all the networks have already run spots on that," Nellie said, straining to hear him. Apex had pledged to finance the costly extraction of toxins that had leached from the dump into Woolsey soil, but it had denied discharging wastes into the Hudson through the old brick factory pipes. Nevertheless, the dogged team of Nellie and William had found evidence that wastes had recently been flushed through the pipes. They had done this by entering the Apex hot-fuel lab in the dark of night, their faces rubbed with burnt cork, ostensibly so they wouldn't be seen, but actually for the dramatic demands of the television cameras that recorded their entry through a cellar window.

"You two hams have no shame," Augusta assumed a scolding voice. "You've sold out to the media. Why, if I were your publicity agent, I wouldn't let you do half of these crass shenanigans."

"These shenanigans have a purpose, love," William said, waving the pictures of the pipes. "Apex may have to clean up the Hudson River from here down to Tarrytown."

"With apologies to Daddy, sometimes the means do justify the ends," Nellie said.

"By the way, have you figured out what Daddy really thinks about this museum idea? About living in a house open to the public?" Augusta asked.

"I think he loves it," Nellie said. "It means he can stay here as long as he wants, even after William and I move. He can keep his bees. He'll have the upstairs to himself, and he can always take part of the barn and make it into an apartment. He loves to be asked questions—you know how he likes to give those long, thorough explanations of things. I think he'll love having the house full of people."

"As long as he doesn't shoot them!" Augusta said.

"Shoot who?" Henry said, coming into the room. There was a spring in his step, and Augusta knew that Nellie was right; all his life he too had been smothered by the family chauvinism of the Woolseys. All these outside people calling, coming through the orchard, the prospect of more people—it was a breath of fresh air for him. And now, at last, with all the women gone, he would really be head of his own household.

"They're doing a terrific job down there, all your mother's friends," he said. He was wearing a clean shirt and was freshly shaved. "Channel Four wants to film the 'community picking,' and I said yes, but it won't be fair to our friends at the other stations if we don't alert them, so that's what I'm going to do now."

He went back to the telephone and William turned to Augusta. "Will you be a brick and go down and get Coert? I think I hear the truck. I want to ask him something."

Augusta agreed, but halfway down the lawn she rather wondered why William couldn't go get Coert himself. He had gotten very big for his britches with all this publicity. She met Coert as he was getting out of the pickup. He greeted her casually. Not a word about her birthday.

"William wants to see you," she said.

But Coert seemed to want to linger by Auntie Mame. He

fingered the old Newtown Pippin's uncharacteristically large and well-shaped green apples. In fact, the Pippins looked healthier than they ever had. "Just incredible. Look at the fruit this old dame's putting out. And I wanted to cut her down. Well, she was probably too old and too wise to be fooled by the hostile elements."

"Have you been down to the Christmas Orchard? Are they still taking samples?" Augusta asked.

Coert shook his head. "All this hullabaloo," he said, chewing his plug. "The EPA and the BoH and the EPS and God knows what other initials down there nosing around, acting like this was a nuclear staging ground. I figure that fifty years ago, that stream by the brick factory created as much of a health hazard as Apex is doing now, what with people dumping pig slop and everything else into it. Only thing is, then they didn't put it in the newspaper. People knew about it, but they just didn't think it was important."

"Hmm," Augusta said. "Let's go up to the house."

They walked up the lawn, past the porch. As they rounded the corner to the back door, the blast of a trumpet nearly sent Augusta sprawling back on the ground. There stood Nellie, Henry, and William, grinning like Cheshire cats, and to the side . . . a three-man band. In Nellie's hands was a red, round frosted cake shimmering with lighted candles. The band—two trumpets and a drummer—began playing "Happy Birthday to You," and Nellie, William, Coert, and Henry pelted out the words in three different keys.

Augusta sat down at the garden table piled with presents. "I thought you had forgotten!" she said, laughing.

"We couldn't bear to fool you any longer," Nellie said, sitting down beside her. "It was a conspiracy in the grandest Woolsey tradition. Coert was supposed to keep you in the driveway while we set this up. Now you have to open each present, remark on the paper, fold it, and then ooh and aah over it the way Great-grandma Millie always did."

"The band, a real band! Where did you get it?" The men, boys really, had stationed themselves over by the trees and were now playing Sousa marches.

"The high school. Remember what Mother said to you when you went away to college—'Come home, and there'll be a brass band to greet you.' "

"Open your presents," Henry said. "Look how nicely mine is wrapped. I did it myself."

"Oh Daddy, this is beautiful." Augusta took up a large package covered in purple paper with little pansies. "And it's not wrapped in Kleenex! And it's not from the drugstore! And it's not a gun!" Augusta took out a hair dryer with a converter for European current and a large first-aid and travel kit, with dozens of items in it, including bandages, a tourniquet, a toothbrush, laundry soap, a portable clothesline. "This is wonderful, Dad."

"That has everything you need when you're in any foreign country," Henry said. "There's even a package of water purifier that I want you to use if you're anyplace they don't speak English, French, or German."

Coert put a flat package rather shyly in front of her. It was an impressionistic watercolor of Lydia, Henry, Nellie, and Augusta standing in front of an apple tree. "Done it from a photograph," Coert said. "In case you get lonely so far from home."

Augusta kissed Coert, thinking how very grateful she was to get this watercolor, to know that he was and would always be her Coert.

Augusta opened William's present next. It was a journal bound in black suede, its pages deliciously blank. She stared at it. "I thought it was time for you to record your own life," William said, smiling.

Henry got up and disappeared around the far corner of the house. "And it wouldn't be a Woolsey celebration if Dad didn't leave in the middle," Augusta laughed.

"I don't think he'll be gone for long," Nellie said smugly. Coert got up and followed Henry.

"Open my present now, Augusta," Nellie said. She watched with suppressed excitement while her sister carefully unwrapped the rectangular package.

It was a framed needlepoint sampler, stitched in red and gold and yellow and orange, like autumn leaves. Beneath the figure of two delicately sewn hands, one reaching out to the other, was a poem:

> Sharer of Womb
> Companion in Love
> Thank you this Day
> For a Hand to Share
> A Spot in the Universe
> Mentor of Achievement
> Supporter of Dreams
> Thank you this Day
> For being there Always
> Guider of Hopes
> Strengthener in Weakness
> Thank you this Day
> For all our Laughter
> I who stand by your side Forever
>
> Thank you this Day for Being
> My Sister.

Augusta stared at the sampler, reread the poem, then she looked at Nellie and her eyes filled. "Did you *make* this?"

"I've worked on it since Mother died."

Augusta hugged her sister, and was about to speak again when suddenly the band clustered nearer and sent up a loud, heraldic fanfare. Henry and Coert came around the corner pushing a cannon—the cannon that had been found in the barn when Cornelius bought the property 105 years ago. They wheeled it over so it was faced out to the Southeast Orchard leading down to the Apex property. Then Henry took out his lighter and lit a rag torch.

"Oh no," Augusta stood up. "He's not going to light that thing, is he?"

Nellie smiled placidly at her sister. "Tell me you're going to be sorry to leave this luscious loony bin. They won't make them in Europe like they make them here at Woolsey Orchards."

The cannon's fuse burned down quickly. Henry and Coert jumped back just before the big black gun bucked, and with a thunderous bang disgorged the cannonball.

"Oh my God," Augusta gasped, watching the ball arc through the air above the orchards and down into the Apex fields below the trees. Thank God, Augusta thought, that the friends and neighbors helping them—secure in the illusion that this was a sane American family battling technological insanity—were all safely busy back down in the northwest orchards.

Nellie nudged Augusta. "He was determined to do it. Act pleased."

Henry strolled over to them. On his sooty face was the little new-moon grin that had so delighted the young Lydia when they were first courting. "So! You thought your thirty-fifth birthday would go out with a whimper, not a bang!"

"Oh Daddy," Augusta put her arms around him, "thank you."

"You're the one who deserves the thanks," he said, putting his cheek to hers.

Just then, a group of cameramen and reporters came running across the lawn. They went straight to the smoking cannon, photographed it, and then hurried down toward Apex to see if the cannonball had, by some stroke of fortune, hit the factory.

"Look, they think we've fired on Apex. They think it's war!" cried Nellie.

"Oh no," groaned Coert. Henry only looked amused.

Nellie turned to Augusta and said quietly, "Do you remember long ago when Great-great-grandpa was still alive, when Grandpa and all the grandmothers were always about, when we were this big, multigenerational family? Kind of like a Brueghel painting, with everybody on the landscape busy doing some private little task? Even when it was quiet, even in winter with no one working in the orchards, it wasn't ever really quiet."

Augusta smiled and nodded. "Always bacon popping or some invention clattering or the white Imperial backfiring, or someone belting out 'Rock of Ages' in a deep contralto. Those were happy times—for a little while, anyway."

"And then, after Mother died, it seemed so quiet. Like a morgue. Like a shroud," Nellie said. "Like the house was holding its breath, keeping some big secret."

"Well, I don't think we have a single secret left now," Augusta said, cutting a piece of cake. It was banana and it looked delicious. "We've wrung them out, we've squeezed the old house dry."

Nellie shivered. "God, it was so quiet that you could hear the dead. You know how things seem so normal, and then after they're over, you look back and realize how abnormal they were? I hope the house never gets that silent again."

The cameramen were doubling back across the lawn now, coming toward them. And through the trees came the shrill voices of Peggy and Betsey, brandishing poles, asking if everyone was all right, asking what that terrific explosion was.

ABOUT THE AUTHOR

LUCINDA FRANKS, a former *New York Times* reporter, won the Pulitzer Prize for national reporting for her United Press International newspaper series "The Making of a Terrorist." She covered the war in Northern Ireland, the draft-resistance movement in Canada and Sweden, and other European stories for U.P.I. Her investigative reporting on the cancer-causing effects of red dye number 2 for the *Times* led to a federal ban on the food coloring.

She has written for numerous publications, including *The New York Times Magazine, New York, The Nation, People,* and *The Saturday Review,* and is the author of the nonfiction book *Waiting Out a War: The Exile of John Picciano.*

She lives with her husband and two children in New York City. This is her first novel.